FABLEHAVEN
RISE OF THE EVENING STAR

SITTING STILL
WOULD BE
A MISTAKE

IGNORANCE
IS NO LONGER
A PROTECTION

FABLEHAVEN

RISE OF THE EVENING STAR

BRANDON MULL

ILLUSTRATED BY
BRANDON DORMAN

SHADOW
MOUNTAIN

✻ ✻ ✻

To Mom and Dad,
for their endless love and support

Library of Congress Cataloging-in-Publication Data
Mull, Brandon, 1974-
  Fablehaven : rise of the Evening Star / Brandon Mull.
    p.   cm.
  Summary: When Kendra and Seth go to stay at their grandparents' estate, they discover that it is a sanctuary for magical creatures and that a battle between good and evil is looming.
  ISBN-13 978-1-59038-742-9 (hardbound : alk. paper)
  [1. Magic—Fiction.   2. Grandparents—Fiction.   3. Brothers and sisters—Fiction.]   I. Title.
PZ7.M9112Fa   2006
[Fic]—dc22   2006000911

Printed in the United States of America
R. R. Donnelley and Sons, Crawfordsville, IN

10   9   8   7   6   5   4   3   2   1

Contents

CHAPTER ONE

The New Student

Crowding into homeroom with the other eighth graders, Kendra found her way to her desk. In a moment the bell would ring, signaling the start of the last week of school. One final week and she would leave middle school behind forever and start anew as a high school freshman, mingling with kids from two other junior highs.

A year ago that had sounded like a more exciting prospect than it did now. Kendra had been stuck in a nerd rut since around fourth grade, and a fresh start in high school might have meant an opportunity to shed the quiet, studious image. But this had been a renaissance year. Amazing how swiftly a little confidence and a more outgoing attitude could elevate your social status. Kendra no longer felt as desperate for a new beginning.

Alyssa Carter sat down in the desk next to her. "I heard we get yearbooks today," she said. She had short blonde hair and a slender build. Kendra had met Alyssa after making the soccer team back in September.

"Great, I looked hypnotized in my picture," Kendra groaned.

"Yours was adorable. Remember mine? My braces look the size of train tracks."

"Whatever. You could hardly even notice them."

The bell rang. Most of the kids were in their seats. Mrs. Price entered the room accompanied by the most disfigured student Kendra had ever seen. The boy had a bald, scabrous scalp and a face like a chapped welt. His eyes were puckered slits, his nose a malformed cavity, his mouth lipless and crusty. He scratched his arm, crooked fingers lumpy with bulging warts.

The hideous boy was otherwise nicely dressed in a black and red button-down shirt, jeans, and stylish tennis shoes. He stood in front of the class beside Mrs. Price while she introduced him.

"I'd like you all to meet Casey Hancock. His family just moved here from California. It can't be easy starting at a new school so late in the year, so please give him a warm welcome."

"Just call me Case," the boy rasped. He spoke like he was strangling.

"Would you look at that," Alyssa murmured.

"No kidding," Kendra whispered back. The poor kid barely looked human. Mrs. Price directed him to a desk near the front of the room. Creamy pus leaked from multiple sores on the back of his scabby head.

"I think I'm in love," Alyssa said.

"Don't be mean," Kendra muttered.

"What? I'm serious. Don't you think he's a hottie?"

Alyssa was acting so sincere that Kendra found herself repressing a smile. "That's just cruel."

"Are you blind? He's amazing!" Alyssa sounded genuinely offended that Kendra didn't agree.

"If you say so," Kendra placated. "Just not my type."

Alyssa shook her head as if Kendra were crazy. "You must be the pickiest girl on the planet."

Morning announcements were droning over the loudspeaker. Case was talking with Jonathon White. Jonathon smiled and laughed. That was strange—Jonathon was a jerk, not the sort of kid to befriend a circus freak. Kendra noticed Jenna Chamberlain and Karen Sommers sharing looks and whispers as if they too found Case attractive. Like Alyssa, they didn't seem to be joking. Scanning the room, Kendra didn't see a single student who seemed repulsed by his appearance.

What was going on? Nobody who looked this weird could come into a class without raising any eyebrows.

And suddenly the truth was apparent.

Casey Hancock looked inhumanly deformed and hideous because he was not a human. He had to be some sort of goblin who looked like a normal kid to everybody else. Kendra alone could see his true form, the aftereffect of having been kissed by hundreds of giant fairies.

Since leaving Fablehaven nearly a year ago, Kendra had seen magical creatures only twice. Once she had noticed a bearded man barely a foot tall pulling a length of pipe out of a pile of rubble behind the movie theater. When she tried to move in for a closer look, the tiny man scurried away into a storm drain. On another occasion she spotted what looked like a golden owl with a human face. She made eye contact with the creature for an instant before it took flight in a flurry of gilded feathers.

Such odd sights were usually veiled from mortal eyes. Her Grandpa Sorenson had introduced her to magical milk that enabled people to see through the illusions that normally concealed mystical creatures. When the fairy kisses had made that ability permanent, he had warned Kendra that sometimes it was safer to leave certain things unseen.

And here she was, staring at a grotesque monster posing as a new student in her homeroom! Mrs. Price came down the aisle handing out yearbooks. Kendra doodled absently on one of her book covers. Why was the creature here? Surely it had something to do with her. Unless repulsive goblins routinely infiltrated the public school system. Was he here to spy? To cause trouble? Almost certainly he was up to mischief.

Glancing up, Kendra caught the goblin staring at her over his shoulder. She should be glad to be aware the new kid had a hidden identity, right? The knowledge made her nervous, but it would help her prepare to counter any threat he might pose. With her secret ability, she could keep an eye on him. If she played it cool, Case would have no idea she could see his true form.

* * *

Shaped like a huge box, Roosevelt Middle School was constructed so that in winter the students never needed to go outdoors. Interior hallways connected everything, and the same room where they held assemblies doubled as an indoor cafeteria. But beneath the June sun, Kendra found herself seated outside for lunch with three friends at a circular table connected to curved benches.

Kendra signed Brittany's yearbook while munching on a croissant sandwich. Trina was signing Kendra's, Alyssa was signing Trina's, and Brittany was signing Alyssa's. It was important for Kendra to write a long, meaningful message—after all, these were her best friends. "Have a great summer" might work for acquaintances, but true friends required something more original. The key was to mention specific jokes you had shared, or fun things you had done together during the year. At the moment, Kendra was writing about the time Brittany couldn't stop laughing while trying to give an oral report in History.

Suddenly, uninvited, Casey Hancock plopped down at their table holding a lunch tray loaded with cafeteria lasagna, sliced carrots, and chocolate milk. Trina and Alyssa scooted aside to make room for him. It was almost unprecedented boldness for a lone boy to settle in at a table with four girls. Trina appeared slightly annoyed. Alyssa shot

Kendra a look as if she had just won the lottery. If only Alyssa could see what her new crush actually looked like!

"I don't think we've met," Case announced, his voice pinched and gravelly. "I'm Case. I just moved here." Just hearing him speak made Kendra's throat sore.

Alyssa introduced herself and the others. Case had been in two of Kendra's classes since homeroom. He had been well received each time he had stood up front for an intro- duction, particularly by the girls.

Case lifted a forkful of lasagna to his toothless mouth, affording Kendra a glimpse of his narrow black tongue. Watching him chew made her stomach churn.

"So what do you do for fun around here?" Case asked around a mouthful of carrots.

"We start by sitting with people we know," Trina said. Kendra covered a smile. She had never been so grateful to see Trina giving somebody a hard time.

"Is this the cool kids' table?" Case replied with mock sur- prise. "I'd planned to start at the bottom and work my way up." The comeback left Trina speechless. Case winked at Alyssa, to show he meant no harm. For a scab-faced goblin, he was pretty smooth.

"You've been in some of my classes," Case said to Kendra, wolfing down more lasagna. "English and Math." It was hard to look into those squinty eyes and keep her face pleasant.

"That's right," Kendra managed.

"I don't have to take the finals," he said. "I finished up

at my old school. I'm just here to hang out and meet people."

"That's how I feel," Brittany said. "But Kendra and Alyssa get like straight A's."

"You know," Case said, "I hate going to the movies alone, but I have no friends yet. You guys want to catch a show tonight?"

"Sure," Brittany said.

Kendra was stunned by the outlandish bravado of asking out four girls all at once on the first day at a new school. This was the smoothest goblin of all time! What was he after?

"I'll come," Alyssa said.

"Okay," Trina agreed. "If you're on your best behavior, I might even let you sign my yearbook."

"I don't give autographs," Case replied offhandedly. "Kendra, you coming?"

Kendra hesitated. How could she sit through an entire movie beside a foul monster? But how could she abandon her friends when she was the only person who knew what they were getting into? "Maybe," she conceded.

The crusty goblin took a final bite of lasagna. "How about we meet outside the theater at seven? The one on Kendall by the mini mall. Just trust to luck that something good will be playing." The other girls agreed as he stood up and walked away.

Kendra watched her friends talk animatedly about Case. He had won Alyssa at first sight. Brittany was an easy sell. And Trina was the sort of girl who liked to be catty but then got attracted if the guy stood up to her. Kendra supposed she would have been impressed herself if she didn't know he was a revolting monster.

There was no way she could tell her friends the truth about Case. Any accusations would sound crazy. But he was almost certainly up to something shady.

There was only one person in her whole town whom Kendra could tell about her situation. And he wasn't exactly her most reliable acquaintance.

✄   ✄   ✄

Seth lined up against Randy Sawyer. Randy was quick, but short. Seth had started the school year a bit shorter than most of the boys in his grade, but was finishing the year taller than average. The best strategy against Randy would be to go long and make the most of his height advantage.

Spencer McCain hiked the football to himself and dropped back. Four boys went out, while four others covered. One defender stayed at the line counting alligators. Seth juked like he was going to cut across the field, then raced straight for the end zone. Spencer lofted a high spiral. The pass was a little short, but coming back for it, Seth out-jumped Randy and hauled it in. Randy immediately tagged Seth with both hands, downing him just shy of Chad Dupree's sweatshirt, which marked the front of the end zone.

"Third and goal," Spencer declared, jogging down the field.

"Seth!" a voice exclaimed. Seth turned. It was Kendra. His sister didn't usually talk to him at school. Roosevelt

Middle School was sixth through eighth grades, so Seth was at the bottom of the pecking order after having ruled his elementary school the previous year.

"Just a second," Seth called to Kendra. The guys were lining up. Seth got into position. Spencer hiked the football to himself, then threw a short interception to Derek Totter. Seth didn't even bother chasing Derek. He was the fastest kid in their grade. Derek dashed all the way to the opposite end zone.

Seth trotted over to Kendra. "Bringing good luck as usual?" he said.

"That was a weak pass."

"Spencer only gets to quarterback because he throws the best spirals. What's up?"

"I need you to come see something," Kendra said.

Seth folded his arms. This was all very uncommon. She wasn't just talking to him at school, she wanted him to go someplace with her?

"We're kicking off!" Randy yelled.

"I'm in the middle of a game," Seth told her.

"This is Fablehaven-type stuff."

Seth turned to his friends. "Sorry! I have to quit for a while." He and Kendra headed off together. "What is it?"

"You know how I can still see magical creatures?"

"Yeah."

"There was a new student in some of my classes today," she explained. "He's pretending to be human, but he's actually an ugly monster."

"No way."

"My friends think he's cute. I can't see what he looks like. I want you to describe him to me."

"Where is he?" Seth asked.

"Over there, talking to Lydia Southwell," Kendra said, pointing subtly.

"The blond kid?"

"I don't know. Red and black shirt?"

"He *is* cute!" Seth gushed.

"What does he look like?"

"He has the dreamiest eyes."

"Knock it off," Kendra demanded.

"He must be thinking the most beautiful thoughts."

"Seth, I'm serious!" The bell rang, announcing the end of lunch.

"He's really a monster?" Seth asked.

"He looks a little like the creature who came in through the window on Midsummer Eve," Kendra said.

"The one I salted?"

"Yes. What is he pretending to look like?"

"Is this a joke?" Seth asked suspiciously. "He's just some new kid you have a crush on, isn't he? If you're scared, I can go ask for his phone number."

"I'm not messing around." Kendra swatted him on the arm.

"He looks athletic. He's got a dent in his chin. Blond hair. It's kind of messy, but cool. Like it's on purpose. He could probably get a part on a soap opera. Good enough?"

"Not bald and covered in scabs and pus?" Kendra verified.

"Nope. Is he really all disgusting?"

"He makes me want to puke. Thanks, see you later." Kendra hurried away.

Mr. Soap Opera was also moving away, still chatting with Lydia Southwell. For a monster, he had good taste. She was one of the cutest girls in the school.

Seth figured he had better get to class. Mr. Meyers had threatened to give him detention if he was late again.

※　※　※

Kendra sat in silence as Dad chauffeured her to the movie theater. She had tried to persuade Alyssa not to go. Alyssa had started to act suspicious that Kendra secretly wanted Case all to herself, and since Kendra could not tell her friend the truth, she had to drop it. In the end, Kendra had decided to join them, concluding that she could not leave her friends alone with a scheming goblin.

"What movie are you seeing?" Dad asked.

"We're going to figure it out when we get there," Kendra said. "Don't worry—nothing racy." Kendra wished she could tell her father about her predicament, but he knew nothing about the magical properties of the preserve Grandpa and Grandma Sorenson managed. He thought it was just a normal estate.

"You're sure that you're ready for finals?"

"I've been keeping up with my assignments all year. It will just take a quick review. I'll ace them." Kendra wished she could talk to her Grandpa Sorenson about the situation. She had tried to call. Unfortunately, the only number her parents had for him led repeatedly to a recorded message informing her that the call could not be completed as dialed. The only other way she knew to contact him was through the mail. So, just in case the phone was out for a while, she had written Grandpa a letter describing the situation, which she planned to mail the next day. It felt good to lay out her predicament to somebody besides Seth, even if it was just on paper. Hopefully she would get through by phone even before the letter arrived.

Dad pulled into the movie theater parking lot. Alyssa and Trina were standing out front. Beside them stood a hideous goblin wearing a T-shirt and khakis.

"How do I know when to pick you up?" Dad asked.

"I told Mom I would call on Alyssa's cell phone."

"Okay. Have fun."

Not very likely, Kendra thought as she stepped out of the SUV.

"Hey, Kendra," Case rasped. She could smell his cologne ten feet away.

"We were getting worried you weren't coming," Alyssa said.

"I'm right on time," Kendra insisted. "You guys were early."

"Let's pick a movie," Trina said.

"What about Brittany?" Kendra asked.

"Her parents wouldn't let her come," Trina said. "They're making her study."

Case clapped his hands together. "So what are we seeing?"

They negotiated for a couple of minutes. Case wanted to see *Medal of Shame*, about a serial killer addicted to terrorizing veterans who had won the Congressional Medal of Honor. He finally relented on watching his action movie when Trina promised to buy him popcorn. The winning movie was *Switching Places*, the story of a nerdy girl who gets to date the guy of her dreams after her mind gets swapped into the body of the most popular girl in school.

Kendra had wanted to catch that movie, but now she worried it would be ruined. Nothing like cuddling up to a bald goblin during a cheesy chick flick.

As she had suspected, Kendra had a tough time focusing on the movie. Trina sat on one side of Case, with Alyssa on the other. Both were vying for his attention. They all shared a jumbo bucket of popcorn. Kendra declined whenever they offered her some. She wanted no part of anything those warty hands had pawed.

By the time the credits were rolling, Case had an arm around Alyssa. The two of them kept whispering and giggling. Trina sat with her arms crossed, wearing a disgruntled expression. Monster or not, when had any good come from multiple girls going out together with a guy they were all interested in?

Case and Alyssa held hands as they exited the theater. Trina's mom was waiting in the parking lot. Trina said a terse good-bye and stalked away.

"Can I use your cell phone?" Kendra asked. "I need to call my dad."

"Sure," Alyssa said, handing it over.

"You want a ride?" Kendra asked as she dialed.

"I'm not that far," Alyssa said. "Case said he would walk me."

The goblin gave Kendra a strange, sly smile. For the first time, she wondered if Case was aware that she knew his true identity. He seemed to be gloating that there was nothing she could do about it.

Kendra tried to keep her expression neutral. Mom answered the phone, and Kendra reported that she needed to be picked up. She handed the phone back to Alyssa. "Isn't that a pretty long walk? You can both have a ride."

Alyssa gave Kendra a look that questioned why she was deliberately trying to ruin something spectacular. Case put an arm around her shoulders, leering.

"Alyssa," Kendra said firmly, taking her hand, "I need to talk to you in private for a second." She tugged Alyssa toward her. "Is that all right, Case?"

"No problem. I need to run and use the rest room anyhow." He went back inside the theater.

"What is your deal?" Alyssa complained.

"Think about it," Kendra said. "We hardly know anything about him. You just met him today. He's not a little guy. Are you sure you want to go walking alone in the dark with him? Girls can get in a lot of trouble that way."

Alyssa gave her an incredulous look. "I can tell he's a nice guy."

"No, you can tell that he's good-looking, and pretty funny. Lots of psychos seem like nice guys at first. That's why you hang out a few times in public places before you spend time alone. Especially when you're fourteen!"

"I hadn't thought of it that way," Alyssa conceded.

"Let my dad give both of you a ride. If you want to talk with him, do it in front of your house. Not on a dark, lonely street."

Alyssa nodded. "Maybe you have a point. It wouldn't hurt to hang out within screaming distance of home."

When Case got back, Alyssa explained the plan, minus the part about him potentially being a psychopath. He resisted at first, saying it was such a nice night that it would be a crime not to walk, but finally consented when Kendra reminded him that it was after nine.

Dad showed up in the SUV a few minutes later, and agreed to give Alyssa and Case a ride. Kendra climbed up front. Alyssa and Case rode in the back, whispering and holding hands. Dad dropped the lovebirds off at Alyssa's house. Case explained that he lived just down the street.

As she drove away, Kendra looked back at them. She was leaving her friend alone with a creepy, conniving goblin. But there was nothing else she could do! At least Alyssa was in front of her house. If something happened she could cry out or run inside. Under the circumstances, that would have to suffice.

"Looks like Alyssa has a boyfriend," Dad remarked.

Kendra leaned her head against the window. "Looks can be deceiving."

CHAPTER TWO

Talking to Strangers

Kendra arrived at her homeroom several minutes early the next day. As kids trickled in, Kendra sat with her heart in her throat, waiting to see Alyssa. Case walked in, and although Kendra watched him, he paid her no attention. He went to the front of the room and stood near Mrs. Price's desk talking to Jonathon White.

Was Alyssa's face going to end up on milk cartons? If so, Kendra could only blame herself. She shouldn't have left her friend alone with that goblin for a second.

Less than two minutes before the bell, Alyssa entered the room. She glanced at Case, but did not acknowledge him. Instead, she came straight to her desk and sat down next to Kendra.

"Are you okay?" Kendra asked.

"He kissed me," Alyssa said through a tight smile.

"He *what?*" Kendra tried to conceal her revulsion. "You don't sound too thrilled."

Alyssa shook her head regretfully. "I was having so much fun. We talked in front of my house for a while after you drove away. He was being really cute and funny. Then he moved in close. I was terrified—I mean, I hardly know him, but it was also sort of exciting. Until we actually kissed. Kendra, he had dog breath."

Kendra could not resist laughing.

Alyssa relished the reaction, becoming more animated. "I'm serious. It was rancid. Putrid. Like he had never brushed his teeth since birth. It was worse than I could ever describe. I thought I was going to throw up. I swear, I almost did."

Staring at the leprous scalp of the thing Alyssa had kissed, Kendra could only imagine how bad his mouth would have tasted. At least the illusion concealing his true identity had not disguised his rank breath.

The bell rang. Mrs. Price was encouraging a few noisy boys at the back of the classroom to take their seats.

"So what did you do?" Kendra whispered.

"I think he could tell how shocked I was by his breath. He had this weird smile like he'd been expecting it. I was totally grossed out, so I wasn't very nice. I told him I had to go and rushed inside."

"Is the crush over?" Kendra asked.

"I don't mean to be shallow, but yes. Trina can have him. She'll need a gas mask. It was that foul. I went straight to the bathroom and gargled mouthwash. When I look at him now, he makes me shiver. Have you ever eaten food that made you puke, then not been able to imagine ever eating it again?"

"Alyssa," Mrs. Price interrupted. "The school year does not end for four more days."

"Sorry," Alyssa said.

Mrs. Price crossed to her desk and sat down. Yelping, she jumped up, swatting at her skirt. Mrs. Price squinted at the class. "Did somebody put a tack on my chair?" she asked incredulously. She patted her skirt and checked her chair and the floor. "That really hurt and was far from funny." She put her hands on her hips, glaring at the class. "Somebody must have seen. Who did it?"

The class members were silent, exchanging sidelong glances. Kendra could not imagine anybody doing something so hurtful, not even Jonathon White. Until she remembered that Case had been standing near Mrs. Price's desk at the start of class.

Mrs. Price leaned against her desk, one hand rubbing her forehead. Was she going to cry? She was a fairly nice teacher—a middle-aged woman with curly black hair. She had narrow features and wore a lot of makeup. She didn't deserve to have a goblin play hurtful pranks on her.

Kendra considered speaking up. She would have ratted out the monster in a heartbeat. But to her classmates it would look like she was telling on a cool kid. And although he was a prime suspect, she hadn't actually seen him do it.

Mrs. Price was blinking and swaying. "I don't feel so . . ."

she began, her words slurred, and then she toppled to the floor.

Tracy Edmunds screamed. Everybody stood for a better look. A couple of kids hurried over to the fallen teacher. One boy was feeling her neck for a pulse.

Kendra pressed forward. Was Mrs. Price dead? Had the goblin pricked her with a poisonous needle? Case was crouching beside her.

"Get Mr. Ford," Alyssa shouted.

Tyler Ward ran out the door, presumably to fetch the principal.

The kid feeling for a pulse, Clint Harris, declared that her heart was beating. "She probably just fainted because of the tack," he speculated.

"Elevate her feet," someone said.

"No, elevate her head," someone else said.

"Wait for the nurse," a third voice instructed.

Mrs. Price gasped and sat up, eyes wide. She appeared momentarily disoriented. Then she pointed toward the desks. "Get back in your seats, pronto."

"But you just passed—" Clint began.

"Back in your seats!" Mrs. Price repeated more forcefully.

Everyone complied.

Mrs. Price stood at the front of the classroom, arms folded, eyeing the students as if trying to read their minds. "I have never in my life met such an unruly group of vipers," she spat. "If I have my way, you'll all be expelled."

Kendra furrowed her brow. This was not like Mrs. Price,

even under the current circumstances. Her voice had a different edge to it, cruel and hateful.

Mrs. Price grabbed the lip of Jonathon White's desk. He sat in the front row because of repeated discipline issues. "Tell me, my little man, who put a tack on my chair?" She was gritting her teeth. Veins bulged in her neck. She looked like she was about to explode.

"I . . . didn't see," Jonathon stuttered. Kendra had never heard him sound scared before.

"Liar!" Mrs. Price yelled, heaving the front of his desk up so that it tipped over backwards. The seat was connected to the desk, so Jonathon went down as well, banging his head on the desk behind him.

Mrs. Price moved over to the next desk, to Sasha Goethe, her favorite student. "Tell me who did it!" the crazed teacher demanded, spittle flying from her lips.

"I don't—" was all Sasha managed before her desk was upended as well.

Despite her shock, Kendra realized what was going on. Case hadn't poisoned Mrs. Price. Whatever pricked her had cast some sort of spell over her.

Kendra stood up and shouted, "It was Casey Hancock!"

Mrs. Price paused, staring at Kendra through narrow eyes. "Casey, you say?" Her voice was soft and lethal.

"I saw him by your desk before class started."

Mrs. Price advanced toward Kendra. "How dare you accuse the one person in this class who would never harm a fly?" Kendra started backing away. Mrs. Price continued speaking in a low voice, but she was clearly furious. "You did this, didn't you, and now you're pointing fingers, blaming the new kid, the one with no friends. Very low, Kendra. Very low."

Kendra reached the back of the classroom. Mrs. Price was closing in. She was only an inch or two taller than Kendra, but her fingers were hooked into claws, and her eyes boiled with malice. The normally even-tempered teacher looked like she had murder on her mind.

Only a few steps away from Kendra, Mrs. Price leaped forward. Kendra dodged sideways and raced down a different aisle toward the door at the front of the classroom. Mrs. Price was right behind her until Alyssa stuck out a foot and sent the rabid teacher sprawling.

Kendra yanked open the door and found herself face-to-face with Mr. Ford, the principal. Behind him stood a panting Tyler Ward.

"Mrs. Price isn't herself," Kendra explained.

Shrieking, Mrs. Price lunged at Kendra. Mr. Ford, a heavy man with a sturdy build, intercepted the manic teacher, pinning her arms to her sides. "Linda!" he said in a tone that suggested he could not believe what was going on. "Linda, calm down. Linda, stop."

"They're all maggots," she hissed. "They're all vipers. Devils!" She continued struggling vigorously.

Mr. Ford was looking around the room, taking in the overturned desks. "What's going on here?"

"Somebody put a tack on her chair and she freaked out," Sasha Goethe sobbed, standing near her overturned desk.

"A tack?" Mr. Ford said, still trying to control the

squirming teacher. Mrs. Price suddenly whipped her head back, slamming Mr. Ford square in the face. He staggered backwards, losing his grip on her.

Mrs. Price shoved Kendra aside and sprinted out the door and down the hall. A stunned Mr. Ford was catching blood from his nostrils in a cupped hand.

Across the room, Casey Hancock, the goblin in disguise, grinned wickedly at Kendra.

* * *

By the end of the school day, Kendra was sick of recounting the drama in homeroom. The school was buzzing with the news that Mrs. Price had lost her mind. The frazzled teacher had run off school property, leaving her car in the parking lot, and had not been seen since. As word spread that Kendra had spoken up against Case and been specifically attacked, she was bombarded with endless questions.

Kendra felt terrible for Mrs. Price. She was certain it was some strange goblin magic that had led to the outburst, but that was an impossible theory to present to the principal. In the end, Kendra had to admit that she had not actually seen Case put anything on the chair. Nor had anyone else, apparently. They couldn't even find the tack. And of course she could not say anything about Case's secret identity, because there was no way to prove it short of convincing Mr. Ford to kiss him on the mouth.

Walking out to catch her bus, Kendra brooded over the unjust situation. The reputation of an innocent teacher had been ruined, and the obvious culprit was totally getting away with it. Thanks to his disguise, the goblin would keep on causing mayhem without any consequences. There had to be a way to stop him!

"Ahem." A man walking beside Kendra cleared his throat in order to get her attention. Lost in thought, she had failed to notice his approach. The man was dressed in a fancy suit that looked about a hundred years out of style. The coat had tails, and he wore a vest with it. It was the sort of suit Kendra would have expected to see in a play, not in real life.

Kendra stopped walking and faced the man. Kids heading for the buses passed them on either side. "Can I help you?" she asked.

"Beg your pardon, but do you have the time?"

His vest had a watch chain. Kendra pointed at it. "Isn't that a watch?"

"Just the chain, my girl," he said, patting his vest. "I parted with the watch some time ago." He was fairly tall, with wavy black hair and a pointy chin. Although the suit was fancy, it was rumpled and worn, as if he had slept in it for several consecutive nights. He seemed a little seedy. Kendra resolved immediately not to let him lure her into a windowless van.

She was wearing a watch, but did not check it. "School just got out, so it's a little after two-forty."

"Allow me to introduce myself." He held up a business

card in his white-gloved hand, in a way that suggested he meant for her to read it, not take it. The card said:

Errol Fisk
*Cogitator * Ruminator * Innovator*

"Cogitator?" Kendra read dubiously.

Errol glanced at the card and flipped it over.

"Wrong side," he apologized with a smile.

The back side said:

Errol Fisk
Street Performer Extraordinaire

"Now, *that* I believe," Kendra said.

He glanced at the card and, with a look of chagrin, flipped it over again.

"I already—" Kendra began, but she hadn't.

Errol Fisk
Heaven's Special Gift to Women

Kendra laughed. "What is this? Am I on a hidden-camera show?"

Errol checked the card. "My apologies, Kendra, I could have sworn I tossed that one out long ago."

"I haven't told you my name," Kendra said, suddenly on guard.

"You didn't have to. You were the only one of these youngsters who looked fairystruck."

"Fairystruck?" Who *was* this guy?

"I take it you've noticed an unwanted visitor in your school recently?"

Now he had her full attention. "You know about the goblin?"

"The kobold, actually, though the two are often confused." He flipped the card again. It now read:

Errol Fisk
Kobold Exterminator

"You can help me get rid of him?" Kendra asked. "Did my grandpa send you?"

"He did not. But a friend of his did."

At that moment, Seth came up to them, his backpack slung over one shoulder. "Who's the ringmaster?" he said to Kendra.

Errol held the card up for Seth to see. "What's a kobold?" Seth patted Kendra on the shoulder. "Hey, you're going to miss the bus." Kendra could tell he was trying to give her an opening to get away from the stranger.

"I might be walking home today," Kendra said.

"Four miles?" Seth said.

"Or I'll catch a ride with somebody. The goblin who kissed Alyssa and framed Mrs. Price is a kobold." She had told Seth about the disastrous incident at lunch. He was the one person who could understand the real story.

"Oh," Seth said, sizing up Errol anew. "I get it. I thought you were a salesman. You're a magician."

Errol fanned out a deck of playing cards that had appeared out of nowhere. "Not a bad guess," he said. "Pick a card."

Seth pulled out a card.

"Show it to your sister."

Seth showed Kendra the five of hearts.

"Put it back in the deck," Errol instructed.

Seth replaced it so that Errol could not see the face of the card. Errol flipped all the cards around, so they faced the kids, still fanned out. They were all the five of hearts. "And there's your card," Errol announced.

"That's the lamest trick ever!" Seth protested. "They're all the same. Of course you know what I picked."

"All the same?" Errol said, reversing the cards and thumbing through them. "No, I'm sure you're mistaken." He turned them back around, and it now looked like a normal deck of fifty-two different cards.

"Wow!" Seth said.

Errol held the cards face down and fanned them out again. "Name a card," he said.

"Jack of clubs," Seth said.

Errol held the cards up. They were all the jack of clubs. He flipped them over again. "Kendra, name a card."

"Ace of hearts."

Errol displayed an entire deck full of the ace of hearts. Then he tucked the deck away into an inner pocket.

"Whoa, you really are magic," Seth said.

Errol shook his head. "It's just legerdemain."

"Leger-what?"

"Legerdemain. A word of French origin meaning sleight of hand."

"What, you've got a bunch of decks up your sleeve?" Seth asked.

Errol winked. "Now you're on the right track."

"You're good," Seth said. "I was watching close."

Errol tweezed his business card between two fingers, folded it into his palm, and then immediately opened his hand. The card was gone. "The hand is quicker than the eye."

The buses started pulling out. They always left in a caravan of five. "Oh no," Seth said. "My bus!"

"I can give you kids a ride," Errol offered. "Or I suppose calling you a cab might be more appropriate. My treat. Either way, we need to talk about this kobold."

"How did you find out about this so fast?" Kendra asked suspiciously. "The kobold only showed up yesterday. I just mailed my letter to Grandpa Sorenson this morning."

"Cogent question," Errol said. "Your grandfather has an old friend named Coulter Dixon who lives in the area. He asked Coulter to keep an eye on you two. When Coulter caught wind of the kobold, he called me. I'm a specialist."

"So you know our grandpa?" Seth asked.

Errol held up a finger. "I know a friend of your grandpa's. I've never actually met Stan."

"Why do you wear that weird suit?" Seth asked.

"Because I'm terribly fond of it."

"Why are you wearing gloves?" Seth pursued. "It's hot out."

Errol glanced furtively over his shoulder, as if he was about to share a secret. "Because my hands are made of pure gold and I'm worried somebody will steal them."

Seth's eyes widened. "Really?"

"No. But remember the principle. Sometimes the most preposterous lies are the most believable." He tugged off a glove and flexed his fingers, revealing a normal hand with black hairs on the knuckles. "A street magician needs places to hide things. Gloves serve that purpose. Same with a coat on a warm day. And a vest with lots of pockets. And a wrist-watch or two." He pulled back his sleeve, revealing a pair of watches.

"You asked me for the time," Kendra said.

"Sorry, I needed an opener. I have three watches. A watch can be a great place to hide a coin." Errol squeezed his wrist and then held up a silver dollar. He put his glove back on, and the coin vanished in the process.

"So you *do* have a pocket watch," Kendra said.

Errol held up the empty chain. "Sadly, no, that was true. Pawn shop. I needed to buy combs for my girlfriend."

Kendra smiled, getting the reference. Errol did not explain it to Seth. "So, do I pass inspection?" he asked.

Kendra and Seth looked at each other. "If you get rid of the kobold," Kendra said, "I'll believe anything you say."

Errol looked a little concerned. "Well, see, the thing is, I'm going to need your help to do it, so we're going to need to trust one another. You could call your grandpa, and he could tell you about Coulter, at least. And then he could get in touch with Coulter, who would tell him about me. Or maybe Coulter has already contacted him. For now, consider this—your grandfather has hardly told a soul that you were fairystruck, and I am certain he urged you to keep that infor-mation private as well. Yet I am privy to that knowledge."

"What do you mean by fairystruck?" Kendra asked.

"That the fairies shared their magic with you. That you can see whimsical creatures without assistance."

"You can see them too?" Seth asked.

"Sure, if I use my eyedrops. But your sister can see them all the time. I got that information directly from Coulter."

"Okay," Kendra said. "We'll check with our grandpa, but until we hear back, we'll trust that you're here to help."

"Fabulous." Errol tapped his temple. "I'm already hatching a plan. What are the chances of you two sneaking out tomorrow night?"

Kendra winced. "That's going to be tough. I have finals the next day."

"Whatever," Seth said, rolling his eyes. "We'll pretend to go to bed early and slip out the window. Would it work to meet around nine?"

"Nine would be nearly perfect," Errol said. "Where should we rendezvous?"

"You know the service station on the corner of Culross and Oakley?" Seth suggested.

"I'll find it," Errol said.

"What if Mom and Dad notice we're missing?" Kendra said.

"Which would you rather do: risk getting grounded, or keep putting up with your ugly friend?" Seth asked.

Seth was right. It was a no-brainer.

CHAPTER THREE

Extermination Procedures

The sky was nearly dark when Kendra and Seth entered the service station's convenience store. Inside, one of the fluorescent bulbs was flickering, interrupting the harsh, even glow. Seth fingered a candy bar. Kendra turned around in a circle. "Where is he? We're almost ten minutes late."

"Play it cool," Seth said. "He'll be here."

"You're not in a spy movie," Kendra reminded him.

Seth picked up the candy bar, closed his eyes, and smelled it from end to end. "Nope. This is the real thing."

Kendra noticed the headlights of a battered Volkswagen van flashing in the parking lot. "Maybe you're right," she said, approaching the window. The lights flashed again. Squinting, she saw Errol behind the wheel. He motioned her over.

Kendra and Seth crossed the parking lot to the van.

"Are we really going to drive away with him in that thing?" Kendra mumbled.

"Depends on how badly you want to get rid of the kobold," Seth replied.

The creature had not caused any new commotion that day at school, although he had taunted Kendra with several knowing looks. The horrid imposter was reveling in his victory. He kept hanging around with her friends, and there was nothing she could do about it. Who knew what his next act of sabotage might be?

Kendra had continued to try to reach Grandpa Sorenson, and had repeatedly gotten the recorded message that the call could not be completed as dialed. Had he stopped paying his phone bill? Maybe he had switched telephone numbers? Whatever the cause, she had still not been able to speak with him to confirm whether Errol could be trusted.

Errol leaned across the van and pushed the door open. Once again he was wearing his rumpled, antiquated suit. Kendra and Seth climbed inside. Seth shut the door behind them. The motor was already running.

"Here we are," Kendra said. "If you're going to kidnap us, tell me now. I can't handle the suspense."

Errol put the van into gear and pulled out of the service station onto Culross Drive. "I'm really here to help you," Errol said. "Although, if I had kids, I'm not sure I would want them climbing into a vehicle late at night with a man they'd just met, no matter what story he told them. But do not fret, I'll deliver you safe and sound to your home before long."

Errol turned onto a different street. "Where are we going?" Seth asked.

"Nasty vermin, kobolds, very tenacious," Errol said. "We need to get something that will enable us to drive the interloper away permanently. We are going to steal a rare item from a wicked and dangerous man."

Seth leaned forward on the edge of his seat. Kendra leaned back with her arms folded. "I thought you said you were a kobold exterminator," Kendra said. "Don't you have your own gear?"

"I have expertise," Errol said, turning onto a new street. "Exterminating a kobold is a trifle more complicated than spraying your yard with chemicals. Each situation is unique and demands improvisation. Be glad that I know where to get what we need."

They rode in silence for a few miles. Then Errol pulled off to the side of the road and switched off his lights. "We're already here?" Seth asked.

"Fortunately, what we need is close by," Errol said. He indicated a stately building half a block down the road. A sign out front read:

"We're going to break into a mortuary?" Kendra asked.

"Are we going to steal a body?" Seth said, sounding too eager for Kendra's liking.

"Nothing so morbid," Errol assured them. "The owner of the mortuary, Archibald Mangum, lives on the premises. He owns a stylized figurine in the likeness of a toad. We can use the figurine to drive away the kobold."

"He wouldn't just lend it to us?" Kendra asked.

Errol smiled. "Archibald Mangum is not a kind man. In fact, he is not a man at all. He is a vampiric abomination."

"He's a vampire?" Seth asked.

Errol cocked his head. "Strictly speaking, I have never encountered an actual vampire. Not like you see in the movies, turning into bats and hiding from the sun. But certain orders of beings are vampiric in nature. These beings are probably where the notion of vampires originated."

"So what exactly is Archibald?" Kendra pressed.

"Hard to say for certain. Most likely a member of the blix family. He might be a lectoblix, a species that ages swiftly and must drain the youth of others to survive. Or a narcoblix, a fiend capable of exerting control over victims while they are asleep. But given his residence, my best guess would be that he's a viviblix, a being with the power to temporarily reanimate the dead. Like the vampires of legend, blixes connect with their victims through a bite. All varieties of blixes are highly uncommon, and here you are, with one just a few miles from your home!"

"And you want us to break into his mortuary!" Kendra said.

"My dear," Errol said. "Archibald is away. I wouldn't dream of sending you anywhere near his funeral home if it were otherwise. It would be far too perilous."

"Will he have zombie guards?" Seth asked.

Errol spread his gloved hands. "If he is a viviblix, there may be a few reanimated corpses about. Nothing we can't handle."

"There has to be some other way to deal with the kobold," Kendra muttered nervously.

"None that I know of," Errol said. "Archibald will return tomorrow. After that, we can forget about procuring the figurine."

The three of them sat in silence, looking down the street at the gloomy windows of the funeral home. It was an old-style mansion with a covered porch, a circular driveway, and a large garage. The lighted sign out front provided the only illumination besides the moonlight.

At last Kendra broke the silence. "I don't feel good about this."

"Oh, toughen up," Seth said. "It won't be so bad."

"I'm glad to hear you say that, Seth," Errol said. "Because you will have to go into the house alone."

Seth swallowed. "You're not coming with us?"

"Nor Kendra," Errol said. "You're not yet fourteen, correct?"

"Right," Seth said.

"Protective spells guarding the home will prevent anybody over the age of thirteen from entering," Errol explained. "But they neglected to make it childproof."

"Why not protect it from everybody?" Kendra asked.

"The young enjoy an innate immunity to many such spells," Errol said. "Creating enchantments to divert children requires greater skill than erecting barriers to foil adults. Almost no magic works on children under the age of eight. The natural immunity diminishes as they age."

For the first time since entering the van, Kendra was amused. Seth looked as sober as she had ever seen him. No matter what the circumstances, it was always a pleasure to see him have to eat his words. He shifted in his seat and glanced at her.

"Okay, well, what do I do?" he said. The bravado had faded.

"Seth, don't—" Kendra began.

"No," he said, holding up his hand. "Leave the dirty work to me. Just tell me what to do."

Errol unscrewed the cap of a small bottle. An eyedropper was attached to the cap. "First, we need to sharpen your vision. These drops will work like the milk you drank at Fablehaven. Tilt your head back."

Seth obeyed. Errol leaned forward, placed a finger under Seth's right eyelid to pull it down, and squeezed out a drop. Blinking wildly, Seth recoiled. "Whoa!" Seth complained. "What is that, hot sauce?"

"It tingles a little," Errol said.

"It burns like acid!" Seth wiped tears from the afflicted eye.

"Other eye," Errol said.

"Don't you have any milk?"

"Sorry, fresh out. Hold still, it will only take a second."

"So would branding my tongue!"

"Isn't the first eye already feeling better?" Errol inquired.

"I guess so. Maybe I can just look out of one eye."

"I can't send you in there blind to the dangers you might face," Errol said.

"Here, let me do it." Seth accepted the eyedropper from Errol. With his untreated eye squinted almost shut, Seth put a drop on the eyelashes. Blinking, he grimaced and growled. "Of course, the one person who doesn't need these is too old to help out."

Kendra shrugged.

"I use the drops every morning," Errol said. "You get accustomed to it."

"Maybe after your nerves die," Seth said, brushing more tears away. "What now?"

Errol held up an empty hand. His fingers fluttered, and a garage-door opener materialized. "Enter through the garage," Errol said. "You will probably find the door from the garage to the house unlocked. If not, force it open. Once inside, to the left of the door, on the wall you will see a keypad. On top of the protective charms, the funeral home has a conventional security system. Press 7109 and then hit enter."

"7109 enter," Seth echoed.

"How do you know that?" Kendra asked.

"The same way I know Archibald is gone," Errol replied. "Reconnaissance. I wouldn't send Seth in there unprepared.

What do you think I've been doing since I first contacted you?"

"How do I find the statue?" Seth asked.

"My best guess would be down in the basement. Access it by the elevator adjoining the viewing room. If you turn right after entering, you can't miss it. You'll be looking for a toadlike statue not much bigger than my fist. Very likely in plain view. Look in off-limits areas. When you find the figurine, feed it this." Errol held up a dog biscuit shaped like a bone.

"Feed the statue?" Seth questioned doubtfully.

"Until you feed it, the figurine will be immovable. Feed the statuette, pick it up, bring it to us, and I will drive you home." Errol handed Seth the garage-door opener and the dog biscuit. He also gave him a small flashlight, with the warning to use it only if necessary.

"We haven't covered what I do if I run into the living dead," Seth reminded Errol.

"You run," Errol said. "Reanimated corpses are not particularly swift or nimble. You won't have trouble staying ahead of them. But don't take any chances. If you encounter any undead adversaries, statue or no statue, retreat to the van."

Seth nodded gravely. "So just run, huh?" He did not sound fully satisfied with the plan.

"I doubt you'll have any trouble," Errol reassured him. "I've scouted this location thoroughly, and there has been no hint of undead activity. Should be a snap. In and out."

"You don't have to do this," Kendra said.

"Don't worry, I won't blame you if my brain gets eaten," Seth said. He opened the door and hopped out. "Although I can't help it if you blame yourself."

Seth jogged across the street and walked toward the lighted sign. A few cars came down the road toward him, and he averted his eyes from the bright headlights until they passed. On his way to the mortuary, Seth passed a small house that had been converted into a barber shop, and then a larger one that housed dental offices.

Even though he knew Kendra and Errol were close by, facing the forbidding mortuary was a lonely feeling. Glancing back at the Volkswagen van, Seth could not see the occupants inside. He knew they could see him, though, so he tried to look relaxed.

Beyond the illuminated sign at the edge of the yard was a neatly trimmed lawn bordered by tidily rounded hedges that came no higher than his knees. Large potted plants crowded the shadowy porch. Three balconies with low railings projected from the upper story. All the windows were dark and shuttered. A pair of cupolas crowned the mansion, along with several chimneys. Even forgetting the dead bodies inside, the house looked haunted.

Seth considered turning back. Going into the funeral home with Errol and Kendra had sounded like an adventure. Going inside alone felt like suicide. He could probably stomach a spooky house full of dead bodies. But he had seen amazing things at Fablehaven—fairies and imps and monsters. He knew such things really existed, and so he knew there was a serious possibility that he was walking into an actual zombie lair, presided over by a real-life vampire (regardless of what Errol called him).

Seth fidgeted with the garage-door opener. Did he really care this much about getting rid of the kobold? If Errol was such a pro, why was he having kids do his dirty work? Shouldn't somebody with more experience tackle this sort of problem, instead of a sixth-grader?

If he had been unaccompanied, Seth probably would have walked away. The kobold alone was just not worth it. But people were watching, expecting him to do this, and pride would not allow him to wimp out. He had followed through on some intimidating dares—going down steep hills on his bike, fighting a kid two grades older, eating live insects. He had almost died climbing an escalating series of wooden poles. Yet this was the worst so far, because going into a zombie lair alone not only meant you could die, it meant you could die in a really upsetting way.

No cars were coming down the road. Pressing the button on the garage-door opener, Seth hustled across the driveway. The door opened loudly. It made him feel conspicuous, but he told himself that anybody who saw a person going into a garage would not think twice about it. Of course, any zombies inside the mortuary now knew he had arrived.

An automatic light brightened the garage. The black, curtained hearse did little to make the mansion feel more cheery. Neither did the assemblage of taxidermic animals positioned on a workbench along one wall: a possum, a raccoon, a fox, a beaver, an otter, an owl, a falcon—and, in the corner, a huge black bear standing upright.

Seth entered the garage and tapped the button again. The garage door shut with a prolonged mechanical groan. He hurried to the door that would lead into the funeral home. The knob turned, and Seth eased the door open. He heard an immediate beeping. Light from the garage spilled into a hallway.

To the left of the door was a keypad, exactly where Errol had described. Seth punched in 7109 and hit enter. The beeping stopped. And the growling started.

Seth whipped around. The door was still open, and light from the garage revealed a mass of white dreadlocks approaching down the carpeted hall. At first Seth thought it was a monster. Then he realized it was a huge dog with such thick cords of fur that one of its ancestors must have been a mop. Seth did not know how the animal could see, it had so much hair dangling in its eyes. The growls continued rumbling, deep and steady, the kind of sound that meant at any second the dog might make a violent charge.

Seth had to reach a quick decision. He could probably leap out the door and shut it behind him before the dog reached him. But that would be the end of going after the statue. Maybe it would serve Errol right, for carrying out such lousy reconnaissance.

Then again, he was holding a dog biscuit. Surely the statue would not need the whole thing. "Sit," Seth commanded, calmly but firmly, extending his hand palm outward.

The dog grew silent and stopped advancing.

"That's a good dog," Seth said, trying to exude confidence. He had heard that dogs could sense fear. "Now sit," he ordered, repeating the gesture.

The dog sat, its shaggy head higher than Seth's waist. Seth snapped the biscuit in two and tossed half to the dog. The canine caught the biscuit on the fly. Seth had no idea how it saw the treat coming through all that fur.

Seth approached the dog and let it sniff his hand. A warm tongue caressed his palm, and Seth rubbed the top of the animal's head. "You're a good boy," Seth said in his special voice reserved for babies and animals. "You're not going to eat me, right?"

The automatic light in the garage switched off, plunging the hall into darkness. The only glow came from a tiny green bulb on the security keypad, so faint that it was useless. Seth remembered the shutters covering the windows. Even moonlight and the light from the sign could not penetrate the house. Well, that probably meant that people on the outside would not notice his flashlight, and he could not risk zombies sneaking up on him in the blackness, so he turned it on.

Once again he could see the dog and the hall. Seth moved down the hall to a large room with plush carpeting and heavy drapes. He swung the beam of his flashlight around, checking for zombies. Several couches and armchairs and a few tall lamps lined the perimeter of the room. The center of the room was empty, apparently so mourners could mingle. There was a place on one side where Seth figured they laid the casket for people to view the deceased. He had visited a room not too different from this one when his Grandma and Grandpa Larsen had died just over a year ago.

Several doors led out of the room. The word *Chapel* was written above a set of double doors. Some other doors were unmarked. A brass gate blocked access to an elevator. A sign above it announced, "Authorized Personnel Only."

The dog followed Seth as he crossed the room to the elevator. When Seth pushed the gate sideways, it collapsed like an accordion. Seth entered the elevator and shut the gate, preventing the dog from following. Black buttons projected from the wall, looking very old-fashioned. The floor buttons were marked "B," "1," and "2." Seth pushed "B."

The elevator lurched downward, rattling enough that Seth wondered if it was about to break. Through the gate Seth could see the wall of the elevator shaft scrolling by. Then the wall of the shaft disappeared. With a final squeal the ride came to an abrupt halt.

Without opening the gate, and keeping one hand near the elevator buttons, Seth shone the flashlight around the room. The last thing he wanted was to get cornered by zombies inside of an elevator.

It appeared to be the room where the bodies were prepared. It was much less fancy than the parlor above. He saw a worktable, and a table with wheels that had a casket on it. There were multiple storage cabinets and a big sink. Seth estimated that the casket would barely fit inside the elevator. One side of the room had what appeared to be a large refrigeration unit. He tried not to dwell upon what was kept in there.

He saw no statues, toadlike or otherwise. There was a door marked *Private* on the wall opposite the elevator. Satisfied that the room was zombie-free, Seth slid the gate open. He stepped out, tense, ready to leap back into the elevator at the slightest provocation.

The room remained silent. Walking between the worktable and the casket, Seth tried the private door. It was locked. The knob had a keyhole.

The door looked neither particularly strong nor unusually flimsy. It was built to open into the next room. Seth tried kicking it near the knob. It shuddered a bit. He tried a few more times, but, despite the repeated shuddering, the door showed no sign of weakening.

Seth supposed he could use the wheeled table to ram the door with the casket. But he doubted he could generate enough speed to strike the door much harder than he could kick it. And he could picture knocking the casket off the table and creating a huge mess. The casket might not be empty!

Another door, this one unmarked, also led out of the room. It was against the same wall as the elevator, so Seth had not seen it until after he had stepped into the room. Seth found that door unlocked. Behind it was a bare hall with doors along one side and an open doorway at the end.

Seth cautiously ventured down the hall. He realized that if zombies came at him from behind, he could become pinned in the basement, so he listened very carefully. The large room at the end of the hall was crammed almost from floor to ceiling with cardboard boxes. Seth hurried through the narrow aisles that granted access to the room, scanning for the statue. All he found was more boxes.

Back in the hall, Seth tried the other doors. One led to a bathroom. Behind the other door was a large storage closet full of cleaning supplies and various tools. One object among the mops and brooms and hammers caught his attention: an ax.

Seth returned with the ax to the private door. So much for stealth. If the garage door and elevator had not alerted the zombies, this should do the job. The ax was fairly heavy, but, choking up a little, he gave it a solid swing, and the bit crunched into the wood about a foot away from the doorknob. He wrenched it free and attacked the door again. A few more strokes and he had chopped a hole in the door large enough to reach his hand through. Seth wiped the handle of the ax with his shirt before setting it aside, just in case vampires knew how to check for fingerprints.

Seth shone his flashlight through the hole in the door. He could not see any reanimated corpses, but a zombie could easily be standing off to the side, out of view, waiting for his hand to appear. Reaching into the splintery hole, worried that clammy fingers might close around his wrist at any second, Seth felt the doorknob on the far side and unlocked it. Twisting the knob, he pushed the door open. Seth used the flashlight to examine the room. It was large and L-shaped, so the entirety was not in view at once. Funeral paraphernalia littered the room: nameless headstones, caskets lying horizontal or upended, easels with colorful wreaths of fake flowers. A long desk with a rolling chair and a computer was covered with a mess of papers. Beside the desk stood a row of tall filing cabinets.

Half-expecting slobbering zombies to burst from the caskets at any moment, Seth wove through the cluttered room until he could see around the corner of the "L." He found a red felt pool table underneath a ceiling fan. Inside an arched niche beyond the table, a statuette squatted atop a variegated block of marble.

Seth rushed to the recess in the wall. The statue was not on all fours like a toad. Rather, it sat upright on two legs with a pair of short arms folded across its chest. The figurine looked like a pagan idol with froglike features. A polished dark green, it appeared to be carved out of speckled jade, and stood about six or seven inches tall. Above the statue a sign read:

The brief message filled Seth with foreboding. What exactly would happen once he fed the frog? Errol had made it sound like it would simply enable him to carry the statue out of the mortuary.

The statue did not look too heavy. Seth tried to pick it up. The figurine would not budge. It felt welded to the block

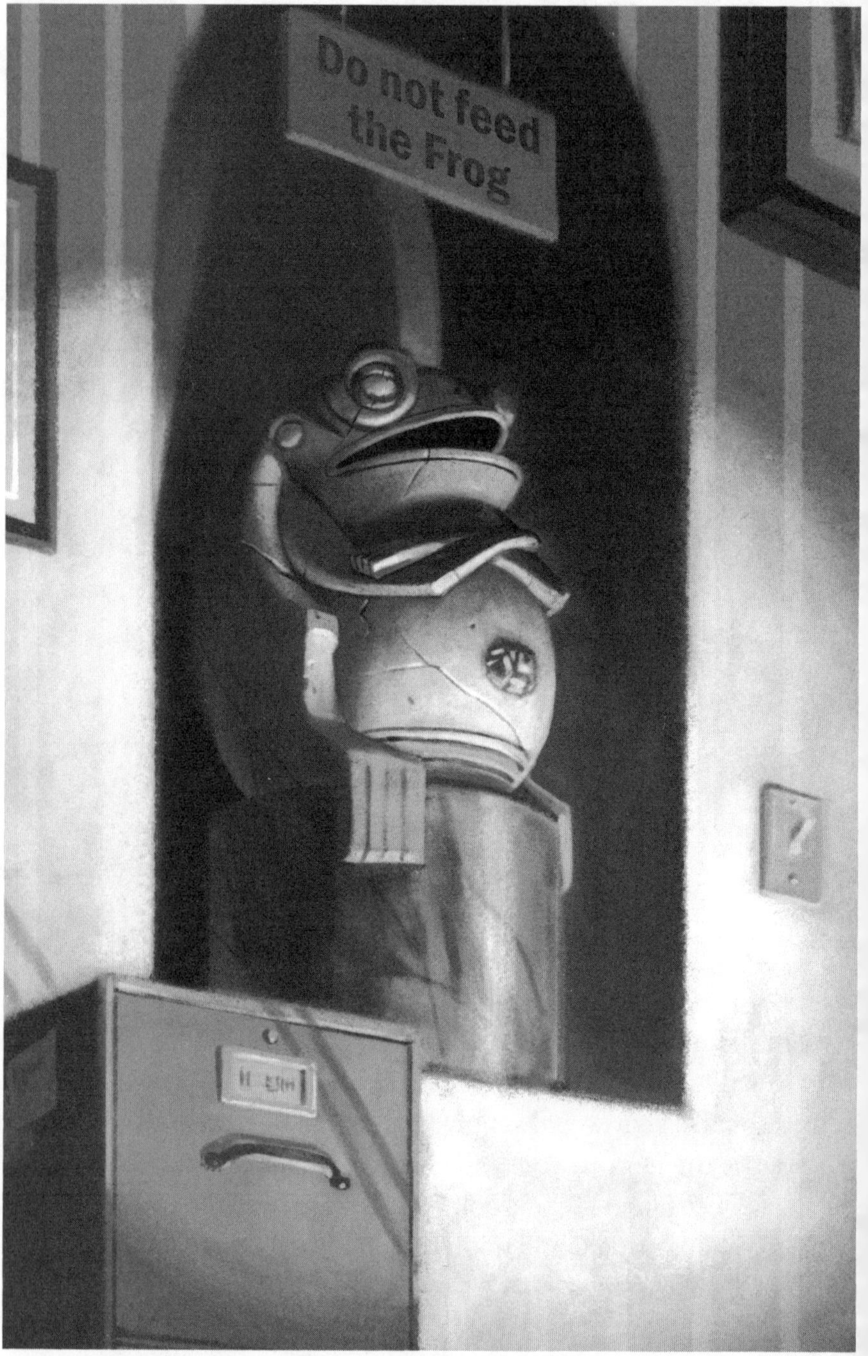
Do not feed
the Frog

of marble, which in turn felt firmly anchored to the base of the niche. Seth could not even slide the statuette or slightly tip it. Maybe Errol knew what he was talking about after all.

Not wanting to spend more time than necessary inside the funeral home, Seth held out the remaining half of the dog biscuit. Would the statuette actually eat it? Seth inched the treat forward. When the biscuit was almost touching the mouth, the froglike lips began to twitch. He moved the treat back, and the lips stopped moving. Holding the biscuit closer than ever, he saw the lips pucker outward, quivering.

Apparently it was going to work! Seth slid the biscuit into the eager jade mouth, careful not to let the figurine nip his fingertip. The statue gulped down the food, and once again sat motionless.

Nothing seemed to have changed, except that when Seth tried to pick up the statuette, it lifted off the marble block easily. Without warning, the statue squirmed and bit the side of his thumb. Yelling in surprise, Seth dropped the figurine and the flashlight onto the carpeted floor. The sensation of a jade statue wriggling like a living thing was extremely unnerving. Retrieving the flashlight, Seth checked the side of his thumb and found a row of tiny puncture wounds. The frog had teeth.

Seth nudged the fallen figurine with his foot. It did not twitch. Warily he picked it up, holding it near the base so if it tried to bite him again he could avoid the tiny fangs. The statue did not move. He tapped it on the head. The statuette was once again inanimate.

Seth hurriedly backtracked, exiting the room. There was nothing he could do to hide the damage to the door, so he opened the accordion gate and entered the elevator. It squealed up one floor and rattled to a stop. He opened the gate and stepped out.

The dog padding toward him made him jump, and he almost dropped the statue again. Fortunately, the shaggy animal seemed to have accepted his presence. Seth stooped and petted it for a moment, and then went to the door to the garage. He paused at the keypad and reset the alarm by pressing the "Away" button.

Closing the door behind him, Seth pressed the button to open the garage door. When the automatic light came on, he switched off the flashlight. Seth jogged out onto the driveway and pressed the button again to shut the garage.

Seth knew running would look more conspicuous, but he could not resist racing to the Volkswagen van. Errol opened the door and Seth climbed in.

"Well done," Errol said, starting the engine. It took a second to turn over.

"You were in there for a long time," Kendra said. "I was getting worried."

"I found a computer and played some video games," Seth said.

"While we were out here stressing about you?" Kendra exclaimed.

"I'm kidding," Seth said. "I had to whack down a door with an ax." He turned to Errol. "By the way, thanks for telling me about the dog."

They were now driving down the road, the lighted sign of the funeral home receding behind them. "There was a dog?" Errol said. "Archibald must really keep him hidden. Was he big?"

"Enormous," Seth said. "One of those dogs that looks like a giant mop. You know, with hair covering its eyes?"

"A komondor?" Errol said. "You're fortunate; that breed can be really unfriendly to strangers. They were originally bred to guard livestock in Hungary."

"I played nice and gave it half of the dog biscuit," Seth said. "The statue bit me!"

"Are you all right?" Kendra said.

"Yeah." Seth held up his thumb. "It's hardly bleeding."

"I should have warned you," Errol said. "Once the statue eats, it temporarily gets aggressive. Nothing to worry about, but they do nip at you."

"Tell the truth, you knew about the dog, didn't you?" Seth accused.

Errol knitted his brow. "What makes you say that?"

"Why send me in with a dog biscuit? You could have given me any food for the statue. I think you were worried I might not go if I knew there was a dog."

"I'm sorry, Seth," Errol said. "I assure you the biscuit was a coincidence. Why would I warn you about the undead, yet not mention a dog?"

"Good point," Seth admitted. "At least I didn't see any zombies. That was a relief."

"So how does this statue get rid of the kobold?" Kendra asked.

"For that," Errol said, "you need simply follow my instructions."

CHAPTER FOUR

Vanessa

The following morning in homeroom, well before the bell sounded, a steady murmur filled the air as students huddled in abnormal clusters. At the center of the clusters were the smartest kids, leafing through their notes. The others were trying to leech information, in hopes that some last-minute cramming might earn them a few extra right answers on the forthcoming finals.

Alyssa hovered near Sasha Goethe, gleaning information for Science. Alyssa normally got impressive grades, but she worried a lot nonetheless. Kendra felt confident about the upcoming exams. They were not weighted as heavily as they would be next year in high school, and she had kept up on her readings and homework all year. She had skimmed her notes and reviewed her old tests. Even with the distraction of the excursion to the mortuary the night before, she was unconcerned.

Besides, she had more pressing matters on her mind. The scabby kobold was the only other student in the room who appeared indifferent to the looming exams. Which made sense, considering he didn't have to take them. He sat at his desk with his hands folded. Mr. Reynolds, the same prematurely balding substitute from yesterday, sat behind Mrs. Price's desk.

A wrapped package rested in front of Kendra. The paper had a pattern of reindeer and snowflakes. She had found it on a closet shelf, left over from the previous Christmas. Inside the paper was a shoebox, and inside the box was the stolen statue.

The night before, prior to dropping off Kendra and Seth around the corner from their house, Errol had explained how to proceed. The figurine was apparently sacred to kobolds. Once a kobold took possession of it, he would be compelled to return it to the shrine where it belonged, hidden deep in the Himalayas. Errol also stressed that kobolds were suckers for gifts, so all they needed to do was wrap up the statue like a present and give it to him. The rest would take care of itself.

It sounded almost too easy to be true. But Kendra had learned at Fablehaven that sometimes powerful magic was worked through simple means. For example, keeping a captured fairy indoors overnight would turn her into an imp.

Kendra studied the kobold. The instant popularity Case had initially enjoyed was fading as his rancid breath became legendary. He had now also kissed Trina Funk and Lydia Southwell, and, along with Alyssa, they had wasted no time spreading the word about his chronic halitosis.

The bell would ring in less than a minute. Kendra had been toying with having somebody else deliver the gift, in case the kobold knew to distrust her. But with time running out, she decided that she could always rewrap it and have somebody less suspect give the figurine to him later if this attempt failed. By now he had seen the present in her possession anyway.

Kendra took the wrapped shoebox to his desk. "Hi, Case."

He leered up at her. "Kendra."

"I know I haven't been very kind since you arrived," Kendra said. "I thought I would make a peace offering."

The kobold glanced down at the present and back into her eyes. "What? More mouthwash?"

Kendra stifled a laugh. "No, something nice. If you don't want it—"

"Give it." He reached for the present, and she let him take it. He shook the package, revealing nothing, because Kendra had packed the statue snugly amid wadded newspapers.

The bell rang. "You're welcome to open it," Kendra said. Study groups disbanded and everyone went to their desks. Kendra returned to her desk as Case unwrapped the gift.

By the time Kendra sat down, Case had the lid off the shoebox and was rummaging through the newspapers. He froze, staring. Then he slowly pulled out the statuette, holding it gingerly. Glancing over his shoulder, he glowered at Kendra.

The substitute gave a couple of announcements and then welcomed the class to use the remainder of homeroom as a review session. Alyssa asked if he knew anything about Mrs. Price. He replied that he had not been informed.

The study clusters re-formed rapidly. The kobold collected his things, placing the statue in his backpack, and walked toward the door, giving Kendra a final venomous glare.

"Hey, where are you going?" the substitute asked.

"The rest room," Case replied.

"You need a hall pass," the substitute said.

"Ten to one I can manage without one," Case sneered.

The substitute could not have been older than thirty. He had a laid-back air and did not look accustomed to having students behave with such insolence. "Ten to one you're heading to the principal's office," the sub said, his face becoming stern.

The class was growing silent as the exchange continued. Case smirked. "I'll take that bet. Five hundred dollars. That would be, what, three years' earnings?"

Case opened the door. The substitute stood up. "You're not going anywhere!"

Case exited and dashed down the hall. The substitute remained impotently by the desk. "What's his name?" he asked, bewildered.

"Casey Hancock," Alyssa reported. "But you can call him dog breath."

✻ ✻ ✻

Seth was heading for the bus when he recognized a familiar man in an outmoded suit. He diverted from his course to speak with Errol.

"Did you hear?" Seth said. "Kendra gave Case the package this morning and he left immediately."

Errol nodded. "I followed the kobold out of town. You will never see him again. A kobold seldom travels far unless compelled."

"Thanks for your help," Seth said. "I better catch my bus."

"Can you spare a moment?" Errol asked. "You did an exceptional job at the funeral home last night. Better than many of the trained professionals I have partnered with in the past. I could use some assistance with one other task."

"What?"

"A similar mission, actually. I need to recover an amulet from a member of the Society of the Evening Star. It would issue quite a blow to their organization."

"They're the people trying to destroy all the magical preserves like Fablehaven," Seth said. "And free the demons."

"Sharp lad."

"Is it a vampire again?" Seth asked.

"Nothing so exotic," Errol assured him. "The amulet is on a houseboat. The owner is out of the country, so the boat is currently vacant. The only catch is, we'll have to drive a few hours to get there. It would take all night. If we left at ten or so, I could have you back before six in the morning."

"Tonight is a school night," Seth said.

"Which is why I was planning on tomorrow night," Errol said. "The school year will be over. Your sister can help with this one. The barrier on the houseboat functions only against those eighteen and older."

"I'll talk it over with her. How should I confirm?"

"I will be at the service station tomorrow night. Come as close to ten as you can. Show up before ten-thirty, and I'll be waiting. Otherwise I'll assume you declined."

"Got it. I better go; the buses will leave any minute."

"By all means," Errol said. "By all means."

※   ※   ※

Kendra placed a period after the final sentence of the final essay of her final exam. English. She knew she had aced it, just as she had sailed through the others. Once she handed in the test, middle school would be officially over. It was Friday afternoon, and there were almost three months between her and the next homework assignment.

Yet as Kendra turned in the exam, she did not experience the euphoria she had earned. Instead she was weighed down by the question of whether she should sneak out of her house to break into a houseboat hundreds of miles away with a virtual stranger and her younger brother.

As of that morning, she still had not reached her grandpa by telephone, and he still had not replied to the letter she had mailed Tuesday. She had told Seth that until she confirmed the identity of Errol Fisk with Grandpa, they were not going on a road trip with him in the middle of the night.

The thing with the kobold had been a desperate situation. Now they could afford to wait a day or two.

Seth had ranted about her being a traitor and a coward. He had complained that if there was a chance to harm the Society of the Evening Star, they had better take it. He had finished by threatening to join Errol with or without her.

Having completed the exam early, Kendra had about twenty minutes before the buses would be leaving. She went to her locker and took her time loading everything she wanted to keep into her backpack, including the pictures she had clipped from magazines and taped to the inside of the door. Maybe Seth had a point. Checking with Grandpa was more of a formality at this stage. Errol had already helped them dispose of the kobold. If he had wanted to harm them, he'd had his chance when he took them to the mortuary.

Kendra tried to be completely honest with herself. She was afraid of going to the houseboat. If it belonged to some-body from the Society of the Evening Star, it would be very dangerous. And this time she would have to go inside, not just wait in the van.

She zipped her backpack. What she wanted was for Grandpa Sorenson to tell her that Errol was a friend but that stealing amulets from houseboats in the middle of the night was no job for children. Or teenagers. And it was true! Barriers or no barriers, it seemed peculiar that Errol recruited kids for tasks like this.

She headed down the hall and out the doors. The sun was shining. The buses idled in a line along the curb. Only a few kids were on them. Ten minutes remained before school would officially let out.

Was Seth right? Was she a coward? She had been brave on the preserve when she sought help from the Fairy Queen and rescued everybody. She had been brave when trying to get rid of the kobold. Brave enough to sneak out of the house and go with Errol. But those were emergencies. She had been forced to be brave. What happened to her courage without an immediate threat? How dangerous was sneaking onto an empty houseboat? Nothing had happened at the mortuary; Seth had gone in and out. Errol would not take them to the houseboat if it was too dangerous. He was a professional.

Kendra climbed onto her bus, walked to the back, and plopped down onto a seat. Her last bus ride from Roosevelt Middle School. She was now in high school. Maybe she ought to start acting more like an adult and less like a scaredy-cat.

※　※　※

Seth whistled as he inventoried his emergency kit. He clicked the flashlight on and off. He examined an assortment of firecrackers. He inspected the slingshot he had received for Christmas.

Kendra sat on his bed, chin in her hand. "You really think firecrackers are going to come in handy?" she asked.

"You never know," Seth answered.

"I get it," Kendra said. "Somebody might want to have an early Fourth of July celebration."

Seth shook his head in exasperation. "Yeah, or we might need a diversion." He ignited a flame with his cigarette lighter to make sure it worked. Then he held up a couple of dog biscuits. "I added these since the mortuary. I might have been eaten alive without one."

"I can't believe you talked me into this," Kendra said.

"Neither can I," Seth agreed.

Mom opened the door, holding the cordless telephone. "Kendra, Grandpa Sorenson wants to speak with you."

Brightening, Kendra jumped off the bed. "Okay." She took the phone. "Hi, Grandpa."

"Kendra, I need you to go someplace where you can speak freely," Grandpa said, his tone urgent.

"Just a second." Kendra rushed into her room and shut the door. "What is it?"

"I fear you and your brother may be in danger," Grandpa said.

Her grip tightened on the phone. "Why?"

"I have just received reports of some disturbing activity in your area."

Kendra relaxed a little. "I know, I've been trying to call you. There was a kobold in my school."

"A what?" Grandpa exclaimed.

"It's okay, a guy named Errol Fisk helped us get rid of it. He knows your friend Coulter."

"Coulter Dixon?"

"I guess. Errol said Coulter found out about the kobold and recruited him to help us get rid of it."

"When did this happen?"

"This week."

Grandpa paused. "Kendra, Coulter has been here at Fablehaven for more than a month."

She squeezed the phone, knuckles white. A sick feeling was creeping into her stomach. "What do you mean?"

"I'll confirm with Coulter, but I'm sure this man approached you under false pretenses. You must not go near him."

Kendra was silent. She looked at her digital clock. It was 8:11 P.M. In less than two hours they were supposed to meet Errol at the service station. "He was going to pick us up tonight," she said.

"Pick you up?"

"To take us to steal an amulet from a houseboat. He said it would harm the Society of the Evening Star."

"Kendra, this man is almost certainly a member of the Society of the Evening Star. They recently stole something from a friend of mine."

Kendra's mouth was dry. Her heart was sinking. "What did they steal?"

"No matter," Grandpa said. "The problem is—"

"Not a little statue of a frog," Kendra said.

Now Grandpa was silent. "Oh, Kendra," he finally muttered. "Tell me what happened."

Kendra recounted how Errol had told them the only way to get rid of the kobold was to acquire the statue. She related how he had told them the owner of the mortuary was an evil viviblix in order to convince Seth to steal the frog.

"So that's how they did it," Grandpa said. "There was a

spell on the mortuary that would have prevented all but children from entering. Archibald Mangum is an old friend. He is no blix. He was away at his eightieth birthday party in Buffalo the night Seth stole the statue from his house. He phoned me a few minutes ago."

"I've been trying to call you all week," Kendra said. "And I wrote you a letter Tuesday."

"There has been foul play," Grandpa said. "I have not received your letter. I suspect it was intercepted, perhaps from my mailbox. I didn't know the phone was down until yesterday. We hardly use it except for emergencies. The phone company came out to fix it a few hours ago. They found where the line had been damaged, not far beyond the front gates. I asked if it looked like the line had been deliberately cut, and they said no, but I have my doubts. When Archibald called, my worries were multiplied. He has quietly kept an eye on you and Seth for me. Of course, I realized that any action taken against him could also involve you, but I did not expect this. The Society of the Evening Star is on the move."

"What do I do?" Kendra asked, feeling unbalanced.

"I have already set a plan in motion," Grandpa said. "Now I see that my suspicions were more warranted than I had anticipated. I told your mother that I was in an accident, and asked if you and Seth could come stay with us while I recover."

"What did she say?" Kendra asked.

"Your parents are willing as long as you and your brother want to come," Grandpa said. "I told her I wanted to invite you myself. Assuming you would agree, I already dispatched somebody to pick you up."

"Who?"

"You have not met her," Grandpa said. "Her name is Vanessa Santoro. She'll give you a code word: *kaleidoscope*. She should be there within a couple of hours."

"What should we do until then?"

"You said this Fisk character is expecting to meet you tonight?"

"We haven't confirmed with him," Kendra said. "I wanted to talk to you first." She deliberately neglected to mention that although she had not confirmed the rendezvous, she had already resolved to go. "He's going to wait for us at a gas station near our house. If we aren't there by ten-thirty, he'll know we aren't coming."

"I don't like the interest the Society is showing in you," Grandpa said pensively, as if talking to himself. "We'll have to puzzle that out later. For now, pack your things. Vanessa should arrive around ten-thirty herself. Be on the lookout. It may be tough to anticipate how Errol will react when the two of you fail to keep his appointment."

"Can you tell your friend to hurry?"

"She'll hurry," Grandpa said, chuckling. "For now, let your mother know your decision. Then I'll need to speak with her again, get her used to the idea that a friend of mine is going to swing by and pick you up tonight. I'll tell her Vanessa is a trusted neighbor who happens to be returning from a trip to Canada."

"Grandpa?"

"Yes?"

"You weren't really in an accident?" she asked.

"Nothing life-threatening, but yes, I'm rather banged up. There have been many interesting developments over the past months, and whether I like it or not, you are becoming involved. Right now, as dangerous as Fablehaven can be, it is the safest place for you."

"Grandma's not a chicken again or anything."

"Your grandmother is fine," he assured her.

"What about Mom and Dad? What if Errol Fisk goes after them?"

"Oh, no, Kendra. Don't worry about your parents. Their ignorance of the secret world we know about should be all the protection they need. With you and Seth out of the house, they will be much safer than any of us. Now, pass me off to your mother."

Kendra found her mom and handed her the telephone. She then raced to Seth's room and filled him in on everything she had discussed with Grandpa Sorenson.

"So Errol was using us," Seth said. "And if we'd gone with him tonight . . . I never learn my lesson, do I?"

"This wasn't your fault," Kendra said. "Errol had me fooled too. You were just being brave. That isn't always a bad thing."

The compliment seemed to buoy him up. "I bet Errol thought he had us in the bag. I wonder what he would have done with us. I wish I could see his face when we don't show up tonight."

"Hopefully by then we'll already be on the road."

Dad entered the room. He clapped his hands together and rubbed them. "We need to get you guys packed," he said. "You two must have really done a number on your grandparents last summer. Dad falls off the roof, and he wants you there to help him. I hope he knows what he's getting himself into."

"We'll be good," Seth said.

"Are those firecrackers?" Dad asked.

"Just little ones." Seth stuffed them into his emergency kit.

✤ ✤ ✤

Kendra paced in her room, watching the clock. She peeked out between her blinds every few minutes, hoping to see Vanessa pull up. The closer the time got to ten-thirty, the more anxious she became.

Her suitcase and her duffel bag were on her bed. She tried to distract herself by putting on her earphones and listening to music. She sat on the floor, closed her eyes, and leaned against the bed. Any minute Vanessa would pull up, and she and Seth would be on their way.

She heard a voice calling her name from far away. She opened her eyes and took off her earphones. Dad was standing over her. "She's here?" Kendra asked, standing up.

"No, I said you have a phone call. Katie's dad, he's wondering if you know where Katie might be."

Kendra accepted the phone. Katie Clark? Kendra barely knew her. "Hello?"

"You disappointed me, Kendra." It was Errol. Dad left the room.

Kendra spoke quietly. "Sorry, we decided tonight wouldn't work. How did you get our number?"

"The phone book," Errol said, sounding hurt by the accusation in her tone. "Sorry about pretending to be the parent of a schoolmate. I didn't want to startle your parents."

"Good thinking," Kendra said.

"I was wondering if I might persuade you to join me after all. I'm down the street from your home, right where I dropped you off the other night. You see, tonight is the last night the houseboat will be unoccupied, and that amulet could cause great harm to your grandparents and their preserve."

"I'm sure it could," Kendra said sincerely. Her mind was racing. Errol could not possibly know she and Seth planned to escape to Fablehaven tonight. She had to pretend she still thought of him as a friend. "Isn't there some other way? I was so scared the other night."

"If I knew of another solution, I would not trouble you. My predicament is dire. The amulet could cause tremendous harm in the wrong hands. Please, Kendra, I helped you. I need you to return the favor."

Kendra heard a vehicle pulling to a stop outside. The engine quit. Parting the blinds, she saw a woman climbing out of a sleek sports car. "I don't think I can," Kendra said. "I'm really sorry."

"Looks like you have a visitor," Errol said, a trace of

suspicion entering his voice. "That's quite a car. Friend of the family?"

"I'm not sure," Kendra said. "Look, I need to go."

"Very well." The line went dead.

Dad poked his head in. "Everything okay?"

Kendra put the phone down, trying not to let her anxiety show. "Katie's dad was just freaking out a little," she said. "I don't hang out with Katie much, so I couldn't really help him. I'm sure she's fine."

There was a knock at the door.

"That must be your ride." Dad grabbed the suitcase and the duffel bag off the bed. Kendra followed him to the living room, where Mom stood chatting with a statuesque woman. Tall and slender, the woman had a lustrous cascade of black hair and an olive complexion. She looked Spanish or Italian, with generous lips and a playful arch to her eyebrows. Her cosmetics were applied with an expertise Kendra had never seen outside of fashion magazines. She wore trendy jeans, brown boots, and a snug, stylish leather jacket.

As Kendra entered the room, the woman smiled, her expressive eyes lighting up. "You must be Kendra," the woman said warmly. "I'm Vanessa Santoro." She had the faint remnant of an accent.

Kendra extended her hand. Vanessa clasped only her fingers. Dad introduced himself and Vanessa offered him a similar handshake. Despite her polished looks and demeanor, her fingernails were incongruously short. Seth came into the room and stopped in his tracks. Kendra felt embarrassed for him—he was so unable to disguise his amazement at Vanessa's striking appearance.

"I've looked forward to finally meeting the famous Seth Sorenson," Vanessa said.

"Me?" Seth replied inanely.

Vanessa smiled tenderly. She seemed accustomed to making boys tongue-tied. Kendra was starting not to like her.

Vanessa glanced at her small, fashionable watch. "I hate to be in a rush, but we have a lot of ground to cover before the night ends."

"You're welcome to stay the night here and get a fresh start in the morning," Mom said. "We could make up the spare bed."

Kendra experienced an acute moment of distress. They had to get out of there. Errol was waiting outside, and he had acted suspicious of Vanessa. Who knew what he might try during the night?

Vanessa shook her head with a regretful smile. "I have an appointment tomorrow," she said. "No worries, I'm a night owl. I slept in late. We'll get to Stan's in one piece."

"Can I get you some refreshments?" Mom pursued.

Vanessa held up a hand. "I have goodies in the car," she said. "We should get on the road."

Dad had pulled out his wallet. "At least let us chip in on gas."

"I wouldn't think of it," Vanessa insisted.

"You're saving us a long drive," Dad persisted. "It's the least—"

"I was going there anyhow," Vanessa said, picking up Seth's suitcase, the largest of the bunch. "Giving your children a lift is my pleasure." Dad snatched Kendra's suitcase before Vanessa could grab it as well. Instead Vanessa seized Seth's duffel bag.

Mom opened the door, and Vanessa walked out, followed by Dad. "I can get my bags," Seth said from behind.

"I'm quite capable," Vanessa assured him, striding easily toward her car.

"Whoa!" Seth said when he got a look at her dark blue sports car.

Dad whistled. "Ferrari?"

"No," Vanessa said. "Custom made. I got a deal through a friend."

"You'll have to introduce me," Dad said.

"In your dreams," Mom muttered.

Standing beside the sports car, Kendra could not believe she was going to get to ride in it all the way to Fablehaven. Low and aerodynamic, the glossy vehicle had twin tailpipes, a sunroof, and fat tires like a race car. In spite of the dead insects plastered to the front, it looked like the sort of vehicle you would expect to see in a showroom or at a car expo—not something that anybody would actually drive.

Vanessa pressed a couple of buttons on her key chain. The passenger door swung open and the trunk popped up. "There should just be room for the suitcases in the trunk," she said. She leaned the passenger seat forward and tucked Seth's duffel bag behind the driver's seat.

"Shotgun," Seth called.

"Sorry," Vanessa said. "House rules. Tallest passenger gets shotgun. The back is a bit cramped."

Seth drew himself up to his full height. "I've almost caught up with her," he said. "Besides, she's more flexible."

"Good," Vanessa said, "because we'll have to slide her seat forward to fit the two of you. I don't often have riders in the back." Dad handed Kendra's duffel bag to Vanessa and then loaded the suitcases into the trunk.

Seth slouched into the backseat and fastened his seat belt. Vanessa slid the passenger seat forward a bit and pushed the back upright. "Can you live with that?" Seth nodded glumly. His legs were twisted sideways with the knees together. "Kendra might be able to spare an extra inch or two once she gets settled," Vanessa soothed.

Vanessa stepped aside so Kendra could get in the car. Kendra met her eyes and glanced at the Volkswagen van parked down the road. Vanessa winked in a way that suggested she was aware of the threat. Kendra hesitated for another moment. "Kaleidoscope," Vanessa murmured.

Kendra got into the car and Vanessa shut the door. The engine roared to life spontaneously. Vanessa thumbed her key chain again and the driver's door opened.

Mom and Dad stood together on the curb, waving. Doubting whether her parents would be able to see her through the tinted glass, Kendra rolled down her window and waved back. According to Grandpa, with her and Seth out of the house, Mom and Dad would be out of danger. Although Kendra was unsure what new hazards awaited at

Fablehaven, at least she could take comfort knowing her departure would ensure the safety of her parents.

Vanessa scooted behind the wheel and closed the door. Her demeanor instantly changed as she tugged on a pair of black driving gloves. "How long has he been there?" she asked, switching on the lights, throwing the manual transmission into gear, and pulling forward.

Calling a final good-bye, Kendra rolled up the window. "Only a few minutes, I think," Kendra said. "He showed up after we skipped out on meeting him at the service station."

"Why didn't you tell me?" Seth complained.

"I just found out," Kendra said. "He called. I was getting off the phone with him when Vanessa pulled up. He was trying to talk me into going."

They drove past the Volkswagen van. Looking back, Kendra saw the headlights come on and the van pull into the street behind them. "He's following us," Seth said.

"Not for long," Vanessa promised. "Once we're out of earshot from your parents, we'll get rid of him quick." She put on a pair of sunglasses.

"Isn't it a little dark for sunglasses?" Seth said.

"Night vision," Vanessa explained. "I can kill the lights and go as fast as I like."

"Awesome!" Seth said.

They turned a corner, heading toward the interstate. Vanessa looked over at Kendra. "You were just on the phone with him?"

"Watch out!" Kendra yelled, pointing straight ahead. A gigantic humanoid figure made of straw shambled out into the road, waving a pair of crude arms. Having just rounded a corner, they were not going very fast. Vanessa swerved, but the monstrous figure leapt sideways to continue blocking their path. Vanessa slammed on the brakes. The seat belts locked, and the car stopped about ten yards shy of the creature.

Yellow and bristly under the bright headlights, the oafish figure towered at least ten feet above the asphalt, straddling the yellow line in the center of the road. It had short legs with large feet, a massive torso, and long, thick arms. The bushy head lacked eyes, but a gaping mouth appeared when the monstrosity let out a raspy roar.

"A haystack?" Seth said, sounding bewildered.

"A dullion," Vanessa corrected, throwing the car into reverse. "A pseudo golem."

The dullion charged. The engine growled and the tires squealed as they backed away. Vanessa expertly whipped the car around and switched gears, wheels shrieking. They were suddenly going forward again, away from the creature. The sharp odor of burnt rubber filled the car.

As they neared the intersection where they had just turned, the Volkswagen van screeched to a stop, blocking their escape. A second car, an older-model Cadillac, pulled up beside it, completing the barricade. The road was only two lanes wide, and the scant shoulder was steep and rocky.

Vanessa cranked the car into a slide and, after a wild fishtail, tires spinning and smoking, they were again facing the lumbering strawman. The bulky creature shuffled toward them. Vanessa gunned the engine. As the screaming tires gained traction, the car picked up speed, but with the dullion rapidly drawing closer, there was not enough space to get going really fast.

Without much room to maneuver, Vanessa did her best, bringing the car to the right edge of the road, then cutting across to the left just before they reached the monster. The tactic kept them from plowing directly into the dullion, but the lunging strawman pounded the car with its huge fists as they roared past. It sounded like they had been struck by a rocket. The car trembled and skidded, and for a terrible moment Kendra thought they were going to sail off the road, but Vanessa regained control and they raced away.

Part of the roof had crumpled above Kendra, and cracks webbed her window and the sunroof. The wheels smelled like they were on fire. But the engine purred and the car seemed to be driving smoothly as the speedometer topped ninety.

"Sorry about the turbulence," Vanessa said. "Everybody all right?"

"I bet we left some sweet skid marks," Seth gushed. "What was that thing?"

"A golem made out of straw," Kendra said.

"It looked ridiculous," Seth said. "Like a moving haystack."

Kendra realized that Seth had not seen the true form of the creature that had assailed them. "You haven't had milk, Seth."

"Oh, yeah. Did he look like Hugo?"

"Sort of," Kendra said, "but bigger and sloppier."

"The thing bashed us hard," Seth said. "He caved in the roof."

They turned onto a wider road, tires whining mildly, then accelerated aggressively. "We were lucky to get away with so little damage," Vanessa said. "The body of the car has been reinforced and the windows are bulletproof. A lesser vehicle would no longer be running. They chose the right spot for an ambush."

"How could something made of hay hit us so hard?" Seth asked.

"Who knows what was underneath the straw?" Kendra said.

"Which is why I didn't just ram him in the first place," Vanessa said. "Good thing for us."

Kendra checked the speedometer. They were going faster than a hundred miles per hour. "Don't you worry about speed traps?"

Vanessa grinned. "Nobody will be able to catch us without a helicopter."

"Really?" Seth said.

"I've never had a ticket," Vanessa bragged. "But I've been chased. I'm tough to catch, especially outside of metropolitan areas. I'll have you to Fablehaven in a little over two hours."

"Two hours!" Kendra exclaimed.

"How do you think I reached your house so soon after you spoke with Stan? We can comfortably average a hundred and fifty on the interstate. Late at night, with our lights off, anybody holding a radar gun will think they clocked a UFO."

"This might be the coolest day of my life," Seth said. "Except that I don't have anyplace to put my legs."

"I don't normally speed for fun," Vanessa explained. "But we might have enemies following us. Tonight, it's the smartest course of action. By the way, Seth, your grandma sent you this." She opened a small ice chest between the front seats and removed a little bottle of milk.

"Now you tell me, after I missed the dullion." He accepted the milk and drank it. "What's the difference between a dullion and a golem?"

"Quality, mostly," Vanessa said. "Dullions are a bit easier to create. Although I haven't seen one in ages. Like golems, they're nearly extinct. Whoever was after you has unusual resources."

They drove in silence for a moment. Kendra folded her arms. "I'm sorry we wrecked your beautiful car."

"It wasn't your fault," Vanessa said. "Believe it or not, I've given cars bigger bruises than that one."

Kendra frowned. "I feel so stupid for letting Errol take advantage of us."

"Your grandfather filled me in," Vanessa said. "You were trying to do the right thing. It was a textbook Society infiltration—setting up a threat, then making it look like they helped you solve the problem in order to build trust. I'm sure they also cut off your communication with Stan. Speaking of Stan . . ."

Vanessa flipped open a small cell phone. Kendra and Seth sat in silence while Vanessa reported to Grandpa that they were on the road and all right. She briefly related the incident with Errol and the dullion, then snapped the phone shut.

"What did I steal from Grandpa's friend?" Seth asked.

"A demon called Olloch the Glutton," Vanessa said. "I'm assuming you fed it?"

"Errol said it was the only way to move it," Seth said wretchedly.

"Errol was right," Vanessa said. "You broke the spell that bound it. It bit you?"

"Yeah, is that bad?"

"They'll tell you more about it at Fablehaven," Vanessa promised.

"Did it poison me?"

"No."

"Am I going to turn into a frog or something?"

"No. Wait until Fablehaven. Your grandparents have much to share with you."

"Please tell me now," Seth said.

"I'll check the wound when we stop for gas."

"Wouldn't *you* want to know?" Seth pleaded.

She paused. "I suppose I would. But I told your grandparents I would let them deliver the news, and I like to be true to my word. There is some danger involved, but nothing immediate. I'm sure we will get it resolved."

Seth fingered the tiny scabs on his hand. "Okay. Is there anything you *can* tell us?"

They reached the on-ramp for the interstate. "Keep those seat belts fastened," she replied.

CHAPTER FIVE

New Arrivals

When the car finally slowed and pulled onto the gravel driveway, Kendra was fighting to keep her eyes open. She had learned that even rocketing along the freeway at one hundred and forty miles per hour became monotonous after a while. It did not take long to lose the sense of how fast you were going. Especially in the dark.

After they left the highway, the road curved more, and Vanessa slowed considerably. She had warned that if there were another ambush, it would most likely come near the entrance to Fablehaven.

As they crunched over the gravel, a single headlight came toward them from around a bend. It belonged to a four-wheeler. Dale rode on it, and waved when he saw them.

"All clear," Vanessa said. They followed Dale past the

No Trespassing signs and through the tall, spiked, wrought-iron gates. He stopped to close the gates behind them while Vanessa proceeded to the house.

Kendra felt a vast sense of relief to be back at Fablehaven. Part of her had wondered whether she would ever return. At times, the previous summer seemed unreal, like a long, strange dream. But there was the house, lights shining in the windows. The stately gables, the weathered stonework, and the turret on the side. Come to think of it, she had never found her way into the turret, even though she had accessed both sides of the attic. She would have to ask Grandpa about it.

Amid the shadowed shrubs of the garden, Kendra noticed the colorful twinkle of fairies flitting about. They were rarely out in great numbers after sundown, so she was mildly surprised to see at least thirty or forty drifting throughout the yard—flickering in red, blue, purple, green, orange, white, and gold. Kendra supposed the unusual quantity could be explained by the increased fairy population resulting from the hundreds of imps she had helped restore to fairy form the previous year.

It was sad to think that her friend Lena would not be there to welcome her. The fairies had returned the housekeeper to the pond from which Patton Burgess had lured her years ago. Lena had not seemed eager to go back, but then the last time Kendra had seen her, Lena had tried to pull her into the pond. Even so, Kendra felt determined to find a way to free her friend from her watery prison. She remained convinced that, deep down, Lena preferred life as a mortal to life as a naiad.

Vanessa brought the damaged sports car to a stop in front of the house. Grandma Sorenson started walking from the front porch to the driveway. Kendra climbed out and pulled the seat forward to release Seth from his confinement. He scrambled out, then paused to stretch.

"I'm so relieved to see you're all right," Grandma said, giving Kendra a hug.

"Except my legs are numb," Seth groaned, rubbing his calves.

"He means we're happy to see you, too," Kendra apologized.

Grandma embraced Seth, who seemed a little reluctant. "Look at you," she said. "You've grown a mile."

Dale skidded to a stop on the four-wheeler, leapt off, and helped Vanessa take the suitcases out of the trunk. Seth hurried over to help. Kendra reached into the backseat and retrieved the duffel bags.

"Looks like you took quite a hit," Grandma said, surveying the gash in the roof of the otherwise streamlined vehicle.

"She still handled surprisingly well," Vanessa said, picking up Seth's suitcase. Seth reached for it.

"We'll cover any costs for repairs," Grandma said.

Vanessa shook her head. "I spend a fortune on insurance. Let them foot the bill." She rewarded Seth's persistence by relinquishing his suitcase.

Together they walked to the front door and entered the house. Grandpa sat in a wheelchair in the entry hall. His left leg was in a cast that went from his toes to the top of his shin. A second cast covered his right arm from wrist to shoulder. Fading bruises marked his face, yellowish and gray splotches. But he was grinning.

A pair of men flanked Grandpa. One was a hulking Polynesian with a broad nose and cheerful eyes. His tank top revealed massive, sloping shoulders. A thorny green tattoo wreathed his thick upper arm. The other man was an older fellow a few inches shorter than Kendra, thin and wiry. His head was bald except for a gray tuft in the middle and a fringe around the sides. He wore several trinkets around his neck, affixed to leather cords or dull chains. He also wore a couple of braided bracelets and a wooden ring. None of it looked valuable. The pinky finger was missing from his left hand, as was part of the ring finger.

"Welcome back," Grandpa cried, beaming. "It's so good to see you." Kendra wondered if he was trying to compensate for his injured appearance with exuberance. "Kendra, Seth, I would like you to meet Tanugatoa Dufu." Grandpa gestured at the Polynesian man with his unbroken arm.

"Everyone calls me Tanu," he said. He was soft-spoken, with a deep voice and clear enunciation. His playful eyes and mild voice went a long way toward offsetting his otherwise intimidating appearance.

"And this is Coulter Dixon, a name Kendra has heard before," Grandpa said.

Coulter regarded them with a measuring gaze. "Any friend of Stan's is a friend of mine," he said, sounding less than sincere.

"Nice to meet you," Kendra said.

"Any friend of Grandpa's . . ." Seth added.

Dale and Vanessa collected the bags Kendra and Seth were holding and started up the stairs.

"And of course the two of you have met Vanessa Santoro," Grandpa said. "Tanu, Coulter, and Vanessa have joined us here at Fablehaven to help with the workload. As you can see, I took a tumble last week, so their assistance has become even more valuable in recent days."

"What happened?" Seth asked.

"We'll reserve that discussion, and many others, for tomorrow. Midnight is long gone. You've had an eventful day. Your room is ready and waiting. Get some sleep, and we'll make sense of the situation in the morning."

"I want to know what bit me," Seth said.

"Tomorrow," Grandpa promised.

"I don't think I could sleep now," Kendra said.

"You may surprise yourself," Grandma said from behind, ushering Kendra and Seth toward the stairs.

"Morning will come soon enough," Grandpa said. As Kendra started up the stairs, Tanu wheeled Grandpa in the direction of the study.

Kendra ran her hand along the smooth finish of the banister. She had seen this house in ruins after Seth had foolishly opened the attic window on Midsummer Eve. And she had seen it restored after an army of brownies had repaired it overnight, making unpredictable improvements in much of the furniture. As Kendra entered the attic playroom, it felt familiar and safe, in spite of the night when she and her brother were pinned inside a circle of salt by ferocious invaders.

"Here's your things," Dale said, indicating the bags beside the beds. "Welcome back."

"Sweet dreams," Vanessa said, exiting the room with Dale.

"Can I offer you anything?" Grandma asked. "Some warm milk?"

"Sure," Seth said. "Thanks."

"Dale will bring it up momentarily," Grandma said. She gave each of them a hug. "I'm so glad you arrived safely. Have pleasant dreams. We'll catch up properly in the morning." She left the room.

Seth dug into his suitcase. "Can you keep a secret?" he asked.

Kendra crouched to unzip her duffel bag. "Yes, but you can't, so I'm sure you'd tell me either way."

He pulled a jumbo pack of size C batteries from his suitcase. "I'm going to leave here a millionaire."

"Where'd you get those?"

"I picked them up a long time ago," Seth said. "Just in case."

"You think you're going to sell them to the satyrs?"

"So they can watch TV."

Kendra shook her head. The satyrs they had met in the woods after stealing soup from the ogress had promised Seth gold if he would bring them batteries for their portable television. "I'm not sure I would trust Newel and Doren to pay up."

"That's why all payments have to be made in advance," Seth said, replacing the batteries in his suitcase and taking out the oversized T-shirt and shorts that he used as pajamas. "We've already talked about it."

"When?"

"Last summer, while you were sleeping forever after the fairies kissed you—during one of those rare moments when somebody wasn't scolding me. I'll be in the bathroom." He headed out the door and down the stairs.

Kendra took advantage of the opportunity to change into her nightclothes. Not long after she changed, there came a soft knock at the door. "Come in," she said. Dale entered with two mugs of warm milk on a tray. He left the drinks on the nightstand.

Pulling back her sheets, Kendra climbed into bed and began sipping at her milk. Seth came into the room, picked up his mug, and chugged the contents. Wiping his mouth on his arm, he walked over to the window. "There's lots of fairies out tonight."

"I bet they'll be happy to see you again," Kendra said. Seth had started a feud with the fairies during their previous visit after he had captured one and inadvertently turned her into an imp.

"They forgave me," he said. "We're friends now." He switched off the light and jumped into bed.

Kendra finished her milk and placed the empty mug on the nightstand. "You're not going to do anything stupid this time, are you," she said.

"I've learned my lesson."

"Because it sounds like something bad is going on," Kendra said. "They don't need you making it worse."

"I'll be the perfect grandchild."

"Once you get your gold from the satyrs," Kendra said.

"Yeah, after that."

She lay back, letting her head sink into the feathery pillow, and stared up at the sharp angles of the attic ceiling. What would Grandpa and Grandma tell them in the morning? Why had Errol taken such an interest in them? Why had he ambushed them? What had bitten Seth? What about Vanessa, Tanu, and Coulter? What were their stories? Where had they come from? How long would they stay? Why replace Lena with three people? Wasn't Fablehaven supposed to be a big secret? Even though it was late and she felt drowsy, her mind was too full of questions for sleep to find her quickly.

❧ ❧ ❧

The next morning, Kendra awoke with Seth shaking her shoulder. "Come on," he said, hushed and excited. "It's time for answers."

Kendra sat up. She blinked several times. She wanted answers too. But why not sleep in a little first? It was this way every Christmas—Seth awakening the whole house at the crack of dawn, anxious and impatient. She swung her legs out of bed, grabbed her duffel bag, and walked down the stairs to the bathroom to freshen up.

When Kendra finally descended the stairs to the entry hall, she found Vanessa carrying a tray laden with steaming scrambled eggs and dark toast. Once again, Vanessa was dressed in a stylish outfit and her makeup was applied with subtle artistry. She looked too sophisticated to be holding a tray of food like a maid. "Your grandparents want you to join them in the study for a private breakfast," Vanessa said.

Kendra followed Vanessa into the study. Another tray with drinks, jam, and butter was already on the desk. Grandpa sat in his wheelchair, Grandma sat in the chair behind the desk, and Seth sat in one of the oversized armchairs in front of the desk. An empty plate rested on his lap. Kendra noticed a cot in the corner where Grandpa now apparently slept.

The study was an eye-catching room, full of odd knick-knacks. Strange tribal masks lined a shelf, golfing trophies crowded another, a collection of fossils vied for attention on a third. Half of a large geode glittered in a corner. Plaques, certificates, and a framed display of medals and ribbons decorated a portion of one wall. The savage head of a boar hung mounted not far from the window. Younger versions of Grandpa and Grandma Sorenson grinned from multiple pictures, some black and white, others in color. On the desk, inside a crystal sphere with a flat bottom, floated a fragile skull no bigger than Kendra's thumb. She settled into the other leather armchair.

"Thank you, Vanessa," Grandma said.

Vanessa nodded and exited.

"We take turns cooking meals these days," Grandma said, spooning eggs onto her plate. "Come dish up before it gets cold. Nobody can match Lena, but we try our best. Even Stan was in the rotation before the accident."

"Even Stan?" Grandpa blustered. "Have you forgotten my lasagna? My omelets? My stuffed mushrooms?"

"I meant because you're so busy," Grandma soothed. She raised a hand to partly hide her mouth, as if confiding a secret to her grandchildren. "He's been a bit crabby since the accident."

Grandpa was visibly biting his tongue, probably because another indignant outburst would only confirm Grandma's words. Under his bruises, his face was reddening. Kendra scooped some eggs onto her plate while Seth buttered a piece of toast.

"What happened to you?" Kendra asked Grandpa.

"Mom said you fell off the roof," Seth said, "but we weren't buying it."

"That would take us into the middle of the story," Grandpa said, regaining his composure. "Better to start at the beginning."

"You'll get to the part about what bit me?" Seth verified hopefully.

Grandma nodded. "But first a question for Kendra. Did Errol ever indicate that he knew anything about what transpired between you and the fairies?"

"Yeah," Kendra said, sitting back down and picking up a piece of toast. "That was partly how he convinced me to trust him. He said that he knew I had been fairystruck, and offered the information as proof that he knew Grandpa's friend Coulter." She put some eggs onto her toast and took a bite.

"The imp," Grandpa growled, drumming the fingers of his good hand on his cast. He shared a glance with Grandma.

"What imp?" Seth asked.

"The imp that put him in that wheelchair," Grandma said.

"I thought all the imps changed back into fairies," Kendra said.

"Apparently a few imps were not at the chapel when the empowered fairies were curing the others," Grandpa said. "But we're getting ahead of ourselves." He stared at Grandma for a moment. "We tell them, right?"

She gave a single, small nod.

Grandpa leaned forward in his wheelchair and lowered his voice. "What we are about to tell you must not leave this room. You must not discuss it even with others we trust, like Dale, or Vanessa, or Tanu, or Coulter. Nobody should know that you know. Or the danger will only increase. Am I understood?"

Kendra and Seth both agreed.

Grandpa eyed Seth. "I mean nobody, Seth."

"What?" he said, squirming a little in his seat. "I promise I won't tell anyone."

"See that you don't," Grandpa admonished solemnly. "I am taking a risk allowing you to return to Fablehaven after the harm you caused. I do it partly because I trust that you have learned a hard lesson about caution, and partly because it may be necessary for your protection. This is information we would prefer not to share with anyone, let alone children. But your grandmother and I feel that you have become too deeply involved for us not to reveal the whole story. You have a right to understand the hazards you face."

Kendra glanced at Seth. He looked so excited that he could hardly contain himself. Although she was also curious, she dreaded to hear the specifics of any threat so somber and secretive.

"I have already related part of the story," Grandma said. "Last summer, in the attic, before we went to rescue your grandfather, I mentioned some reasons why Fablehaven is different from most other magical preserves. I told you in case your grandpa and I perished and you survived."

"Fablehaven is one of five secret preserves," Kendra said.

"Very good, Kendra," Grandpa said.

"The five secret preserves each have a powerful item hidden on them," Kendra continued. "Not many people know about the secret preserves."

"Very few indeed," Grandma said. "And none know the location of all five."

"One probably does," Grandpa corrected.

"Well, if he does, he has never let on," Grandma replied.

"I've wondered a lot about what you told us," Kendra said. "It seems really mysterious."

Grandpa cleared his throat. He looked almost hesitant to speak. "Did Errol ever allude to Fablehaven as a secret preserve housing a special artifact?"

"No," Kendra said. Seth shook his head.

"And he did nothing to cajole that information out of you?" Grandpa pursued.

"No," Seth said. Kendra agreed.

Grandpa leaned back. "That, at least, is a relief."

"But we must continue with our plan," Grandma said.

Grandpa waved his hand. "Of course. We'll proceed as if the secret is out."

"You think they know?" Kendra asked.

Grandpa frowned. "The Society of the Evening Star should not even be aware that this preserve exists. Enormous efforts have been taken to maintain our anonymity. Yet we know the Society colluded with Muriel and nearly managed to overthrow Fablehaven last summer. And so we must assume that they are aware Fablehaven is a secret preserve, and realize what it contains."

"What?" Seth asked. "What is the artifact?"

"By itself, an ancient talisman of tremendous power," Grandpa said. "In connection with the other four, the key to Zzyzx, the great prison where literally thousands of the most powerful demons from every age of this world are incarcerated."

"None remain who know its location," Grandma whispered.

"Except, perhaps, the Society," Grandpa murmured, scowling at the floor. "If the five talismans were ever brought together and used to open Zzyzx, the results would be . . . catastrophic. Apocalyptic. The end of the world."

"Endless night," Grandma echoed. "Across all the earth. The mighty fiends inside of Zzyzx would make Bahumat look like an infant. A lapdog. In their absence, we long ago lost the ability to contend with beings of their power. Even the fairy army you summoned would quail before them. Our only hope is to keep them imprisoned."

The room was silent. Kendra could hear the grandfather clock ticking. "So how do we stop them?" Seth finally said.

"That is the right question," Grandpa said, jabbing a finger at Seth for emphasis. "I put that same query to the unofficial leader of the Conservators' Alliance."

"What's that?" Seth asked.

"The caretakers of all the preserves around the world, along with their allies, belong to the Conservators' Alliance," Grandma explained.

"Each caretaker has an equal say, with none officially presiding," Grandpa said. "But for centuries we have benefited from the advice and aid of our greatest ally—the Sphinx."

"Like in Egypt?" Kendra asked.

"Whether he is actually a sphinx, we do not know," Grandpa said. "Surely he is more than mortal. His service dates back to the twelfth century. I have spoken with him face-to-face only twice, and on both occasions he was in the likeness of a man. But many of the most powerful creatures, like dragons, can assume human form when it suits them."

"You asked the Sphinx what to do?" Seth asked.

"I did," Grandpa said. "Face-to-face, as a matter of fact. He suggested we move the artifact. You see, at roughly three hundred years old, Fablehaven is among the youngest preserves. Of the secret preserves, it is by far the newest. One of the secret preserves was compromised not long before Fablehaven was founded. The vault housing the artifact was transported here, and Fablehaven was kept a secret thereafter. So the idea is not without precedent."

"Have you moved it yet?" Kendra asked.

Grandpa scratched his chin. "We have to find it first."

"You don't know where it is?" Seth blurted.

"To my knowledge," Grandpa said, "none of the caretakers of the secret sanctuaries know where the artifacts on their preserves are hidden. The vaults that hold them were concealed so as to never be found."

"And they are protected by lethal traps," Grandma added.

"Which is the true explanation for our visitors," Grandpa said softly.

"They're here to find the artifact!" Kendra said.

Grandpa nodded. "I do not envy their task."

"Have they found anything yet?" Seth asked.

"Vanessa has had some luck poring through the journals of former caretakers," Grandpa said. "Patton Burgess, Lena's husband, was fascinated by the secret artifacts. In a coded reference in one of his journals, he made mention of an inverted tower on the property where he believed Fablehaven's artifact resides. His notes were inconclusive, but they gave us some idea of where to concentrate our search. We may find the artifact tomorrow. Or it might take many lifetimes."

"No wonder Vanessa has such an awesome car," Seth said. "She's a treasure hunter."

"They all have different specialties," Grandpa said. "Tanu is a potion master. Coulter collects magical relics. Vanessa focuses on capturing mystical animals. Their various occupations have taken them to some of the most dangerous corners of the world, and qualify them for this perilous assignment."

"As caretakers, we hold as an heirloom the key that will allow us to access the vault," Grandma said. "We keep it safely hidden. Once we discover the location of the vault, the key will allow us the chance to get inside and retrieve the artifact."

"Even with the key, avoiding the many traps guarding the artifact promises to be no small task," Grandpa said. "Tanu, Coulter, and Vanessa will need to be in top form."

"Did they know about Fablehaven beforehand?" Kendra asked.

"None of them," Grandpa said. "I counseled long with the Sphinx and others to select them. Coulter is an old friend. I know him the best. Tanu has an impeccable reputation. As does Vanessa. The Sphinx and several other caretakers vouched for both of them."

"Despite their careful selection," Grandma said, "there is a chance, however small, that the Society could have gotten to one of them. Or that one of them has been an agent for the Society all along. The Society of the Evening Star has an uncanny ability for infiltration. An endorsement from the Sphinx virtually clears them of suspicion, but the Sphinx himself cautioned that we should remain mindful of the possibility."

"Which is part of the reason we selected three instead of one," Grandpa said, "along with the desire for extra help. Even with three seasoned experts, finding the artifact is an overwhelming assignment."

"Together they serve the added benefit of providing extra security around here," Grandma said, "which is obviously a comfort, considering the recent unrest."

"There have been reports of unparalleled activity by the Society," Grandpa said. "Since last summer, two more preserves have fallen, one of them a secret preserve like Fablehaven."

"So they got one of the artifacts?" Kendra asked, gripping the arms of her chair.

"We don't know," Grandpa said. "We hope not. You remember Maddox, the fairy broker? He went into the preserve after it fell to perform reconnaissance. We have not heard back."

"How long ago?" Seth asked.

"More than three months," Grandma said.

"The secret preserve was in Brazil," Grandpa said. "They thwarted an infiltration there two years ago. Then this past February . . . we don't know what happened."

"What artifact was hidden there?" Seth asked, wide-eyed.

"Impossible to say," Grandpa said. "We have a rough idea of what the artifacts are, but no clue which is hidden where."

"What are they?" Kendra asked.

Grandpa looked at Grandma, who shrugged. "One

grants power over space, another over time. A third grants unlimited sight. A fourth can heal any ailment. And one bestows immortality."

"The details have been deliberately shrouded in mystery," Grandma said.

"The magic they wield is greater than any we know," Grandpa said. "For example, there are ways to get from one place to another besides walking, but the artifact that grants power over space does so in ways superior to any known spell or relic or creature."

"And somehow, used together, they can open the demon prison?" Kendra clarified.

"Exactly," Grandpa confirmed. "Which is why they must remain apart and out of the hands of our enemies at all costs. One concern is that if the Society could get their hands on one, they could use it to help retrieve the others."

"But they may already have one," Seth said.

"We can only hope that the fallen preserve in Brazil was as inhospitable for them as it apparently was for Maddox," Grandma said. "Others have been sent since Maddox vanished. None have returned. Naturally we must take precautions as if the worst has happened."

"So where do Seth and I come into all of this?" Kendra asked.

Grandpa took a sip from a tall glass of orange juice. He furrowed his brow. "We're not entirely sure. We know the Society has taken a serious interest in you two. We worry that they may know something more than we do about the change the fairies wrought in Kendra, something that makes them believe she could be of use to them. They infiltrated your school and tried to win your trust. They used Seth to free a captive demon. Almost certainly they meant to abduct you. Their ultimate goal is hard to divine."

"The Sphinx himself wants to meet Kendra," Grandma said.

"He's here?" Seth exclaimed.

"Nearby," Grandpa said. "He never stays in one place long. Most recently he was doing damage control in Brazil. But he has become concerned that Fablehaven may be the next target. There have been numerous rumors of Society activity in the area, even beyond what happened with the two of you. I got in touch with him last night. He wants to meet Kendra and see if he can discern why the Society has become so interested in her."

"I want to meet him too," Seth said.

"We plan to bring you as well," Grandpa said, "to see if something can be done about that bite."

"I'm sick of waiting; what's the story?" Seth sounded exasperated.

"Olloch the Glutton is a demon enchanted by a peculiar spell," Grandpa explained. "He remains in a petrified state, inert, until somebody feeds him. He bites the hand that feeds him and, after that, gradually awakens, driven by an insatiable hunger. He eats, and as he eats, he grows. As his size increases, so does his power, and he does not stop eating until he consumes the person who initially awakened him."

"He's going to eat me?" Seth cried.

"He's going to try," Grandpa said.

"Can he get into Fablehaven?"

"I don't think so," Grandpa said. "But the day will soon come when he will prowl our borders, searching for an opportunity to strike, gaining more power every day as he continues to gorge himself. He will be inexorably drawn to you. The only places to hide are those he cannot access."

"There has to be something we can do!" Seth said.

"That is why I want to bring you to the Sphinx," Grandpa said. "His wisdom has proven equal to situations more challenging than this. Don't worry, we won't let Olloch devour you."

Seth put his face in his hands. "Why does everything I do go wrong?" He looked up. "I thought I was being helpful."

"This was not your fault," Grandma said. "You were being very brave, and trying to do the right thing. Sadly, Errol was taking advantage of you."

"Do you know anything about Errol?" Kendra asked.

"Nothing," Grandpa said.

"How did he find out about the fairies?"

Grandpa sighed. "We have a theory. Last week, we found an imp, one of the big kind, passing information to a caped figure through the border fence. We could not catch the person he was informing—the stranger made a hasty retreat. But we managed to apprehend the imp."

"The rogue would have gotten away if not for your grandpa," Grandma said.

"Choosing between me and Tanu, the imp tried to get past me," Grandpa said. "I tackled him, but he was amazingly strong. He hurled me into a gully. I felt my arm snap beneath me, and fractured my tibia. But I managed to slow the brute long enough for Tanu to use a concoction that paralyzed him."

"Where is he now?" Seth asked.

"In the dungeon," Grandpa said.

"The basement," Grandma clarified.

"So that's what's down there!" Seth cried.

"Among other things," Grandpa said. "Unaccompanied, the dungeon is absolutely off-limits to you two."

"Big surprise," Seth mumbled.

"Anyhow," Grandpa said, "the point is, we believe that the imp, and perhaps others, must have leaked the experience Kendra had with the fairies to the Society. Imps are crafty spies."

"Are we going to have to hide here for the rest of our lives?" Kendra asked.

Grandpa slapped his hand down on the arm of the wheelchair. "Who said anything about hiding? We'll be taking action. Finding and moving the artifact. Investigating why the Society is interested in you. Consulting with the Sphinx."

"And offering you two world-class training from some of the most skilled adventurers anywhere," Grandma said. "You need to learn about the world you are being drawn into, and you could find no better teachers than Tanu, Vanessa, and Coulter."

"They're going to teach us?" Seth asked, eyes shining.

"They will be your mentors," Grandpa said. "At this point, sitting still would be a mistake. You two will have opportunities to accompany them on some of their outings as they search for the artifact."

"Not when they do anything truly dangerous," Grandma amended.

"No," Grandpa said. "But you'll get to see a new side of Fablehaven. And learn a trick or two that may help you in the future. Ignorance is no longer a protection for either of you."

"Coulter may be tough to work with, particularly for Kendra," Grandma said with a trace of bitterness. "He has a prehistoric outlook on certain issues, and a difficult personality. But he also has a lot to offer. If all else fails, Vanessa has agreed to take up the slack."

"They do not know the extent of what we have told you," Grandpa said. "They think we informed you that they are hunting for a hidden relic, and they understand that you are to accompany them when prudence will allow it. They have no idea that we revealed the true nature of the artifact or the fact that Fablehaven is a secret preserve. You must keep those details to yourselves. I don't want anyone learning how much you know."

"No problem," Seth said.

"What do they think we believe the artifact is?" Kendra said.

"A magical relic that will help us in our fight against the Society," Grandma said. "An unknown talisman rumored to be hidden on the property. We told them we would keep it vague, and that they should do the same."

"If we find it," Seth said, "why don't we use it against Errol and his friends?"

"The artifacts have remained in our possession for millennia precisely because we have not sought to use them," Grandpa said. "Those watching over them have not even known where they are hidden. If we use them, it will be only a matter of time before we misuse them, and they fall into the wrong hands."

"That makes sense," Kendra said. "When will we see the Sphinx?"

"He should let me know shortly," Grandpa said, dabbing the corner of his mouth with his napkin. "You now know all we know about the new threat we are facing. We have treated you as adults, and expect you to behave accordingly."

"Get to know our new arrivals," Grandma said. "Learning from them will be a once-in-a-lifetime experience."

"When do we start?" Seth asked.

"Immediately," Grandpa answered.

CHAPTER SIX

Tanu

When Kendra and Seth exited the study, Dale was waiting on the other side of the door. "Ready to start summer school?" he asked.

"If it means we get to see cool monsters, absolutely," Seth replied.

"Follow me," Dale said. He led them into the parlor, where Tanu sat reading a leather-bound book. "Your pupils have arrived," Dale announced.

Tanu stood up. Dale was tall, but Tanu was half a head taller. And much thicker. He wore a rugged, long-sleeved shirt and jeans. "Please have a seat," he said in his deep, mild voice. Kendra and Seth sat down on a sofa, and Dale departed. "Your grandparents told you about the relic we are hunting?" he asked.

"They weren't very specific," Kendra said. "What exactly is it?" She figured that if she didn't sound curious, it would look suspicious.

"We don't know many of the details," Tanu said, his dark eyes flicking back and forth between the two of them. "Only that it is rumored to be quite powerful, and could help us keep the preserves safe from the Society. You two will be helping in the pursuit of this hidden treasure. But first we need to get acquainted."

Tanu asked them several standard questions. He found out that Seth was going into seventh grade, that he liked to ride his bike and play practical jokes, and that he had once captured a fairy using a jar and a mirror. He learned that Kendra was heading into ninth grade, that her favorite subjects were history and English, and that she played halfback on the school soccer team. He did not ask Kendra about the fairy army.

"It's only fair that I now tell you about myself," Tanu said. "Do you have any questions?"

"Are you from Hawaii?" Seth asked.

"I grew up in Pasadena," Tanu said. "But my ancestors are from Anaheim." He flashed a broad smile, showing big white teeth. "I'm Samoan. I've only been there as a visitor, though."

"Have you traveled a lot?" Kendra asked.

"More than my fair share," he admitted. "I've been around the world many times, seen many strange sights. My father made potions, and his father before him, going back many generations. My dad taught me what I know. He retired a few years back. He lives in Arizona in the winter, Idaho in the summer."

"Do you have a family?" Kendra asked.

"I have my folks, some brothers and sisters, and a bunch of nieces and nephews and cousins. No wife, no kids. Drives my folks crazy. Everybody wants me to settle down. Dad once tried to slip me a love potion to make me fall for some neighbor girl that he liked. He already has seventeen grand-kids, but he says he wants some from his eldest. I'll throw down roots someday. Not yet."

"You know how to make love potions?" Seth asked.

"And avoid them," Tanu grinned.

"What else can you make?" Seth asked.

"Potions to cure illnesses, potions to induce sleep, potions that awaken lost memories," Tanu said. "It all depends on what I have to work with. The toughest part of being a potion master is collecting ingredients. Only magical ingredients yield magical results. I study cause and effect, and I benefit from the studies of many who came before me. I try to figure out how to combine different materials to achieve a desired outcome."

"Where do you get ingredients?" Kendra asked.

"The most powerful ingredients are usually by-products of magical creatures," Tanu explained. "Viola, the milch cow, is a potion master's dream. Her milk, her blood, her dung, her sweat, her tears, her saliva—they all have differ-ent magical properties. At an icy preserve in Greenland, on the coast, they get their milk from a gigantic walrus, nearly a thousand years old, one of the eldest animals on the planet.

The derivatives of the walrus have different properties from the cow's. Along with certain similarities."

"Cool," Seth said.

"It is fascinating," Tanu admitted. "You never know what skills you'll need. I've climbed mountains, picked locks, ventured deep underwater, and learned foreign languages. Sometimes you can trade for ingredients, or purchase them. But you have to be careful. Some potion makers are unscrupulous. They get their ingredients in horrible ways. Dragon tears, for example. A very potent ingredient, but hard to come by. Dragons cry only when they are in the deepest mourning or when they have committed a terrible betrayal. They cannot fake the tears. There are bad people out there who would capture a young dragon and then murder its dear ones just to collect the tears. You don't want to support that kind of barbarity, so you have to be careful who you trade with, and who you buy from. Most of the best potion makers prefer to find their own ingredients. Which is why some of the best potion makers don't live very long."

"Do you collect your own ingredients?" Seth asked.

"Most of the time," Tanu said. "Every now and again I barter with reputable dealers. I can find much of what I need on preserves. Other items I locate in the wild. My grandfather lived to retirement and died in his sleep. My dad lived to retirement and is still with us. They taught me some good tricks that help keep me safe. Hopefully I can pass some of that knowledge along to you."

Tanu picked up a pouch that was sitting next to his chair. He began removing small bottles with narrow necks

and arranging them in a single row on the coffee table. "What are those?" Seth asked.

Tanu glanced up. "Part of a demonstration, to prove that I know my trade. A family specialty—bottled-up emotions."

"Drinking them will make us feel a certain way?" Kendra asked.

"Temporarily, yes," Tanu said. "In large doses the emotions can be overpowering. I want each of you to choose an emotion to sample. I'll mix you a small dose. The emotions will pass quickly. You can try fear, rage, embarrassment, or sorrow." He removed more items from his pouch—jars, vials, and a small sandwich bag full of leaves.

"Are they all bad emotions?" Kendra asked.

"I can do courage, calm, confidence, and joy, among others. But the negative emotions make better demonstrations. They are more shocking, and less addictive."

"I want to try fear," Seth said, coming to stand near Tanu.

"Good choice," Tanu responded. He unscrewed the lid of a jar and used a tool that looked like a small tongue depressor to scoop out some beige paste. "I'm mixing this so the effect will come and go very quickly, just giving you a brief sample of the emotion." Removing a small leaf from the bag, Tanu scraped the paste onto the leaf. He then dripped four drops from one of the bottles onto the leaf, added a single drop from a different bottle, and mixed the liquid into the paste with the tongue depressor. He handed the leaf to Seth.

"Eat the leaf?" Seth asked.

"Eat it all," Tanu said. "Sit down first. When the emotion hits, it will be distressing, much more real than you probably expect. Try to remember that it is artificial and that it will pass."

Seth sat down on a brocaded armchair. He sniffed the leaf, then popped it into his mouth. He chewed and swallowed quickly. "Not bad. Tastes a little like peanuts."

Kendra watched him intently. "Is he going to freak out?" she asked.

"Wait and see," Tanu said, suppressing a grin.

"I feel fine so far," Seth announced.

"It takes a few seconds," Tanu said.

"A few seconds for what?" Seth asked, an edge of anxiety creeping into his voice.

"See?" Tanu said, winking at Kendra. "It's starting."

"What's starting?" Seth asked, eyes darting. "Why'd you wink at her? Why are you talking like I'm not in the room?"

"I'm sorry, Seth," Tanu said. "We mean no harm. The effects of the potion are hitting you."

Seth's breathing was becoming ragged. He was shifting in his seat, rubbing his thighs with his palms. "What did you give me?" he said, raising his voice and sounding paranoid. "Why'd you have to mix so much stuff? How do I know I can trust you?"

"It's all right," Kendra said. "You're just feeling the effects of the potion."

Seth looked at Kendra, his face contorting, tears brimming in his eyes. He raised his voice more, sounding hysterical. "Just the potion? Just the potion!" He chuckled bitterly. "You don't get it? He poisoned me! He poisoned me, and you're next. I'm going to die! We're all going to die!" He was curling up on the chair, quivering and hugging his knees. A single tear leaked from one eye and slid down his cheek.

Kendra looked at Tanu, distressed. Tanu raised a calming hand. "He's already coming out of it."

She looked back at her brother. He sat still for a moment, then straightened his legs and sat up, wiping the remnants of the tear from his cheek. "Wow," Seth said. "You weren't kidding! That felt so real. I couldn't think straight. I thought you had tricked me into drinking poison or something."

"Your mind was searching for threats to justify the emotion," Tanu said. "It helped that you knew beforehand the emotion was coming. Had I drugged you by surprise, it would have been much more difficult to make sense of the experience afterwards. Let alone if I used a higher dosage. Imagine if I made that emotion much more intense and longer lasting."

"You have to try it," Seth said to Kendra.

"I'm not sure I want to," Kendra said. "Can't I feel something happy?"

"You should try an emotion you would normally resist if you want to appreciate the potency," Tanu said. "It's alarming in the moment, but you'll feel fine afterwards. In a way, it's cleansing. An occasional foray into negative emotions makes feeling normal that much sweeter."

"He's right, I feel great now," Seth said. "Like the riddle.

Why do you hit yourself in the head fifty times with a hammer?"

"Why?" Kendra asked.

"Because it feels so good when you stop!"

"Try an emotion other than fear," Tanu said. "For the sake of variety."

"Pick one for me," Kendra said. "Don't tell me what it is."

"You sure?" Tanu asked.

"Yeah, if I'm going to do it, I want you to surprise me."

Tanu put another glop of beige paste on a leaf and mixed in drops from three bottles. He gave the leaf to Kendra, and she popped it into her mouth and chewed it up, sitting down on the carpet in the middle of the room. The leaf was a little tricky to chew. It did not taste like something you were supposed to eat. The paste was pretty good. It melted in her mouth and was a little sweet. She swallowed.

Seth edged over to Tanu and whispered something to him. Kendra realized he was probably asking what emotion to expect. Kendra focused on remaining aware that a phony emotion was about to surface. If she concentrated hard enough, she should be able to keep it under control. She'd feel it, but she wouldn't let it overwhelm her. Tanu whispered something back to Seth. They were both staring at her expectantly. What was their deal? Did she have a piece of the leaf caught in her teeth? Seth whispered something else to Tanu.

"Why are you whispering?" Kendra accused. It came out a little harsher than she intended, but they were being so secretive all of a sudden. Had she whispered to Tanu? No! She had spoken so everyone could hear her. It seemed obvious they were no longer talking about the potion—they were gossiping about her.

Seth laughed at her question, and Tanu grinned.

Tears stung Kendra's eyes. "Did I say something funny?" she challenged, her voice cracking a bit. Seth laughed harder. Tanu chuckled. Kendra ground her teeth, her face flushing. Once again, she was the outcast. Seth always made friends so quickly. He had already turned Tanu against her. It was fourth grade all over again; she was eating lunch alone, silently hoping for somebody to talk to her. Hoping somebody besides a teacher would notice and include her.

"It's all right, Kendra," Tanu said kindly. "Remember, it isn't real."

Why was he trying to reassure her? All of a sudden she realized what Seth must have whispered to him. He had pointed out the pimple on her chin! Seth had said that her face was erupting like a volcano, that grime was clogging her pores and turning her into a freakish sideshow. That was why they had laughed! Seth had probably accused her of not washing enough, even though she scrubbed her face every night! But of course Tanu would believe Seth, because the evidence was right there on her chin, as subtle as a lighthouse. And now that Tanu had noticed, the pimple would be all he saw. She hung her head. Tanu would almost certainly tell Grandpa. And all the others! They'd laugh behind her back. She would never be able to show her face again!

Her cheeks burned. She began to weep. Grudgingly, she

glanced up. They both looked astonished. Seth was approaching her. "It's okay, Kendra," he said.

She buried her face in her arms, sobbing. Why did they keep staring at her? Why wouldn't they leave her alone? Hadn't they done enough? Enduring their pity was much worse than suffering their scorn. She wished she could just disappear.

"It'll be over soon," Tanu assured her.

What did he know? This could be just the beginning! She had been lucky so far, with only the occasional pimple now and again, but soon she might be disfigured by vast constellations of acne. Red lumps would pile up until she looked like she had thrust her head into a beehive. Now that Seth had set the tone of mocking her, things would never be the same. From here on out, all she could look forward to were cruel jokes and false sympathy. She had to get away.

Kendra jumped to her feet. "I hate you, Seth!" she yelled, not caring what anyone would think of the outburst. Her reputation was already damaged beyond repair. She ran from the room. Behind her, she heard Tanu telling Seth to let her go. Where could she hide? The bedroom! She raced to the stairs and started charging up them two at a time. And suddenly she realized how ridiculous it would look for her to run away. She stopped, her hand gripping the banister. The situation abruptly seemed much less tragic.

Was she sure Seth had pointed out the pimple to Tanu? Even if he had, was it that big of a deal? Almost every teen got pimples from time to time. Now that she thought about it, was it even likely that Seth had mentioned anything about the pimple? No! She had jumped to that conclusion on her own, with very little evidence. It was the potion! This was just like when Seth assumed he had been poisoned! Even though she had tried to anticipate it, the emotion had blindsided her. It seemed ridiculously obvious now.

Kendra returned to the parlor, wiping away the tears. She had cried a lot. Her sleeves were damp, and her nose was congested. "That was incredible," she said.

"What emotion do you think it was?" Seth asked.

"Embarrassment?" Kendra guessed.

"Close," Tanu said. "It was shame. A hybrid of embarrassment and sorrow."

"I thought," Kendra said, hesitating for a moment to divulge her ridiculous assumption, "I thought that Seth was pointing out the pimple on my chin. And it suddenly seemed like he had revealed the guiltiest secret of all time. I thought you two were making fun of me. Not that I love getting pimples, but it was suddenly blown all out of proportion."

"Again, your mind was seizing on something to try to make sense of the emotion," Tanu said. "Can you see the power emotion has to distort our outlook? Makes you wonder, did you *have* a bad day, or did you *make it* a bad day?"

"I thought if I stayed focused I could keep the emotion under control," Kendra said.

"Not unreasonable," Tanu said. "We can exert a lot of control over our emotions. But sometimes they run away with us. These bottled-up emotions hit you with a lot of force. It would take a shockingly strong will to resist them. In large enough doses, I don't see how anybody could."

"What do you use them for?" Seth asked.

"Depends," Tanu said. "Sometimes people need a little dose of courage. Other times you want to cheer somebody up. And every now and then, you can avoid an unwanted confrontation with a little fear, or use a mix of emotions to extract information. We save those uses for the bad guys."

"Can I try some courage?" Seth asked.

"You already have plenty," Tanu said. "You don't want to overuse these emotions. Their potency wears thin if they're overused, plus you can put your natural emotions out of balance. Artificial emotions are useful only in certain situations. They must be combined by an expert. If you drink straight courage, you can become reckless and foolhardy. For a good result, you have to temper the courage with a little fear, a little calm."

"That makes sense," Kendra said.

"I know my trade," Tanu said, vials and jars clinking as he collected them into his pouch. "I hope that you weren't too shaken up by the experience. An occasional dose of fear or sorrow can be cathartic. Same with a good cry."

"If you say so," Kendra said. "I'll probably pass next time."

"I'd do the fear again," Seth said. "It was sort of like a roller coaster. Except so scary, you don't really like it till after the ride is over."

Tanu folded his hands on his lap and adopted a more formal air. "Now that I've let you glimpse what I can do, I want to establish some common goals. They are the same goals I have set for myself, and if we're going to work together, I think we should share them. Assuming you want to work with me."

Kendra and Seth both enthusiastically agreed that they were excited to learn from Tanu.

"My first goal is to protect the integrity of Fablehaven," Tanu said. "I want to keep this preserve safe from any dangers without or within. That includes protecting the people who live here. That objective stands as my top priority. Will you commit to help me do that?"

Kendra and Seth both nodded.

"Second," Tanu continued, "I want to find the missing relic. It may be a tedious hunt, but working together I know we will succeed. And in accordance with our top priority, we must find the relic without putting Fablehaven or ourselves at risk. Which means we use sense and caution. Sound good?"

"Yes," Kendra and Seth said together.

"And third, without jeopardizing our other missions, I want to find a cure for Dale's brother, Warren. I understand you two have not met him?"

"Nope," Seth said.

"Grandpa told me about him," Kendra said. "He said Warren vanished into the woods. When Warren showed up a few days later, he was white as an albino, and catatonic."

"Those are the basics," Tanu said. "It happened almost two years ago. Truthfully, I think your grandparents have almost given up on ever healing him. But they are willing to let us try. If anybody can find a cure, I think we're the team to do it."

"Do you know what happened to him?" Seth asked.

"Not yet," Tanu said. "And it is hard to cure a malady without diagnosing the problem. I have put some thought into it, and I remain puzzled, so the cabin where Warren lives will be our main stop today. Dale has been waiting in the other room to take us. Sound like a plan?"

"Sounds perfect," Seth said.

"Then we're agreed on our goals?" Tanu asked.

"All of them," Kendra said.

Tanu grinned. "We have a lot of work ahead of us."

❦ ❦ ❦

The June sun glared down as Kendra, Seth, Tanu, and Dale rounded a corner on the grassy cart track. Up ahead, a picturesque log cabin rested on the side of a slope, not far from the rounded crest of a gentle hill. A dilapidated outhouse stood a fair distance from the cabin, and Kendra spotted a hand-operated water pump near the porch. Off to one side of the cabin, the ground had been leveled, and numerous vegetables flourished in tidy rows. As a consequence of the slope, a retaining wall encompassed three sides of the garden, low in the front, high in the back. The area immediately around the cabin had been cleared, but trees bordered the yard on all sides.

"That's where he lives?" Seth asked.

"Warren doesn't do well around people," Dale explained.

"He doesn't respond well to commotion. We'll want to speak in low voices inside."

"I thought you said he was catatonic," Seth said.

Dale stopped. "He hasn't spoken since he turned albino," he said. "But you can sometimes read reactions in his eyes. It's subtle, but I can tell. And he responds to touch. If you guide him, he'll move around. If you put food to his lips and prod the corner of his mouth, he'll eat. Left to himself, he'd starve."

"Tell them about the hoeing," Tanu prompted.

"That's right," Dale said. "One evening I started him hoeing out in the garden. I put the hoe in his hands and started moving his arms. After a while he was doing it on his own. I'd had a long day, so I sat down to watch him. He kept going and going, hoeing and hoeing. I rested my eyes, leaned back against the retaining wall, and fell asleep.

"Next thing I know, I wake up in the dead of night, during the chill before dawn. Warren was still hoeing. He'd churned up the whole garden, and much of the yard beyond. His hands were a bloody mess. I could hardly get the gloves off."

"How terrible," Kendra said.

"Can't say I'm proud of dozing," Dale said. "But it taught me never to let him do anything unsupervised. Once you get him started at something, he just goes on and on until you stop him."

"Is it safe for him to be here?" Kendra asked. "I mean, with all the creatures in the woods?"

"The cabin enjoys the same protections as the house," Dale said. "Although creatures can come into the yard."

"What if he has to go to the bathroom?" Seth asked.

Dale looked at him as if the question were perplexing. Then the lanky man tipped his head back in realization. "Oh, you mean the outhouse. The cabin has an indoor toilet now."

Dale started walking again. They reached the plank porch of the cabin, and Dale used a key to open the front door. The cabin had a large central room with a door in the rear that led to another room, and a ladder that granted access to a loft. On pegs beside the front door hung a sombrero, a slicker, and an overcoat. A long table dominated the room, surrounded by six chairs. Pyramids of firewood flanked the dark fireplace. A bed stood against the wall, and a man was curled up under the covers, eyes staring flatly toward the door.

Dale crossed to Warren. "You have some visitors, Warren," Dale said. "You remember Tanu. And this is Kendra and Seth Sorenson, two of Stan's grandkids." Dale pulled back the covers and straightened his brother's legs. Then he placed a hand behind Warren's head and guided him into a sitting position. Warren wore a dark orange T-shirt and gray sweatpants. Contrasted against the shirt, his arms looked white as milk. Dale turned him so that he was seated on the edge of the bed. When Dale let go, Kendra half-expected Warren to topple over, but he remained seated upright, eyes vacant.

He looked to be in his twenties, at least ten years

younger than Dale. Even with pale skin, white hair, and empty eyes, Warren was unexpectedly handsome. Not quite as tall as his brother, Warren had broader shoulders and a firmer jaw. His features were more finely sculpted. Looking at Dale, she would not picture his brother handsome. Looking at Warren, she would not picture his brother plain. And yet seen together, a family resemblance persisted.

"Hi, Warren," Seth said.

"Pat him on the shoulder," Dale suggested. "He's more aware of touch."

Seth patted Warren. The action elicited no response. Kendra wondered if this was how people acted after a lobotomy.

"I like to think that in some corner of his mind, he might be aware of us," Dale said. "Although he doesn't show much recognition, I suspect he absorbs more than it seems. Left to himself, he curls up into a fetal position. Does it faster if things get too noisy."

"I've tried some doses of different emotions," Tanu said. "I was hoping something might pierce the fog. But that style of therapy looks like a dead end."

Kendra gently patted his shoulder. "Hi, Warren." Warren turned his head and looked at her hand, a slow smile creeping onto his face.

"Would you look at that!" Dale gasped.

Kendra left her hand on Warren's shoulder, and he kept staring at it. He was not smiling with his eyes, they still appeared far away, but the grin on his face was as wide as it could be. He lifted a hand and placed it over Kendra's.

"In all this time, this is the biggest reaction I've seen," Dale marveled. "Put your other hand on his shoulder."

Standing in front of Warren, Kendra rested her other hand on his other shoulder. The action caused Warren to take his eyes off her hand. Instead, he looked up into her face. The grin appeared artificial, but for an instant, Kendra thought she saw a flicker of life in his gaze, as if he almost focused on her.

Dale stood with his hands on his hips. "Wonders never cease."

"She was fairystruck," Tanu said. "It must have left a lingering effect that Warren can sense. Kendra, come stand by me."

Kendra walked over to Tanu. Warren did not follow her with his eyes. He stared directly ahead, unmoving, as if the flicker Kendra noticed had been only her imagination. Once again, Warren looked utterly mindless—except tears were welling up in his eyes. It looked peculiar, those vacant eyes brimming with tears above a slack expression. The tears overflowed and streamed down both white cheeks.

Dale had a fist in his mouth. Warren's tears stopped flowing, though his cheeks remained damp. Warren made no move to wipe the tears away, showed no evidence he knew he had cried. When Dale pulled his fist from his mouth, there were teeth marks on his knuckles. "What does this mean?" Dale asked Tanu.

"Kendra transmitted something to him by touch," Tanu said. "This is very encouraging. Somewhere deep inside, I believe his mind is intact. Kendra, take his hand."

Kendra approached Warren and took his left hand in her right. Again, he came half to life—glancing down at her hand, the dazed smile returning.

"See if you can pull him to his feet," Tanu said.

Kendra did not have to pull hard before Warren arose.

"I'll be jiggered," Dale said. "He never moves so willingly."

"Lead him around the room," Tanu said.

Keeping hold of Warren's hand, Kendra led him around the room. He followed wherever she went, taking shuffling steps.

"She didn't have to move his legs to get him walking," Dale murmured to Tanu.

"I noticed," Tanu replied. "Kendra, lead him over to that chair and have him sit. Keep hold of his hand."

Kendra did as instructed, and Warren complied woodenly.

Tanu came and stood beside Kendra. "Would you mind giving Warren a kiss?"

The thought of it made her feel shy, mostly because Warren was nice-looking. "On the lips?"

"Just a peck," Tanu said. "Unless it makes you too uncomfortable."

"You think it might help him?" she asked.

"Fairy kisses have potent restorative powers," Tanu said. "I realize you're not a fairy, but they did work a change in you. I want to see how he responds."

Kendra leaned in toward Warren. Her face felt warm. She hoped desperately that she wasn't blushing. She tried to think of Warren as a catatonic patient who needed a strange cure, tried to make the kiss something detached and clinical. But he was cute. It put her in mind of the crush she'd had on a teacher, Mr. Powell, a couple of years ago.

How would she have felt about kissing Mr. Powell, had circumstances ever called for it? About how she felt right now. Secretly excited in a very embarrassing way.

They all crowded around as Kendra gave Warren a quick peck on the lips. He blinked three times. His mouth twitched. He tightened his grip on her hand for a moment. "He squeezed my hand," Kendra reported.

Tanu had Kendra stroke Warren's face and lead him around some more. Whenever she stopped touching him, all signs of life would vanish, but he never wept again. Whenever they were in contact, he wore the smile, and occasionally he made simple fidgety motions, like rubbing his shoulder, although all his actions seemed to lack deliberateness.

After having experimented with how Warren reacted to Kendra for more than an hour, they stood outside, watching the albino perform jerky jumping jacks. Dale got him going by patiently moving his arms and legs until Warren began repeating the action on his own. Warren was wearing the sombrero. Dale had explained that Warren sunburned easily.

"This is not what I expected," Tanu said. "I'm hoping this response to Kendra will help us as we seek a cure. It is the first real breakthrough we've had so far."

"What did those fairies do to me?" Kendra asked.

"Nobody has been fairystruck in a long time, Kendra," Tanu said. "We know *of* it—we don't know much about it."

"What about when the fairies attacked Seth?" she asked. "Was he fairystruck then?"

"That's different," Tanu said. "Fairies use their magic all the time, sometimes for mischief, sometimes to beautify a garden. Being fairystruck is when fairies mark you as one of their own and share their power with you. We can't even be sure that is what happened to you, but the evidence looks very suspicious. The Sphinx should be able to tell you more."

"I hope someone can," Kendra said.

"You really think this is a breakthrough?" Dale asked.

"Figuring out what Warren's condition is, and what variables affect that condition, will be the key to curing it," Tanu said. "What happened here today is a big step in the right direction."

"He'll just keep doing jumping jacks forever?" Seth asked.

"Eventually he'd collapse, I guess," Dale said. "Otherwise, he'll go until I stop him."

"You just leave him out here alone?" Kendra asked.

"Many nights I stay with him," Dale said. "Some nights Hugo watches over him. An interesting consequence of his condition is that the creatures of Fablehaven never come near him, even when I bring him outside. Foul or fair, they keep their distance. Of course, I'm out here every day, to check on him and feed him and see to his hygiene."

"If we were all quiet, couldn't we find him a room back at the house?" Kendra asked.

"I take him there from time to time, like on his birthday. But he never seems comfortable. He curls up more, goes limp more. Out here he seems more peaceful. This is where he stayed before it happened."

"He lived out here even before he became albino?" Seth asked.

Dale nodded. "Warren enjoyed his privacy. Unlike me, he was never a permanent fixture at Fablehaven. He came and went. He was an adventurer, like Tanu here, or Coulter, or Vanessa. He belonged to a special brotherhood—the Knights of the Dawn. It was all very hush-hush. They worked to combat the Society of the Evening Star. The last time Warren visited, he stayed for quite a while. He was on some sort of secret mission. He didn't tell me the details; he was always tight-lipped about his assignments until after the fact. I have no idea if it had anything to do with what turned him white. But he was as good a brother as a guy could hope for. Never hesitated to help me out. Now I get to return the favor, make sure he gets exercise, eats right, stays healthy."

Kendra watched Warren performing his awkward jumping jacks in the absurd sombrero. He was sweating. It was heartbreaking to picture him as an intelligent adventurer fulfilling dangerous assignments. Warren was no longer that person.

"Want to see something nice?" Dale asked, apparently trying to change the subject.

"Sure," Kendra said.

"Follow me up to the belvedere," Dale said over his shoulder.

Leaving Tanu with Warren, Dale led Kendra and Seth back into the cabin and up the ladder to the loft. From the loft, he led them up a second ladder through a hatch in the ceiling. They came out on the roof of the cabin, on a small platform with a low railing. The platform was high enough to see over the nearest treetops down the slope from the cabin, which extended their view quite a distance. The hill was not terribly high, but it was the highest point in the area.

"It's beautiful," Kendra said.

"Warren used to like to come up here and watch the sunset," Dale said. "It was his favorite place to think. You should see it in the fall."

"Isn't that where the Forgotten Chapel used to be?" Seth asked, pointing to a lower hill not far away, brilliant with flowers and blossoming shrubs and fruit trees.

"Good eyes," Dale said.

Kendra recognized the place as well. Up until they had veered off onto the cart track that brought them to the cabin, she knew they had been walking along the same path Hugo had taken them down when they went to rescue Grandpa the previous summer. Her army of fairies had leveled the chapel when they defeated and imprisoned Bahumat and Muriel. Then the fairies had mounded up the surrounding earth over the spot the chapel had occupied and made it bloom as brightly as the gardens back at the house.

"Must look better now without that moldy old church," Seth said.

"The chapel had a certain charm," Dale said. "Especially from a distance."

"I'm getting hungry," Seth grumbled.

"Which is why we brought food," Dale replied. "And there is more in the cupboards. Let's go fetch Tanu and Warren. I bet my brother has worked up an appetite."

"What'll you do if you can't find a way to cure him?" Seth asked.

Dale paused. "I'll never know that day has come, because I'll never stop trying."

CHAPTER SEVEN

The Dungeon

The next morning, Kendra, Seth, Grandpa, Grandma, and Tanu sat around the kitchen table eating breakfast. Outside, the sun was rising on a clear, humid day.

"What are we doing today?" Seth asked, using his fork to chop up his omelet.

"Today you're going to stay here at the house with me and your grandmother," said Grandpa.

"What?" Seth cried. "Where's everybody going?"

"And what are we?" Grandpa asked.

"I mean, where are the others going?" Seth restated.

"This omelet is delicious, Grandpa," Kendra said after swallowing a mouthful.

"I'm glad you're enjoying it, my dear," Grandpa replied

with dignity, shooting a glance at Grandma, who pretended not to notice.

"They have some unpleasant business to attend to," Grandma told Seth.

"You mean awesome business," Seth accused, whirling on Tanu. "You're ditching us? What was all that about teamwork yesterday?"

"Keeping you and your sister safe was one of our goals," Tanu replied calmly.

"How are we ever supposed to learn anything if you only let us do wimpy stuff?" Seth complained.

Coulter entered the room holding a walking stick. The top of the stick was forked and strung with an elastic strap that turned it into a slingshot. "You don't want to come where we're going today," he said.

"How do you know?" Seth said.

"Because *I* don't want to come," Coulter said. "Omelets? Who made omelets?"

"Grandpa," Kendra said.

Coulter suddenly looked cautious. "What is this, Stan? Our last meal?"

"I just wanted to lend a hand in the kitchen," Grandpa said innocently.

Coulter eyed Grandpa suspiciously. "He must love you kids," Coulter finally said. "He's been exploiting those broken bones to stay as far from chores as possible."

"I'm not okay with being left behind," Seth reminded everyone.

"We're going to an unmapped portion of Fablehaven,"

Tanu explained. "We're not sure what to expect, except that it will be dangerous. If all goes well, we'll bring you next time."

"You think the relic might be hidden there?" Kendra asked.

"It is one of several possible places," Tanu said. "We expect to find the relic in one of the less hospitable areas of the preserve."

"All we'll probably find are hobgoblins, fog giants, and blixes," Coulter spat, taking a seat at the table. He shook some salt into his palm and tossed it over his shoulder, then rapped his knuckles on the tabletop. The motions seemed automatic.

Vanessa strolled into the room. "I have some unhappy news," she declared. She wore a U.S. Army T-shirt and black canvas pants, and had her hair tied back.

"What?" Grandma asked.

"My drumants got loose last night, and I only recaptured a third of them," Vanessa said.

"They're loose in the house?" Grandma exclaimed.

Coulter jabbed his fork toward Vanessa accusingly. "I told you no good would come from bringing that menagerie indoors."

"I can't imagine how they got out," Vanessa said. "I've never had trouble like this before."

"You obviously weren't bitten," Tanu said.

"Think again," Vanessa replied, holding up her arm and displaying three pairs of puncture wounds. "More than twenty bites, all over my body."

"How are you still alive?" Grandpa said.

"These were a special strain of drumants I bred myself," Vanessa said. "I've been experimenting with eliminating the toxicity of venomous whirligigs."

"What's a whirligig?" Kendra asked.

"And what's a drumant?" Seth added.

"Any magical animal of subhuman intelligence is a whirligig," Grandma explained. "It's jargon."

"Drumants look kind of like tarantulas with tails," Tanu said. "Very furry. They hop around, and can warp light to distort their location. You think you see one, and you go to grab it, but you only touch an illusion, because the drumant is actually two or three feet away."

"They're nocturnal," Grandpa said. "Aggressive biters. They normally wield a deadly poison."

"Somehow the door to the cage got open," Vanessa said. "All nineteen escaped. When I woke up, they were all over me. I managed to catch six. The rest scattered. They're in the walls by now."

"Six of nineteen is less than a third," Coulter pointed out while chewing.

"I know I shut and locked the cage," Vanessa said firmly. "To be plain, if I were anywhere else, I would suspect foul play. Nobody knew those drumants weren't poisonous. If they had been, I would be dead right now."

An awkward silence stretched out.

Grandpa cleared his throat. "In your shoes, regardless of where I was, I would suspect sabotage."

Kendra stared at her plate. Had one of the people eating

breakfast with her just tried to kill Vanessa? Certainly not her or Grandpa or Grandma or Seth! Tanu? Coulter? She didn't want to make eye contact with anybody.

"Could an outsider have sneaked in?" Vanessa said. "Or could someone have escaped the dungeon?"

"Not likely," Grandpa said, wiping his hands on a napkin. "Brownies and mortals are the only beings permitted to enter this house freely. Brownies would never cause mischief like that. Besides Dale and Warren, the only mortals free to roam this preserve are in this room. Dale stayed at the cabin last night. Any other mortals would have to get past the gate before they could get to the house, and getting past the gate is nearly impossible."

"Somebody could have been hiding on the grounds for a long time, and waited until now to strike," Coulter theorized.

"Anything is possible," Vanessa said. "But I would swear that I left that cage locked. I haven't opened it in three days!"

"Nobody saw anything peculiar last night?" Grandpa asked, fixing his stare on everyone in turn.

"I wish I had," Tanu said.

"Not a thing," Coulter murmured, narrow eyes thoughtful.

Kendra, Seth, and Grandma shook their heads.

"Well, until we find out more, we have to consider this an accident," Grandpa said. "But be doubly vigilant. I have a hunch that several pieces are missing from this puzzle."

"None of the drumants were poisonous?" Grandma asked.

"None," Vanessa said. "They'll be a nuisance, but they won't cause any lasting harm. I'll put out traps. We'll get them rounded up. If you sprinkle sawdust and garlic on your sheets, it should help keep them away."

"Might as well add some broken glass while we're at it," Coulter grumbled.

"With all these drumants loose," Seth said, "maybe we'd be safer going with you guys today."

"Nice try," Kendra said.

"Ruth will keep you entertained," Grandpa said.

"I have some fascinating things to show you," Grandma agreed.

"Cool things?" Seth asked.

"You'll think so," Grandma promised.

Vanessa pulled a white mesh fabric from her pocket. "I'll leave a few of these around the house. If you spot a drumant . . ." She tossed the fabric and it fell to the floor like a parachute, spreading to cover nearly an eight-foot diameter. "The lump will tell you where the little rascal is actually hiding. Use the surrounding mesh to scoop him up. If he tries to hop away, he'll just get tangled. Might take a little practice, but it works. Don't just take a swat at them or try to pick them up with your bare hands."

"No worries about that," Kendra said. "Do you have other animals, too?"

"Several varieties, yes," Vanessa said.

"Are any of them poisonous?" Kendra asked.

"None are lethal. Although some of my salamanders could put you to sleep. I use their extracts for my darts."

"Darts?" Seth asked, perking up.

"For my blowgun," Vanessa said.

Seth was practically jumping out of his seat. "I want to try it!"

"All in due time," Vanessa said.

※　※　※

The air felt significantly cooler at the bottom of the long flight of steep stairs to the basement. The iron door looked ominous at the end of the gloomy corridor, illuminated only by the flashlight Grandma Sorenson carried. At the base of the door was the smaller portal the brownies used, matching the other tiny portal in the door at the top of the stairs.

"The brownies get in and out through the dungeon?" Seth asked.

"Yes," Grandma replied. "At least one visits every night, to see if we left anything for them to fix."

"Why don't you let the brownies do all your cooking?" Kendra asked. "They make tasty food."

"Delicious," she agreed. "But no matter what ingredients we leave, they try to make everything into a dessert."

"Sounds good to me," Seth said. "Have the brownies ever made you brownies?"

Grandma winked. "Where do you think brownies got their name? The little masterminds invented the treat."

They reached the metal door. Grandma produced a key.

"Remember, keep your voices down, and stay away from the cell doors."

"Do we have to do this?" Kendra asked.

"Are you nuts?" Seth asked. "They're locked up, there's nothing to worry about."

"There is plenty to worry about," Grandma corrected. "I know you're just trying to encourage your sister, but never treat the dungeon casually. The creatures down here are imprisoned for a reason. Your grandfather and I bring the keys to the individual cells into the dungeon only when transferring prisoners. That should tell you something."

"I'm not sure I want to see what's down here," Kendra said.

Grandma placed a hand on her shoulder. "Running toward danger is foolhardy. As your brother has hopefully learned. But so is closing your eyes to it. Many perils become less dangerous once you understand their potential hazards."

"I know," Kendra said. "Ignorance is no longer a shield, and all that."

"Good," Seth said. "That's settled. Can we go in now?"

Grandma inserted the key and pushed open the door. It squealed a bit. A cool, damp breeze greeted them. "We need to oil those hinges," Grandma said in a hushed voice, shining the beam of her flashlight down a long corridor. Iron doors with small, barred windows lined the hall. The floor, walls, and ceiling were all made of stone.

They entered and Grandma closed the door behind them. "Why only flashlights?" Seth asked.

Grandma pointed the flashlight beam at a light switch.

"From here forward, the dungeon is wired for lighting." She shone the beam on some naked lightbulbs dangling from the ceiling. "But most of our guests prefer the dark. To be humane, we generally stick to flashlights."

Grandma walked over to the nearest door. The barred window was about five feet off the ground—low enough for all of them to see into the vacant cell beyond. Grandma pointed to a slot near the base of the door. "The keepers slide in trays of food through the slot."

"The prisoners never leave their cells?" Kendra asked.

"No," Grandma said. "And escape is difficult. All of the cells are magically sealed, of course. And we have a few stronger containment areas for more powerful occupants. In the event of a jailbreak, a whisper hound serves as a fail-safe."

"Whisper hound?" Seth asked.

"It's not a living creature—just an enchantment," Grandma said. "Every now and then down here you brush past an icy cold pocket. That is the whisper hound. It becomes quite ferocious if a prisoner breaks out of a cell. I've never heard of that happening here."

"It must be a lot of work feeding the prisoners," Kendra said.

"Not for us," Grandma said. "Most of the cells are empty. And we have a pair of keepers, lesser goblins who make and serve the glop and keep things reasonably tidy."

"Wouldn't goblins let the prisoners out?" Kendra asked.

Grandma led them down the corridor. "Smart ones might. Our keepers are the type of goblins that have managed dungeons for millennia. Scrawny, servile creatures who live to take and execute orders from their superiors—meaning your grandfather and myself. Besides, they have no keys. They enjoy dwelling in the dark, supervising their dismal domain."

"I want to see some prisoners," Seth said.

"Trust me, there are many you don't want to meet," Grandma assured him. "Several are quite ancient, transfers from other preserves. Many speak no English. All are dangerous."

The corridor ended in a T. They could turn left or right. Grandma shone the flashlight both ways. There were more cell doors down both halls. "This hallway is part of a large square. You can go either left or right and end up back here. A few other corridors branch off, but nothing too complex. There are some noteworthy features I want to show you."

Grandma turned right. Eventually the corridor elbowed to the left. Seth kept trying to peek into the cells they were passing. "Too dark," he reported quietly to Kendra. Grandma had the light pointed ahead of them.

Kendra peered into one of the windows and saw a wolflike face glaring back at her. What was Seth's problem? Were his eyes bad? He had just looked into the same cell, reporting he could see nothing. It was dim, but not black. After seeing the wolfman, she did not peek through any of the other barred windows.

Some distance down the hall, Grandma stopped at a door carved out of blood-red wood. "This leads to the Hall of Dread. We don't ever open it. The prisoners in those cells need no food." As they continued down the hall, Seth's eyes lingered on the door.

"Don't even think about it," Kendra whispered.

"What?" he said. "I'm dumb, but I'm not stupid."

The hall angled to the left again. Grandma shone the flashlight into a doorless room where a cauldron bubbled over a low fire. A pair of goblins squinted and held up their long, narrow hands against the light. Short, bony, and greenish, they had beady eyes and batwing ears. One balanced on a three-legged stool, stirring the foul-smelling contents of the cauldron with what looked like an oar. The other grimaced and cringed.

"Introduce yourselves to my grandchildren," Grandma said, shining the flashlight away from them so it illuminated them indirectly.

"Voorsh," said the one stirring the cauldron.

"Slaggo," said the other.

Grandma turned and continued down the corridor. "The food smells awful," Kendra said.

"Most of our guests rather like glop," Grandma said. "Humans aren't normally fond of it."

"Do any of the prisoners ever get released?" Seth inquired.

"The majority are serving life sentences," Grandma said. "For many mystical creatures, that is a very long time. Because of the treaty, we have no death penalty for captured enemies. As you may recall, under most circumstances, to kill on Fablehaven property is to destroy all protection afforded you by the treaty and render yourself so vulnerable to retaliation that the only option is to depart and never return. But certain offenders cannot be permitted to roam free. Hence the dungeon. Some lesser offenders are kept here for prescribed periods of time and then released. For example, we have a former groundskeeper imprisoned here for selling batteries to satyrs."

Seth compressed his lips.

"How long is his sentence?" Kendra prodded.

"Fifty years. By the time he gets out, he'll be in his eighties."

Seth stopped walking. "Are you serious?"

Grandma grinned. "No. Kendra mentioned you were planning on doing a little business while you were here."

"Way to keep a secret!" Seth accused.

"I never said I would," Kendra replied.

"She was right to tell me," Grandma said. "She wanted to make sure it wouldn't endanger you or the preserve. It should be all right, if you keep it simple. Just don't leave the yard. And don't let your grandpa know. He's a purist. Tries hard to keep technology off the grounds."

As they progressed down the long corridor, they passed a couple of hallways that branched off. At the third, Grandma paused, seemingly deliberating. "Come with me, I want to show you something."

The hall had no cell doors. It was the narrowest passage they had seen. At the end was a circular room, and in the center of the room was a metal hatch in the floor. "This is our oubliette," Grandma said. "There is a cell at the bottom for a most dangerous prisoner. A jinn."

"Like a genie?" Kendra asked.

"Yes," Grandma said.

"Sweet! Does he grant wishes?" Seth asked.

"Theoretically," Grandma said. "True jinn are not much like the genies you have heard of in stories, though they are the entities through which the myths arose. They are powerful, and some, like our prisoner, are cunning and evil. I have something to confess."

Kendra and Seth waited quietly.

"Your grandfather and I were very distraught over what happened to Warren. I took to conversing with the jinn, opening the hatch and calling down to him from up here. As our prisoner, his powers are curtailed, so I did not fear he would escape. I became convinced he could cure Warren. And he probably could have. I talked it over with Stan, and we decided it was worth a try.

"I studied all I could on the subject of bargaining with jinn. If you obey certain rules, you can negotiate with a captured jinn, but you have to take care what you say. In order to open negotiations, you must make yourself vulnerable. They get to ask you three questions, which you must answer fully and with absolute truthfulness. After you answer the questions honestly, the jinn will grant you a favor. If you lie, they are set free and gain power over you. If you fail to answer, they remain captive but get to exact a penalty.

"The one question they are not permitted to ask is your given name, which you must never let them learn by other means. Before asking the formal three questions, the jinn can try to persuade you to agree to a bargain other than the traditional answering of three questions. The petitioner can only wait patiently and speak carefully, because every word you utter to a jinn is binding.

"To make a long story short, I entered the oubliette, with Stan standing watch, and the jinn and I negotiated. It makes me angry thinking about it—the jinn was so devious. He could have talked the devil into attending church. I was out of my depth. The jinn haggled and flattered and cleverly sought hints to what questions he should ask. He offered many alternatives to the questions, several of which were tempting compromises, but I detected traps in all his propositions. We exchanged offers and counteroffers. His ultimate goal was clearly to secure his freedom, which I could not allow.

"After our conversation had consumed many hours, and I had revealed more about myself than I liked, he finally quit dickering and proceeded to the questions. Stan had spent days changing passwords and other Fablehaven protocols so that I knew nothing vital to our security. I had thought through all the questions he could pose, and felt prepared to answer anything. He used his first question to inquire what he could ask that I would be unwilling to answer. As you may imagine, I had anticipated a question like this, and had prepared myself to be able to respond that I would freely answer any possible question. But in the moment of his asking, perhaps called to my remembrance by some power that permeated the proceedings, I realized a piece of information that I could not reveal, and so chose not to answer the question. It was all I could do to prevent him from being set free.

Consequently, I opened myself to retaliation. He couldn't kill me, but he did turn me into a chicken."

"That's how you became a chicken!" Seth exclaimed.

"Yes," Grandma said.

"What was the secret you couldn't reveal?" Seth asked.

"Something I cannot share," Grandma said.

"The jinn is still down there," Kendra said softly, gazing at the hatch.

Grandma started walking back the way they had come. Kendra and Seth followed. "The hatch to the oubliette requires three keys and a word to open it," Grandma said. "At least one living person must know the word that opens the hatch, or the spell is broken and the prisoner freed. If any of the keys are destroyed, the same happens. Otherwise, I would melt the keys and never tell the word to anyone."

"What's the word?" Seth asked.

"It's two words," Kendra said. "*Dream on.*"

"Kendra's right. Perhaps one day you'll be ready for that sort of responsibility." Grandma patted him on the back. "But probably not before I'm long gone."

They returned to the main corridor and followed it until it turned left again. Grandma stopped at a floor-to-ceiling alcove and shone the flashlight on a strange cabinet. A bit taller than a person, it looked like the kind of box a magician would use to make people vanish. Fashioned out of glossy black wood with gold trim, the cabinet was simple and elegant.

"This is the Quiet Box," Grandma said. "It is much more durable than any cell in the entire dungeon. It holds only a single prisoner, but it always holds a single prisoner. The only way to get the captive out is to put another in."

"Who's in there?" Seth asked.

"We don't know," Grandma said. "The Quiet Box was brought here when Fablehaven was founded, and was already occupied. Word has been passed down from caretaker to caretaker never to open it. So we leave it be."

Grandma proceeded down the hall. Kendra stayed near her, while Seth lingered in front of the Quiet Box. After a moment, he hurried to catch up. Near the final elbow of the hall, the one that would complete the square, Grandma paused at a seemingly random cell door. "Seth, you said you wanted to see a prisoner. There is the imp who injured your grandfather."

She shone the flashlight through the little window in the door. Kendra and Seth crowded close to see. The imp stared at them coldly, frowning. He stood nearly as tall as Dale. A short pair of antlers jutted from his brow. Leathery skin sheathed long, muscular limbs. Kendra had seen many imps. Too bad this one had not been changed back into a fairy like the others.

"Go ahead, shine your light, you have no idea the doom hanging over you," the imp snarled.

"What do you mean?" Kendra asked. Grandma and Seth both looked at her strangely. The imp was staring at her. "What?" Kendra said.

"No light will stave off the coming darkness," the imp said, eyes on Kendra.

"What darkness?" Kendra replied.

The imp made a choking sound and looked astonished.

"Can you understand his speech?" Grandma asked in wonder.

"Can't you?" Kendra said. "He's speaking English."

Grandma put a hand to her lips. "No, he's speaking Goblush, the tongue of imps and goblins."

"You understand me, Stinkface?" the imp tested.

"Is this a joke?" Kendra asked.

"Because I understand you," the imp said.

"I've been speaking English," Kendra said.

"Yes," Grandma agreed.

"No," the imp said. "Goblush."

"He says I'm speaking Goblush," Kendra said.

"You are," the imp said.

"That must be what he hears," Grandma said.

"You don't understand him?" Kendra asked Seth.

"You know how imps sound," Seth said. "No words, just growls and snorts."

"What are they saying?" the imp asked. "Tell them I'm going to cook their insides on a stick."

"He's saying gross things," Kendra said.

"Say nothing more," Grandma said. "Let's get you away from here."

Grandma hurried them down the hall. The imp called after them: "Kendra, you don't have long to live. Sleep on that. I'll be out of here before you know it. I'm going to dance on your grave! On all your graves!"

Kendra whirled. "Well, you'll be dancing alone, you ugly wart! All the rest of your kind got changed back into fairies, and they're beautiful and happy. And you're still a deformed freak! You should hear them laugh at you! Enjoy your glop!"

Silence. And then the sound of something slamming against the cell door, followed by guttural snarling. Knobby fingers protruded from the bars of the small window in the door. "Come along," Grandma said, tugging Kendra's sleeve. "He's just trying to upset you."

"How can I understand him?" Kendra asked. "The fairies?"

"It must be," Grandma said, walking swiftly. "We should have more answers tomorrow. Your grandfather got through to the Sphinx this morning and set up a meeting for tomorrow afternoon."

"Me too?" Seth asked.

"Both of you," Grandma said. "But keep it between us and your grandfather. We want everyone else to think we're going on an outing into town. They don't know that the Sphinx is currently nearby."

"Sure," Kendra said.

"What was the imp saying?" Seth asked.

"That he was going to dance on our graves," Kendra said.

Seth spun around and cupped his hands beside his mouth like a megaphone. "Only if they bury us in your cruddy cell," he yelled. He glanced at Grandma. "Think he heard me?"

CHAPTER EIGHT

Coulter

"He's not here," Seth said, checking his wristwatch.

"He'll be here soon," Kendra said.

They sat together on a stone bench at the edge of an oval section of lawn with a marble birdbath near the center. The sun had not been up long, but the day was already getting warm. A cluster of fairies played among the blossoms of a nearby shrub. Others hovered over the birdbath, admiring their reflections.

"The fairies haven't been very friendly lately," Seth said.

Kendra scratched her temple. "They probably just need their space."

"They were so friendly before we left last summer, after you led them against Bahumat."

"They were probably just extra excited."

"Try to talk to them," Seth said. "If you can understand imps, I bet you can understand fairies too."

"I tried last night. They ignored me."

Seth glanced at his watch again. "I say we go do something else. Coulter's like ten minutes late. And he picked the most boring spot in all of Fablehaven to make us wait."

"Maybe we're in the wrong place."

Seth shook his head. "This is where he said."

"I'm sure he'll come," Kendra said.

"By the time he does, we'll have to leave to visit the Sphinx."

Coulter suddenly appeared in front of them, standing on the lawn not ten feet away, blocking their view of the birdbath. One instant there was nothing, the next, he had popped into existence, leaning on his walking stick. "I suppose I wasn't meant to hear that," Coulter said.

Kendra shrieked, and Seth jumped to his feet. "Where did you come from?" Seth yelped.

"Take more care what you say out in the open," Coulter said. "You never know who may be listening. I'm sure your grandparents wanted your visit to the Sphinx kept a secret."

"Why were you eavesdropping?" Kendra accused.

"To prove a point," Coulter said. "Believe me, if I weren't on your side, and you had given me that information, I would not have tipped my hand by revealing myself. By the way, Kendra, fairies are jealous by nature. There's no surer way to earn their dislike than to become popular."

"How did you do that?" Seth asked.

Coulter held up a fingerless leather glove, letting it hang

limp. "One of my prize possessions. I deal in magical trinkets, tokens, and artifacts. Tanu has his potions, Vanessa has her critters—I have my magic glove. Among other things."

"Can I try it?" Seth asked.

"All in good time," Coulter said, pocketing the glove and clearing his throat. "I understand Tanu got you off to a fine start yesterday. He knows his business. You'd do well to heed him."

"We will," Kendra said.

"Before we begin," Coulter said, shifting his feet as if he were feeling a tad uncomfortable, "I want to make one thing clear." He gave Kendra an uncertain glance. "No matter how careful you are about personal hygiene, it is perfectly natural for a teenage girl to develop an occasional pimple."

Kendra hid her face in her hands. Seth grinned.

"Such things are a natural part of the maturation process," Coulter continued. "You may begin to notice other changes as—"

Kendra raised her head. "I'm not embarrassed about it," she insisted. "It was just the potion."

Coulter nodded patronizingly. "Well, if you ever need to talk about . . . growing up—"

"That's very kind," Kendra blurted, holding up both hands to stop him from saying more. "I'll let you know if I want to talk. Zits happen. I'm okay with it." Seth looked like he was about to explode with laughter, but he managed to contain himself.

Coulter wiped a hand across the top of his head, flattening his little tuft of gray hair. He had reddened slightly.

"Right. Enough said about hormones. Shifting gears." He paused for a moment, rubbing his hands together. "What do the two of you want me to teach you?"

"How to make ourselves invisible," Seth said.

"I mean generally," Coulter clarified. "Why do you want to apprentice with me?"

"So we can learn how to protect ourselves from magical creatures," Kendra said.

"And so we can help out around here," Seth said. "I'm sick of staying in the yard."

Coulter wagged a finger. "A preserve like Fablehaven is a dangerous place. In my line of work, any degree of carelessness can lead to disaster. And by disaster I mean death. No second chances. Just a cold, lonely coffin."

The new soberness in his tone had quickly changed the mood. Kendra and Seth listened attentively.

"Those woods," Coulter said, sweeping a hand toward the trees, "are teeming with creatures who would love nothing more than to drown you. To cripple you. To devour you. To turn you to stone. If you let your guard down for a moment, if you forget for a second that every one of the creatures on this preserve is potentially your worst enemy, you won't have any more chance of surviving than a worm on a henhouse floor. Am I getting through to you?"

Kendra and Seth nodded.

"I don't tell you this out of cruelty," Coulter said. "I'm not trying to shock you with exaggerations. I want you to go into this with your eyes wide open. People in my profession die all the time. Talented, cautious people. No matter how careful you are, there is always the chance of running across something more terrible than you are prepared to handle. Or you might find yourself in a situation you've dealt with a hundred times, but you make a mistake, and you never get a second chance. If either of you expects to venture out into those woods with me, I don't want you clinging to a false sense of security. I've had my close calls, and I've seen people die. I'll do my best to keep you safe, but it is only fair to warn you that on any given day, even doing something that might seem routine, if we're out in those woods, we could all perish. I'll not have you along without making that clear."

"We know it's risky," Seth said.

"Something else I ought to tell you now. If we're all in mortal peril, and it looks like saving you means sacrificing myself, or worse, sacrificing both of us, I'm probably going to save myself. I'd expect you to do the same. If I can protect you, I will; if not . . . you've been warned." Coulter raised his hands. "I don't want your ghosts showing up moaning about how I didn't warn you."

"We've been warned," Kendra said. "We won't haunt you."

"I might haunt you a little," Seth said.

Coulter snorted, hawked up some phlegm, and spat. "Now, I intend to keep us far from situations where our lives are in jeopardy, but there's always a possibility the worst could happen, and if that's a risk you're unwilling to take, speak now, because once we're out in the woods, it may be too late."

"I'm in," Seth said. "I'm still sad I didn't get to go yesterday."

"I'm in too," Kendra said bravely. "But I was fine with yesterday."

"That reminds me," Coulter said, "I'm a little old-fashioned in some ways, and that carries over to this arrangement. Call it outdated chivalry, but there are some places I don't feel women should go. Not because they aren't intelligent or able. I just feel there is a certain respect with which a lady should be treated."

"Are you saying there are places you'd take Seth but not me?" Kendra asked.

"That's what I'm saying. And you hold all the feminist rallies you want, it won't shake my opinion." Coulter spread his hands. "If you want somebody else to take you, and they're willing, I can't do much about that."

"What about Vanessa?" Kendra exclaimed incredulously. "What about Grandma?" Although part of her didn't even want to go to the dangerous places Coulter was talking about, the idea that her gender would prevent him from taking her was deeply insulting.

"Vanessa and your grandma are free to do as they please, as are you. But I'm also free to do as I please, and there are some places I would rather not take a woman, no matter how capable she might be, Vanessa and your grandmother included."

Kendra stood up. "But you'd take Seth? He's two years younger than me and practically brain dead!"

"My brain is not the issue," Seth said, enjoying the argument.

Coulter pointed at Seth with his walking stick. "At twelve, he's on his way to becoming a man. There are plenty of places I wouldn't take either of you, if that brings any consolation. Places none of us would take you until you're much older and more experienced. There are even places we wouldn't go ourselves."

"But there are places you'd take my little brother and not me, just because I'm a girl," Kendra pressed.

"I wouldn't have brought it up if I didn't foresee it happening within the next few days," Coulter said.

Kendra shook her head. "Unbelievable. You know that Fablehaven wouldn't be here if it wasn't for me."

Coulter shrugged apologetically. "You did a wonderful thing, and I'm not trying to detract from that. I'm not talking about ability. If I had a daughter and a son, there are certain things I see myself doing with one and not the other. I know everybody is busy trying to pretend boys and girls are exactly the same nowadays, but that isn't how I see it. If it makes you feel better, I'll share everything I know with both of you, and most places we'll be going, we can all go."

"And I'll get somebody else to take me where you won't," Kendra promised.

"That's your prerogative," Coulter said.

"Can we move on to something else?" Seth asked.

"Can we?" Coulter asked Kendra.

"There's nothing else for me to say," Kendra said, still frustrated.

Coulter acted like he didn't notice her tone. "As I was telling you before, my specialty is magical items. There are all sorts of magical items in the world. Many have burned out—they were once magical but have run out of energy and lost their power. Others remain functional but can only be used a limited number of times. And others seem to draw from an endless supply of magical energy."

"Is the glove limited?" Seth asked.

Coulter held up the glove again. "I've been using it for years, and the effects never seem to dwindle. For all I can tell, it will work forever. But like most magical items, it has certain limitations." He slipped it onto his hand and disappeared. "As long as I hold still, you can see nothing. Different story if I move around." Coulter began to flicker in and out of view. He was wiggling his head. When he waved an arm, he flashed into clear view until he stopped.

"The glove only works if you're motionless," Kendra said.

Coulter was no longer visible. "Correct. I can talk, I can blink, I can breathe. Much more movement than that, and I become visible." He took off the glove, reappearing instantly. "Which is quite an inconvenience. Once I've been spotted, this glove isn't very handy for getting away. It also doesn't mask my smell. For maximum effect, I have to slip it on before I've been seen, in a situation where I can hold still, and where no being that can discern my presence through senses other than sight is present."

"That's why you had us meet you here," Seth said. "So you could come early and get ready to spy on us."

"See?" Coulter said to Kendra. "He isn't brain dead. Naturally, if I were really intent on spying on you, I would have stood behind the bench in the bushes. But I wanted to make a dramatic appearance, so I trusted to luck that you wouldn't run into me and ruin my surprise."

"Your footprints must have been obvious on the lawn," Kendra pointed out.

Coulter bobbed his head. "The grass was newly trimmed, and I stamped around a bit before I chose my spot, but yes, had you been paying proper attention, you could have noticed the imprints of my feet on the lawn. But I guessed right. You didn't."

"Can I try out the glove?" Seth asked.

"Some other time," Coulter said. "Listen. I would prefer that you kept my glove a secret. Your grandparents know, but I would rather keep it from the others. Doesn't pay to let the world in on your best tricks."

Seth mimed like he was locking his lips shut and tossing away the key. "I won't tell," Kendra said.

"Keeping secrets is an important skill to master in my line of work," Coulter said. "Especially with the Society out there, always scheming to gather information and exploit weaknesses. I tell my best secrets only to people I know I can trust. Otherwise the secret becomes a rumor just like that." He snapped his fingers. "You practice keeping the confidences I share with you. Believe me, if I learn you've told anyone, you'll never hear another secret from me."

"You better keep an eye on Kendra," Seth said.

"I never promised to keep that secret," she maintained.

"I'll be keeping an eye on both of you. And I'll up the stakes for the test." He held up a small greenish pod. "There is a species of pixie in Norway that loses its wings at the onset of winter. The pixie spends the coldest winter months hibernating in a cocoon like this one. When spring comes, the pixie emerges with a beautiful new set of wings."

Seth wrinkled his nose. "We have to keep that a secret?"

"I haven't finished. After the proper treatments and preparations, these cocoons become valuable items. If I pop this cocoon into my mouth and bite down hard, it will instantly expand and envelop me. I'll be inside an absolutely impervious shelter, completely safe from any external threat. Enough carbon dioxide filters out of the cocoon, and enough oxygen filters into it, to keep me comfortable—even underwater! The moist inner walls are edible. Together with the moisture they absorb from the outside, the cocoon walls could sustain me for months. And despite the impenetrable outer carapace, from inside, with a little work, I can break free whenever I choose."

"Wow," Kendra said.

"This rare, specially prepared cocoon is my insurance policy," Coulter said. "It's my Get Out of Jail Free Card. And it is one of the secrets I guard most carefully, because a day will likely come when it saves my life."

"And you're telling us?" Seth asked.

"I'm testing you. Even your grandparents don't know about this cocoon. You are not to talk about it with anyone, including each other, because you might be overheard. After sufficient time passes, if you keep this secret, I may share others with you. Don't disappoint me."

"We won't," Seth vowed.

Coulter bent down and scratched his ankle. "You kids notice any drumants last night?"

They both shook their heads.

"I got nipped a couple of times on the leg," he said. "Slept right through it. Maybe I ought to try sawdust and garlic after all."

"Vanessa caught two more," Kendra said.

"Well, she has eleven to go then," Coulter said. "I want to show you one more item." He held up a silver sphere. "You heard your grandparents talking about how no mortals can access Fablehaven through the gates. The entire fence surrounding Fablehaven is reinforced by mighty spells. One of those spells can be illustrated by this ball."

Coulter walked over to the birdbath. The fairies scattered at his approach. "In my hand the spell remains dormant. But once I release the ball, it becomes protected by a distracter spell." He plopped the sphere into the birdbath. "Not nearly as strong as the distracter spell protecting the gates, but it should do."

Coulter returned and stood beside them. "Seth, go get that ball for me, would you?"

Seth studied Coulter suspiciously. "It's going to distract me somehow?"

"Just go bring it over here."

Seth trotted over to the birdbath. He stopped and

started looking around in all directions. "What did you want?" he finally called back to Coulter.

"Bring me the ball," Coulter reminded him.

Seth slapped the heel of his hand against his forehead. "Right." He reached into the water with one hand. Then he put his other hand in and rubbed them together. He stepped back from the birdbath without the ball, shaking droplets from his hands and then drying them against his shirt. He started walking back over to Coulter and Kendra.

"That's incredible," Kendra said.

"Forget anything, Seth?" Coulter asked.

He stopped, cocking his head.

"I wanted the ball," Coulter said.

"Oh, yeah!" Seth cried. "What was I thinking?"

"Come back over here," Coulter invited. "Now you've sampled a distracter spell. One of the spells protecting the fences of Fablehaven does essentially the same thing. Anyone who comes across the fence immediately has his or her attention diverted elsewhere. Simple and effective."

"I want to try," Kendra said.

"Be my guest," Coulter offered.

Kendra walked toward the birdbath. She kept repeating in her mind what she was supposed to do. She even mouthed, "The ball, the ball, the ball," repeatedly. When she reached the birdbath, she stared into the water at the silvery sphere. She wasn't distracted yet. She picked it up and brought it back to Coulter. "Here you go."

He looked flabbergasted. "How did you do that?" he asked.

"I'm as surprised as you are. I thought I was just a girl."

"No, really, Kendra, that was most unusual."

"I just focused."

"On the ball?"

"Yeah."

"Impossible! The charge must have run out. After all these years . . . go put it back."

Kendra jogged over to the birdbath and set it inside. Coulter walked over to the birdbath, hands balled into fists. He placed a hand into the water beside the sphere, began rubbing the bottom of the basin, and then quickly snatched the ball. "It still works. I could feel the spell striving to muddle me, potent as ever."

"Then how did you get it?" Kendra asked.

"Practice," Coulter said. "If you focus on the ball it will distract you. So you focus on something near the ball. I was focusing on rubbing the bottom of the birdbath, keeping the ball in the back of my mind. Then, as I'm rubbing the bottom of the birdbath, when I notice the ball, I grab it."

"I concentrated on the ball," Kendra said.

Coulter tossed the ball toward the bench. It came to a rest on the lawn. "Go get it again. Don't even try to focus."

Kendra walked over and picked it up. "Guess I'm immune."

"Interesting," Coulter said thoughtfully.

"I bet I could do it now," Seth said.

"Set it down, Kendra," Coulter said.

Seth walked toward the ball, stooped to pick some grass, and then went and sat on the bench. "What?" he asked, wondering why they were staring, then slapping his forehead again once they reminded him.

"Must be another side effect from the fairies," Kendra guessed.

"Must be," Coulter said thoughtfully. "The mysteries keep piling up around you, don't they. You've reminded me, the fairies have caused some other peculiar effects here at Fablehaven. Let's move on to the fun stuff. We've made a fascinating discovery since your last visit." He raised his voice. "Hugo, come!"

The massive golem came out from behind the barn, loping toward them with long, pounding strides. When Kendra had last seen Hugo, he was blooming with verdure, thanks to the fairies. Now he looked much more like he had before the fairies had resuscitated him: a primitive body of soil, stone, and clay, more apelike in form than humanlike, a few weeds and dandelions sprouting here and there, but no leafy vines or colorful flowers.

Hugo halted in front of them. The top of Coulter's head barely reached the middle of the golem's powerful chest. Hugo was broad, with thick limbs and disproportionately large hands and feet. He looked like he could effortlessly tear Coulter limb from limb, but Kendra knew Hugo would never do something like that. The golem only followed orders.

"You remember Hugo?" Coulter said.

"Of course," Seth said.

"Watch this," Coulter said. He picked up a stone and tossed it toward the golem. Hugo caught it.

"What's that supposed to prove?" Seth said.

"I didn't tell him to catch it," Coulter said.

"He must have a standing order to catch things thrown at him," Kendra guessed.

Coulter shook his head. "No standing order."

Faintly, Hugo smiled.

"Is he smiling?" Seth asked.

"I wouldn't put it past him," Coulter said. "Hugo, do whatever you like."

Hugo squatted, and then jumped high into the air, raising both arms. He landed with enough force to make the ground tremble.

"He's doing things on his own?" Kendra asked.

"Little things," Coulter said. "He's still totally obedient. He completes all his chores. But one day your grandmother spotted him putting a baby bird back into its nest. Nobody had issued a command; he was simply being kind."

"You're saying the fairies did something to him!" Kendra said. "After Muriel destroyed Hugo with a spell, they rebuilt him, but they must have changed him."

"Near as we can tell, they made him a true golem," Coulter said. "Manufactured golems, the mindless puppets who exist only to obey orders, were originally created in imitation of true golems, actual living creatures of stone or mud or sand. True golems long ago passed out of all human knowledge. But apparently Hugo is now one. He is developing a will."

"Awesome!" Seth exclaimed.

"Can he communicate?" Kendra asked.

"Only crudely for now," Coulter explained. "His comprehension is quite good—it had to be, for him to take orders. And his physical coordination is as precise as ever. But he is only just beginning to experiment with expressing himself and acting on his own. Slowly but surely he has been improving. In time, he should be able to interact with us like a normal person."

"So right now he's like a big baby," Kendra said in wonder.

"In many ways, yes," Coulter agreed. "One of the jobs I want the two of you to undertake is to engage in an hour of playtime with Hugo every day. He will not be under any order to heed your commands. I will simply leave him with the mandate to enjoy himself. Then you two are free to talk to him, play catch with him, teach him tricks, whatever you like. I want to see if we can get him functioning more on his own."

"If he gets too smart, will he stop taking orders?" Seth asked.

"I doubt it," Coulter said. "Obedience to his masters is woven too deeply into his being. It is part of the magic that holds him together. He could, however, develop into a much more useful servant, capable of making decisions and sharing information. And he could start enjoying a higher state of existence."

"I like this assignment," Kendra said. "When can we start?"

"How about now?" Coulter offered. "I don't think we have enough time for a real foray into the woods today. You need to be here after lunch so you can go into town with your grandmother. I have no idea what you might be doing there." Imitating Seth, Coulter pantomimed like he was locking his lips and throwing away the key. "Hugo, I want you to play with Kendra and Seth. Feel free to do whatever you want."

Coulter strode away toward the house, leaving Kendra and Seth with the massive golem. For a moment the three stood in silence. "What should we do?" Seth asked.

"Hugo," Kendra said. "Why don't you show us your favorite flower in the garden?"

"Favorite flower?" Seth complained. "Are you trying to bore him to death?"

Hugo raised a finger and then waved for them to follow. He stomped off across the lawn in the direction of the swimming pool. "Picking favorites gives him a chance to practice making choices," Kendra explained as they ran to keep up with Hugo.

"Fine, then how about favorite weapon or monster or something cool?"

Hugo stopped beside a hedge with a flowerbed at the base. He pointed at a large blue and white flower with a trumpet-shaped blossom and vivid, translucent petals. It was delicate and exquisite.

"Good pick, Hugo, I like that one," Kendra complimented.

"Great," Seth said. "You're very sensitive and artistic. Now, how about we have some fun? Want to go jump in the pool? I bet you could make the best cannonballs!"

Hugo crossed and uncrossed his hands, indicating that he did not like the idea.

"He's made of dirt," Kendra said. "Use your brain."

"And rock and clay . . . I thought it would just make him sort of muddy."

"And clog up the filter. You should have Hugo throw you in the pool."

The golem turned his head toward Seth, who shrugged. "Sure, that would be fun."

Hugo nodded, grabbed Seth, and, with a motion like a hook shot, flung him skyward. Kendra gasped. They were still thirty or forty feet away from the edge of the pool. She had pictured the golem carrying Seth much closer before tossing him. Her brother sailed nearly as high as the roof of the house before plummeting down and landing in the center of the deep end with an impressive splash.

Kendra ran to the side of the pool. By the time she arrived, Seth was boosting himself out of the water, hair and clothes dripping. "That was the freakiest, awesomest moment of my life!" Seth declared. "But next time, let me take off my shoes."

CHAPTER NINE

The Sphinx

Kendra stared out the window at a huge, derelict factory as the SUV idled at a stoplight. Rotting boards crisscrossed the lower windows. The yawning upper windows were nearly devoid of glass. Wrappers, broken bottles, crushed soda cans, and weather-worn newspapers littered the sidewalk. Cryptic graffiti decorated the walls. Most of the spray-painted words looked sloppy, but a few had been expertly rendered with gleaming metallic letters.

"Can I take off my seat belt yet?" Seth complained, squirming.

"One more block," Grandma said.

"The Sphinx isn't staying in a very nice part of town," Kendra said.

"He has to keep a low profile," Grandma said. "Often that translates to less than ideal accommodations."

The light turned green, and they drove through the intersection. Kendra, Seth, and Grandma had been on the road quite a while in order to reach the coastal city of Bridgeport. Grandma took a much more leisurely approach to driving than Vanessa, but despite the gentle pace and pleasant scenery, the prospect of meeting the Sphinx had kept Kendra on edge for the entire ride.

"Here we are," Grandma announced, activating the left blinker and turning into the parking lot of King of the Road Auto Repair. The run-down auto shop looked abandoned. There were no cars in the small lot, and all the shop windows were obscured by dust and grime. Grandma avoided a lone, rusty hubcap lying on the asphalt.

"What a dump!" Seth said. "You sure this is the place?"

The SUV was just coming to a stop when one of the three doors to the garage slid upwards. A tall Asian man in a black suit waved them inside. He was lean, with wide shoulders and a humorless face. Grandma pulled into the garage, and the man yanked the door down behind them.

Grandma opened her door. "You must be Mr. Lich," she said. The man lowered his chin briefly, a motion halfway between a nod and a bow. Mr. Lich gestured for them to exit the vehicle.

"Come along," Grandma said, descending from the SUV. Kendra and Seth got out as well. Mr. Lich was walking away. They hurried to follow him. He led them out a door into an alley where a black sedan was waiting. Bland features neutral, Mr. Lich opened the back door. Grandma, Kendra, and Seth ducked inside. Mr. Lich got up front and started the car.

"Do you speak English?" Seth asked.

Mr. Lich fixed him with a steady stare in the rearview mirror, put the car in drive, and started down the alley. None of them made further efforts at conversation. They followed a disorienting series of alleys and side streets before finally reaching a main road. After a U-turn, they were back on side streets, until Mr. Lich brought the sedan to a stop in a dirty alley beside a row of dented garbage cans.

He got out and opened the door for them. The alley smelled like taco sauce and rancid oil. Mr. Lich escorted them to a grimy door that read *Employees Only*. He opened it and followed them inside. They passed through a kitchen into a dimly lit bar. Blinds covered the windows. There were not many patrons. Two guys with long hair were playing pool. A fat man with a beard sat at the bar next to a skinny blonde with a pockmarked face and frizzy curls. Wispy strands of cigarette smoke twisted in the air.

Grandma, Seth, and Kendra entered the room first. The bartender was shaking his head. "No patrons under twenty-one," he said. Then Mr. Lich appeared and pointed toward a stairway in the corner. The demeanor of the bartender changed instantly. "My mistake." He turned away.

Mr. Lich ushered them up the carpeted stairs. At the top, they pushed through a beaded curtain into a room with shaggy, calico carpet, a pair of brown sofas, and four suede beanbag chairs. A heavy ceiling fan spun slowly. A large, old-fashioned radio stood in the corner, softly playing big band music, as if tuned to a station broadcasting out of the past.

Placing a hand on Grandma's shoulder, Mr. Lich motioned toward the couches. He did the same for Seth. Turning to Kendra, he gestured toward a door on the other side of the room. Kendra glanced at Grandma, who nodded. Seth flung himself onto a beanbag.

After crossing to the door, Kendra hesitated. The silent car ride and unusual environment had already made her uncomfortable. The prospect of facing the Sphinx by herself was unsettling. She looked over her shoulder. Both Grandma and Mr. Lich motioned for her to enter. Kendra knocked softly. "Come inside," said a deep voice, barely loud enough to be heard.

She opened the door. A red curtain fringed with gold tassels and embroidery blocked her view. She pushed through the velvet curtain into the room beyond. The door closed behind her.

A black man with short, beaded dreadlocks stood beside a Foosball table. His skin was not merely a shade of brown—it was as close to truly black as Kendra had ever seen. He was of average height and build, and wore a loose gray shirt, cargo pants, and sandals. His handsome face had an ageless quality—he could have been in his thirties or his fifties.

Kendra glanced around the spacious room. A large aquarium held a vibrant collection of tropical fish. Numerous delicate, metallic mobiles dangled from the ceiling. She counted at least ten clocks of eccentric designs on the walls, tables, and shelves. A sculpture made of garbage stood beside a life-sized wooden carving of a grizzly bear. Near the window was an elaborate model of the solar system, intricate planets and moons held in place by wire orbits.

"Would you join me in a game of Foosball?" His accent made Kendra think of the Caribbean, although that was not quite right.

"Are you the Sphinx?" Kendra asked, bewildered by the unusual request.

"I am."

Kendra approached the table. "Okay, sure."

"Would you prefer cowboys or Indians?"

Spitted on rods were four rows of Indians and four rows of cowboys. The cowboys were all the same, as were the Indians. The cowboy had a white hat and a mustache. His hands rested on his holstered six-guns. The Indian had a feathered headdress, and his reddish-brown arms were folded across his bare chest. The feet of each cowboy and Indian were fused together to better strike the ball.

"I'll be Indians," Kendra said. She had played some Foosball at the rec center back home. Seth usually beat her two out of three games.

"Let me forewarn you," the Sphinx said, "I am not very good." There was a mellow quality to his voice that evoked images of old-time jazz clubs.

"Neither am I," Kendra admitted. "My little brother usually beats me."

"Would you like to serve the ball?"

"Sure."

He gave her the bright yellow ball. She put her left hand on the handle that controlled the goalie, dropped the ball into the slot with her right, and started wildly spinning her nearest Indians as it rolled across the center of the table. The Sphinx controlled his cowboys with more calm, using quick, precise jabs to counter Kendra's reckless spinning. It was not long before Kendra scored the first goal.

"Well done," he said.

Kendra marked the goal by sliding a bead along a bar at her end of the table. The Sphinx took the ball out of his goal and served it through the slot. The ball rolled to his men. He passed it up to his front row of cowboys, but the Indian goalie blocked the shot. The Indians spun madly, mercilessly pounding the ball at the cowboys until they scored a second goal.

The Sphinx slid the ball into the slot. Her confidence boosted, Kendra attacked even more aggressively with her Indians, and ended up winning the game five goals to two.

"I feel like General Custer," the Sphinx said. "Well played. Can I offer you something to drink? Apple juice? Cream soda? Chocolate milk, perhaps?"

"Cream soda sounds good," Kendra said. She was feeling more at ease after trouncing him.

"Excellent choice," the Sphinx said. He opened a freezer and withdrew a frosty mug with ice in it. From a small refrigerator he removed a brown bottle, uncapped it with a little tool, and poured the yellow soda into the mug. It was surprisingly foamy. "Please, sit down." He nodded to a pair of chairs facing each other with a low table in between.

Kendra took a seat and the Sphinx handed her the mug. Her first few sips were all froth. When she finally reached the soda, it was a perfect mix of sweet, creamy, cool, and bubbly. "Thanks, this is delicious," she said.

"The pleasure is mine." A miniature gong sat on the table between them. The Sphinx tapped it with a small hammer. "While the gong vibrates, none can overhear our conversation. I have at least part of the answer you came here seeking. You are fairykind."

"I am very kind?"

"Fairy . . . kind," he said, enunciating carefully. "It is written all over your countenance, woven into your speech."

"What does that mean?"

"It means that you are unique in all the world, Kendra. In my long years and many travels, I have never met anyone who was fairykind, though I am familiar with the signs and see them expressed plainly in you. Tell me, did you sample the elixir you prepared for the fairies?"

There was a hypnotic gravity to his voice. Kendra felt like she had to snap out of a trance in order to answer the question. "Yes, actually, I did. I was trying to convince them to try it."

The corners of his mouth lifted slightly, showing dimples in his cheeks. "Then perhaps you gave them an incentive," he said. "They had to either make you fairykind or watch you die."

"Die?"

"The elixir you ingested is fatal to mortals. You would

have eventually suffered a torturous death had the fairies not chosen to share their magic with you."

"The fairies cured me?"

"They changed you, so that you no longer required curing."

Kendra stared at him. "People have said I was fairy-struck."

"I have met individuals who were fairystruck. It is a rare and extraordinary occurrence. This is much more rare, and much more extraordinary. You have been made fairykind. I do not believe it has happened in more than a thousand years."

"I still don't understand what it means," Kendra said.

"Neither do I, not entirely. The fairies have changed you, adopted you, infused you with their magic. A semblance of the magical energy that naturally dwells in them now dwells in you. The diverse effects that could flow from this are difficult to anticipate."

"That's why I don't need the milk to see anymore?"

"And why Warren found himself drawn to you. And why you understand Goblush, along with, I imagine, the other tongues derived from Silvian, the language of the fairies. Your grandfather has been in touch with me regarding the new abilities you have been manifesting." The Sphinx leaned forward and tapped the little gong with the hammer again.

Kendra took another sip from her mug. "This morning, Coulter was showing us a ball protected by a distracter spell. Seth couldn't pick it up; he kept losing focus and getting redirected someplace else. But it didn't work on me. I could grab it just fine."

"You have apparently developed resistance to mind control."

Kendra wrinkled her brow. "Tanu gave me a potion that made me feel ashamed, and it worked just fine."

"The potion would have been manipulating your emotions. Mind control functions differently. Pay close attention to all the new abilities you discover. Report them to your grandfather. Unless I am mistaken, you are only beginning to scratch the surface."

The thought was thrilling and terrifying. "I'm still a human, right?"

"You are something more than human," the Sphinx said. "But your humanity and your mortality remain intact."

"Are you a human?"

He smiled, his teeth shockingly white in contrast to his black skin. "I am an anachronism. A holdover from long-forgotten times. I have seen learning come and go, empires rise and fall. Consider me your guardian angel. I would like to conduct a simple experiment. Do you mind?"

"Is it safe?"

"Completely. But if I am right, it could provide the answer to why the Society of the Evening Star has shown such interest in you."

"Okay."

A pair of short copper rods rested on the table. The Sphinx picked up one and handed it to Kendra. "Hand me the other one," the Sphinx said. After Kendra complied, he held his rod in both hands, one at each end of the rod. "Hold your rod like me," he instructed.

Kendra had been holding the slender rod in one hand. The instant her other hand touched it, she felt a sensation like she was falling backwards through the chair. And then it passed. And she was inexplicably sitting where the Sphinx had been sitting, and he was seated in her chair. They had instantaneously switched places.

The Sphinx released one hand from the rod and then grabbed it again. The moment his hand came back into contact with the rod, Kendra felt her insides lurch again, and suddenly she was sitting back in her former chair.

The Sphinx set the rod down on the table, and Kendra did likewise. "We teleported?" Kendra asked.

"The rods enable users to trade locations over short distances. But that is not what makes what happened unusual. Those rods have been dead for decades, useless, drained of all energy. Your touch recharged them."

"Really?"

"Fairykind are known to radiate magical energy in a unique way. The world is full of burned-out magical tools. Your touch would revitalize them. This amazing ability alone would make you tremendously valuable to the Society of the Evening Star. I wonder how they know. An educated guess, perhaps?"

"Do they have a lot of things that need recharging?"

The Sphinx tapped the gong again. "No doubt, but I refer more directly to the five hidden artifacts your grandparents told you about. The ones on the five secret preserves. If any of them lie dormant, as is likely, your touch would reactivate them. All five would have to be functional in order for the Society to achieve their goal of opening Zzyzx and freeing the demons. Without your gift, reactivating talismans of such monumental power would be most difficult."

"Here's what I don't get," Kendra said. "Why have keys to the prison? Why not make a demon prison without keys?"

The Sphinx nodded as if he approved of the question. "There is a fundamental principle of magic that applies to many other things as well: Everything with a beginning has an ending. Any magic that can be done, can be undone. Anything you can make, can be unmade. In other words, any prison you can create, can be destroyed. Any lock can be broken. To construct an impenetrable prison is impossible. Those who have tried have invariably failed. The magic becomes unstable and unravels. If it has a beginning, it must have an end.

"The wise learned that rather than attempting to make a prison impenetrable, they should focus on making it extraordinarily complicated to open. The strongest prisons, like Zzyzx, were crafted by those who understood that the goal was to make them nearly impenetrable, as close to perfect as possible without crossing the line. Because there is a way to open Zzyzx, the magic that holds the demons bound remains potent. The principle sounds simple, although the details become quite complicated."

Kendra shifted in her seat. "So if the Society just

destroyed the keys, would that unravel the magic and open the prison?"

"Nimble thinking," the Sphinx said, dark eyes twinkling. "Three problems. First, the keys are virtually indestructible—note that I say *virtually*; they were made by the same experts who created the prison. Second, if my research is correct, a fail-safe would cause any destroyed key to be reconstituted in a different form in an unpredictable location, and that process could go on almost indefinitely. And third, if the Society were somehow to free the demons by permanently destroying an artifact, they would become victims like the rest of humanity. The Society must parley with the demons before their release in order to obtain any measure of security, which means they must open the prison properly rather than simply undermine the magic that upholds it."

Kendra drank the last of her cream soda, ice tumbling against her lips. "So they can't succeed without the artifacts."

"Therefore we must keep the artifacts from them. Which is easier said than done. One of the great virtues of the Society is patience. They make no rash moves. They research and plan and prepare. They wait for the ideal opportunities. They understand that they have an unlimited amount of time in which to succeed. To them, it is the same to achieve their aims in a thousand years as it would be to triumph tomorrow. Patience mimics the power of infinity. And nobody can win a staring contest with infinity. No matter how long you last, infinity is just getting started."

"But they aren't infinity," Kendra said.

The Sphinx blinked. "True. And so we attempt to equal their patience and diligence. We do our best to stay far ahead of them. Part of that means moving an artifact once they learn its location, as we fear has happened with the artifact at Fablehaven. Otherwise, somehow, sometime, they will exploit a mistake and lay hands on it."

"Grandpa mentioned another endangered artifact, in Brazil."

"Some of my best people are working on it. I believe the artifact remains on the fallen preserve, and I believe we will retrieve it first." He threw up his hands. "If the Society manages to recover it, we will have to steal it back."

The Sphinx gazed at Kendra with fathomless eyes. Kendra looked away. "What letter of mine did you read?" he finally asked.

"Letter?"

"All of my letters carry enchantments. They leave a mark upon those who read them surreptitiously. You bear the mark."

At first Kendra had no idea what he was talking about. When would she have read a letter from the Sphinx? Then she remembered the letter she had read last summer while Grandpa was sleeping after staying up late with Maddox. Of course! It had been signed "S." For Sphinx!

"It was a letter you sent Grandpa last year. He accidentally left it out in the open. You were warning him about the Society of the Evening Star. I read it because I thought it might have something to do with my grandma. She was missing."

"Be glad you did not read it with malicious intent. The letter would have turned into a toxic vapor." He folded his hands on his lap. "We are nearly finished. Have you any final questions for me?"

Kendra frowned. "What do I do now?"

"You return to your grandfather with the knowledge that you are fairykind. You do your part to keep Fablehaven safe while the artifact is recovered. You take note of any new abilities. You counsel with your grandparents as needed. And you take comfort in the fact that you now know why the Society is interested in you."

He placed a single finger beside his temple. "One last thought. Though secret, and in many ways quiet, the struggle between the Society of the Evening Star and those who manage the preserves is of desperate importance to the whole world. Whatever the rhetoric on both sides, the problem boils down to a simple disagreement. While the Conservators' Alliance wants to preserve magical creatures without endangering humanity, the Society of the Evening Star wants to exploit many of those same magical creatures in order to gain power. The Society will pursue its ends at the expense of all humankind if necessary. The stakes could not be higher."

The Sphinx stood up. "You are an extraordinary young lady, Kendra, with immeasurable potential. The day may come when you want to deliberately explore and channel the power the fairies have granted you. On that day, it would be my pleasure to offer guidance and instruction. You could become a powerful adversary of the Society. I hope we can count on your assistance in the future."

"Okay, wow, thanks," Kendra said. "I'll do all I can."

He extended a hand toward the door. "Good day, my new friend. Your brother can come see me now."

※　※　※

Seth reclined on a beanbag, staring at the ceiling. Grandma sat on a nearby couch, leafing through a thick book. It seemed like all he ever did lately was wait. Wait for somebody to take him into the woods. Wait for the car ride to be over. Wait while Kendra talked forever with the Sphinx. Was the purpose of life learning to endure boredom?

The door opened and Kendra emerged. "Your turn," she said.

Seth rolled off the beanbag and stood up. "What's he like?"

"He's smart," Kendra said. "He said I'm fairykind."

Seth cocked his head. "Very kind?"

"Fairy . . . kind. The fairies shared their magic with me."

"Are you sure, dear?" Grandma said, one hand over her heart.

"That's what he said," Kendra shrugged. "He acted sure."

Seth tuned them out and hurried over to the door. He opened it and shoved through the curtain into the room. The Sphinx stood leaning against the Foosball table. "Your sister tells me you are quite the Foosball player."

"I'm okay. I don't own my own table or anything."

"I do not play often. Would you care to try your hand against me?"

Seth surveyed the table. "I want to be cowboys."

"Good. They were unlucky for me against your sister."

"Are you really part lion?"

"You mean, am I appearing to you as an avatar? I will tell you if you win. Would you care to serve?"

Seth grabbed the handles. "You can."

"As you wish." The Sphinx pushed the ball through the slot. The cowboys started spinning frantically. The Sphinx got control of the ball, nudged it sideways about an inch, and, with a flick of his wrist, blasted it into Seth's goal.

"Wow!" Seth said.

"Your serve."

Seth put the ball in play. Flailing with his cowboys, he knocked it all the way to the Sphinx's goalie. Using controlled movements, the Sphinx passed the ball across the table, from row to row, until he slammed it into Seth's goal from a tricky angle.

"You're amazing!" Seth said. "Did you say Kendra beat you?"

"Your sister needed confidence. Yours is a different problem. Plus there is no chance of me telling you my secret unless you earn it." Seth put the ball back in play, and the Sphinx swiftly scored again. The same thing happened two more times, the final point coming from a shot that put a spin on the ball so it curved into the goal.

"You skunked me!" Seth cried.

"Do not tell your sister that I went easy on her. Tell her

you beat me, if she asks." The Sphinx paused, looking Seth up and down. "You have obviously been cursed."

"A demon statue bit me. You can tell?"

"I knew beforehand, but the evidence of the curse is plain. Olloch the Glutton. How does it feel to be on his menu?"

"Not so good. Can you fix me?"

The Sphinx opened the refrigerator. "I offered your sister a drink."

"You have anything from Egypt?"

"I have apple juice. I suppose Egyptians drink it sometimes."

"Okay." Seth roamed the room, looking at the strange knickknacks on the tables and shelves. A miniature Ferris wheel, a collapsible spyglass, a crystal music box, numerous figurines.

The Sphinx popped open a can of apple juice and poured the contents into a frosty mug. "Here you go."

Seth accepted the mug and took a sip. "I like the frozen cup."

"I am glad. Seth, I cannot remove the curse. It will remain until Olloch either devours you or is destroyed."

"So what do I do?" Seth started guzzling his juice.

"You will have to rely on the barrier the walls of Fablehaven provide. The day will come when Olloch shows up at the gates. The insatiable drive that compels him toward you will only increase over time. Worse, the demon is in the hands of the Society, and I suspect they will ensure he makes his way to you sooner rather than later. When

Olloch makes his appearance, we will find a way to deal with him. Until that day, Fablehaven will be your refuge."

"No more school?" Seth asked hopefully.

"You must not leave Fablehaven again until the glutton has been subdued. Mark my words, he will appear before long. When he does, we will discover a weakness and learn a way to exploit it. You should have no problem returning to school by the fall."

Having finished the juice, Seth wiped his lips with the back of his hand. "No big rush."

"Our conversation is nearly finished," the Sphinx said, taking the mug from Seth. "Take care of your sister. Turbulent times lie ahead. The gift the fairies have given her will make her a target. Your bravery can be a powerful asset if you can keep it unspoiled by recklessness. Do not forget that Fablehaven almost fell because of your folly. Learn from that mistake."

"I will," Seth said. "I mean, I have. And I'll keep Kendra's fairykind thing a secret."

The Sphinx extended a hand. Seth shook it. "One last thing, Seth. Are you aware that Midsummer Eve is scarcely a week away?"

"Yeah."

"Might I make a suggestion?"

"Okay."

"Don't open any windows."

CHAPTER TEN

An Uninvited Guest

Grandpa leaned back in his wheelchair, tapping his lips with the safe end of a fountain pen. Kendra and Seth sat in the oversized armchairs, and Grandma was behind the desk. Kendra and Seth had not seen Grandpa the previous night—Grandma had taken them to a fondue restaurant after their meeting with the Sphinx, and so they had not returned until well after dark.

"Our story is that you were fairystruck, and that there were some residual effects from the incident," Grandpa said, ending the contemplative silence. "It sounds perfectly plausible, and will make you less of a target than if word gets out you are fairykind. Obviously we never let on that the diagnosis came from the Sphinx—we do not mention him at all, to anyone."

"Coulter already knows we went to see him," Kendra confessed.

"What?" Grandma leaned forward.

"He already told me," Grandpa said. "Ruth, he was trying to teach the lesson that spies could be anywhere, eavesdropping on conversations, and in the process learned about the Sphinx. The secret will be safe with Coulter. But he need not hear further details. No discussing it outside of this study."

"So if anyone asks, Kendra was fairystruck," Seth said.

"If someone knows enough to ask, and deserves an answer, that is our story," Grandpa reiterated. "Now I hope we can get back to business as usual. Tanu is off scouting some unexplored territory. Coulter has an outing specifically for Seth. And Kendra can assist Vanessa with research."

"Research?" Kendra asked. "Here in the house?"

Seth bit the side of his hand. He was choking back laughter, which only served to inflame Kendra's indignation.

"She's going through some journals," Grandpa said. "Following up on some hints left by Patton Burgess."

"Why can't I go with Coulter? It's sexist! Can't you make him take me?"

"Coulter is one of the most stubborn men I know," Grandpa said. "I have serious doubts whether anyone could make him do anything. But I'm not sure today need be an issue for you, Kendra. I suspect you would rather skip this outing of your own accord. You see, a certain fog giant shared a valuable lead with us. In return, we promised him a live buffalo. So Coulter, Seth, and Hugo will be handing over a buffalo to the brute to be instantly devoured. It will be a gruesome sight."

"Awesome," Seth whispered reverently.

"Okay, well, I guess I don't mind skipping that," Kendra admitted. "But I still don't like the idea of being left out of Coulter's excursions."

"Complaint noted," Grandpa said. "Now, Seth, I don't want this Olloch the Glutton business keeping you up at night. The Sphinx is right, the walls of Fablehaven will be sufficient protection, and if he says he will help us take care of the glutton once the demon shows up, then I see no cause for worry."

"Sounds good to me," Seth said.

"Well, then," Grandpa said. "Off you go."

❧ ❧ ❧

Seth kept glancing over his shoulder at the buffalo they were leading along the path. Huge shaggy head, short white horns, bulky body, plodding gait. He had never appreciated what large animals they were. Had Hugo not been leading the beast with a bridle, Seth would have scrambled up a tree.

They had started out on paths Seth knew, but quickly turned down unfamiliar roads. Now they had reached lower, wetter terrain than Seth had ever seen at Fablehaven. The trees had more moss and vines, and the first shreds of unexpected mist eddied close to the ground.

Seth clutched his emergency kit. Alongside the more conventional contents, Tanu had added a small potion that would boost his vigor if he became exhausted. This morning

Coulter had added a lucky rabbit's foot and a medallion that was supposed to repel the undead.

"Is this rabbit's foot really lucky?" Seth asked, fingering it.

"We'll see," Coulter responded, eyes scanning the trees.

"Are you superstitious?"

"I like to cover my bases," he said softly. "Keep your voice low. This is not a hospitable area of the preserve. Now might be a good time to put on that medallion."

Seth fished the medallion out of his emergency kit and slipped the chain around his neck. "Where did Hugo find a buffalo in the first place?" he asked quietly.

"There's a complex of corrals and stables on the preserve," Coulter said. "Not filled to capacity, but with plenty of animals for Fablehaven to remain self-sufficient. Hugo does most of the upkeep. He brought the buffalo from there this morning."

"Do you have any giraffes?"

"The most exotic it gets are ostriches, llamas, and buffalo," Coulter said. "Along with more traditional livestock."

The mist was getting thicker. The air remained warm, but the cloying smell of decay was increasing. The terrain became soupier. Seth began spotting clusters of fuzzy mushrooms and rocks slick with slime.

Coulter pointed to a path diverting off to one side. "Normally in Fablehaven you are relatively safe if you stay on the path. But that is only true of the real paths. That path, for example, was created by a swamp hag to lead the unwary to their doom."

Seth stared at the narrow trail meandering off into the mist, trying to memorize it so he would never make the mistake of following it. They did not go much farther before Coulter stopped.

"We are now at the edge of the great marsh of Fablehaven," he whispered. "One of the most perilous, least explored areas of the preserve. A likely region for the inverted tower to be hidden. Come."

Coulter stepped off the path onto muddy ground. Seth squelched after him, with Hugo and the ill-fated buffalo bringing up the rear. Up ahead, through the shroud of white mist, a geodesic dome came into view. The grid of triangles that comprised the dome appeared to be composed of glass and steel. In form, the structure was similar to the domes of interlocking metal bars Seth had seen on playgrounds.

"What's that?" Seth asked.

"A safe hut," Coulter said. "Glass domes strategically placed in some of the more threatening areas of the preserve. They provide the kind of refuge we enjoy back at the main house. Nothing can enter uninvited."

They walked about ten yards past the hut. "Hugo, picket the buffalo here," Coulter ordered. "Then stand watch from behind the hut."

Hugo produced a stake the size of a fence post and thrust it deep into the ground with a single powerful motion. The golem then fastened the buffalo to the stake. Coulter shook something from a pouch into his palm, then cupped his hand near the buffalo's muzzle. "This will anesthetize him,"

Coulter explained. Next he produced a knife and slashed the buffalo on the shoulder. The buffalo tossed its heavy head.

A deep roar came echoing out of the mist. "To the hut," Coulter murmured, wiping the knife clean before stowing it. He tossed the rag that he had used to wipe the knife near the buffalo.

The symmetry of the glass dome was broken only by a small hatch in one side, also made of glass and framed in steel. Coulter opened the hatch and crawled in after Seth. The hut had no floor—just the bare earth. Hugo waited outside.

"We're safe in here?" Seth asked.

"As long as we don't break the glass from the inside, no creature can get us, even a fog giant in a blood frenzy."

"Blood frenzy?"

"You'll see," Coulter assured him. "Fog giants go mad around blood. Worse than sharks. This tribute is the price we agreed to pay for information Burlox gave us about the marshland. After the tribute, he has promised us one more piece of information."

"Burlox is the giant?"

"The most approachable of them, yes."

"What if the wrong giant takes the buffalo?"

Coulter shook his head. "Fog giants are highly territorial. Another would not encroach on Burlox's domain. Their borders are clearly defined."

Despite the condensation on the glass and the intervening mist, Seth had a good view of the buffalo. It was grazing. "I feel bad for the buffalo," Seth said.

"Like most livestock, it was born to be slaughtered," Coulter said. "If not by a fog giant, by your grandfather. The anesthetic will dull its senses. The fog giant will administer a quick death."

Seth frowned, staring through the glass. What had sounded like fun back at the house was no longer very appealing, now that he recognized the buffalo as an actual living thing. "I guess I eat hamburgers all the time," he finally said.

"This isn't much different," Coulter agreed. "Somewhat more dramatic."

"What about the rules of the treaty?" Seth asked. "Won't you get in trouble for killing the buffalo?"

"I won't be doing any killing; that will be the giant," Coulter explained. "Besides, the rules are different for animals. The treaty was meant to keep sentient beings from committing murder and casting spells on each other. The same protection does not extend to animals of a lower order of intelligence. When the need arises, we can slaughter animals for food with no repercussions."

Another roar sounded, much closer and more intense. A gargantuan shadow loomed beyond the buffalo. "Here he comes," Coulter breathed.

Seth's mouth went dry. As the fog giant emerged from the mist, Seth found himself scooting back to the far side of the small dome. Burlox was enormous. Seth was not much taller than his knee. Hugo was shorter than his hip. The buffalo suddenly looked like a house pet.

The fog giant had the proportions of a heavyset man. He

wore tattered, matted furs, and his body was smeared with oily muck. Beneath the filth, his skin was a sickly bluish gray. His long hair and beard were tangled in slime. In one hand he bore a crude, heavy club. The overall impression was that of a fierce, battle-weary Viking who had lost his way in a swamp.

The giant stopped near the buffalo. He turned and looked toward the dome, giving a single nod and leering. Seth was acutely aware that a single swing of the huge club could bash the hut to smithereens. Burlox tossed the club aside and then pounced at the buffalo, tearing off the bridle and hoisting the flustered animal into the air.

Seth looked away. It was too much. He heard a noisy combination of bones crunching and flesh tearing before clamping his hands over his ears. Part of him wanted to watch, but instead he kept his head down and his ears covered.

"You're missing it," Coulter eventually said, kneeling at his side.

Seth peeked. The buffalo no longer looked much like a buffalo. Sections of the hide had been cast aside, and jutting bones were visible. Seth tried to pretend that the leg Burlox was mauling was a gigantic spare rib, and that the feasting giant was drenched in barbecue sauce.

"Not something you get to see every day," Coulter said.

"True," Seth conceded.

"Look at him, munching away—he can't eat it fast enough. He rarely gets meat of this quality. He ought to slow down and savor it. But the brute can't help himself."

"It's pretty disgusting."

"Just one beast consuming the meat of another," Coulter said. "Although I'll admit I glanced away at the start myself."

"It was sadder than I expected."

"Look at him going after the marrow. He doesn't want to waste a thing."

"I can't imagine eating something raw like that," Seth said.

"He can't imagine cooking it," Coulter replied.

They watched as the giant picked the bones clean and sucked them dry. "Here it comes," Coulter said, rubbing his hands. "You'd think he'd be satisfied, but no matter how much fresh meat you give them, it just whets their appetite." The fog giant began rooting around on the ground, apparently lapping up what he could from the mud. Soon his face was masked with sludge, and limp vegetation dangled from his lips. He began hammering his mighty fists against the soggy turf and throwing fragments of bone into the mist. He tossed back his head and let out a long, angry cry.

"He's going berserk," Seth said.

The fog giant wheeled toward the dome, scowling. He picked up his club and charged, eyes ablaze. Seth felt totally exposed. With glass on all sides, held together by narrow strips of metal, it felt worse than no cover whatsoever. One swing of the club and the dome would explode toward him like a thousand daggers. He recoiled and raised his arms to shield his face from flying glass. Coulter sat calmly beside him, as if watching a movie.

Racing at full speed, the giant lifted the club high above

his head and brought it down with terrible force. Just before the club connected with the surface of the dome, it rebounded sharply, making an unnatural pinging sound, and sailed out of the giant's grasp. Burlox's forward momentum instantly reversed, and the giant pitched violently backwards.

Shaken and seething, the fog giant arose and staggered away from the dome. As a hulking silhouette in the mist, Burlox began brutalizing a tree. He tore down huge limbs, and was soon pounding his fists against the sturdy trunk. Groaning and growling, he seized the trunk in a terrible embrace, twisting and wrenching and wrestling until the bole began to split. With a final mighty heave accompanied by a tremendous crack, he toppled the entire tree and knelt panting, hands on his knees.

"Incredible strength," Coulter commented. "He should be cooling down by now."

Sure enough, after a few moments, the giant trudged over and retrieved his club. Then he came and stood towering over the dome. Much of the mud had fallen from his face. After the food and the exertion, his complexion was ruddier. "More," he demanded, pointing at his mouth.

"We agreed on a single buffalo," Coulter called to him.

Burlox grimaced, revealing weeds and bark and fur in his teeth. He stamped a massive foot. "More!" It came across as a roar rather than a word.

"You said you knew a place Warren had been exploring before he turned white," Coulter said. "We had a deal."

"More after," Burlox grunted threateningly.

"If we give you anything else, it will be out of kindness, not obligation. A deal is a deal. Was the buffalo not delicious?"

"Four hills," the giant spat, before pivoting and stalking away.

"The four hills," Coulter repeated softly, watching the enormous figure vanish into the mist. He clapped Seth on the back. "We just got what we came here for, my boy. A bona fide lead."

✤   ✤   ✤

Kendra reached into the sack and then sprinkled raisins into the glass cylinder. The orange mass at the bottom oozed toward the raisins like living pudding, covering them and slowly darkening to a deep red. "You have gross pets," Kendra said.

Vanessa lifted her gaze from the journal she was studying. "Wizard slime looks unappetizing, but no other substance can equal its ability to draw out the poison from infected tissue. All of my darlings have their uses."

Unusual animals occupied most of Vanessa's room. Cages, buckets, aquariums, and terrariums contained a stunning variety of inhabitants. Whether they looked like reptiles, mammals, arachnids, amphibians, insects, sponges, fungi, or something in between, all were magical. There was a colorful lizard with three eyes that was nearly impossible to pick up because it could see slightly into the future and avoid your every move. A hairless mouse that transformed into a fish if you dropped it in water. And a bat who shed her wings biweekly—if the discarded wings were quickly pressed against another creature, they would take hold and grow. Vanessa had used them to create a flying rabbit.

Aside from the dozens of life forms in their respective containers, stacks of books dominated the room. The majority were bulky reference books and leather-bound journals of previous Fablehaven caretakers. Bookmarks protruded from the journals, marking pages of interest Vanessa had discovered during her research.

"I'm not sure I could sleep surrounded by so many freaky animals," Kendra said.

Vanessa closed the journal she was reading, marking the page with a silk ribbon. "I've rendered the truly dangerous whirligigs harmless, like the drumants. None of the creatures I brought into Fablehaven could cause anyone serious harm."

"I got nipped last night," Kendra said, holding out her arm to show the bite marks in the crook of her elbow. "Slept right through it."

"I'm sorry," Vanessa said. "I have fifteen in the cage now."

"Which means four are running loose," Kendra said gruffly, imitating Coulter.

Vanessa smiled. "He means well."

"He's not winning any points by taking off with Seth and leaving me behind. If he gave me the choice, I would probably volunteer to skip some excursions. I mean, I could probably go my whole life without seeing a buffalo eaten alive and be just fine. But being told to stay behind feels different."

Vanessa stood up and crossed to a chest of drawers. "I suspect I would feel the same way." She opened a drawer and started rummaging. "It seems only fair that I should share a secret with you." She removed a candle and what looked like a long, translucent crayon.

"What are those?" Kendra asked.

"In rain forests around the world, you can find tiny sprites called umites that make honey and wax like bees. In fact, they dwell in almost hivelike communities. This marker and candle are both composed of umite wax." Vanessa wrote on the front of the drawer with the clear waxen marker. "See anything?"

"No."

"Watch." Vanessa struck a match and lit the candle. Once a flame burned on the wick, the entire candle glowed yellow, as did the marker, as did a vivid message on the front of the drawer:

Hi Kendra!

"Cool," Kendra said.

"Try to wipe it off," Vanessa said.

Kendra tried to wipe away the words to no avail. As soon as Vanessa blew out the candle, the message vanished. Vanessa handed the crayon and the candle to Kendra. "For me?" Kendra asked.

"I have spares. Now we can send each other secret messages, and none of the boys will know. I always carry one of those markers on me. They write surprisingly well on nearly any surface, the messages are difficult to erase, and only those with a properly enchanted umite candle can read them. I've used umite wax to mark myself a trail, to send a sensitive communiqué to a friend, and to remind myself of important secrets."

"Thanks, what a great gift!"

Vanessa winked. "We're pen pals."

% % %

Seth watched Coulter mount the steps to the back porch and enter the house. He knew his window of opportunity might be brief, so he hurried past the barn to a tree beside a path into the woods. It was the same path that led to the greenhouse where he and Kendra had harvested pumpkins the previous year. That morning, before anyone was awake, Seth had left a note at the base of that tree under a rock.

The year before, after Kendra had saved Fablehaven and while she slept for two days straight, Seth had held a private meeting with the satyrs, Newel and Doren. Most of the inhabitants of Fablehaven were not permitted in the yard uninvited, so the satyrs had stood at the edge of the yard and beckoned Seth over. They had agreed that when Seth returned to Fablehaven, he would bring size C batteries and leave a note under the rock. Newel and Doren would recover the note and leave instructions for a meeting, where they would exchange gold for the treasured batteries that would bring new life to their portable television.

Seth squatted at the base of the tree. Even though he had left the note in the morning and it was now late afternoon, it was almost too much to hope that the satyrs would have already responded. Who knew how often they would check? Knowing them, maybe never. Seth picked up the rock. On the back of his note the satyrs had scrawled a message:

> *If you get this today, follow this path, take your second left, first right, keep on until you hear us. You'll hear us. If you get this tomorrow, it will say something else!*

Excited, Seth stuffed the note in his pocket and set off down the path. He had eight size C batteries in the bottom of his emergency kit. After he sold those, and the satyrs were hooked, he figured he could sell the rest for even more. If everything panned out, he would be retired before reaching high school!

Walking briskly, Seth took about six minutes to reach the second left, and about four more to reach the next right. At least, he hoped it was the next right. It was a scant trail, less inviting than the fake one Coulter had shown him in the swamp. But the satyrs had said "first right," so they must have meant this little trail. He wasn't too far from the yard, so Seth felt confident it would be safe.

The farther he went, the thicker the woods and under-growth around the little trail became. He was beginning to consider doubling back and waiting for a second message from the satyrs when he heard shouting up ahead. It was definitely the goatmen. He jogged forward. The closer he got, the more clearly he could hear them.

"Are you out of your skull?" one voice griped. "That was right on the line!"

"I'm telling you, I saw daylight between the line and the ball, and it's my call," a strident voice answered.

"Is that fun for you? To win by cheating? Why even play?"

"You aren't going to guilt me out of my point, Newel!"

"We better arm wrestle for it."

"What would an arm wrestle prove? It's my call, and I say it was out."

Seth had drawn even with the argument. He could not see the satyrs, but he could hear that they were not far off the path. He started shoving through the undergrowth.

"Your call? Last time I checked, it takes two to play. I'm ahead; maybe I'll quit right now and declare myself champion."

"Then I'll declare myself champion too, because that would be an indisputable forfeit."

"I'll show you an indisputable forfeit!"

Seth pushed between some bushes and stepped onto a level, well-trimmed grass tennis court. The court had neatly chalked lines and a regulation-style net. Newel and Doren stood at the far side of the court, faces red, each clutching a tennis racket. They looked like they were about to come to blows. As Seth emerged onto the court, they turned to face him.

Both of the satyrs were shirtless, with hairy chests and freckled shoulders. From the waist down they had the furry legs and hooves of a goat. Newel had redder hair, more freckles, and slightly longer horns than Doren.

"Glad you found us," Newel said, trying to smile. "Sorry you happened by when Doren was being a knucklehead."

"Maybe Seth can solve this one," Doren said.

Newel closed his eyes in exasperation. "He wasn't here to see the point."

"If you both think you're right, do it over," Seth said.

Newel opened his eyes. "I could live with that."

"Me too," Doren agreed. "Seth, your new nickname is Solomon."

"You mind letting us finish this game?" Newel asked. "Just so we can keep momentum? No fun to start again cold."

"Go ahead," Seth said.

"You be line judge," Doren said.

"Sure."

The goatmen trotted into position. Newel was serving. "Forty-fifteen," he called, tossing a ball into the air and hitting it briskly into play. Doren hit a hard crosscourt forehand, but Newel was in position and hit it back with a gentle slice that took a soft bounce with a lot of spin. It looked unreachable, but Doren dove and managed to get his racket under the ball before the second bounce, popping it over the net. Newel had read the situation well and was already charging forward. As Doren scrambled up, Newel slammed the ball into the far corner of the court, bouncing it deep into the bushes.

"Go fetch it, nitwit!" Doren said. "You didn't have to wail it into the woods. You had an open lane."

"He's sore because I just went up five games to three," Newel explained, twirling his racket.

"I'm sore because you're trying to show off for Seth!" Doren said.

"You're saying you wouldn't have slammed it if I'd hit you a pathetic lob?"

"You were at the net! I would have just tapped it at a brutal angle. Better to win with finesse than to hunt for balls in the shrubbery."

"You're both really good," Seth said.

The two goatmen looked pleased by the compliment. "You know, satyrs invented tennis," Newel said, balancing his racket on the tip of his finger.

"They did not," Doren said. "We learned about it on TV."

"I like your rackets," Seth said.

"Graphite, light and strong," Newel said. "Warren got us our equipment. Back before he went all Boo Radley on us. The net, the rackets, a few cases of balls."

"We built the court," Doren said proudly.

"And we maintain it," Newel said.

"The brownies maintain it," Doren corrected.

"Under our supervision," Newel amended.

"Speaking of tennis balls," Doren said, "most of ours are flat, but with the supply dwindling, it always kills us to open a new can. If our battery arrangement works out, think you might be able to score us some new balls?"

"If this works out, I'll get you whatever you want," Seth promised.

"Then let's get down to business," Newel said, setting down his racket and rubbing his palms together. "You have the merchandise?"

Seth scrabbled through his emergency kit and pulled out eight batteries, lining them up on the ground.

"Would you look at that," Doren marveled. "Have you ever seen such a gorgeous sight?"

"It's a start," Newel said. "But let's face it, they'll run out before long. I assume there are more where those came from?"

"Lots more," Seth assured him. "This is just a test run. If I remember right, you said something about batteries being worth their weight in gold."

Newel and Doren shared a glance. "We think we may have figured out something you'd like more," Newel said.

"Follow us," Doren said.

Seth walked with the satyrs over to a little white shed not far from the net. Newel opened the door and ducked inside. He came out holding a bottle. "What do you say?" Newel asked. "A bottle of fine wine for those eight batteries."

"Potent stuff," Doren confided. "It'll put hair on your chest in no time. Good luck getting something like that from your grandparents."

Seth looked back and forth at the two satyrs. "Are you serious? I'm twelve years old! Do you think I'm an alcoholic or something?"

"We figured something like this might be tough for you to get," Newel said with a wink.

"Good wine," Doren said. "Primo."

"That might be true, but I'm just a kid. What am I going to do with a bottle of wine?"

Newel and Doren shared a nervous glance. "Well done, Seth," Newel said awkwardly, ruffling his hair. "You . . . passed our test. Your parents would be very proud."

Newel elbowed Doren. "Yeah, um, sometimes we test people," Doren said. "And play jokes."

Newel went back into the shed. He returned holding a blue frog with yellow markings. "Seriously, here is what we really had in mind, Seth."

"A frog?" Seth asked.

"Not just any frog," Doren said. "Show him."

Newel tickled the frog's belly. Its air sac swelled up to the size of a cantaloupe, and the frog let out a tremendous belching sound. Seth laughed in surprised delight. The satyrs laughed with him. Newel tickled the frog again and the thunderous belching sound repeated. Doren was wiping away mirthful tears.

"So what do you say?" Newel asked.

"Eight lousy batteries for one incredible frog," Doren said. "I'd take it."

Seth folded his arms. "The frog is pretty cool, but I'm not five years old. If it's between gold and a burping frog, I'll take the gold."

The satyrs frowned, clearly disappointed. Newel nodded

at Doren, who slipped into the shed and returned holding a bar of gold. He handed it to Seth.

Seth turned the bar over and over in his hands. It was about the size of a bar of hotel soap. An "N" was embossed on one side. Otherwise it was a plain, golden rectangle, a little heavier than it looked. Probably enough gold to be worth a lot of money.

"This is more like it," Seth said happily, placing the gold inside his emergency kit. "What does the 'N' stand for?"

Newel scratched his head. "Nothing."

"Right," Doren said hastily. "Stands for 'nothing.'"

"Nothing?" Seth said dubiously. "Why would somebody write an 'N' for 'nothing'? Why not just leave it blank?"

"Newel," Doren tried. "It stands for Newel."

"Used to be my favorite belt buckle," Newel added wistfully.

"You wore pants?" Seth asked.

"Long story," Newel explained. "Let's not dwell on the past. Fact is, there are more—um—belt buckles where that came from, all pure gold. You bring us more batteries, we'll keep trading with you."

"Works for me," Seth said.

"This could be the beginning of a spectacular partnership," Newel said.

Doren raised a cautionary hand, halting the conversation. "You hear that?"

The three of them paused, listening. "Something's coming," Newel said, eyebrows knitting together. No matter how the satyrs behaved, they usually had an air about them that everything they said was tongue-in-cheek. That air was gone.

They kept listening. Seth heard nothing. "Are you guys fooling with me?" he asked.

Newel shook his head, holding up a finger. "I can't place it. You?"

Doren was sniffing the air. "Can't be."

"You better scram, Seth," Newel said. "Get back to the yard."

"With the gold, right?" Seth suspected they might be trying to trick him out of his reward.

"Of course, but you better hur—"

"Too late," Doren warned.

A creature the size of a pony burst out of the bushes onto the tennis court. Seth recognized it immediately. "Olloch?"

"Olloch the Glutton?" Newel asked Seth.

"I thought it smelled like a demon," Doren groaned.

"Yeah," Seth said. "He bit me."

Grotesquely toadlike, Olloch reared back and opened his mouth. It looked like the demon had swallowed a squid, so many flailing tongues emerged. Sitting upright, Olloch was nearly as tall as Seth. After a triumphant roar, the demon lowered his head and charged, advancing in a jerky, scrambling crawl.

Newel grabbed Seth's hand and hauled him away from the demon. "Run!" Newel yelled.

"For television!" Doren cried, brandishing his tennis racket and holding his ground. Olloch pounced at the satyr, but Doren lunged aside, swatting away a pair of tongues with the racket. Several more tongues lashed out, wrenching the racket from Doren's grasp. The tongues pulled the racket into a gaping mouth, and moments later expelled it with the strings missing and a crack in the frame.

Seth had reached the bushes at the edge of the court when Olloch, ignoring Doren, took a huge leap toward him and then charged with frightening speed. Seth knew he wouldn't make it back to the path, let alone to the yard. His mind raced, trying to think if there was anything useful in his emergency kit.

Tongues writhing, the demon sprang. "For batteries!" Newel cried, intercepting the glutton in midair and wrapping both arms around its middle.

"To the shed!" Doren called, retrieving his unstrung racket and running toward the demon.

Seth turned and dashed toward the shed. Growling and slobbering, Olloch squirmed free from Newel and raced after Seth, staying low and gaining quickly. Over his shoulder, Seth glimpsed the demon drawing near, rapidly closing the space between them despite moving with such a choppy gait. The shed was still several steps away.

Jumping into the demon's path, Doren raised his damaged racket. A multitude of tongues snaked around the satyr and slung him aside. His efforts barely slowed Olloch, but bought Seth just enough time to lunge into the shed and slam the door. The demon crunched against the door an instant later. Some of the whitewashed planks split, but they held. The demon crashed against the shed again, rattling the small structure.

"Hang on, Seth," Doren yelled. "Help is coming."

Seth searched for a weapon. The best he could find was a hoe. The door shattered open and Olloch entered, snarling, wet tongues thrashing. Behind the slavering demon, Seth saw Hugo bounding across the tennis court. Grasping tongues stretched toward Seth, and he swung the hoe viciously. A tongue adroitly coiled around the hoe, ripping it from Seth's grasp. And then Hugo arrived.

The golem grasped the demon from behind with one hand and hurled it away from the shed. Olloch landed, rolled, and came charging back toward Seth, who now stood in the empty doorway alongside Hugo. The golem stepped forward, blocking access to Seth.

Dripping tongues whipped toward Hugo. The golem grabbed several tongues, yanked the demon into the air, and began spinning Olloch above his head. The tongues elongated as the golem whirled the glutton faster and faster, finally releasing him, sending Olloch sailing away over the treetops.

Doren whistled, clearly impressed.

"He'll be back straightaway," Newel said. He had grass stains on his chest and arms.

"You should hurry to the yard," Doren agreed.

"We better get some free batteries out of this," Newel said, brushing himself off.

"And a new racket," Doren added.

"We'll talk about it," Seth said, clutching his emergency kit with the gold inside. Hugo unceremoniously lifted Seth and started running, leaving him no opportunity to say or hear another word. Seth could not believe how fast the golem raced through the trees, massive strides eating up ground. Ignoring trails, Hugo bulldozed his own path through undergrowth and tangled limbs.

Before long, they were back in the yard. Grandma stood there, fists on her hips, along with Coulter, Vanessa, and Kendra. Hugo gently set Seth on his feet in front of Grandma.

"Are you all right?" Grandma asked, grabbing his shoulders and checking him for injuries.

"Thanks to Hugo."

"You're lucky Hugo was in the yard," Grandma said. "We heard something roaring in the woods and found you missing. What were you doing in the woods?"

"I was playing tennis with the satyrs," Seth said. "Olloch found me."

"Olloch!" she cried. The others looked shocked as well.

"How could he have gotten onto the preserve?" Coulter asked.

"Are you sure it was Olloch?" Grandma asked.

"I recognized him," Seth said. "He's a lot bigger. He has a bunch of tongues. He went right for me, didn't hardly care about the satyrs."

They heard something rustling in the woods and turned to face whatever was approaching. Olloch scrambled up to the edge of the yard before stopping. The demon reared up, tongues waving like meaty banners, and let out a mournful bellow. He lunged forward but could not step onto the grass.

"He can't enter the yard," Vanessa said.

"Not yet," Grandma agreed.

"Then how did he get onto the preserve?" Coulter repeated.

"I don't know, but we better get to the bottom of it quickly," Grandma said.

"Can Hugo kill it?" Kendra asked.

"Not likely," Grandma said. "In fact, I expect even at this size, if Olloch put his mind to it, he could devour Hugo piece by piece."

Olloch was shaking his head, wagging his tongues, and pawing the ground, obviously furious at having his prey so near yet utterly unreachable. "Now, there's an unusual sight," Coulter murmured.

"Incredible," Vanessa said.

"What do we do?" Seth asked.

"For starters," Grandma said crossly, "you are officially grounded."

CHAPTER ELEVEN

Betrayal

Kendra sat on the love seat beside Seth, resting her elbow on the arm of the couch and her chin on her hand. Ever since Hugo had rescued Seth earlier in the day, an uncomfortable new tension had filled the house. Grandpa had been poring over books and making phone calls. Vanessa and Coulter came and went several times, often accompanied by Hugo. There were many hushed conversations behind closed doors. Now it was getting late, but Grandma had informed everyone they had to meet about something that could not wait until morning. Which could not be a good sign.

Kendra's chief consolation was that she was not Seth. Wandering off into the woods without permission had almost gotten him killed. The thought of what had almost happened had terrified everyone, and he was getting an ear-ful as a result. Undoubtedly he would hear plenty more about it in the impending meeting.

Seated in a chair beside Seth, Tanu was showing him potions, explaining what they did and how he marked the bottles to distinguish them from each other. Only Tanu, who had returned not long ago from an all-day excursion, had refrained from reprimanding Seth. Instead, the Samoan seemed intent on distracting him from his misery.

"This one is for an emergency," Tanu was saying. "It's an enlarger, doubles my height, makes me big enough to wrestle an ogre. The ingredients for enlargers are extremely hard to come by. I've only got one dose, and once I use it, I don't expect to own another. Shrinking is easier. Each of these little vials carries a dose that makes me eight times shorter. I end up just under ten inches tall. Not so helpful in a brawl, but not bad for sneaking around."

Coulter and Vanessa sat on opposite ends of an antique sofa. Dale was perched on a stool he had brought in from another room. Grandma wheeled in Grandpa and took a seat in the last armchair.

Grandpa cleared his throat. Tanu fell silent, returning his potions to his pouch. "Getting to the point, we probably have a traitor among us, so I thought we should talk this through."

Nobody spoke. Kendra made brief eye contact with Vanessa, then with Coulter, then with Tanu. "Ruth and I are fairly certain how Olloch got onto the property," Grandpa continued. "Somebody signed him in on the register within the past two days. He probably waltzed right through the front gate. And he didn't come alone."

"What's the register?" Kendra asked.

"The register is a book that controls access to Fablehaven," Grandma said. "When you come to visit, we write your name in the register, and that action disarms on your behalf the spells guarding the gate. Unless they were signed in on the register, it would be effectively impossible for anyone to get past the fence."

"Somebody signed in Olloch?" Dale asked.

"Between now and two evenings ago, the last time we checked the register, someone signed in Christopher Vogel and Guest," Grandma said. "We blotted out the names, but the damage has been done. Christopher Vogel, whoever that is, came onto the property and turned Olloch loose."

"Therefore we must assume we have two enemies out there," Grandpa said, motioning toward the window. "And one in here."

"Could somebody from outside have gotten to the register?" Dale asked.

"The register was hidden in our room," Grandma said. "Only Stan and I knew where it was. Or so we thought. Now we've moved it. But coming into the house unnoticed after we shut it down for the night is almost as difficult as getting through the gates. Let alone writing in the register right under our noses."

"Whoever wrote in the register is more than likely the same person who released the drumants," Grandpa said. "Is it possible that somebody outside this room accessed our bedrooms twice? Yes. Probable? No."

"Can we trace the handwriting?" Coulter asked.

Grandma shook her head. "They used a stencil. Apparently they weren't in a rush."

"Perhaps all of us should leave," Tanu suggested. "The evidence is too glaring to ignore. Kendra and Seth are above suspicion, as are Ruth and Stan. Maybe the rest of us should depart."

"The thought crossed my mind," Grandpa said. "But now that we have two foes on the preserve, it is hardly a good time to send away our protectors, even if one is probably a traitor. At least until we can summon replacements. I am stuck in this chair, and the children are young and untrained. The situation is maddening. As I consider each of you individually, you seem above suspicion. Yet someone wrote in the register, and since you all appear equally innocent, you consequently appear equally guilty."

"I hope we find another explanation," Grandma said. "For the moment, we must acknowledge the likelihood that one of us is a master deceiver working for our adversaries."

"It gets worse," Grandpa said. "The phone lines are down again. We've been trying to summon aid via Vanessa's cell phone, but our chief contact has not been answering. We will keep calling, but none of this bodes well."

"The other immediate problem is Olloch himself," Grandma said. "As he gorges himself on whatever edible matter he can find, he will continue to gain both size and power. He quit trying to enter the yard hours ago, which means he realizes that if he gets big enough, he could gain sufficient power to overthrow the treaty, access the house, and claim his prize."

"Like how Bahumat almost overthrew the preserve last year," Kendra said.

"Yes," Grandpa said. "Olloch could conceivably muster sufficient power to plunge Fablehaven into lawless chaos."

Kendra glanced at Seth, sitting silently. She had rarely seen him so quiet and contrite. It looked like he wanted to melt away into the love seat and vanish.

"What can we do?" Tanu asked.

"Olloch the Glutton will not stop until he has devoured and digested Seth," Grandpa said. "Slaying Olloch is well beyond our power. We have an ally who suggested there might be a way to subdue the demon, but we have not been able to reach him. The glutton has already reached a size that will allow him to ingest just about whatever he chooses, and his appetite will not abate. We cannot sit idly by. Our peril is literally growing by the minute."

"We must assume our benefactor is on the move," Grandma said. "He is a heavily desired target of the Society. We'll keep trying to telephone him, and assume that he'll make himself available as soon as he can. Otherwise, we're just not sure how to find him. He moves too frequently."

"How long before Olloch becomes strong enough to countermand the treaty?" Vanessa asked.

Grandpa shrugged. "With the kind of game he can find inside Fablehaven, magical and nonmagical, it is a worst-case scenario. He'll grow much faster than he would out in the normal world. He must have had help getting to his current size, probably from that Christopher Vogel character. My best guess? A day, more likely two, maybe three. I can't imagine it would take much longer."

"Maybe you should just feed me to him," Seth said.

"Don't talk nonsense," Grandma said.

Seth stood up. "Wouldn't it be better than letting Olloch destroy all of Fablehaven? Sounds like he'll get me sooner or later. Why should I make him go through all of you first?"

"We'll find another way," Coulter said. "We still have some time."

"He'll have to eat me to get to you," Dale said. "Whether you like it or not."

Seth sat down. Grandpa pointed at him. "Now is not the time to leap to rash solutions. We have not yet spoken with our most knowledgeable ally. Seth, I repeat, you are not culpable for awakening Olloch. You were tricked and are not to blame. You should not have been out in the woods alone— that was a most foolish error in judgment, the exact kind of nonsense I hoped you would have abandoned by now—but you are far from deserving a death sentence. Since the satyrs were involved, I take it you were trading for batteries? I haven't asked, what did they give you?"

Seth lowered his eyes. "Some gold."

"May I see it?"

Seth went and retrieved his emergency kit. He pulled out the gold bar. Grandpa examined it. "You do not want to be caught out in the open with this in your pocket," he said.

"Why?" Seth asked.

Grandpa handed the bar back to Seth. "It was clearly stolen from Nero's hoard. What did you suppose the 'N' stood for? He will be scrying for it in his seeing stone. In fact, the presence of the gold could grant him the power to see within the walls of our home. The satyrs must have only recently stolen it, or Nero would have already reclaimed it."

Seth placed a hand over his eyes and shook his head. "When will I do something right?" he moaned. "Should I go chuck it into the woods?"

"No," Grandpa said. "You should go set it on the porch, and we'll return it to its rightful owner as soon as reasonably possible."

Nodding sheepishly, Seth exited the room. "We also have some encouraging news," Grandpa said. "Coulter made an important breakthrough today. We may be close to uncovering the relic we have been seeking. The latest revelation harmonizes with the information we already possess. At this juncture, I believe there is more wisdom in sharing this information openly than in hiding it. No matter which of us is the traitor, the rest of us must continue functioning. Better we make our knowledge common than become paralyzed."

"Not that the traitor will be sharing secrets with us," Vanessa said bitterly.

"All the same, Coulter will disclose his discovery," Grandpa said.

"The fog giant Burlox reported that Warren was

investigating the four hills area before he turned white," Coulter said.

"One of the main areas Patton mentioned suspiciously," Vanessa said.

"And the same area I investigated today," Tanu said. "The grove on the north end of the valley is definitely cursed. I did not risk treading there."

Seth came back into the room and reclaimed his spot on the love seat.

"Many areas of Fablehaven carry terrible curses and are protected by ghastly fiends," Grandpa said. "The valley of the four hills is one of the most infamous. At the moment, the evidence seems to suggest a pair of related mysteries. We may very well find not only that the grove contains the relic we have been seeking, but also that it is guarded by whatever entity transformed Warren."

"Of course, all that would need to be confirmed," Grandma said.

"Carefully," Grandpa admonished. "As with several of the most dread regions of Fablehaven, we have no idea what evil haunts the grove."

"What is our next move?" Vanessa asked.

"I say we need to focus on Olloch before we try to penetrate whatever secrets lie inside the grove," Grandpa said. "Exploring the grove safely will require all of our resources and focus. Even under ideal circumstances it is a hazardous assignment."

"So we wait to see if Ruth can reach your contact?" Coulter asked.

Grandpa was picking at the frayed edge of his cast. "Ruth will keep calling on Vanessa's cell phone. For now, the rest of us should try to get a good night's sleep. It may be our last chance for a while."

※ ※ ※

Kendra closed the bathroom door, locked it, and set the sheet of paper on the counter. She had found the blank paper beneath her pillow, but with Seth in the room, she dared not light the candle and give away her secret. Alone in the bathroom, Kendra struck a flimsy match and put the flame to the wick until it caught. Shaking out the match, she watched as glowing words came into view on the formerly empty page:

> Kendra,
>   Sorry we didn't get to talk much today. Can you believe all the commotion? We need to keep your brother on a leash!
>   Let me know if this message came through all right.
>   Your friend,
>   Vanessa

Kendra blew out the candle, and the luminous words vanished. Folding up the note, she climbed the stairs to the attic bedroom, pondering how she should reply to the secret message. Seth was setting up toy soldiers on the floor. One in front, with two behind him, then a row of three, and another of four. Kendra crossed the room and climbed into bed. Seth walked several paces away and bowled at the soldiers with a softball. He knocked down seven.

"Turn off the light and come to bed," Kendra said.

"I don't think I can sleep," Seth protested, retrieving the softball.

"I know I can't with you rolling balls around the room," Kendra said.

"Why don't you go sleep someplace else?"

"This is where they put us."

"At home we each have our own room. Here, with way more rooms, we sleep in the same one." He rolled the softball again, claiming two more soldiers.

"This isn't the sort of place I'd want to sleep alone," Kendra admitted.

"I can't believe they took my gold," Seth said, setting up the soldiers again, this time placing them closer together. "I bet it was worth thousands of dollars. It isn't my fault if Newel and Doren stole it from Nero."

"You can't just do whatever you want and always get away with it."

"I've been good! I've tried hard to be careful and keep secrets and follow all the rules."

"You went into the woods without permission," Kendra reminded him.

"Just a little ways. It would have been fine if somebody hadn't let that demon onto the preserve. Nobody saw that coming. If Olloch hadn't caught up with me today, he might have caught up with us tomorrow, when we were out with Vanessa, a lot farther from the house. I might have saved our lives." He rolled the ball again. Missing the front soldier, he still knocked down eight.

"Way to avoid taking any responsibility," Kendra said, leaning back onto her pillow. "I'm glad they grounded you. If it were up to me, I'd lock you in the dungeon."

"If it were up to me, I'd give your face plastic surgery," he said.

"Really mature."

"Do you think they'll figure out a way to stop the demon?" Seth asked.

"I'm sure they'll think of something. The Sphinx seems really smart. He'll have a plan."

"He said you beat him at Foosball," Seth said.

"He wasn't too good. He didn't even spin his cowboys."

Shaking his head, Seth bowled the ball again and picked up the spare. "I don't think Nero could follow me off the preserve. Maybe I should just take the gold and go. Then everyone will be out of danger."

"Stop pitying yourself."

"I'm serious."

"No you're not," Kendra said, exasperated. "If you take off, Olloch will hunt you down and eat you."

"Better than having everyone hate me."

"Nobody hates you. They just want you to be cautious, so you'll be safe. The only reason they get mad is because they care about you."

Seth arranged the soldiers in the tightest formation yet. "Think I can knock them all down with one roll?"

Kendra sat up. "Of course, you set them up like dominoes."

Seth took his position and rolled the ball, totally missing all of them. "Looks like you were wrong."

"You missed on purpose."

"I bet you couldn't knock all of them down."

"I could easily," Kendra said.

"Prove it."

She got out of bed, grabbed the ball, and went and stood by her brother. Taking careful aim, she bowled it hard, right down the center, and all the soldiers fell. "See?"

"Almost like I let you win."

"What's that supposed to mean?"

"Nothing," he said. "Who do you think is the traitor?"

"I don't know. It doesn't seem like any of them."

"My guess would be Tanu. He's too nice."

"And that makes him evil?" Kendra asked, getting back into bed.

"Whoever is guilty would be trying really hard to act nice."

"Or they would know that everyone would expect that, so they would try to throw us off by acting grumpy."

"You think it could be Coulter?" Seth turned out the light and jumped into bed.

"He's known Grandpa for too long. And Vanessa could have handed us over to Errol instead of rescuing us. They all seem innocent. I wouldn't be surprised if it turned out to be another explanation."

"I hope so," Seth said. "They're all really cool. But keep your eyes open."

"You do the same. And please stay out of the woods. You're my only brother, and I don't want you to get . . . hurt."

"Thanks, Kendra."

"Good night, Seth."

⚹ ⚹ ⚹

Seth awoke in the dead of night with a hand covering his mouth. He grabbed at the fingers but was unable to pry them from his lips. "Don't be alarmed," a voice whispered. "It's Coulter. We need to talk."

Seth turned his head. Taking his hand from Seth's mouth, Coulter held a finger to his lips, then curled it beckoningly. What was Coulter up to? It was an odd hour for a conversation.

Turning his head the other way, Seth saw Kendra asleep under her covers, breathing evenly. He eased out of bed and followed Coulter to the door and down the stairs to the hall. Coulter took a seat on the last couple of steps. Seth sat down beside him.

"What's going on?" Seth asked.

"How would you like to set things straight?" Coulter asked.

"Sure."

"I need your help," Coulter said.

"In the middle of the night?"

"It may be now or never."

"No offense," Seth said. "This seems kind of suspicious."

"I need you to trust me, Seth. I'm about to try something I can't do alone. I think you're the only person with the courage to help me right now. You have no idea what is really going on."

"You're going to tell me?"

Coulter looked around, as if he were nervous that somebody might be spying. "I have to. I need somebody like you on my side here. Seth, the artifact we are looking for is very important. In the wrong hands it could be extremely dangerous. It could even lead to the end of the world."

That seemed to agree with what Seth had heard from his grandparents. "Go on," he said.

Coulter sighed and rubbed his thighs, as if hesitant to continue. "I'm taking a big risk here because I believe I can trust you. Seth, I'm a special agent working for the Sphinx. He gave me specific instructions that at all costs, I had to recover the artifact, especially if the integrity of Fablehaven was ever compromised. Now that we're nearly certain where the artifact is hidden, I'm going to go prepare the way to get it, tonight, and I want you to come with me."

"Right now?"

"Immediately."

Seth wiped away an eyelash that was starting to poke his eye. "Why not get help from the others?"

"You heard your grandfather. He wants to wait and take care of Olloch first. That poses a problem because, in a day or two, Olloch could become too powerful, Fablehaven could fall, and the artifact could be placed in extreme jeopardy."

"How could I come with you?" Seth said. "The second I leave the yard, the demon will be after us."

"It's risky," Coulter conceded. "But Fablehaven is a big place, and the demon is off foraging. Hugo is waiting outside. He'll take us to the grove and keep Olloch off of us if the glutton makes an appearance."

"Grandma said the demon could eat Hugo," Seth said.

"Eventually. Until Olloch gets more powerful, it would take him a long time to best Hugo. I wouldn't chance this tomorrow. But Hugo handled the demon just fine not so many hours ago. And Hugo is faster than Olloch. If we have to, we'll just have Hugo escape with us back to the yard."

"Why me?" Seth asked. "I don't get it. Part of me thinks I should go tell Grandpa Sorenson right now."

"I can't blame that instinct. I know this is unusual. Just let me finish. You know that if you go to your grandpa, he will never let you come with me. And he is in no position to help me himself. I came to you because I've spent the evening trying to convince the others to go after the artifact now rather than later, but they are all too afraid to take definitive action. Yet my private mandate from the Sphinx remains—with the threat of Olloch looming, I need to secure the artifact right away."

"Why me?" Seth repeated.

"Who else can I trust besides your grandfather? Your grandmother is good at a lot of things, but she doesn't belong on this kind of mission. Neither does Kendra. I can't do it alone. I think I know what is haunting the grove, a phantom, and I need somebody brave to join me if I'm going to defeat it. You're my only hope. You're young, but honestly, Seth, as far as courage goes, in my book, you've got all the others beat."

"What if you're the traitor?" Seth asked.

"If I were the traitor, I'd already have somebody to help me bypass the phantom. Christopher Vogel and I would be off taking care of business. You and I wouldn't be having this conversation. Also, we can't actually get the artifact tonight. We need a key your grandfather has in order to access it. But if we can get rid of the phantom and confirm the location of the artifact, I'm confident that I'll be able to convince the others to join us in retrieving it tomorrow."

Coulter's mention of the key also corresponded with what Seth had heard from his grandparents. Without the key, Coulter couldn't access the vault. If he couldn't access the vault, his goal couldn't be to steal the artifact. And if Coulter harmed Seth, it would blow his cover and prevent him from ever getting Grandpa to hand over the key. Still, even if Coulter was telling the truth, the adventure would certainly be dangerous. Seth knew that his life would depend on whether Coulter really could handle the phantom in the grove. It had been too much for Warren. He wished he could get advice from somebody else, but Coulter was right—if Seth told anyone, from Grandpa to Kendra to Tanu, they would try to stop them.

"I don't know what to do," Seth said.

"Once we have the artifact, we can all escape and lock

down Fablehaven, trapping Olloch inside until your grand-parents and their not-so-secret friend figure out what to do with him. Everybody wins, and we keep the artifact out of evil hands. I've thought it through, and this is our last chance to set everything right. If we stall, it is going to end badly. By tomorrow night, Olloch will be too strong. I can only do this with your help, Seth. Warren failed because he attempted it alone. If you refuse, we may as well both go back to bed."

"It seems like every decision I make is wrong lately," Seth said. "People keep tricking me. Or I just do stupid things on my own."

"Not everybody is out to fool you," Coulter said. "And bravery is not always a liability. Often it is quite the oppo-site. I happen to know your grandfather has great admiration for your adventurous spirit. This could be your chance to redeem yourself."

"Or to prove that I'm the most gullible person in the world," Seth sighed. "Hopefully this will end the streak. Do I need to bring anything?"

Coulter beamed. "I knew I could count on you." He pat-ted Seth on the shoulder. "I have everything we need."

"Can I grab my emergency kit?"

"Good idea. Quiet, though. We mustn't disturb the others."

Seth slunk back up the stairs and into the attic bedroom. Kendra had shifted position but was still sound asleep. Crouching, Seth pulled the emergency kit out from under his bed.

He felt uncommonly nervous. Was he making a mistake? Or was he just anxious at the prospect of facing a terrible phantom in a cursed grove with a short old man in the middle of the night? Coulter seemed to be the most cautious of all the adventurers. He had known exactly what to do when they met the fog giant, and he seemed confident that together they could handle the phantom. Seth stared at his emergency kit. If he just followed instructions, he would be fine, right?

Coulter did seem a little desperate to comply with the assignment from the Sphinx. He was probably putting them in a situation more dangerous than he would normally prefer because the stakes were so high. But he was right. The stakes really were high. Fablehaven was once again heading toward destruction. And Seth knew it was mainly his own fault. Last time, Kendra had saved the day. Now it was his turn.

Seth crept down the stairs.

"Ready?" Coulter asked.

"I guess."

"Let's get you some milk."

CHAPTER TWELVE

Peril in the Night

Deadfalls snapped and popped like firecrackers as Hugo pounded through the dark woods. No starlight penetrated the balmy darkness beneath the trees. Hugo maintained an unflagging pace, clutching Coulter under one arm and Seth under the other, like a running back with two footballs.

They emerged from the woods briefly and thumped through a covered bridge spanning a deep ravine. Seth recognized it as the same bridge he had seen when Grandma took him and Kendra to barter with Nero. Not far beyond the bridge, Hugo left the path again, resuming their noisy, loping dash through oblivion. Only the occasional clearing allowed the faint glow of the stars to interrupt the blackness.

Seth remained tense, anticipating the appearance of

Olloch. At any minute, he expected a supersized glutton to attack Hugo, splitting the night with a ferocious roar. Instead, Hugo continued tirelessly forward, fluidly dodging obstacles.

When Hugo reached the top of a steep slope, he charged down without hesitation. Seth felt like they were on the verge of tipping over with every step, but the golem never stumbled. When they reached a dead tree leaning against a cliff, without using his hands, Hugo raced up the rotten trunk like a ramp. Seth's stomach lurched as the ground grew distant, and he felt certain they would fall, but although the tree creaked beneath them, the golem did not falter.

At length they reached a large, open valley with a rounded hill at each corner. After the complete darkness of the forest, the starlight proved sufficient to reveal the surrounding terrain. Tall brush covered the ground, mingled with prickly weeds. A dark stand of trees loomed at the far end of the valley, between the two largest hills.

Hugo bounded across the valley, coming to an abrupt stop near the edge of the shadowy grove. "Forward a few more steps, Hugo," Coulter said.

The golem leaned forward, trembling. He rocked back, and the shaking stopped. Slowly Hugo lifted a leg. As he tried to move it forward, he began to shudder.

"Enough, Hugo," Coulter said. "Set us down."

"What's the deal with Hugo?" Seth asked.

"Just as most magical creatures cannot enter the yard back at the house, Hugo cannot enter this grove. There is an unseen boundary here. The ground is cursed. Fortunately, as mortals, we can go wherever we choose."

Seth raised his eyebrows. "We have to go up against the phantom without Hugo?" he said.

"I expected this," Coulter said. "Though I would rather have been mistaken."

"Are we sure we want to go someplace Hugo can't?"

"This has nothing to do with what we want. This is a matter of duty. I don't want to go in there, but I must."

Seth stared at the dark trees. The night seemed suddenly cooler. He folded his arms. "How do you know a phantom is in there?"

"I did some private reconnaissance. I ventured far enough into the grove to read the signs. It's clearly the abode of a phantom."

"How do we stop a phantom?"

Coulter pulled a short, crooked stick from his belt. "You hold this holly wand high. No matter what happens, keep it above your head—change hands if you must. I'll take care of the rest."

"That's all?"

"The holly will protect us while I bind the phantom. No small task, but I've done it once before. The phantom may try to frighten or intimidate you, but if you keep the wand high, we'll both be fine. Now more than ever, whatever you see and hear, you must remain stouthearted."

"I can do that," Seth said firmly. "What if Olloch shows up?"

"Golems make fabulous guardians," Coulter said. "Hugo, keep Olloch the Glutton out of the grove."

"Should I wear my medallion?"

"The one to repel the undead? By all means, put it on."

Seth fished the medallion out of his emergency kit and slipped it around his neck. Coulter turned on a heavy flashlight. The initial glare made Seth squint and blink. The bright beam pierced the darkness of the grove, lighting the space between the trees, allowing Coulter and Seth to see much deeper into the ominous woods. Instead of vague, shadowy trunks, the harsh light revealed the color and texture of the bark. There was almost no undergrowth, just rank upon rank of gray pillars supporting a leafy canopy.

"Find your courage, and hang on tight," Coulter said.

"I'm ready," Seth said, holding the holly wand aloft.

"Hugo, if we fall, return to the house," Coulter said.

"If we fall?"

"Just a precaution. We'll be fine."

"You're not helping my courage a whole bunch," Seth complained. He started impersonating Coulter. "Seth, we'll be just fine. Nothing to worry about. Hugo, when we die, please have us buried in a beautiful cemetery by a stream. I'm sorry, Seth, I meant *if* we die. Be brave. When the phantom kills you, don't scream, even though it's going to hurt a lot."

Coulter was smirking. "Are you finished?"

"Sounds like we're both finished."

"Everyone copes with nerves differently. Humor is among the better ways. Follow me."

Coulter stepped forward, beyond the plane Hugo could not cross, and Seth followed closely. The trees cast long shadows. The flashlight beam swayed back and forth, making the shadows swing and stretch, creating the illusion that the trees were in motion. As they passed the first few trees, Seth glanced back at Hugo, waiting in the shadows. His night vision had already been ruined by the flashlight, so he could barely make out the form of the golem in the darkness.

"Can you feel the difference?" Coulter whispered.

"I'm scared, if that's what you mean," Seth said softly.

Coulter stopped walking. "More than that. Even if you didn't know to be scared, you would be. There's an unshakable sense of foreboding in the atmosphere."

Seth had goose bumps on his arms. "You're sort of freaking me out again," he said.

"I just want you to be aware of it," Coulter whispered. "It may get worse. Keep that holly wand up high."

Seth was not sure whether it was simply the power of suggestion, but as they resumed walking, with each step the air seemed to grow colder, and the feeling inside seemed to become darker. Seth grimly studied the trees, bracing himself for the terrifying form of a phantom to appear.

Coulter slowed and then stopped. The hair rose on the back of Seth's neck. Coulter turned slowly, eyes wide and shimmering. "Uh-oh," he mouthed.

The fear hit Seth like a physical blow, making his knees buckle. He dropped his emergency kit as he collapsed to the ground, keeping the hand with the holly wand high. Seth was instantly reminded of when he had sampled Tanu's fear potion. The terror was an irrational, overpowering force that instantly stripped away all defenses. He struggled to rise and to keep his hand up.

He had made it to his knees and was trying to lift a leg when a second wave of fear washed over him, more powerful than the first, much more potent than the potion Tanu had given him. The medallion around his neck dissolved, evaporating into the chilly air. Vaguely, distantly, Seth was aware that the flashlight was on the ground, and that Coulter was on his hands and knees, quivering. The fear intensified steadily, relentlessly.

Seth crumpled. He was on his back. The wand remained above his head, clenched in a frozen fist. His whole body was paralyzed. He tried to call out to Coulter. His lip twitched. No sound came out. He could barely think.

This surpassed the fear of death. Death would be a mercy if it would make the feeling stop, the uncontrollable panic mingling with the mind-scrambling certainty of something sinister approaching, something with no need to hurry, something that would not be so kind as to let him die. The fear was palpable, suffocating, irresistible.

Seth had always pictured his life ending much more heroically.

* * *

Kendra snapped awake. The room was dark and silent. She did not often awaken in the middle of the night, but she felt strangely alert. She turned to glance over at Seth. His bed was vacant.

She bolted upright. "Seth?" she whispered, scanning the room. There was no sign of her brother.

Where could he be? Had the traitor kidnapped him? Had he gone to sacrifice himself to Olloch? Had he taken his gold and left Fablehaven? Maybe he was just using the bathroom. She leaned down and glanced under his bed, where he kept his emergency kit. She could not see it.

Kendra rolled out of bed. She checked more thoroughly, looking under both beds. No emergency kit. Not a good sign. What could he possibly be thinking?

Kendra clicked on the light and hurried to the stairs, descending them quickly. Vanessa's room was nearest. Kendra rapped gently and opened the door. Vanessa was curled up under her covers. Kendra tried not to think about the unusual creatures inhabiting the containers stacked around the room. She switched on a light and crossed to the bed.

Vanessa rested on her side, facing Kendra. She was perfectly still, except her eyelids were fluttering wildly. Kendra knew from school that R.E.M. sleep was a sign of dreaming. The sight was eerie, her face placid, her closed eyes twitching spasmodically.

Kendra put a hand on Vanessa's shoulder and shook her. "Vanessa, wake up, I'm worried about Seth." The eyelids kept fluttering. Vanessa showed no sign of feeling or hearing Kendra. Shaking Vanessa a second time again elicited no reaction. Kendra lifted an eyelid. The eye was rolled back, white and bloodshot. Kendra jumped back. The sight creeped her out.

There was a half-full cup of water on the nightstand. Kendra hesitated only for a moment. It was an emergency. She poured it onto Vanessa's face.

Gasping and sputtering, Vanessa sat up, hand clutching her chest, eyes wide, looking not only startled but almost paranoid. She glanced around, eyes darting, clearly disoriented. Her gaze settled on Kendra. "What are you doing?" She sounded angry and bewildered. Water dripped from her chin.

"Seth's missing!" Kendra said.

Vanessa inhaled sharply. "Missing?" The anger was gone from her voice, replaced by concern.

"I woke up and he was gone," Kendra said. "So was his emergency kit."

Vanessa swung her legs out of bed. "Oh, no, I hope he hasn't done something rash. Sorry if I sounded harsh; I was having an awful nightmare."

"It's okay. Sorry to splash you."

"I'm glad you did." Vanessa tied on a robe and led the way into the hall. "You fetch Coulter; I'll get Tanu."

Kendra ran down the hall to Coulter's door. She entered after a quick knock. His bed was empty. Made up. There was no sign of him.

Kendra returned to the hall, where Vanessa was leading a bleary-eyed Tanu. "Where's Coulter?" Vanessa asked.

"He's gone too," Kendra reported.

On his back in the dark, Seth tried to get accustomed to the fear. If he could get used to it, maybe he could resist it. The feeling most reminded him of the sensation you experience when somebody startles you and makes you jump—a burst of instinctive, irrational terror and panic. Except this feeling was sustained. Instead of coming in a jolt and quickly subsiding into rational relief, the startled feeling not only lingered but intensified. Seth found it tough to think, let alone move, and so he lay frozen, overwhelmed, inwardly struggling, sensing something drawing inexorably closer. His only similar experience had been when Tanu had given him the fear potion, although by comparison that now seemed harmless and diluted. This was the real thing. Fear that could kill.

"Seth," a strained voice said urgently, "how did we get here?"

Unable to turn his head, Seth shifted his eyes. Coulter lay beside him, leaning up on one elbow. Having something to focus on besides the fear helped, and the fact that Coulter was still able to speak gave him hope. But what kind of pointless question was that? Coulter knew how he had gotten there. It was his idea. Seth tried to ask what he meant but managed only a groan.

"No matter," Coulter grunted. He reached a hand toward Seth, moving like a man on a planet where the gravity was much greater than on Earth. "Take it."

Seth could not see what Coulter held. He tried to move his arm but failed. He tried to sit up and failed again.

"Look," Coulter said. The flashlight was on the ground

near his feet. He kicked it softly, changing the angle of the beam. Then Coulter fell flat.

With the light turned and Coulter lower to the ground, Seth could now see what was drawing nearer through the trees: an emaciated, raggedly dressed man with a large thorn protruding from the side of his neck. His skin looked sickly, leprous, with open sores and blotchy discolorations. Because the flashlight was on the ground, the bottom half of the figure was better illuminated than the top. He had knobby ankles. Dried mud rimmed the cuffs of his tattered trousers. Seth studied his shadowy face. He had a pronounced Adam's apple, and wore the unnatural smile of a shy man posing for a photograph. The eyes were empty but uncannily aware. His expression did not change. He was still about forty feet away, treading slowly, as if in a trance.

Panting, sweating, Coulter propped himself back up on one elbow. "Revenant," he growled through clenched teeth. "Talismanic . . . uses fear . . . remove the nail." He scooted closer to Seth. "Open . . . mouth."

Seth focused all his attention on his jaw. He could not stop grinding his teeth. Opening his mouth was not a current option. "Can't," he tried to say. No sound came out.

Coulter pressed something into his hand. It felt like a handkerchief. "Warn," Coulter coughed, barely getting the word out. He tried to say more, but it sounded like he was strangling.

Coulter lurched at Seth. Both his hands were on Seth's face. One brusquely jerked his jaw down. The other thrust something past his lips. When Coulter released him, Seth automatically bit down hard on whatever Coulter had inserted, his jaw clenching involuntarily, flattening the object between his molars.

Suddenly Seth experienced the sensation that his tongue was rapidly inflating. It was like it had suddenly turned into an emergency airbag, exploding out of his mouth. Then his inflated tongue seemed to turn inside out, doubling back and enfolding him. The stark scene before him instantly vanished. He was shrouded in complete darkness. For the first time since he had begun to feel it, the overwhelming fear was significantly reduced.

He could move again. He was inside spongy darkness, totally encased by something. Seth touched his tongue. It was intact. Normal. His tongue had not actually ballooned; it must have been whatever Coulter had crammed in his mouth. The cocoon! That was the only explanation! Somehow Coulter had found the strength to shove his failsafe into Seth's mouth. Seth pressed against the confining walls of his snug enclosure. They felt soft at first, but when he pressed hard, they did not budge. According to what Coulter had said, nothing could get to him now. He could survive for months.

Coulter! The older man had sacrificed himself! Though it was now muted, Seth could still feel the fear increasing. Somewhere beyond the pillowy darkness enfolding him, the creature was nearing Coulter. Even he would be petrified by now, no matter how resistant he was to the smothering fear. It had seemed like he'd used his last strength to give away the cocoon.

Seth examined the object Coulter had placed in his hand. It was not a handkerchief; it was a glove with no fingertips, presumably the glove that turned Coulter invisible. It would not come in very handy inside the cocoon, but if he ever got out, it would certainly prove useful.

Seth squeezed the glove. There could be only one reason Coulter had passed it to him. The older man did not expect to survive.

Coulter started screaming. Although the sounds were muffled by the cocoon, Seth had never heard such unrestrained expressions of pure terror. Seth resisted the impulse to start tearing the cocoon apart. He wanted to help, but what could he do? Coulter did not scream long.

※ ※ ※

Grandpa sat on the edge of his cot, surrounded by Vanessa, Dale, Tanu, Grandma, and Kendra. His hair was sticking up in a way Kendra had never seen. But his hard eyes were not sleepy.

"The traitor is unmasked," Grandpa said, as if to himself.

"Not Coulter," Grandma said in disbelief.

"They're gone," Tanu said. "He took his gear; Seth took his kit. Glancing at the tracks, it looked like Hugo carried them."

"Can you follow them?" Grandpa asked.

"Easily," Tanu said. "But they have a good start on us, and Hugo is not slow."

"What do you suppose he's up to?" Vanessa asked.

Grandpa glanced worriedly at Kendra. "We'll discuss that later."

"No," Kendra said. "Go ahead. We have to hurry."

"Coulter is missing an essential object for uncovering the lost relic," Grandpa said. "Right?"

Grandma nodded. "We still have it."

"I can only imagine that he has some reason for offering Seth to Olloch," Grandpa said. "It does not strike me as very strategic, which is unlike Coulter. He may know something we don't."

"Time is wasting," Dale said.

"Right," Grandpa agreed. "Dale, Vanessa, Tanu, find where Coulter took Seth. Recover Seth and Hugo."

The three of them ran out of the room. Kendra heard them thumping around the house collecting gear. She stood still, stunned. Was this really happening? Was her brother really gone, kidnapped by a traitor? Was Coulter really going to feed him to Olloch? Or did Coulter have something unforeseeable in mind?

Seth might already be dead. Her mind recoiled at the thought. No, he had to be alive. Tanu and Vanessa and Dale would rescue him. As long as she had room to hope, she should not lose faith. "Is there anything I can do?" Kendra asked.

Grandma rubbed her shoulders from behind. "Try not to worry. Vanessa, Tanu, and Dale will find them."

"Do you think you could go back to bed?" Grandpa asked.

"Not likely," Kendra said. "I've never felt more awake. And I've never wished more that I was dreaming."

※　※　※

Merciless silence followed the end of Coulter's cries. Seth could not tell if it was an aftereffect of the screaming, but the fear seemed to be intensifying again, welling up inside of him. Something jostled Seth's cocoon. Again. And again.

Seth pictured the gaunt man with the lank hair and the unphotogenic smile rocking the cocoon. "He can't get in, he can't get in, he can't get in," Seth repeated softly to himself.

The fear was leveling off. It was uncomfortable, but bearable after what he had sampled outside of the cocoon. What would he do now? He was trapped. Sure, the zombie man could not get in, but Seth could not get out either. The instant he ripped open the cocoon he would become vulnerable. So it was a standoff. He would have to wait to be rescued.

A roar interrupted his thinking. It sounded distant, though it was difficult to be sure how much of that was the cocoon. Seth waited, listening. The next roar was definitely nearer. He knew the sound. It was deeper and fuller in a way that implied bigger, but it was certainly Olloch.

Seth heard another fierce roar. And another. What was going on? A showdown with Hugo? What would happen if Olloch got into the grove? If Olloch had the potential to become as powerful as Bahumat, strong enough to overthrow the foundational treaty of Fablehaven, wasn't it possible that the demon could become stronger than the cocoon?

All Seth could do was wait in the close, soft confines of his enclosure, ignoring whenever it was shaken by the zombie. Actually, Coulter had called the creature a revenant, whatever that meant. Apparently he had been mistaken about the grove being home to a phantom. Coulter had said to remove the nail, which had to be the thornlike thing in the side of the revenant's neck. Easier said than done. Hard to pull out a nail when a fear you can't control has you frozen solid.

An earsplitting roar caught Seth unprepared. He flinched, covering his ears. It sounded like Olloch was right outside the cocoon. And then Seth was harshly flung about. It felt like the cocoon had been catapulted into a web of bungee cords. He was grateful the snug interior was padded.

After Seth had been whipped about until he was unsure which direction was up, the cocoon settled to a stop. A moment later, he felt the cocoon start moving linearly. Then it stopped. Then it started again. The motion was a lot smoother now. It felt like the cocoon was in the back of a pickup truck that kept accelerating, decelerating, and turning. And occasionally hopping.

It did not take long for Seth to deduce what it meant. Olloch had swallowed him, cocoon and all.

CHAPTER THIRTEEN

The Thief's Net

K endra slowly stirred her oatmeal. She lifted a glob on her spoon, turned the utensil over, and watched the wet clump plop back into the bowl. Her toast was growing cold. Her orange juice was growing warm. She just wasn't hungry.

Outside the sun was rising, casting a golden glow over the garden. Fairies flitted about, coaxing blossoms into brighter bloom. The mellow, peaceful morning seemed indifferent to the fact that her brother had been kidnapped.

"You should eat something," Grandma said.

Kendra put a bite of oatmeal in her mouth. In other circumstances it would have tasted good, dusted with cinnamon and sweetened with sugar. But not today. Today it was like chewing Styrofoam. "I'm not in the mood."

Grandpa sucked butter from his thumb, having finished

another piece of toast. "Eat, even if it feels like a chore. You need your energy."

Kendra took another bite. "You couldn't get the Sphinx last night?" she asked Grandma.

"Nor this morning. It just rang and rang. Which is unfortunate but not uncommon. He answers when he can. I'll try again after breakfast."

Grandpa sat up straight and craned his neck, looking out the window. "Here they come," he said.

Kendra sprang to her feet and ran to the back porch. Tanu, Vanessa, Dale, and Hugo had emerged from the woods and were approaching through the garden. Hugo cradled Coulter in one arm. The golem's other arm was missing. Kendra saw no sign of Seth.

Distressed, Kendra turned to Grandma, who was wheeling Grandpa out to the porch. "I don't see Seth," she said.

Grandma put an arm around her. "Don't jump to conclusions."

As Hugo and the others drew nearer, Kendra realized that Coulter looked different. His expression was blank, and his skin was bleached. His hair, which had been gray, was now white as snow. He had apparently suffered the same fate as Warren.

"What news?" Grandpa asked as the others gathered on the grass beneath the porch.

"Nothing good," Tanu said.

"What about Seth?" Grandpa pressed.

Tanu looked down. The action said it all. "Oh, no," Grandma whispered. Kendra burst into sobs. She tried to stifle them by biting her sleeve. Squeezing her eyes shut did not stop the tears.

"Maybe we should wait," Vanessa said.

"I want to hear," Kendra managed. "Is he dead?"

"All signs suggest he has been consumed by Olloch," Tanu said.

Kendra hunched against the porch railing, shoulders shaking. She tried not to believe what she was hearing, but there was no other choice.

"Tell us everything," Grandma said, voice quavering.

"Hugo was simple to track, though he traversed some rugged terrain," Tanu said. "We met him heading back toward the house, returning along the same route he had used to reach the grove."

"So Coulter did go to the grove," Grandpa said angrily.

"Yes. For the life of me, Hugo looked dejected when we found him. He was missing an arm, had his head hung low, and was trudging slowly. Once we found him, we ordered him to take us to where he had left Coulter."

"And Hugo went directly to the grove in the valley of the four hills," Grandma said.

"Followed his own tracks," Tanu said. "When we got to the grove I studied what evidence I could find. I saw where Coulter and Seth entered the grove together. It did not appear Hugo was able to join them. Working my way around the perimeter of the grove, I found where Coulter's tracks departed. On the far side of the grove, I discovered where Hugo had scuffled with Olloch. I'm sure that is where Hugo lost his arm. Nearby I saw where Olloch entered the grove.

Not far from there, I found where Olloch left the grove. We searched and searched, but located no sign of Seth leaving the grove."

"How could Olloch enter the grove if Hugo couldn't?" Kendra asked.

"Different barriers work in different ways," Tanu said. "My guess is that the grove is less repellent to creatures of darkness. A demon like Olloch would be immune to many black curses."

"Did you go into the grove?" Grandma asked.

"There is a malevolent evil there," Vanessa said.

"We felt unprepared for what we might face below those cursed trees," Tanu said. "We had to physically restrain Dale. In the end, we followed Coulter's departing tracks and found him roaming in the woods as you now see him."

Kendra could hardly listen to the news. She clutched the railing and fought the overpowering grief throbbing inside of her. Each time fresh sobs shook her, she tried to weep quietly. After all that had happened last summer, how close they had all come to losing their lives, it seemed unfair that death should now take Seth so suddenly and unexpectedly. It was unimaginable that she would never see her brother again.

"Could he be alive, swallowed whole?" Kendra asked in a small voice.

Nobody would look at her. "If the demon devoured him, he is no more," Grandpa said gently. "We'll give it a day. If Olloch consumed Seth, he should slow down and return to his dormant state until somebody else makes the mistake of feeding him. I don't mean to give you false hope, but we won't know for certain that Olloch has ingested Seth until we locate the demon in his dormant state."

"Should we look sooner?" Kendra asked, wiping her eyes. "What if Seth's still out there, running?"

"He isn't running," Tanu said. "Believe me, I looked. At best he may have found a place to hide inside the grove."

"Which is unlikely if the demon came and went," Grandma said sadly.

"Can we get anything out of Coulter?" Kendra asked.

"He seems no more responsive than Warren," Dale said. "Want to see if he reacts to you, Kendra?"

Kendra pressed her lips together. The thought of going near Coulter was revolting. He had killed her brother. And now, like Warren, his mind had flown. But if there was a chance he might reveal something useful, she had to try.

Kendra climbed over the porch railing and dropped to the grass. "Hugo, set Coulter down," Dale ordered.

Hugo complied. Coulter stood still, looking even smaller and more frail now that he was albino and expressionless. Kendra placed a hand on his white neck. Coulter cocked his head and looked her in the eye. His lips trembled.

"We never got Warren to say anything," Kendra said.

"Try asking him," Vanessa said.

Kendra placed a hand on either side of Coulter's face and stared into his eyes. "Coulter, what happened to Seth. Where is he?"

Coulter blinked twice. The corner of his mouth

twitched toward a smile. Kendra pushed him away. "He looks happy about it," she said.

"I'm not sure you were getting through," Dale said. "I think he just liked your touch."

Kendra gazed up at the golem. "Poor Hugo. Can we fix his arm?"

"Golems are resilient," Grandpa said. "They frequently shed and accumulate matter. Over time the arm will reform. Kendra, perhaps you should come in and lie down."

"I don't think I can sleep," Kendra moaned.

"I could give her a mild sedative," Vanessa offered.

"That may not be a bad idea," Grandma said.

Kendra considered it. The idea of falling asleep and temporarily leaving all the heartache behind was appealing. She was not sleepy, but she was weary. "Okay."

Placing a supportive hand on Kendra's elbow, Vanessa guided her up to the porch and back into the house. In the kitchen, Vanessa put some water on the stove. She left and returned with a tea bag.

Kendra sat at the table, absently handling a salt shaker. "Seth really is dead, isn't he?"

"It doesn't look good," Vanessa admitted.

"I didn't picture this happening. It was all starting to feel like a wonderful game."

"It can be wonderful, but it is definitely not a game. Magical creatures can be deadly. I have lost several loved ones to them."

"He was always asking for it," Kendra said. "Always looking for risks."

"This wasn't Seth's fault. Who knows what kind of pressure Coulter might have applied to lure him away?" Vanessa poured warm water into a mug, inserted the tea bag, and stirred in some sugar. "I'm guessing you would prefer your tea drinkable versus scalding." She pulled out the tea bag and set it on the counter. "This should be plenty potent."

Kendra sipped at the herbal tea. It was minty and sweet. Unlike the rest of breakfast, it tasted like something she could finish. "Thanks, this is good."

"Let's start walking to your room," Vanessa said. "In a moment, you'll be glad to be near a bed."

Kendra continued sipping from the mug as they climbed the stairs and passed down the hall. The drowsiness hit her on the way up the steps to the attic. "You weren't kidding," Kendra said, leaning against the wall to steady herself. "I feel like I could just curl up right here and fall asleep."

"You could," Vanessa said. "But why not go a few more steps and sleep on your bed." Vanessa took the mug from Kendra. It was not yet half empty.

The rest of the way to her bed, Kendra felt like she was moving in slow motion. After the painful news about her brother, the numb, detached sensation was welcome. She climbed into bed and instantly faded into a deep sleep, unable to process the final words Vanessa spoke to her.

※　※　※

Waking up from her drugged slumber was a delicious, gradual process for Kendra, like lazily floating upward out of deep water. The surface was not far off, and when she reached it, she knew she would feel perfectly rested. No desire to slap a snooze button, no grogginess from sleeping too long. She had never noticed herself awakening so smoothly.

When she was finally fully awake, Kendra hesitated to open her eyes, hoping the contentment would linger. Wasn't there a reason she shouldn't feel so perfect? Her eyes shot open, and she looked over at Seth's empty bed.

He was gone! Dead! Kendra closed her eyes again, trying to pretend it had all been a miserable dream. Why hadn't she awoken when Coulter came and took him? How had Coulter gotten him out of the house so stealthily?

She opened her eyes. Judging from the light, it was late afternoon. She had slept the day away.

Kendra went downstairs and found Grandma in the kitchen, chopping cucumbers. "Hello, dear," she said.

"Any news while I was out?"

"I've tried to contact the Sphinx twice. Still no answer. I hope he's all right." Grandma stopped cutting and wiped her hands on a towel. "Your grandfather wanted to talk to us in the study once you awakened."

Kendra followed Grandma to the study, where Grandpa sat reading a journal. He closed the book as they entered. "Kendra, come in, we need to talk."

Kendra and Grandma sat down on the cot near Grandpa. "I've been thinking," Grandpa said, "and the way everything played out last night doesn't add up. I know Coulter well. He is a cunning man. The more I ponder the situation, the less strategic sense I see to his actions, especially with him ending up an albino like Warren. His behavior was so clumsy that I suspect he was not acting under his own volition."

"You think somebody was controlling him?" Kendra asked.

"Such things are possible in numerous ways," Grandpa said. "I may be wrong, and I have no concrete proof, but I suspect we may have yet to discover our traitor. And so I have set a plan in motion. It may cause some commotion tonight, so I thought it was only fair to warn you. Look under my cot."

Under the cot Kendra saw a six-foot-long, ornately carved box. Grandma peeked as well. "What's in the box?" Kendra asked.

"Less than an hour ago I called in Vanessa, Tanu, and Dale. I told them I believed we had caught our traitor, but that I was worried about Christopher Vogel's presence on the property, undoubtedly with designs for more mischief. I told them that I had decided to hide the key to the artifact vault under my cot, and that I wanted them to know where it was in case of an emergency. Then we went on to discuss plans for tracking Olloch tomorrow, as well as how we might discover the whereabouts of our other uninvited guest."

"Big box for a key," Kendra said.

"It's no ordinary key," Grandpa said.

"You're not actually using the key as bait," Grandma said, sounding certain he would not be so foolish.

"Of course not. The box contains a thief's net. The key is hidden elsewhere."

Grandma nodded approvingly.

"A thief's net?" Kendra asked.

"If anyone opens the box without deactivating the trap, the net will spring out and wrap them up," Grandpa explained. "A magical tool for apprehending would-be robbers."

"Where's the key?" Kendra asked.

"I'm not sure you should be burdened with that knowledge," Grandma said. "That kind of information could make you more of a target. Your grandfather and I are the only people aware of the key's location."

"Okay," Kendra said.

Grandpa rubbed his chin. "I've debated over whether to send you away, Kendra. On one hand, I strongly suspect that the crisis here at Fablehaven has not ended. On the other, the Society of the Evening Star will start trying to track you down the moment you exit the gates. At least the fences of Fablehaven provide a barrier against them. With the register hidden in a new place, we should have no new undesired visitors."

"I'd rather stay here," Kendra said. "I don't want to put my parents in danger."

"I think for now that is the best move," Grandpa said. "I recommend you sleep with your grandmother tonight in our room. I don't want you sleeping alone. The attic provides extra protection against magical creatures with bad intentions, but I'm afraid our remaining foes are mortal."

Because Olloch ate Seth and is now out of the picture,

Kendra thought morbidly. "Whatever you want," Kendra said.

❧ ❧ ❧

Bedtime arrived much too soon for Kendra. Before she knew it, dinner was eaten, painful condolences were shared, and she was lying in a king-sized bed beside Grandma Sorenson. Kendra loved her grandma, but she was becoming aware that she smelled too much like cough drops. Plus she snored.

Kendra tossed and turned trying to find a comfortable position. She tried lying on her side, her stomach, and her back. She bunched the pillow in different ways. It was no use. Having slept all day, she was more ready to go play soccer than she was to fall asleep. It didn't help that she was sleeping with her clothes on in case somebody really did get caught in Grandpa's net during the night.

In her own home she would have watched TV. Or made herself a snack. But the only ones at Fablehaven with a television were the satyrs. And she was afraid to get up for a snack for fear of running into somebody trying to sneak into Grandpa's study.

There was no visible clock, so time began to feel indefinite and endless. She kept trying to construct a scenario in which Seth was not dead. After all, nobody had seen Olloch eat him. They weren't a hundred percent sure. In the morning, after they tracked the demon, it would be more certain, but for tonight, she could still hope a little.

A sudden disturbance downstairs broke the restless

monotony. Someone shouted and something clattered. Grandma awoke with a start. Grandpa started calling for help.

Kendra tugged on her shoes and raced into the hall. She turned a corner to the hall that led to the stairway. Grandpa was yelling excitedly from downstairs.

On the stairs Kendra met Vanessa and Tanu. Vanessa carried her blowgun; Tanu held his pouch full of potions. Kendra could hear Grandma right behind her.

After tromping down the stairs, they all dashed across the entry hall and into the study, where Dale lay tangled in a net on the floor. Grandpa sat at the edge of his cot, a knife in his uninjured hand. "We caught somebody with a hand in the cookie jar," he announced.

"I told you, Stan," Dale panted. "I don't know how I got here."

Tanu put the potion he was holding back into his pouch. Vanessa lowered her blowgun. Grandma engaged the safety on her crossbow.

"Why don't you explain to everyone?" Grandpa suggested.

Dale was on his stomach. The net was so tight it squished his features and only allowed him to partially turn his head to try to face them. His arms were crossed awkwardly on his chest, and his legs were bound together.

"I went to sleep and woke up like this on the floor," Dale asserted. "Simple as that. I know it looks bad. Honestly, I had no intention of stealing the key. I must have been sleepwalking."

Dale looked and sounded desperate. Grandpa narrowed his eyes. "Went to sleep and woke up here," he repeated thoughtfully. Understanding dawned in his gaze. "The traitor is clever enough to realize that I now know the secret, so it will do no good to pretend otherwise—the clues lead to an obvious conclusion. Trusted friends acting out of character. Drumants released to explain the bite marks. And now Dale asserts that his strange behavior happened in his sleep. I should have connected the dots earlier. I'm afraid this will end in a scuffle. Dale, I'm sorry you're stuck in a net. Tanu, we mustn't blow this."

Grandpa threw his knife at Vanessa. Raising the blowgun to her lips, she arched her body, barely dodging the knife, and fired a dart at Tanu. The large Samoan caught the dart on his pouch. Vanessa lunged gracefully at Grandma, swinging the blowgun like a switch and knocking the crossbow from her grasp. Tanu charged Vanessa. She dropped the blowgun, producing a pair of tiny darts, and pricked Tanu on the forearm as he reached for her. Instantly his eyes went wide and his knees turned rubbery. His potion pouch tumbled from unfeeling hands and he fell hard to the study floor.

Grandma reached for her fallen crossbow, a red welt already rising on her hand. Vanessa sprang at her, stabbing her with the other tiny dart. As Grandma swayed and toppled, Kendra dove, snatched the crossbow, and tossed it across the room to Grandpa an instant before Vanessa slammed into her.

Grandpa pointed the crossbow at Vanessa, who scrambled behind the desk, putting herself out of his line of fire. Kendra saw Vanessa close her eyes. Her face became serene.

Clutching the crossbow, Grandpa rose from his bed and hopped toward the desk. "Careful, Kendra, she's a narcoblix," he warned.

Moving swiftly, Tanu pulled out the dart lodged in his potion pouch and pounced at Grandpa, tackling him and wrenching the crossbow from his grasp. "Get away, Kendra!" Grandpa cried as Tanu pricked him with the dart. Vanessa remained trancelike on the floor.

Tanu had left the potion pouch behind when he attacked Grandpa. Kendra grabbed the pouch and dashed out the door. She hadn't digested all the details, but it was clear that Vanessa was controlling Tanu. "Run," Grandpa panted groggily.

Kendra raced to the back door and out to the porch. She jumped the railing to the grass below. The yard was dark. Most of the lights in the house were off. Kendra ran away from the porch through the garden. Glancing back, she saw Tanu burst out of the doorway and vault the railing.

"Kendra, don't be rash, come back!" he called.

Kendra offered no reply and ran even faster. She could hear Tanu gaining behind her. "Don't make me hurt you!" he shouted. "Your grandparents are fine; I just put them to sleep. Come back, we'll talk." His voice sounded strained.

Kendra sprinted toward the woods, taking the most direct route she could, tromping through flowerbeds and knifing between blossoming shrubs. The thorns of a rosebush raked her arm. Playing soccer during the previous school year had led to a habit of jogging. She appreciated her added speed and stamina as she reached the woods well ahead of the hulking Samoan and still going strong.

"The woods are deadly at night!" Tanu hollered. "I don't want any harm to come to you! It's pitch black, you're going to have an accident. Come back." His phrasing was labored as he tried to run and yell at the same time.

The woods were dim, but Kendra could see well enough. She jumped a fallen limb and dodged around some thorny briars. There was no way she was going back. Vanessa had staged a coup. Kendra knew that if she could get away, maybe she could return later with a plan.

Kendra no longer heard Tanu pursuing her. Chest heaving, she paused and looked back. Tanu stood at the edge of the woods, hands on his hips in a feminine stance. He looked hesitant to enter. "I really am your friend, Kendra. I'll see that no harm comes to you!"

Kendra had her doubts. She stayed low and tried to pick her way more quietly, worried that if she gave away her exact location Tanu might be encouraged and give chase. He held his hands up to his eyes, as if he was having trouble seeing. It was apparently more shadowy where she was walking than where he stood. He did not come after her, and Kendra worked her way deeper into the woods.

She was not on a path. But this was roughly the route she and Seth had taken when they first came upon the naiad pond. If she kept going straight, she would reach the hedge surrounding the pond, and from there she knew how to find a path. Not that she had any idea where she should go from there.

Walking briskly, swerving through the bracken, Kendra tried to piece together what had happened. Grandpa had called Vanessa a narcoblix. She remembered that Errol had told her and Seth about blixes before Seth snuck into the mortuary. There was a type of blix that drained away your youth, and another that could animate the dead. Narcoblixes were the kind that could control people in their sleep.

Which meant that Grandpa was right—Coulter was innocent. He had been under Vanessa's influence. Vanessa didn't care if Seth got eaten or if Coulter was turned into a mindless albino. She was just doing reconnaissance on the grove so she could figure out how to get to the artifact. She may have even wanted for Seth to be eaten in order to get Olloch out of the way.

Kendra was seething. Vanessa had killed her brother. Vanessa! She never would have guessed it. Vanessa had saved them from Errol and acted so kindly. And now she had backstabbed them and taken over the house.

What could Kendra do? She considered going back to the Fairy Queen, but something deep inside warned against that course of action. It was hard to explain—it simply felt wrong. She had a quiet certainty that if she returned, she really would end up turning into dandelion fluff, like the ill-fated man who had ventured to the island in the middle of the pond in the story Grandpa had told her last summer.

Were Grandma and Grandpa really all right? Was

Vanessa going to hurt them? Kendra wanted to believe that Vanessa meant it when she said she meant them no harm. There was reason to hope she was sincere. Taking a life on Fablehaven soil would strip Vanessa of the protections afforded by the treaty. She couldn't have that happen if she planned to go after the artifact, right? The need to respect the treaty should protect her grandparents if nothing else. Then again, Vanessa had already indirectly killed Seth by leading him out of the yard. Maybe that didn't count, since Olloch had actually done the killing.

To make matters worse, somewhere Vanessa had an accomplice—the unseen intruder, Christopher Vogel. How long before he found out she had usurped the house and joined her there? Or was he off working some other aspect of a plan more complex than Kendra could guess at?

Kendra had to do something. Where was Hugo? Would he help her if she could find him? He didn't have to take orders from her, but his free will was blossoming, so maybe she could persuade him to lend a hand. On second thought, Vanessa had been authorized to issue commands to Hugo, so chances were the treacherous narcoblix could instantly turn the golem into an enemy if Kendra brought him near.

There was nobody else. Grandpa, Grandma, Dale, and Tanu were captured. Coulter was an albino just like Warren. Seth was dead. She tried not to let the thought derail her.

What were her assets? She had grabbed the potion pouch, although she wasn't very confident which potion was which. She wished she had paid closer attention when Tanu was showing Seth. At least the potions couldn't be used against her.

What about Lena? The thought sent a thrill of hope through her. Kendra was headed toward the pond. She hadn't seen her former friend yet during this return visit to Fablehaven. The last time Kendra had seen her, Lena was a full-fledged naiad again and had tried to drown her. After the full-sized fairies saved Fablehaven from Bahumat, while undoing much of the harm the demon had caused, they restored Lena to her state as a naiad. Decades ago she had voluntarily left the water and married Patton Burgess. The decision had made her mortal, although she had aged more slowly than he. After he passed away, she toured the world, eventually returning to Fablehaven with plans to end her days at the preserve. Lena had resisted the fairies when they hauled her off to the pond. But once she was back in the water, she had appeared content.

Maybe Lena could be tempted to leave the water if Kendra explained the dire situation! Then Kendra wouldn't have to face the situation alone! It certainly beat having no plan. New purpose entered Kendra's stride.

Before long Kendra reached the tall hedge. She knew that the hedge ringed the pond, and if she followed it she would eventually reach an opening with a path. When she and Seth had first visited the pond, he had found a low opening where they had managed to crawl under the hedge. She kept an eye out for such an aperture, since it would certainly save some time.

She did not travel too far along the thick hedge before

she noticed a pronounced indentation. When she investigated more closely, she found it was impassable—the foliage was too dense. The next indentation she noticed was less obvious, but when she crouched she found it went all the way through.

She wriggled through the hedge on her belly, wondering what other animals or creatures used this cramped entrance. At the far side she stood and surveyed the pond. A whitewashed boardwalk connected a dozen wooden pavilions around the dark water. Face tilting toward the sky, Kendra noticed there were no stars, and no moon either. It was overcast. Still, enough light was apparently filtering through the clouds to illuminate the night, for although the clearing was gloomy, she could make out the contours of the lawn and the latticework of the gazebos and the foliage on the island in the middle of the pond.

Kendra crossed the lawn to the nearest gazebo. Somebody certainly took pride in caring for this area. The grass was always tidy, and the paint on the woodwork was never peeling. Maybe it was the result of a spell.

Projecting from the boardwalk below one of the pavilions was a little pier attached to a floating boathouse. The last time Kendra had seen Lena was at the end of that pier, so it seemed as good a place as any to call for her.

Kendra noticed no evidence of life in the clearing. At times she had seen satyrs and other creatures, but tonight all was silent. The tenebrous water of the pond was still and impenetrable. Kendra tried to walk quietly, out of reverence for the silence. The tranquil night was ominous. Somewhere below the inscrutable surface of the pond waited Kendra's old friend. With the right plea, hopefully Lena would renounce life as a naiad and come to her aid. Lena had decided to leave the pond once—she could do it again.

Walking along the pier, Kendra kept away from the edges. She knew the naiads would enjoy nothing more than to pull her in and drown her. Kendra gazed at the island. Again a sense of foreboding filled her. Returning to the island would be a mistake. The feeling was so tangible that she wondered if it had something to do with being fairykind. Perhaps she could sense what the Fairy Queen considered permissible. Or maybe she was just scared.

Stopping just short of the end of the pier, Kendra licked her lips. She felt hesitant to speak and desecrate the silence. But she needed help, and could not afford to waste time. "Lena, it's Kendra, I need to talk."

The words seemed to die the instant they left her lips. They did not carry or reverberate. The dark pond remained inscrutable. "Lena, this is an emergency, please come speak to me," she tried in a louder voice.

Again, she felt she had spoken for her own ears alone. There was no hint of response from her shadowy surroundings.

"Why is she back again?" a voice said from off to her right. The sound came up out of the water, the words soft but undistorted.

"Who said that?" Kendra asked.

"She's here to show off, what else?" another voice answered from directly below the pier. "Mortals get so proud when they know our language, as if speaking it weren't the easiest and most natural ability."

"I'll allow that it beats her clumsy honking," a third voice giggled. "Barking like a seal."

Several voices giggled from under the obscure water. "I need to speak with Lena," Kendra pleaded.

"She needs to find a new hobby," the first voice said.

"Maybe she should take up swimming," the third voice suggested. Laughter rippled all around her.

"You don't have to talk like I'm not here," Kendra said. "I can hear every word just fine."

"She's an eavesdropper," the voice under the pier said.

"She should come closer to the water so we can hear her better," said a new voice near the end of the pier.

"I'm just fine where I am," Kendra said.

"Just fine, she says," said another new voice. "A big clumsy scarecrow glued to the ground, plodding around on stilts." The comment initiated the longest bout of tittering yet.

"Better than being trapped in an aquarium," Kendra said.

The pond became silent. "She is not very polite," the voice under the pier finally said.

A new voice chimed in. "What do you expect? Her feet are probably sore." Kendra rolled her eyes at the giggles that followed. She suspected the naiads would gladly trade insults all night.

"Fablehaven is in danger," Kendra said. "The Society of the Evening Star has taken my Grandma and Grandpa prisoner. My brother Seth has been killed. I need to talk to Lena."

"I'm here, Kendra," said a familiar voice. It was slightly more light and musical, slightly less warm, but it was definitely Lena.

"Hush, Lena," said the voice under the pier.

"I'll speak if I choose," Lena said.

"What do you care of mortal politics?" one of the earlier voices chided. "They come and go. Have you forgotten what mortals do best? They die. It's the one talent they have in common."

"Kendra, come close to the water," Lena said. Her voice was nearer. Kendra could vaguely see her face beneath the surface of the pond to the left of the pier. Her nose was nearly breaking the surface.

"Not too close," Kendra said, squatting well out of reach.

"Why are you here, Kendra?"

"I need your help. The preserve is at the brink of falling again."

"I know you think that matters," Lena said.

"It does matter," Kendra said.

"It seems to matter for a moment. Just like a lifetime."

"Don't you care about Grandma and Grandpa? They could die!"

"They will die. You'll all die. And at the time it will seem like it matters."

"It does matter!" Kendra said. "What do you mean, nothing matters? What about Patton? Did he matter?"

There came no answer. Lena's face broke the surface of

the water, gazing up at Kendra with liquid eyes. Even in the weak light, Kendra could see that Lena looked much younger. Her skin was smoother and more evenly colored. Her hair had only a few strands of gray. The water around Lena sloshed and churned and she vanished.

"Hey," Kendra said. "Leave her alone."

"She's through talking with you," said the voice under the pier. "You are not welcome here."

"You pulled her away!" Kendra accused. "You jealous little airheads. Waterheads. What do you do, brainwash her? Lock her in a closet and play songs about living under the sea?"

"You do not know of what you speak," said the voice under the pier. "She would have perished and now she will live. This is your final warning. Go face your fate. Leave Lena to enjoy hers."

"I'm not going anywhere," Kendra said resolutely. "Bring Lena back. You can't do anything to me if I stay away from the water."

"Oh, no?" said the voice under the pier.

Kendra did not like the knowing tone of the speaker. Too much confidence. She had to be bluffing. If naiads left the water, they became mortal. Still, Kendra looked around, worried that somebody might be sneaking up on her to push her into the water. She saw nobody.

"Hello?" Kendra said. "Hello?"

Silence. She felt certain they could hear her.

"Don't say we didn't warn you," one of the earlier voices sang.

Kendra crouched, trying to be ready for anything. Were the naiads going to throw something at her? Maybe they could collapse the pier? The night remained quiet and still.

A hand reached up out of the water at the end of the pier. Kendra jumped back, her heart in her throat. A wooden hand. Little golden hooks served as joints. Mendigo scrambled out of the dark water and crawled onto the pier.

Kendra backed away as Mendigo stood, the wooden limberjack Muriel had changed into a fearsome servant. The overgrown primitive puppet had been pulled into the water by the naiads the year before. It had not crossed Kendra's mind that they might release him. Or even that he would still be functional. Muriel had been imprisoned. She was locked up with Bahumat deep beneath a verdant hill. Apparently nobody had told Mendigo.

The wooden figure rushed at Kendra. Although she had grown since she last saw the limberjack, he was still an inch or two taller. Kendra turned and ran along the pier back to the boardwalk. She could hear him gaining, wooden feet clacking against wooden planks.

He caught up to her at the bottom of the gazebo stairs. Kendra whirled and tried to grab at him, hoping to catch hold of a limb and unhinge it. He nimbly evaded her grasp and caught hold of her around the waist, flipping her upside down. She struggled and he changed his grip, pinning her arms to her sides.

Kendra was caught in a helpless position—facing away from him, upside down, arms immobilized. She tried to wriggle and flail, but Mendigo was alarmingly strong. As the oversized puppet trotted away from the pond, it became apparent she was going wherever he wanted.

Reunion

Seth stripped off another piece of the spongy wall and placed it in his mouth. The texture reminded him of citrus pulp. He chewed until he was left with a small amount of tough, tasteless matter, which he swallowed. Puckering his lips, Seth pressed his mouth against the wall of the cocoon. The harder he kissed the wall, the more moisture flowed into his mouth. Water with a hint of honeydew.

Olloch roared again, and the cocoon shuddered. Seth flopped around as the cocoon lurched from side to side. By the time he braced himself, the movement stopped. Seth was growing accustomed to the roars and the flurries of motion, although the thought that he was listening to a roar from inside a cocoon inside the belly of a demon remained peculiar.

Seth had tried to sleep. When he had first started dozing, the roars had awakened him every time. Eventually, with the help of his mounting fatigue, he had managed a few fitful stretches of slumber.

Time was becoming meaningless in the endless blackness. Only the growls and motion of the demon interrupted the monotony. That and snacking on fragments of the padded walls. How long had he been inside of Olloch? A day? Two days? Three?

At least Seth remained reasonably comfortable inside his womblike enclosure. It fit him rather snugly. There was just enough room to move his arms when he wanted to pick at the walls. Even when he was flung around, he never got injured, because the walls were soft, and there was not enough room for him to get shaken into dangerous positions.

With so little space, it seemed the air would run out in a matter of minutes, but his breathing remained unstrained. Being swallowed by Olloch had made no difference—the air remained fresh. The closeness of the cocoon made him a little claustrophobic, but in the darkness, when he lay still, he could pretend the enclosure was spacious.

Olloch gave a particularly ferocious roar. The cocoon quaked. The demon emitted a couple of prolonged growls followed by the loudest roar Seth had yet heard. Seth wondered if the demon was in a fight. The snarls and roars continued. It felt oddly like the cocoon was being squeezed, first by his head, then near his shoulders, then at his waist, then at his knees and feet. The vicious growls continued unabated.

The cocoon was jostled one final time and silence followed. Seth lay in stillness, waiting for the turbulence to resume. He waited for several minutes, expecting more roaring at any moment. The growls had been almost desperate. Now all was eerily calm. Could Olloch have been killed? Or perhaps the demon had won a battle and then collapsed in exhaustion. It was easily the longest interval of motionless silence Seth had experienced since being swallowed. Uneventful minutes accumulated until Seth felt his eyelids drooping. He slipped into a deep slumber.

*   *   *

Mendigo dumped Kendra onto the ground. A thick carpet of wildflowers cushioned her landing. The air smelled of blossoms and fruit. As disoriented as the dash through the woods had left her, Kendra knew where they were: at the site where the Forgotten Chapel once stood. The last order from Muriel to Mendigo must have been to bring Kendra to the chapel.

During the entire run through the woods, Kendra had wriggled and twisted and squirmed. She had kicked Mendigo in the head and tried to unhinge his limbs. But the oversized puppet had just shifted his grip and continued doggedly onward. She had been carried upside down, over his shoulder, and curled up in a ball. No matter how vigorously she struggled, Mendigo had adjusted.

Kendra lay sprawled on a bed of wildflowers beneath a starless sky, the dim night pungent and mild. Mendigo crouched and started digging, clawing at the soil with wooden fingers, tossing stones aside when he encountered them. Somewhere under the hill, Muriel was buried, imprisoned with Bahumat. Apparently the order had not merely been to bring Kendra to the chapel but to bring Kendra to Muriel.

Kendra sprang to her feet and bolted down the hillside. She had not traveled six steps before Mendigo slammed into her from behind, tackling her near the trunk of a peach tree. They rolled and she wrenched her back. Kendra shrieked as Mendigo clung to her with unnatural strength, wrapping her up with his arms and legs.

At least if he was clinging to her, he wasn't digging. What would happen if he tunneled down to Muriel? Would the witch issue new commands to her wooden servant? Would she get in touch with Vanessa and figure out a way to escape?

"You're in a fine predicament," a tiny voice giggled. It was high and musical, like the tinkling of a little bell.

Kendra turned her head. A yellow fairy hovered near her face, emitting a golden glow. She wore a shimmering slip of gossamer and had wings like a bumblebee and a pair of antennae. "I wouldn't mind some help," Kendra said.

"A heroine of your reputation should have no trouble escaping such a feeble adversary," the fairy said airily.

"You'd be surprised how strong he is," Kendra said.

"His magic is weak," the fairy sniffed. "Muriel is sealed in a mighty prison. Her will no longer supports the enchantments she left behind. And yet you can do nothing but beg for help. Forgive me if I am unimpressed."

Mendigo was dragging Kendra up the hill toward the spot where he had started digging. "Obviously I'm having trouble," Kendra said. "I don't know what to do."

The fairy laughed, a twittering sound. "This is priceless! The great Kendra Sorenson being hauled through the dirt by a puppet!"

"You act like I think I'm some big shot," Kendra said. "I think you're projecting. I know I'm just a girl. Without the help of all the fairies I would have died last summer."

"False humility is more insulting than open pride!" the fairy sniffed.

Mendigo picked up Kendra, cradling her in his arms, folding her knees up to her chin and keeping her arms trapped at her sides. He resumed digging with his feet. "Do I look like I could possibly be feeling superior to anyone?" Kendra demanded.

The fairy drifted close, hovering in front of Kendra's nose. "The magic inside you is dazzling. By comparison, he is like a faint star next to the noonday sun."

"I don't know how to use it," Kendra said.

"Don't ask me," the fairy said. "You're the gifted luminary our Queen chose to honor. I can't show you how to unlock your magic any more than you can teach me how to use mine."

"Could you use your magic on him?" Kendra asked. "Change him back into a little puppet?"

"The spell that animates him remains potent," the fairy said. "But the command guiding his actions is weak. With some help, I could probably turn him."

"Oh, please, would you?" Kendra asked.

"Well, I am here to guard the prison," the fairy said. "All of us who were imps take turns as sentries."

"You were an imp?" Kendra said.

"Don't remind me. It was a graceless existence."

"He's trying to dig down to Muriel," Kendra said. "If you're a guard, shouldn't you stop him?"

"I suppose I should," the fairy conceded. "But the plums smell so wonderful right now, and the night is so fine . . . rounding up fairies is such drudgery."

"I'd be so grateful," Kendra said.

"We fairies crave nothing more than your gratitude, Kendra. We look up to you so. One kind word and our little hearts start racing! All we wish for is the love of big, clumsy girls."

"You're terrible," Kendra said.

"I am, aren't I," the fairy said, finally sounding flattered. "Tell you what. It is my responsibility to guard Muriel and Bahumat, you were right about that, so maybe I could check if anybody else is bored enough to lend you a hand."

The little fairy zipped away. Kendra hoped she was really going for help. The fairy didn't sound very reliable. Kendra tried to force the limberjack's arms apart by straightening her legs. The effort strained her back. Mendigo was too strong.

As Mendigo dug deeper, Kendra's hope that the fairy would return began to dwindle. Mendigo was nearly waist deep in a hole before a small group of fairies swarmed around them, glimmering in prismatic colors.

"See, I told you," the little yellow fairy tinkled.

"He's certainly tunneling toward Muriel," another fairy said.

"Not very efficiently," a third chimed in.

"Would you like us to turn him to obey your will?" a fourth fairy asked. Kendra recognized the speaker as the silver fairy who had led the charge when the fairies attacked Bahumat.

"Sure, that would be great," Kendra said.

The fairies hovered in a ring around Mendigo and Kendra. When they began chanting, colors flared and sparked, making Kendra blink. Kendra could no longer comprehend what they were saying. It felt like trying to listen in on multiple conversations at once. All she caught were tangled fragments of meaning that together made no sense.

After a final blazing flash, the fairies fell silent. Most soared away. Mendigo continued digging. "He is now yours to command," the silver fairy reported.

"Mendigo, stop digging," Kendra tried. Mendigo stopped. "Mendigo, set me down." He set her down.

"Thank you," Kendra said to the yellow fairy and the silver fairy, the only two who remained.

"Our pleasure to help," the silver fairy said. Though pitched high, her voice was richer than the others.

The yellow fairy shook her head and buzzed away.

"Why are they hurrying away?" Kendra asked.

"They have done their duty," the silver fairy said.

"None of the fairies have been very friendly," Kendra said.

"Friendliness is not always our forte," the silver fairy said.

"Especially to one who was shown kindness by our Queen. You are much envied."

"I was only trying to protect Fablehaven and save my family," Kendra said.

"And you succeeded, which only elevates your status," the silver fairy said.

"Why are *you* speaking with me?" Kendra asked.

"I suppose I am peculiar," the silver fairy said. "I am of a more serious mind than many of the others. I am called Shiara."

"I'm Kendra."

"Fortunately for you, we all have an interest in keeping Bahumat imprisoned," Shiara said. "Otherwise I question whether I would have been able to rally sufficient help to turn Mendigo. Although Bahumat rightly blames you above all others, his vengeance against the fairies would be merciless were he to escape."

"Couldn't you just imprison him again?" Kendra said.

"Your elixir augmented our size and our power. Without it we would be no match for a demon like Bahumat."

"Couldn't I get the elixir again?" Kendra asked.

"My dear girl, you truly are naïve, which may be partly why our Queen condescended to share her tears with you. Your decision to tread near her shrine would normally have been rewarded with a swift departure from this life. I suspect she spared you because of your innocence, though her reasons are her own."

"Fablehaven is in danger again," Kendra said. "I could use some help."

"Do not seek favors from her again unless she invites you," Shiara said. "Now that you know better, irreverence will not be tolerated."

Kendra recalled how she had sensed that going to the island again would be a mistake. "Could you help me?"

"Obviously I could, because I have," Shiara said, twinkling.

"Have you seen Olloch the Glutton? He's a demon who is after my brother."

"The glutton is becoming dormant. He will not bother you."

Kendra felt a stab of grief at the news. If the demon was slowing down, it meant Seth truly was gone. "There is more to the problem than Mendigo and the demon," Kendra said. "Bad people have taken over the house. They captured my grandparents and Dale and Tanu. They want to steal something precious from Fablehaven. If they have their way, they'll release all the demons from their prisons."

"It is challenging for us to mind the affairs of mortals," Shiara said. "Dwelling on such concerns is not in our nature. You made the binding of Bahumat our duty with authority from our Queen. And we continue to attend to that duty. I keep a sentinel stationed here always."

Kendra scanned the surrounding area, her gaze settling on the hill where Warren's cottage sat, some ways off. "Could you help me heal Warren, Dale's brother?"

"The curse upon him is much too strong," Shiara said. "All the fairies in Fablehaven together could not break it."

"What if you had the elixir?"

"That might be another matter. I wonder, why did you fail to return the bowl to the shrine?"

Kendra scrunched her eyebrows. "Grandpa thought it would be more appropriate to toss it onto the water. He thought it would be disrespectful to go back."

"The naiads have claimed it as a tribute," Shiara said. "In the future, bear in mind, if you take something in need, you will not be punished for returning it in gratitude. Such action would not have harmed your standing with Her Majesty."

"I'm sorry, Shiara," Kendra said. "We thought they would return it."

"The naiads fear and respect our Queen, but elected to accept the bowl as a gift freely given," Shiara said. "I sought to retrieve it but they would not yield, blaming you for awarding it to them. Some among the fairies hold you culpable." The silver fairy hovered higher. "It appears the situation here is now under control."

"Wait, please don't leave," Kendra said. "I don't know what to do."

"I will try to make the others mindful of the threat you named," Shiara said. "But do not count on aid from our kind. I admire your goodness, Kendra, and wish you no harm."

Shiara streaked away, vanishing into the night. Kendra turned and studied Mendigo. He stood motionless, awaiting instructions. Kendra sighed. The only person on her side was a big, creepy puppet.

❧ ❧ ❧

Groaning, Seth stirred. He tried to stretch but the effort was thwarted by the snug confines of the cocoon. The realization of where he was caused him to snap awake. How long had he been asleep?

Opening his eyes, he was surprised to find the inside of the cocoon illuminated by a soft green glow, as if light were filtering in from outside. The cocoon remained unusually still. Was Olloch sleeping? Why was there suddenly light? Was the light passing through both Olloch and the cocoon?

Seth waited. Nothing changed. Eventually he started yelling and tried to rock the cocoon by flinging himself from one side to the other. There came no roars, no growls, no movement except a slight tilting as he shifted his position. Just silence and the even, muted glow.

Was the cocoon no longer inside Olloch? Had he been coughed up like a hairball? Perhaps the cocoon was indigestible! He dared not hope for such good fortune. But it would explain the lack of growls and the new illumination. Had Grandpa come to his rescue? If so, why wasn't anyone encouraging him to open the cocoon?

Could it be some sort of trick? If he opened the cocoon, would Olloch gobble him up again, this time without a cocoon to impede digestion? Could he still be in the evil grove with the revenant? He didn't think so. He felt no hint of the chilling, involuntary fear.

Seth decided to wait. Acting rashly had gotten him in trouble before. He folded his arms and listened, straining his senses for any indication of what was going on outside the cocoon.

Seth quickly became fidgety. He had never coped well with boredom. When the cocoon had swayed and jostled with the movements of the demon, and when the silence had been interrupted by ferocious growls, Seth had remained on edge, which kept him occupied. The motionless silence was relentless.

How much time had passed? Time always moved slower when he was bored. He could remember certain classes at school where it used to feel like the clock was broken. Every minute felt like a lifetime. But this was worse. No classmates to joke with. No paper to doodle on. Not even the drone of a teacher to give shape to the monotony.

Seth began picking at the wall of the cocoon. He didn't have to break all the way out, he just wanted to see how tough it would be. He ate part of the wall as he went.

Soon he had made a pretty good hole in the wall in front of his face. As he dug deeper, the texture of the wall was changing, becoming goopy, like peanut butter. It was the best-tasting part of the wall so far, reminding him vaguely of eggnog.

After scooping away the eggnog paste, he reached a membrane. It was slick, and it rippled when he prodded it. Seth ruptured the membrane by jabbing it with his fingers, and clear liquid gushed out, soaking him.

Now light was really pouring into the cocoon through the hole. He had reached a hard, translucent shell. Silvery light shone through it, overpowering the green glow. He was obviously no longer inside Olloch. And as he had dug, Seth had neither heard nor felt any indication that Olloch was near.

Who knew if he would get another chance like this? He had to try to escape. The demon might return anytime. Seth began punching at the shell. The blows hurt his knuckles, but the shell began to crack. Soon his hand burst through, and unfiltered sunlight flooded in.

Seth worked furiously to widen the hole. The effort took longer than he liked. Now that his protective cocoon was breached, he wanted to get out as quickly as possible, before some creature came along and cornered him.

Finally the hole was big enough for Seth to squirm through. With his head, shoulders, and arms out of the cocoon, Seth froze. Olloch sat not twenty feet away, back to him. The demon had grown considerably. Olloch was bigger than the elephants Seth had seen at the zoo, not just taller, but much broader as well. No wonder the demon had been able to swallow him. The glutton was immense!

Seth realized he had made the worst mistake of his life, and that now he would die. Why hadn't he waited to open the cocoon? Why was he so impatient?

But Olloch did not turn. The huge demon continued to sit motionless, back to him. Seth began to notice a terrible stench. He looked at the shell of the cocoon. It was smooth, with a luster like mother-of-pearl, except that it was streaked with smelly brown matter. Huge clumps of mushy brown excrement sat on the ground nearby, buzzing with flies.

Suddenly Seth understood. He had passed right through

the demon, safe inside the cocoon! It was the only explanation. In one end, and out the other!

Olloch remained still. The demon did not even seem to breathe. He was like a statue. And judging from what Seth could see, the clearing he was in was not the haunted grove.

Seth squirmed the rest of the way out of the cocoon, trying his best to avoid touching the excrement. Once free of the cocoon, he picked his way through the minefield of reeking demon pies, slinking away from the enormous glutton. While he was stepping around one stinking pile, a dry branch cracked loudly underfoot. Seth's entire body tensed. After a breathless moment, he hazarded a glance at the demon. The glutton had not budged, and continued to hold perfectly still.

Deciding he had to confirm that the demon was no longer a threat, Seth started looping around so he could view Olloch from the front, giving the demon a wide berth. Coming around to the front, Seth found the demon seated in the same sitting position as when he had first laid eyes on him in the funeral home. The texture of his skin had changed. The demon was a statue once more. Seth could not help smiling. He was no longer doomed! And until some new victim made the mistake of feeding him, Olloch the Glutton was frozen.

Seth surveyed his surroundings. He was in a small clearing encircled by trees. He realized he could be anywhere on the preserve. He needed to get his bearings.

Seth wished for his emergency kit. He had dropped it back in the grove. His only remaining asset was the glove

Coulter had thrust into his hand. Seth had stowed the glove in his pocket. He tugged it out and pulled it on.

The instant he put on the glove, Seth could no longer see himself. It was a strange sensation, like all that was left of him was a pair of transparent eyeballs. He held up his hands in front of his face. When he moved them, his body flickered back into view. But when he held still, he didn't just see right through them, he saw no sign of himself. It was as if he had been completely disembodied.

The glove was a little loose on his hand, but it did not fit him badly. Fortunately it had belonged to Coulter and not Tanu. Keeping it on should afford him some protection as he tried to figure out where he was.

The sun was high in the sky, so for the moment it would be no help determining direction. And since he had no idea where on the preserve he was, identifying north would not help him much yet anyhow. He needed a landmark. Seth stepped into the center of the clearing, weaving around the piles of dung. The biggest stack was as high as his waist. Seth stood with his hands on his hips. The trees circling the clearing were too tall—he could see nothing beyond them.

He glanced at the demon. Climbing Olloch would give him an extra fifteen feet or so, but he did not want to get anywhere near that mouth.

There were no apparent trails leading out of the clearing, but the undergrowth was not heavy, so he chose a direction and set off. After a while, he became used to how his body would vanish whenever he paused, then reappear as he continued walking. His first priority was to find a landmark or a vantage point that would allow him to get his bearings. For all he knew, each step was carrying him farther from the main house.

He came across a pair of deer. They paused and looked toward him. He held still, vanishing from sight. After a moment they bounded away. Had they caught his scent?

Farther along he glimpsed a great black owl roosting in a tree. The feathery head swiveled toward him, round eyes staring. Seth had never known owls could be so large or so black. Even as he stood motionless and invisible, the golden eyes seemed to stare into his. In that instant, Seth realized he had not consumed any milk. It was a new day, and he had slept. He could not see the true forms of any of the magical creatures. The owl could be anything. The deer could have been anything.

He thought back to Olloch. Had the demon really looked as much like a statue as it had seemed to him? Or was that another illusion?

Seth backed away from the owl, eyeing the large bird as he distanced himself and circled around it. The dark owl did not turn, but the head pivoted, golden eyes trained on Seth until he passed out of sight.

Before long, Seth came to an unusual path. Once it had been a wide road paved with flagstones, though now it was choked with weeds and slender young trees. Many of the paving stones were out of place or hidden beneath vegetation, but plenty were visible to help him follow the road. Seth had never seen a paved path at Fablehaven, and even though the road was in disrepair, he decided that following an old road was probably safer than roaming aimlessly through the forest.

The path was not level, and many of the lichen-covered flagstones were crooked and loose, forcing Seth to watch his step or risk turning an ankle. At one point he stopped as a long snake slithered through the weeds. He held his breath, unsure whether it was really a snake or something more dangerous in disguise. The serpent did not appear to notice him.

Seth passed the decaying remnants of a humble cabin not far off the path to one side. Two walls and a stone chimney remained partially intact. Farther along he spotted the jumbled remnants of a smaller shelter, splintered and rotten beyond recognition. It might have once been a shack or a lean-to.

He passed a few more ruins of crude shelters before the road led him into an open area, where he stood facing an impressive manor, surprisingly undamaged compared to the road and the other dwellings he had passed. The manor was three stories tall, with four large pillars in the front. White walls were now gray, and all the windows were covered by heavy green shutters. Flowering vines twisted around the pillars and climbed the walls. The road formed a circular driveway in front of the manor, doubling back on itself.

Seth remembered hearing about an abandoned mansion somewhere on the property. It had once been the main house at Fablehaven, and the center of a community, of which the dilapidated shelters were probably remnants. He could not recall ever hearing why the mansion had been abandoned.

Given his current situation, one detail about the manor stood out above the rest. It occupied high ground. He suspected that from the roof he would be able to get his bearings.

Did he dare risk entering the house? Normally he would intrude in a heartbeat. He loved exploring. But he knew that barging into an abandoned mansion on Fablehaven property was a risky proposition. Here, ghosts and monsters were not only real, they were everywhere. And the manor had to be vacant for a reason. It was larger and more grand than the house his grandparents occupied.

He had to find out where he was. Although the sun was still fairly high, nightfall would inevitably come, and he didn't want to get caught in the woods after dark. Plus, everybody had to be terribly worried. If entering the house would help him figure out where he was on the property, it would be worth the risk. Also, it would be cool to see what the manor looked like inside. Who knew? There might even be treasure.

Seth walked cautiously toward the house. He decided to take it slow, keeping himself tensed to bolt at the first sign of trouble. The day was hot and still. Clouds of gnats twirled above the lawn. He could imagine carriages pulling up to the house, being greeted by uniformed servants. Those days were long gone.

He mounted the steps to the front porch, passing the pillars. He had always liked houses with pillars. They seemed so stately, like true mansions. The front door was ajar. Seth went to the nearest shuttered window. The green paint of the shutters was blistered and peeling. When he tugged on the shutters, they rattled but would not swing open.

Seth returned to the front door and eased it open. With the windows shuttered and no other lights on, the house was gloomy. Beyond the cavernous entry hall, he could see into a spacious living room. The furniture looked expensive, even under a heavy layer of dust. Everything was quiet.

Stepping inside, Seth left the door wide open. His passage stirred up dust off the floor. Standing inside the house was barely cooler than standing under the sun outside. It smelled musty, with a hint of mildew. Great sheets of cobwebs hung from the high ceiling and veiled the chandelier. He decided it might be wise to hurry.

A grand staircase led up from the entry hall to the second floor. Seth charged up the stairs, kicking up dust with each step, leaving footprints on the dingy carpeting. At the top of the stairs hung a sepia portrait of a man and a woman. The man looked serious and wore a mustache. The woman was Lena—much younger than when Seth had known her, but even under the film of dust on the glass, her identity was unmistakable. She had a slight, knowing smile.

Seth hurried down the hall until he found another staircase, which granted access to the third level. Climbing to a higher, narrower hall, he tried a random door and found it locked. The next door he tried was locked as well, but the third opened onto a bedroom. He hurried to the window, opened it, and unfastened the shutters. Already he had a good view, but only in one direction, so Seth stepped out onto the roof. The roof was steep enough that if he fell, he could conceivably roll off the edge and fall three stories to the driveway. Treading gingerly, wood creaking, Seth moved to the crest of the roof.

Standing atop the manor, he found himself just high enough to get a decent view of the surrounding area. Unfortunately, not much looked familiar. He identified the four hills that surrounded the valley where Coulter had led him. But he was not sure from what direction he was looking at the four hills. Slowly he turned, scanning the horizon, searching for clues. In one direction he could see what he suspected was the beginning of the marshland. In another direction he saw a single hill. On the hill, he saw a rooftop peeking above the trees.

Warren's cottage! It had to be. He could barely see the top of it from his current vantage point. He stood on his tip-toes, trying to improve his angle. It was a good distance away, but if he could reach the cottage, he knew how to find his way back to the main house from there.

Sweeping the area with a final look, Seth soaked up all the details he could. Back on the ground the way would not be plain. But the sun was moving, casting enough shadow now for him to feel confident which way was west. And by knowing west, he should be able to maintain his heading as he hiked to the cottage.

He returned to the window and climbed back into the room, closing and latching the shutters. Seth surveyed the room. It was well appointed, but he didn't see anything worth carrying all the way back to the cottage. Of course, now that he had been here, he could probably find his way back. Maybe there was money or jewelry lying around some-place, perhaps in the master bedroom. Might be worth tak-ing a look around for a few minutes before he departed. After all, it wouldn't be stealing since the house was abandoned.

He guessed a good place to start looking would be the second floor, where the rooms had seemed bigger. After quickly checking a few dresser drawers and glancing inside a nightstand, Seth exited the room. He stopped, staring down at the far end of the hall, where the dust on the floor was swirling in a low circle. The sight was unsettling, eddying dust at the height of his shins. Where was the breeze com-ing from?

The staircase that accessed the second floor was about halfway down the hall toward the swirling dust. Seth found that his mouth was suddenly dry. He did not want to move toward the dust, but the hall came to a dead end in the other direction.

Seth moved lightly toward the unnatural disturbance. Suddenly the dust began whirling more fiercely, rising in a column from floor to ceiling. Seth ran toward the dust devil as it moved down the hall toward him. Something told him that if he lost the race to the staircase, he would deeply regret it.

His pounding footfalls kicked up dust, but it was hardly noticeable as the wind from the oncoming vortex filled the hall with blinding particles. Seth squinted and tucked his head. When he reached the staircase, the whirlwind was scarcely ten feet away. Wind lashed at his clothes.

Seth darted down the stairway, the whoosh of the vortex close behind. At the bottom of the stairs he turned quickly down the hall toward the grand staircase. It sounded like a hurricane was on his tail. A wave of dust engulfed him from behind as he reached the top of the grand staircase.

Not daring to look back, Seth plunged down the stairs two at a time. Something smashed against the wall just behind him. Howling wind filled his ears. Coughing, Seth felt like he was lost in a sandstorm as decades of dust saturated the air.

At the bottom of the stairs, as he dashed for the front door, Seth glanced back. The vortex had grown. It was floating down toward him across the high entry hall, skipping the stairs and growing taller by the instant. Tentacles of dust stretched out from the center of the whirlwind. An icy gale hurled stinging dust into his eyes.

Seth lunged out the open door and slammed it behind him. Choking on dust, he raced down the steps to the driveway and sprinted across the yard in the direction of the cottage. Only when the manor was out of sight did he relax his pace.

※ ※ ※

Kendra sat at the table with Warren, wracking her brains to decide her next move. Mendigo stood guard outside the window. Despite the company of the mute albino and the oversized puppet, she had rarely felt so alone.

Mendigo had proved to be quite useful. After he had gathered fruit for her on the small hill that covered the

Forgotten Chapel, the puppet had carried her piggyback to Warren's cottage as dawn began to streak the sky.

But now the day was starting to fade, and she still had no plan, except to keep watch out the window in case Vanessa decided to pay her a visit. Kendra had spread out all the potions from Tanu's pouch on the table. She knew which containers held the bottled-up emotions, but was unsure which emotion was which. The rest of the potions could be just about anything. She had thought about sampling one, but became worried that some might be poisons or otherwise harmful concoctions meant for enemies. Kendra concluded she should save testing random potions as a last resort.

She needed to find a way to free her grandparents. There were tools in the cottage, plenty of items she could use as weapons, but if Vanessa was still controlling Tanu, Kendra had a hard time picturing herself succeeding. Mendigo could help, but Kendra would be surprised if the puppet was able to enter the yard, since he could not enter the cabin. She was pretty sure Grandpa had to grant special permission to any nonmortal visitors. The fairies were permitted in the garden only by his consent.

Mendigo started tapping on the window. She had told him to warn her if anyone approached. What could she do? "Mendigo, protect Warren and me from harm, but stay out of sight until my command."

Mendigo crouched behind a bush near the porch as Kendra made her way to the window. She peeked out, moving her head slowly, and could not believe what she saw.

Seth was emerging from the trees, walking up the path to the cottage.

Initially she was shocked. When she recovered, Kendra ran to the door and flung it open, tears of happiness and relief springing to her eyes. "Seth!" she cried.

"Kendra?" he said, stopping in his tracks.

"You're not dead!"

"Sure I am. I'm a ghost. I've been sent back with a warning."

Kendra could not stop smiling. "I thought I'd never hear you say something idiotic again!"

"Who else is with you?"

"Just Mendigo and Warren. Hurry, come inside."

"Ha-ha," Seth said, continuing toward the cottage at a leisurely pace.

"I'm serious," Kendra said. "Come inside. Bad things have happened."

"And I'm serious too," he said. "Muriel called me back from beyond the grave to deliver a singing telegram."

Kendra put her hands on her hips. "Mendigo, show yourself."

The limberjack jumped out from behind the bush. "Holy cow!" Seth exclaimed, recoiling. "What's he doing here? And why is he taking orders from you?"

"Get inside and I'll tell you!" Kendra said. "I've never been gladder to see anybody. We have a big problem on our hands."

CHAPTER FIFTEEN

Satirical Assistance

Seth sat across the table from Kendra, looking totally shell-shocked. After he had told Kendra about the cocoon and passing through Olloch, she had explained how Vanessa had been revealed while he was absent. "So Vanessa was controlling Coulter," he said. "That was why he suddenly seemed so disoriented. He woke up with the revenant right on top of us, and still managed to save me."

"If we fall asleep, she may be able to control us," Kendra said.

"How?" He picked up another cookie from the plate Kendra had left at the center of the table. She had discovered the cookies in a cupboard.

"Since she's a narcoblix, I think the drumants were a diversion so she could bite us in the night without anybody worrying about the marks. You were bitten by drumants. So was I. So was Coulter. So was Tanu. But who knows if all those bites were actually drumants?"

"I bet you're right," Seth said, munching on the cookie. "You know, I fell asleep inside the cocoon a couple of times. Once for quite a while. She might know I'm still alive."

"To be safe, we better not fall asleep until we solve this problem," Kendra said.

"You look tired," Seth said. "Your eyes are getting blood-shot."

"Vanessa gave me a sleeping drug yesterday, and I slept most of the day. But then I was up all night, and didn't want to risk napping today." Kendra yawned. "I'm trying not to think about it."

"Well, I had a good sleep after Olloch . . . got rid of me, so I should be able to go all night," Seth said. "I agree we need to free Grandpa and Grandma, but we also need to find the key and keep it away from Vanessa. We have to protect the artifact."

"For all we know, she may already have the key," Kendra said. "She might even have the artifact!"

"I doubt it. It will be hard to get past that revenant. I mean, the thing just froze me with pure terror—there was nothing I could do. But maybe Vanessa knows a trick."

"It can't be too easy for her," Kendra said. "I think she sent you and Coulter to the grove as an experiment. I'm not sure she knows what she's doing."

"Well, if she sent Coulter, she might send others," Seth said. "She and that Christopher Vogel guy are here to get the artifact. They're going to find a way if we don't stop them. And they might hurt everybody they captured in the process."

"You think we should go spy on them?"

"Right away. While we still have light. We don't have time to waste."

Kendra nodded. "Okay, you're right." She stood and put a hand on Warren's shoulder. "We're going to the house, Warren. We'll be back." He smiled up at her blankly.

"I know some of these potions," Seth said, indicating the potions on the table.

"Do you know which emotions are which?" Kendra asked.

"I'm pretty sure," he said. "And I know these ones turn you small. Like under a foot high. And this one is an antidote for most poisons. And this one makes you resistant to fire. Or was that this one?"

"Do you know which one was fear?" Kendra asked. "That might come in handy."

"This one is fear," Seth said, picking up one of the bottles. "But we should bring all of them." He began placing the potions in the pouch. "Oh, and this jar has something important." Seth unscrewed the lid of a small jar. He dipped his finger in and withdrew it with a pale yellowish paste on it. He sucked the paste off his fingertip.

"What was that?" Kendra asked.

"Walrus butter," Seth said. "From a walrus on a preserve up in Greenland. Works like the milk. It's what Tanu uses out in the field."

"Hopefully they haven't found the key yet," Kendra said. "Grandpa hid it in a new place. Of course, we might not be able to find it either."

"We'll figure something out," Seth said. "We can't really plan until we check out what's going on. I should be able to use the glove to get a good look."

Kendra walked to the door, opened it, and spoke to the giant puppet. "Mendigo, obey all the instructions Seth gives you as if I were giving them." She turned back to Seth. "You ready?"

"Just a second," Seth said, carefully placing the final potions into the pouch. He kept the fear potion in his hand. "I lost my emergency kit, but gained a bag of magical potions and an invisibility glove. Pretty good trade."

They went outside. "Mendigo," Kendra said, "carry Seth and me to the yard as fast and as comfortably as you can, trying not to let us be heard or seen."

The wooden puppet slung Seth over one shoulder and Kendra over the other. Showing no sign of strain, Mendigo trotted briskly down the path away from the cottage.

※　※　※

Crouched, choosing their steps carefully, Kendra and Seth approached the yard. Mendigo waited several paces behind them, with orders to retrieve them and retreat to the cottage if they called. Kendra had tried to send him into the yard, but he had been unable to set foot on the grass. The same barrier that had kept Olloch out of the yard was in full effect for the limberjack as well.

Seth squatted behind a leafy shrub near the edge of the woods. Kendra settled in beside him. "Look on the porch," he whispered.

Kendra raised her head to peek over the shrub, but Seth pulled her down. "Look through the bush," he hissed. She leaned back and forth until she found a gap that let her see the porch.

"Imps," she whispered.

"Two of them," Seth said. "The big kind. How could they get in the yard?"

"That big one looks like the imp from the dungeon," Kendra said. "I bet they were both prisoners. They didn't enter the yard from the woods; they came up out of the basement."

"We've seen what they can do," Seth said, backing away from the shrub. "Imps are tough. We can't risk them spotting us."

Kendra retreated with Seth back to where Mendigo stood waiting. The shadows were long as the sun dipped toward the horizon. "How do we get past them?" Kendra said.

"I don't know," Seth said. "They're fast and strong." He put on the glove and vanished. "I'll go in for a closer look."

"No, Seth. They're on the lookout. They'll spot you. You can't hold still and run away at the same time."

"So we give up?"

"No. Take the glove off." She didn't like talking to his disembodied voice.

Seth reappeared. "I'm not sure we have many options. It's front door, back door, or a window."

"There's another way in," Kendra said. "And we might be able to use it."

"What way?"

"The brownie doors. They lead in through the dungeon."

Seth frowned pensively. "But how would we . . . wait a minute—the potions."

"We shrink ourselves."

"Kendra, that is the best idea you've ever had," Seth said.

"But there's a problem," she said, folding her arms. "We don't know where the brownies enter. We know they pass through the dungeon and into the kitchen, but we don't know where to start."

"My turn," Seth said. "Let's go ask the satyrs."

"You think they'll help us?"

Seth shrugged. "I have something they want."

"Do you know how to find them?"

"We can try the tennis court. If that fails, there's a place where I leave them messages."

"I wonder if the fairies would tell me," Kendra said.

"If you can get any to speak to you," Seth said. "Come on, if we hurry we can get there before sundown. It isn't far."

"They really built a tennis court?"

"A nice one. You'll see."

Seth ordered Mendigo to pick them up, and then guided the limberjack around the perimeter of the yard to the path that would lead them to the tennis court. Mendigo jogged down the path, hooks jingling. As they neared the court, they could hear arguing.

"I'm telling you, it's too dark, we have to call the game," one voice said.

"And you say that makes it a draw?" the other voice replied incredulously.

"That's the only fair conclusion."

"I'm up 6–2, 6–3, 5–1! And it's my serve!"

"Doren, you have to win three full sets to take the match. Count your blessings—I was getting ready to make my move."

"The sun isn't even down!"

"It's below the trees. I can't see the ball in these shadows. You played some solid games. I'll grant that you had a fair chance of winning had we continued. Sadly, nature has intervened."

Mendigo left the path at Seth's prompting and started through the undergrowth toward the hidden court.

"Can't we start again tomorrow at the same score?" the second voice tried.

"Unfortunately, tennis is a game of inertia. Restarting cold wouldn't be fair to either of us. Tell you what. We'll begin earlier tomorrow, so we can get a full match in."

"And I suppose if you're behind and can find a cloud somewhere in the sky, you'll say there's a chance of showers and call the game. I'm serving. You're welcome to return it, or you're welcome to stand there."

Mendigo pushed through the bushes at the edge of the

tennis court. Doren stood waiting to serve. The racket he had broken while swatting Olloch had been beautifully mended and restrung. Newel stood at the net.

"Hello," Newel said. "Look, Doren, we have visitors. Kendra, Seth, and . . . Muriel's weirdo puppet."

"Would you kids mind if I serve one last game?" Doren asked.

"Course they'd mind!" Newel shouted. "Terribly rude of you to ask!"

"We're sort of in a hurry," Kendra said.

"We'll make it quick," Doren said with a wink.

"In this blackness, one game could be all it takes to cause a serious injury," Newel insisted desperately.

"It isn't very dark," Seth observed.

"Line judge says we should play on," Doren said.

Newel shook his fist at Seth. "Okay, one last game, winner take all."

"Sounds good to me," Doren said.

"That isn't fair," Kendra mumbled.

"No problem," Doren said. "He hasn't broken my serve all day."

"Enough chitchat!" Newel called grumpily.

Doren tossed the ball up and blasted it over the net. Newel returned the blistering serve with a limp lob, allowing Doren to rush forward and hit a winner at a vicious angle. Doren's next two serves were aces. The fourth serve Newel returned briskly, but after a fierce volley, Doren took the point with a wicked slice that died before Newel could reach it.

"Game, set, match!" Doren trumpeted.

Growling, Newel ran over to the shed and started bashing his racket against the wall. The frame cracked and several strings popped.

"Booooo," Seth cried. "Poor sportsmanship."

Newel stopped and looked up. "Has nothing to do with sportsmanship. Ever since the brownies mended his racket, his shots have more zip. I just want to level the playing field."

"I don't know, Newel," Doren said, tossing his racket and catching it. "Takes quite a satyr to handle a racket of this caliber."

"Relish the moment," Newel said. "Next time we'll be playing under the light of day, and we'll have comparable equipment!"

"Funny you guys should mention brownies," Seth said. "We need a favor."

"Does the favor involve demons trashing our shed?" Newel asked.

"I took care of Olloch," Seth said. "We need to know how the brownies get into the house."

"Through the little doors," Doren said.

"He means we need to know where their entrance is so we can get in through the little doors," Kendra clarified.

"No offense, but it might be a bit of a squeeze," Newel said.

"We have potions to shrink ourselves down," Seth said.

"Resourceful kids," Doren commented.

Newel studied them shrewdly. "Why would you want to

get into the house that way? There may be barriers to prevent you. And who says the brownies will grant you access? They keep to themselves."

"We have to sneak inside," Kendra explained. "Vanessa is a narcoblix. She drugged my grandparents and took over the house, and will probably try to destroy Fablehaven next!"

"Wait a minute," Doren said. "Vanessa? As in, smoking-hot Vanessa?"

"As in betrayed-us-all Vanessa," Kendra said.

"I'm not sure how the brownies would feel about us giving away their secret entrance," Newel said, rolling his tongue against his cheek and winking at Doren.

"True," Doren said, nodding sagely. "We'd be violating a sacred trust."

"I wish we could help," Newel said, folding his hands. "But a promise is a promise."

"How many batteries do you want?" Seth asked.

"Sixteen," Doren said.

"Deal," Seth said.

Newel elbowed Doren. "Twenty-four, is what he meant."

"We've already got a deal for sixteen," Seth said. "We could make it less."

"Fair enough," Newel said. He gave Seth a sly glance. "I'm assuming you have said batteries on your person."

"In my room," Seth said.

"I see," Newel said, scowling dramatically. "And suppose you get caught and never make it back? We're out sixteen batteries, and we've broken our sacred promise to the brownies. I could live with sixteen up front, but with deferred payment, we're going to have to up our fee by fifty percent."

"Okay, twenty-four," Seth said. "I'll pay up as soon as I can."

Newel grabbed Seth's hand and shook it vigorously. "Congratulations. You just found yourself a secret entrance."

"So, seriously," Doren said. "What's with the puppet?"

* * *

Dusk was deepening when the satyrs, Kendra, Seth, and Mendigo reached the driveway to the main house, not far from the front gates of Fablehaven. Kendra had seen a few twinkling fairies in the woods, but when she tried to get their attention, they darted away.

"Now I'd say it's getting dark," Doren said.

"Save it," Newel replied, kneeling beside a tree and pointing. "Seth, go straight not more than twenty paces, and you'll find a tree with a reddish hue to the bark. At the base of the tree, between a fork in the roots, you'll see a good-sized hole. That is the entrance you're looking for. Don't blame me if they don't roll out the red carpet."

"And don't tell them we told you how to find them," Doren said.

"But be a pal and leave this near the entrance," Newel said, handing Seth his freshly broken racket.

"Thanks," Kendra said. "We'll take it from here."

"Unless you want to help us," Seth tried.

Newel winced. "Yeah, about that, see, we've got a thing—"

"We promised some friends," Doren said.

"It's been scheduled for a while . . ."

"We've already canceled twice . . ."

"Next time," Newel promised.

"Take care," Doren said. "Don't get eaten by a brownie."

The satyrs gamboled away and passed out of sight.

"Why'd you even ask?" Kendra said.

"Didn't think it could hurt," Seth replied. "Come on."

They rushed across the gravel driveway. The house was not in sight, so they felt relatively safe from Vanessa and her imps. Mendigo followed a few paces behind them.

They continued in the direction the satyrs had indicated. "That must be it," Seth said, touching a tree with rosy bark. "There's the hole. Good thing we found it before it was totally dark." Seth leaned the broken tennis racket against the tree.

The hole looked big enough to roll a bowling ball into. It fell away at a steep angle. "Get the potions out," Kendra said.

Seth rummaged in the pouch. He pulled out a pair of small vials. "These should do the trick."

"You're sure they're the right ones?" Kendra verified.

"They're the easiest to remember—the potion in the smallest bottles makes you small." He handed one of the vials to Kendra. She frowned at it, her brow furrowed. "Now what?" he asked.

"Do you think our clothes will shrink too?" she asked.

Seth paused. "I hope so."

"What if they don't?"

"Tanu said the potions leave him about ten inches tall. So we'd be what, around seven or eight inches? What could we wear?"

"Tanu wraps handkerchiefs around some of his bottles," Kendra said.

Seth scrabbled through the bag and removed two silk handkerchiefs. "These should do."

"Hopefully whoever made the potions took clothes into account," Kendra said.

"Should we sprinkle some on our clothes to be safe?" Seth said. "We have four extra shrinking potions."

"Couldn't hurt," Kendra said.

Seth dug out an extra vial of shrinking potion. "At the same time?" he asked.

"Drink yours first," Kendra said.

Seth unstopped the vial and downed the contents. "Tingly," he said. His eyes widened. "Really tingly!"

His clothes suddenly looked very loose. He looked up at Kendra, craning his neck at his much taller sister. He sat down on the ground. His feet slipped easily out of his oversized shoes as his legs shortened. His head sank into his collar. The shrinking accelerated, and he seemed to disappear.

"Seth?" Kendra asked.

"I'm in here," answered a chipmunk version of his voice. "Could you give me a hankie?"

Kendra placed a handkerchief into the shirt. A moment later Seth emerged, the handkerchief wrapped around his waist like a towel and dragging behind him. He looked up.

"Now you really are my big sister," he shouted. "Sprinkle some on my clothes."

Removing the stopper from another vial, Kendra sprinkled the contents over Seth's clothes. They waited, but there was no reaction. "Looks like we'll have to save the day wearing handkerchiefs," Kendra sighed.

"They're nice and silky," Seth called.

"You're a nut," Kendra said. She turned to Mendigo. "Mendigo, collect our clothes and our things and watch for us to come out of the house. When we come out, you need to hurry and meet up with us."

Mendigo started tugging at her shirt. "Mendigo, wait to collect my clothes until after I shrink, and leave us with the handkerchiefs."

Mendigo picked up Tanu's pouch and Seth's clothes. "Hey," Seth cried, "let me see if I can carry the glove."

Kendra retrieved the glove from the pocket of Seth's pants, telling Mendigo to leave the glove with them. She handed it to Seth. He draped it over his shoulder and started walking. It looked cumbersome. "Is it too big?" Kendra asked.

"I can handle it," Seth said. "When we turn big we'll be glad we have it. Speaking of which, drink your potion and let's get going. I don't want to turn big and get crushed in the brownie hole."

Kendra unstopped a third vial and drank it. Seth was right, it made her tingle. It felt like her limbs were on pins and needles, as if they had fallen asleep and now feeling was returning most uncomfortably. As she shrank, the tingling sensation intensified. Whenever Seth knew her leg had been asleep, he always tried to poke the tingly limb. It drove her crazy. This was much worse, stinging tingles starting at her fingertips and toes and racing through her whole body.

Before Kendra fully recognized what was happening, her shirt was all around her like a collapsed tent. She crawled to an opening through one of her sleeves. "Close your eyes, Seth," she called, noticing how high and squeaky her voice sounded.

"They're closed," he said. "I don't want nightmares."

Kendra found the other handkerchief, turning it into a makeshift toga. "Okay, you can look."

"You know," Seth said, "if we turn big while we're in the dungeon we'll be trapped down there."

Kendra walked over to one of the empty vials lying on the ground. Grunting and shoving, she tipped it upright. Relative to her new size, it was nearly as big as a garbage can. "The glass is thick," Kendra said. "I can barely move this empty one."

Setting down the bulky glove, Seth tried to lift the bottle. He could barely hold it off the ground. "Too bad we can't bring a spare," he said. "We'll just have to hurry."

"Mendigo, remember, watch for us and meet up with us when we come out." Mendigo now looked enormous, like some eerie monument.

Seth slung the glove over his shoulder. "Come on."

Kendra looked up. Through the gaps in the branches above her, she saw stars coming out. She followed her brother down into the yawning hole.

CHAPTER SIXTEEN

Brownie Doors

Although the dirt near the opening of the brownie hole was crumbly and loose, the ground soon became smooth and firm as the tunnel sloped downward. Near the entrance Kendra and Seth needed to crouch in some places, but before long the tunnel increased in diameter so they could comfortably walk upright. At first roots poked through the walls and ceiling, but as they descended deeper, roots became scarce, and the floor of the tunnel leveled out. The dirt felt cool against their bare feet.

"I can't see a thing," Seth said.

"Your eyes will adjust," Kendra said. "It's dim but it isn't black."

Seth turned around. "I can see a little light looking back, a very little, but it is pitch black looking forward."

"You must be going blind, I can see way down the tunnel."

"Then you take the lead."

Kendra led them deeper into the tunnel. She wasn't sure what Seth was talking about. Sure, it was dim, but there was enough light from the entrance even to reveal the texture of the different stones embedded in the tunnel walls.

"Can you still see?" Seth asked.

"Haven't your eyes adjusted yet?"

"Kendra, it is totally black. No light. I can't see you. I can't see my hand. And I can't see any light looking back."

Kendra looked over her shoulder. The way back appeared equally as dim as the way ahead. "You see nothing?"

"My night vision is fine, Kendra," Seth said. "I could see pretty well when I went to the grove, and there wasn't much light there. If you can still see, then you can see in the dark."

Kendra thought about the overcast night at the pond when she had assumed light was filtering through the clouds. She remembered seeing into cells in the dungeon that Seth thought were black. And now here she was, deep underground, and despite the dwindling twilight outside, no matter how far they walked from the entrance, it had stopped getting dimmer.

"I think you're right," Kendra said. "I can still see pretty well. The light hasn't faded for a while."

"I wish those fairies had kissed me a little," Seth said.

"Just be glad one of us can see. Come on."

The tunnel wound back and forth several times before Kendra came to a stop. "I see a door up ahead."

"Does it block the way?"

"Yes."

"Well, let's go knock."

Kendra started forward.

"Just a second," Seth said. "I lost my handkerchief. No peeking. Here it is. Okay, lead the way."

A round wall filled the entire tunnel. In the wall was an oval-shaped door. When they got close, Kendra tried the knob. It was locked. So she knocked.

An instant later the door opened swiftly, and she was looking at a thin man about her same height. He had a long nose, leaflike ears, and smooth skin, like a baby's. He looked Kendra and Seth up and down. "Brownies only," he said, closing the door.

"What happened?" Seth asked. "Could you understand that?"

"Brownies only," Kendra translated. "A little guy opened the door, said that, and closed it." She slapped the door. "Please, we need to get into the house, it's an emergency!"

The door opened a crack. The little man peered out with one eye. "Now, why would you go and learn Rowian when everyone knows brownies don't talk to strangers?"

"Rowian?" Kendra asked.

"Don't play coy with me, young lady. I've met a few fairies and nymphs who knew the rudiments of the brownie tongue, but never a miniature human."

"I'm Kendra," she said. "I love brownies. You cook

wonderful food and you repaired my grandparents' house after it was ruined."

"We all do what we do," the brownie said humbly.

"My brother and I need desperately to get into the house, and this is the only way. Please let us pass."

"This way is meant only for brownies," he said. "I may be the least of your troubles. There are magical barriers in place to prevent others from entering the house through our passage."

Kendra glanced at Seth, who was watching the exchange dumbfoundedly. "But we're allowed to enter the house, we're guests there."

"Curious way for guests to enter."

"My grandparents are the caretakers of Fablehaven. Somebody has sabotaged them, so we are trying to sneak in to help. We have to hurry. If this potion wears off, we'll clog up your tunnel."

"Can't have that," the brownie said thoughtfully. "Very well, seeing as you're brownie-sized, and seeing as you belong to the house, and seeing as you explained yourself so patiently, I see no harm in letting you pass. On one condition. You both must wear blindfolds. You are about to enter a brownie community. Our secrets are our own."

"What's he saying?" Seth asked.

"He says we have to wear blindfolds."

"Tell him to get on with it," Seth said.

"What's he saying?" the brownie asked.

"He says he'll wear a blindfold."

"Fair enough," the brownie said. "One moment." The

brownie closed the door. Kendra and Seth waited. She tried the knob. It was locked.

"What's he doing?" Seth asked.

"I don't know," Kendra said.

Just as Kendra was beginning to wonder if she had been abandoned, the door opened. "Two blindfolds," the brownie said. "And two blankets, more your size. I can't abide that fine material dragging in the dirt."

"What's he saying?" Seth said.

"He brought blindfolds," Kendra relayed.

"Ask if I have to wear one since I can't see in the first place," Seth said.

"Just wear it," Kendra said. "And he wants us to switch our handkerchiefs for blankets."

Kendra and Seth traded the handkerchiefs for the blankets, making the exchange in such a way that they remained strategically covered throughout. Then the brownie tied on the blindfolds. "I'll be your guide, dear," a female voice said to Kendra. "Put your hand on my shoulder."

"Tell your friend I'll be guiding him," the male brownie said.

"He's going to guide you, Seth."

The brownies led them through the door and along the tunnel. Soon the ground became hard. It felt like polished stone. Even with the blindfold on, Kendra could tell that they had entered a lighted area. The brownies gave occasional instructions like "step up" or "duck your head," which Kendra relayed to Seth. Occasionally she heard murmuring, as if their passage was stirring hushed comments from a crowd.

After they had walked for some time, the glow faded, and the polished floor became dirt once more. The brownies came to a halt. The male brownie removed the blindfolds. They were standing at a door that looked very much like the previous one. "Is it dark?" Kendra asked.

"I can't see a thing," Seth said.

"Just follow this passage," the brownie instructed. "It will lead straight to the dungeon. I suppose you know your way from there. I can't say whether the barriers will impede you. That risk is yours to take."

"Thank you," Kendra said.

"Here are your clothes," the female brownie said. She held up a lovely dress and a pair of moccasins, all made from the silk of the handkerchief. Kendra accepted the dress, and the female brownie handed Seth a shirt, jacket, pants, and slippers fashioned from the same material.

"Now, that is improvising," Kendra said. "The clothes look wonderful."

"We all do what we do," the female brownie responded with a small curtsy.

The brownies held up the blankets in such a way as to allow Kendra and Seth privacy as they put on their clothes. Kendra could not believe how comfortably the dress fit her.

"Just my size," Seth said, pulling on the slippers.

Kendra turned the knob and opened the door. "Thanks again," she said.

The brownies nodded congenially. She and Seth stepped

through the door, closed it behind them, and proceeded down the gloomy tunnel. "These are the silkiest clothes ever," Seth said. "I'm going to use them as pajamas."

"If you drink a shrinking potion every night," Kendra reminded him.

"Oh, yeah."

Eventually the curved dirt walls of the tunnel gave way to stone, and the corridor became more square. The air began to smell less earthy and more dank. "I think we're getting close," Kendra said.

"Good—I'm sick of the dark," Seth said.

"I'm not sure the dungeon will be any brighter," Kendra said.

"Maybe we'll find a way to reach a light switch," he said.

"We'll see."

The corridor ended at an elaborately engraved brass door. "I think this is it," Kendra said. She tried the handle, and the door swung open to reveal a room illuminated by trembling firelight. The source of the light was off to the left along the same wall as the tiny door, so they could not yet see it.

"I can see," Seth whispered excitedly.

"I think we must have made it past the barriers," Kendra said.

Seth pushed by her and stepped out into the room. Like the walls, the floor was composed of stone blocks mortared together. Seth stared off to the left. "Hey, it's the room where they make the—"

A huge, veiny hand suddenly seized him. The glove he

was carrying dropped to the ground as Seth was yanked out of sight.

"Seth!" Kendra cried. A second hand shot through the doorway into the tunnel. She tried to dodge the grasping fingers and retreat, but the nimble hand grabbed her without difficulty.

The hand pulled Kendra from the tunnel and lifted her high in the air. At her diminished height, the room looked vast. When she saw the large cauldron bubbling over a low fire, she realized it was simply the room where the goblins prepared the glop. In the wavering firelight, Kendra recognized her captor as Slaggo.

"Voorsh, I caught some strays to sweeten the glop," Slaggo grated in his guttural voice.

"Are you daft?" Voorsh sneered. "No snatching brownies." He sat on a table in the corner picking his teeth with a knife.

"I know that, you twit," Slaggo griped. "They aren't brownies. Have a smell."

Kendra was trying to pry apart the fingers that were clutching her. It was no use; they were thicker than her leg and covered in calluses as hard as stone. Slaggo held her up to Voorsh's snout, and he took a couple of sniffs, slit nostrils flaring.

"Smells like people," Voorsh said. "Something familiar to the odor . . ."

"We're Kendra and Seth," Kendra shouted in her squeaky voice. "Our grandparents are the caretakers of Fablehaven."

"It speaks Goblush," Slaggo said.

"Thinks she's an imp," Voorsh chuckled.

"You have to help us," Kendra cried.

"Pipe down," Slaggo said. "You're in no position to issue orders. I remember these two. Ruth brought them through here not long ago."

"Right you are," Voorsh agreed. "And considering how things have changed . . ."

"What do you mean how things have changed?" Kendra yelled.

"He means seeing as your grandsires are now prisoners in their own dungeon," Slaggo said, "it might be a fine prank to watch them gobble down their own flesh."

"You read my mind," Voorsh gurgled.

"What are they saying?" Seth asked.

"They're talking about cooking us," Kendra said. "Grandma and Grandpa are imprisoned here."

"If you cook us, you'll pay," Seth shouted. "You'll be guilty of murder. Grandma and Grandpa won't be imprisoned forever!"

"This one speaks like people," Slaggo grunted.

"It has a point," Voorsh sighed.

"You can't cook us," Kendra called. "The treaty protects us."

"Trespassers in our dungeon forfeit all protection," Voorsh explained.

"But the runt may be right about Stan and Ruth," Slaggo said.

"Course, if Stan and Ruth don't know, they can't rightly punish us," Voorsh mused.

"Why don't you set my grandparents free?" Kendra proposed. "They're the rightful caretakers here. You'll be rewarded."

"Vanessa freed the big imps," Slaggo croaked. "She is master of the situation."

"Besides, we couldn't spring Stan even if we wanted," Voorsh said. "We have no keys to the cells."

"So we may as well have a little fun," Slaggo said, giving Kendra a squeeze that made her ribs creak.

"If you let us go, we may be able to help my grandparents," Kendra said. "Vanessa has no real authority here. My grandparents will be back in charge sooner or later. And when they are, they will reward you greatly for helping us now."

"Desperate words from cornered prey," Slaggo said, striding toward the cauldron of roiling gray sludge.

"Hold, Slaggo, she may be right," Voorsh said.

Slaggo hesitated at the cauldron. Hot, foul steam fumed up, washing over Kendra. She glanced over at Seth, who returned a worried look. Slaggo turned to face Voorsh. "You think?"

"Stan and Ruth have repaid loyalty in the past," Voorsh said. "If we spare their spawn, there may be more reward in it than watching the runts boil."

"A goose?" Slaggo asked hopefully.

"Or better. This would merit much gratitude, and Stan has always dealt with us justly."

"I'm sure they'd give you huge rewards," Kendra said.

"You'd say anything at present to save your neck," Slaggo growled. "All the same, my ears agree with Voorsh. Stan will likely return to power, and he has a history of fair rewards." Slaggo set Kendra and Seth on the floor.

"Could you take us to their cell?" Kendra asked.

Seth looked at her like she was crazy.

"Wouldn't go over well if the new mistress caught us aiding enemies," Voorsh said.

"If you take us to the cell, you can be sure Stan will fully appreciate your involvement," Kendra said. "You can always cut and run if somebody comes."

"Might not hurt," Slaggo muttered. "Can you keep your traps shut as we go?"

"Absolutely," Kendra said.

"Have you lost it?" Seth hissed.

"This could save us lots of time," Kendra whispered back.

"You'll deny our involvement if you're caught," Voorsh said.

"Of course," Kendra said.

"Because we could make things very uncomfortable for you if you land us in hot water," Slaggo snarled.

"If we get caught, we'll keep you out of it," Kendra promised.

"Make sure the other one understands," Voorsh said. "My tongue gets tangled speaking your vile language."

Kendra explained the situation to Seth, who asserted his

compliance. Slaggo stooped and picked them up in one hand.

"Can you hold us a little looser?" Kendra asked.

"Be glad I don't cripple you," Slaggo said, slightly relaxing his crushing grip.

"Ask him to grab the glove," Seth said.

"Could you also get that glove on the floor?" Kendra asked. "We'll want it when we're big again."

"I understood the other one fine," Slaggo said. "I'll wager I grasp more languages than the two of you together. What good is a glove?" He bent down and picked it up.

"Better than nothing," Kendra replied weakly.

Slaggo shook his head. "Be right back," he said to Voorsh. "Don't forget to stir the glop."

"Don't get discovered," Voorsh said. "Swallow them if it comes to it."

Slaggo grabbed a torch and lit it in the fireplace. He exited the room and moved swiftly down the hall. When the hall ended, he rounded a corner and continued. They passed the Quiet Box that Grandma had shown them. Kendra was grateful for each cell they passed, because they were progressing toward the front of the dungeon. If she and her brother returned to their normal sizes before they made it up to the kitchen, they would be trapped underground. Which meant every second counted.

"Here we are," Slaggo said quietly, setting them down in front of a cell door. "Now, keep your word and don't cause any trouble for us." He laid the invisibility glove on the ground beside them. "And if things go well, give credit where it's due."

As the goblin scurried away, taking the torch with him, Kendra and Seth wormed through the slot meant for food trays. "Grandma, Grandpa!" Kendra called.

"Is that Kendra?" Grandpa Sorenson said. "What are you doing here?"

"Not just Kendra," Seth said. "We shrunk ourselves."

"Seth?" Grandma Sorenson gasped, her voice trembling with emotion. "But how?"

"Coulter woke up just before the revenant got us," Seth said. "He gave me a magical cocoon that wrapped around me. Olloch swallowed me like a pill. I went in one end and out the other."

"Which would have satisfied the spell and bound him," Grandpa said. "What a stroke of good fortune! I can't say how relieved I am. I have many more questions but little time to ask them. I take it you gained entry through the brownie doors?"

"I got away with Tanu's potion bag," Kendra said. "We made ourselves small. Do you know how long it lasts?"

"I can't say," Grandpa said.

"Clever children!" Grandma said. "You had better hurry if you hope to enter the house. The spell will not last forever."

"We want to steal back the artifact key," Seth said.

"Do they have it?" Kendra asked.

"I'm afraid they do," Grandpa said. "I was talking with your grandmother, and she does not recall certain recent conversations. Before she was revealed, I believe Vanessa controlled your grandmother to gather information from me. That would explain how she wrote those names in the register. I remember Ruth asking me to confirm where the key to the vault was hidden, as well as to remind her of the combination to access the secret attic."

"I have no recollection of asking any such questions," Grandma said.

"With that knowledge, Vanessa should already have the key in her possession," Grandpa said.

"Do they know where the register is?" Kendra asked. "Can they let more people onto the preserve?"

"I don't believe they know where the register is now hidden," Grandpa said. "But they have released at least one of the big imps, a brute who occupied this very cell, the same savage who broke my leg."

"I thought this was the cell with the imp," Kendra said. "The one who yelled at me when Grandma showed us the dungeon."

"That's right, dear," Grandma said.

"We had two other giant imps in confinement, so you can bet she released them as well," Grandpa said. "In addition, she probably has help from Christopher Vogel by now, and I would wager that she is still inhabiting Tanu. You kids will need to use extreme caution."

"Dale and Coulter are down here in another cell," Grandma said. "Voorsh was kind enough to confirm that."

"The goblins almost cooked us," Seth said. "Then

Kendra said that you would reward them if they helped us. So they did. I think they want a goose."

"I'll give them ten geese if we get out of this," Grandpa said. "Quickly, what is your plan?"

"We're going to get the artifact key and then free you guys," Seth said. "We have Coulter's invisibility glove, so when we get big again, we can still be sneaky."

"At least one of us can," Kendra said.

"The key to the vault is large, like a staff," Grandpa said.

"Like five feet?" Seth said.

"More like six," Grandpa said. "Taller than I am. Vanessa will keep it close. Be on guard; she is most dangerous. Seth, have no illusions: whether or not she is inhabiting Tanu, you stand no chance against her in a fair fight. You have seen the dungeon keys?"

"Yes," Kendra said.

"We used to keep them on a peg by our bed," Grandpa said. "She may be keeping those close as well. Depending on how everything plays out, it may be impossible for you to return to us with the dungeon keys. For all but the brownies, there is only one way out of here, so you could easily become trapped down here with us. If worse comes to worst, get the artifact key and flee the preserve. We can hope the Sphinx will find you."

"If all else fails, leave the artifact key and save yourselves," Grandma said. She turned to Grandpa. "We had better let them go."

"By all means," Grandpa said. "Should the potion wear off before you reach the kitchen, all will be lost."

"You'll find that the brownies have a staircase all their own," Grandma said. "Look for the hole at the base of the stairs."

"Can you find your way in the dark?" Grandpa asked.

"Kendra can see in the dark," Seth said.

"I think it's another fairykind thing," Kendra said.

"You know the way, then?" Grandma asked.

"I think so," Kendra said. "Out the door, turn right, then left, then right, then through the door and up the stairs."

"Good girl," Grandpa said. "Make haste."

Kendra and Seth scooted back through the slot in the door. "Good luck!" Grandma called. "We're very proud."

CHAPTER SEVENTEEN

Recovering the Key

K endra held Seth's hand as they raced along the hall. At their current size, the corridor felt as wide as a ballroom. Seth's speed began to flag as they reached the end of the hall where they needed to turn left. "This glove gets heavier and heavier," Seth panted.

"Let me take it for a while," Kendra offered. He handed it over with no protest. The glove was not terribly heavy, but it was hard to hold, like trying to carry a couple of unrolled sleeping bags. Burdened by the glove, she hurried as best she could.

"I wish I had infrared vision like you," Seth said.

"Infrared?"

"Or ultraviolet. Whatever. Is normal light too bright for you now?"

"It's the same as ever. Can we talk later? I'm running out of wind."

They trotted along in silence. The hall seemed endless. Kendra's heart was hammering, and sweat was drenching her silky clothes, making them feel slimy. The bulky glove flopped around as she ran.

"I have to walk for a minute," Kendra gasped finally. They slowed their jog to a walk.

"I can take the glove back," Seth said. Kendra handed it over.

"I still need to walk, just a little," Kendra said. "Hey, I see our last turn up ahead."

"Still a pretty good ways to the door, and then the stairs after that," Seth reminded her.

"I know, I'll be good in a second, sorry to slow us down."

"Are you kidding? I'm tired too, and you carried that glove a long way." They walked in silence until they reached the hall where they needed to turn right.

"Should we run again?" Kendra asked.

"We'd better," Seth said.

Kendra was reminded of running laps around the field with her soccer team. She was naturally a pretty good runner, but those first few practices had really tested her. She had almost thrown up a couple of times during the first week. She could run through the stitches in her side and the burning muscles, but once she became nauseated, her willpower to run faded fast. She had been at that point when she asked Seth to stop, and she could feel the unwelcome sensation returning.

She tried to ignore the dank smell of the dungeon. The humid stench alone was enough to make her queasy. She reminded herself that Seth was carrying the glove and doing just fine. The taste of bile rose in her throat. She fought to choke back the sensation until she involuntarily flopped forward, hands slapping the stone floor, and dry heaved.

"That's sick, Kendra," Seth said.

"Keep going," she gasped. Nothing had come up, but she had a foul taste in her mouth. She wiped her lips on her sleeve.

"I think we should stay together," he said.

"You'll get big first," she said. "I'll catch up."

"Kendra, I can't see. I can't run without you with me. Maybe if you let loose and yack you'll feel better."

Kendra shook her head and stood up. "I hate puking. I'm already feeling better."

"We can walk for a minute," he said.

"Just for a minute," she replied.

Before long Kendra was feeling much steadier. She picked up the pace, not charging as hard as before, trying to conserve energy. "I see the door up ahead," she finally said.

The tall iron door loomed into view. Kendra led Seth to the small opening in the bottom of the door. They passed through the brownie entrance and hustled toward the stairs.

"Do you see the hole Grandma was talking about?" Seth asked.

"Yes, off to the left. It's small, looks like a mouse hole."

She led Seth to the hole in the wall near the first step. She had not remembered how steep and numerous the stairs were from the basement to the kitchen. They would barely be able to reach the top of each step. With the glove, scaling the stairs could have taken hours.

Kendra and Seth wriggled through the hole. Inside they found a brownie tunnel like the one they had followed to get into the dungeon, except it was a stairway entirely of stone. The stairs were steep but just the right size for brownies. They started scaling the long staircase two steps at a time. Kendra's legs soon felt rubbery. "Can we rest for a second?"

They paused, both of them breathing hard. "Uh-oh," Seth said after a moment.

"What?" Kendra said, looking around, worried he had seen a rat.

"I'm starting to tingle," he said.

"Give me the glove and run," Kendra said.

He handed it off and bolted up the stairs. Kendra followed, finding new energy in her desperation. He was ten steps ahead, then twenty, then thirty. Soon he was out of view. Before long she could see where the steps ended. There was a little extra light filtering in through the door from the kitchen.

She reached the top of the long staircase and crammed the glove through the hole ahead of her. Then she squirmed through the hole.

"Kendra, the glove," Seth hissed from beyond the brownie door. His voice was pitched lower again. She raced to the little door, dragging the glove, and lunged through into the kitchen.

Seth was almost back to his normal size. The clothes the

brownies had made lay in tatters. Kendra heard footsteps coming toward them from around the corner. Seth's face was a mask of panic as he snatched the glove and hastily tugged it on, vanishing instantly. Flashing back into view, he picked up Kendra, and she disappeared as well. They both flickered briefly back into view as Seth grabbed the remnants of the clothes the brownies had made. Then he held still and became transparent.

A second later Vanessa rounded the corner and looked right through them. "Did you hear something?" she asked uncertainly.

"Course not, love," a male voice answered from around the corner. "You've been hearing things all day. The imps are on guard. All is well." Kendra recognized the voice. It was Errol!

Vanessa frowned slightly. "I suppose I have been on edge." She walked back out of sight.

Kendra realized she had been holding her breath. It made her feel lightheaded. She started breathing again, as controlled as she could. Seth grabbed a large green dish towel off the counter and wrapped it around his waist.

Suddenly, Kendra started tingling. She slapped Seth's hand. He held her up to his ear. "I'm tingling," she whispered.

He tiptoed away from the door. Vanessa had walked away toward the dining room, so he went in the opposite direction. As they entered the living room, Kendra felt the tingling spreading and intensifying. "Won't be long," she warned.

He stuck her behind a sofa. As soon as she was out of view, she started pulling off her dress, which was feeling tight. After a couple of moments, the tingling became severe, and she felt herself growing. Before she knew it, she was back to her normal size, her body pushing the sofa away from the wall, the unbearable tingles subsiding.

Seth straightened the sofa. Kendra peeked her head up. "If you hold my hand, will I turn invisible too?"

Seth grabbed her hand and held still. He became invisible, but she did not. "It must just work for small stuff," he said.

"Try to find me some clothes," she whispered.

Voices and footsteps were approaching. Seth hushed her, moved to the side of the sofa, and held still.

Errol came striding into the room, wearing the same antiquated suit Kendra and Seth had become familiar with. "A minor setback," he remarked over his shoulder. "Why not just send Dale?"

Vanessa followed him into the room. "We're running out of people. Our job here is far from complete. We must conserve. Tanu is a major loss. He was strong as a bull."

Kendra bit her lip. What had happened to Tanu?

Errol crossed the room and flung himself down on the sofa, kicking off his shoes. "At least now we know what we're up against," he said.

"We should have known last time," Vanessa said. "Kendra awoke me at just the wrong moment, right before I glimpsed what was approaching. Many creatures radiate fear.

The feeling was so strong, I suspected a demon. And of course I missed seeing what happened to Seth."

"You're sure he's alive?" Errol said.

"I'm sure I felt him," Vanessa said. "But I couldn't take possession of him. He was slippery, protected. It was like nothing I've ever felt."

Errol laced his hands behind his neck. "Sure he isn't just a mindless albino?"

Vanessa shook her head. "After Coulter and Tanu were attacked by the revenant I lost all contact. It's as if Seth found some kind of shielded area."

"But there was no escape! You saw enough to know that."

"Which is why I'm perplexed," she said. "I know what I felt."

"You haven't sensed him since this morning?"

"True. He could be free, he could be dead, though dead would be a reckless assumption. My instincts tell me something unforeseeable has happened."

"Are you sure you don't want to send the imps out hunting for him and Kendra?" Errol asked.

"Not yet," Vanessa said. "Once the imps pass out of the yard they will not be able to return. If we find the register, that would change things. We mustn't take unnecessary risks. There's too much at stake. I want the imps on guard until we resolve how to handle the revenant. Kendra will surely return to try to help her grandparents. If we are patient and keep careful watch, she will come to us. And if not, she will have to sleep before long."

Kendra fought the urge to leap to her feet and shout at Vanessa. She reminded herself that getting caught would only make matters worse, no matter how satisfying an angry tirade might feel. Not to mention the awkward fact that she had no clothes on.

"You're sure she won't meet up with Hugo?" Errol asked.

"I sent Hugo to the farthest corner of Fablehaven with strict instructions to wait there for at least two weeks. The golem is out of the picture."

"Yet the problem of the revenant remains," Errol mused.

"We know the location, we have the key, we just need to get past the undead guardian," she said.

"Along with whatever traps protect the tower itself," Errol added.

"Naturally," she agreed. "Which is part of the reason I would hate to waste Dale on the revenant as well. I would like to use him to explore the tower."

Errol sat up. "Then send Stan or Ruth."

"Or when Kendra falls asleep I can send her," Vanessa said. "But I don't want to send anyone until we have a strategy to remove the nail."

"Can't you divorce yourself from the situation?" Errol said. "Just focus on the consoling fact that you are not actually in the grove, that you're just using someone else as a puppet."

"You'd have to sample the fear to understand," she said. "It is overwhelming and irrational. It left me utterly paralyzed both times. There is no room for creating intellectual distance. All I intended to do when I was inhabiting Tanu was get a look at the creature and run away, but I lost all bodily control. It poses quite a problem."

"Perhaps it would do us good to sleep on it," he said.

"That may be your best idea of the evening," Vanessa said.

Errol got to his feet. All he had to do was notice that the sofa was pushed a little farther away from the wall than usual, look behind it, and see Kendra lying there utterly exposed. He picked up his shoes. Not five feet away the invisible presence of Seth remained dutifully motionless.

Kendra heard somebody else entering the room. "Still no sign of activity," a raspy voice reported. It had to be one of the imps.

"Keep a sharp lookout, Grickst," Vanessa said. "I would not be surprised if Kendra tried to slip into the house under the cover of darkness."

Kendra could hear Grickst sniffing. "Their stink is everywhere," he said. "If I didn't know better, I'd say they were right here in this room, the girl and her brother."

"They have been, for days on end," Errol said. "Don't forget the scent. Keep your nostrils open. Kendra will be getting sleepy and desperate by now."

"That will be all, Grickst," Vanessa said. "We are going to turn in. Tell Hulro and Zirt to raise the alarm at any sign of either of the children. Otherwise you can refrain from reporting until sunrise."

"Very well," Grickst said. Kendra heard him leaving. Vanessa and Errol were walking away as well.

"Really is a fine house," Errol remarked. "I rather enjoy lounging in Stan's bed."

Kendra could hear them climbing the stairs.

"The shorter our stay, the better," Vanessa said. "Keep alert. We'll finalize our plans in the morning."

Kendra waited quietly, listening to the sounds of Vanessa and Errol moving around on the floor above. She heard a toilet flush, and then the sound of water running in a sink. "We just need to be patient," Seth whispered.

"Yeah," Kendra said. "Wait for them to settle down."

"Do you think Errol is Christopher Vogel?" Seth asked.

"If they haven't found the register yet, that seems like the only explanation," she said. "It must be his real name."

"I'll be right back," Seth said.

Before she could protest, he was creeping away. He returned shortly wearing Grandpa's white bathrobe. He tossed a sheet over the back of the couch, and Kendra wrapped herself in it. "These were in the study," he whispered. "The cot is still a mess. Nobody will miss the sheet, even if they look. Back in a sec."

Seth exited the room again. He did not return for a few minutes. When he finally came back, he said, "I checked out the windows. There are two imps on the back porch, and a big fat one out front. The sides of the house look unguarded. If you slip out through the study window, you might be able to sneak into the woods."

"We should wait and make a break for it together," she said. "Nobody is going to look behind the couch between now and when you steal the keys."

"How long do you think we should wait?" he asked.

"Longer than you think," Kendra said. "The clock on the wall says 10:47. I say we wait a full hour before you go upstairs, just to be safe."

"In that case, I'm going to make a sandwich."

"No way," Kendra said firmly.

"All I've eaten for two days is cocoon pulp," he said.

"You had snacks at Warren's," she said.

"Right, snacks. I wasn't that hungry then. Now I feel like my stomach is digesting itself."

"If they hear you rustling around, we could all die. There's plenty of food at the cabin. I say wait."

"What if they end up catching us?" Seth asked. "Then we'll be stuck eating glop! Did you smell that stuff?"

"If we get caught, we'll have bigger problems than what to eat."

"I bet I could make a sandwich about ten times quieter than you whisper," he accused.

"Are you trying to make me angry?"

"Are you trying to make me hungry?"

"Fine," Kendra said. "Go make a sandwich. We've got an hour, maybe you can bake some cupcakes too."

"I've got a better idea. I'll make us smoothies in the blender. With lots of ice."

"I wouldn't be surprised."

"Fine. You know what? You win, Kendra. I'll sit here and starve."

"Good. Starve quietly."

Time crawled. Seth spent most of the hour sitting

invisibly on the couch. Kendra tried to picture what escape route she would use if things went bad. Eventually the hour passed.

"Can I go get the keys?" Seth asked.

"Do we need more of a plan?" Kendra said.

"My plan is to be really quiet and bring the keys downstairs," Seth said.

"And then only one of us should go to the basement, so at least one of us can get away," she said. "We don't want to both get trapped down there."

"Okay. What if somebody wakes up and sees me?" Seth asked.

"Run for it," Kendra said. "I'll play it by ear. Just because they see you won't mean they'll know *I'm* in the house. Maybe I can lie low and save the day after things settle down."

"Or maybe somebody else will save the day for a change," Seth said. "Besides, if they find me I bet they'll search the house."

"Where's the best hiding place on this floor?"

"If I were you, I'd hide in the study, like behind the desk. You'll have quick access to a window that will take you outside. Going out through the side should give you a chance to avoid the imps. If they catch me, you should probably take off. Maybe you can leave the preserve and try to find the Sphinx."

"We'll see," Kendra said.

"Wish me luck. Hopefully my growling stomach won't give me away."

Wrapped in her sheet, Kendra walked to the entry hall with her brother. As he started climbing the stairs, staying close to the wall and treading lightly, she went to the study. She unlocked the window and squatted behind the desk. She noticed a letter opener on top of a pile of papers. She picked it up. It felt comforting to have some sort of weapon in her grasp.

All she could do now was wait. Maybe she should be the one wearing the glove and creeping into Vanessa's room. Seth would never have let her, since sneaking around was more his specialty. But it was an awful lot of responsibility to give to somebody who liked sticking French fries in his nostrils.

❧ ❧ ❧

At the top of the stairs, Seth moved stealthily down the hall to Vanessa's door. A light had been left on in the bathroom, so the hall was fairly bright. The door to Vanessa's room was closed. There was no light shining underneath it. Cupping his ear against the door, he waited invisibly, but heard nothing.

Gently he turned the knob. It made a faint clicking sound, and he paused. After several slow breaths, he turned the knob the rest of the way and eased the door open. The room was darker and more shadowy than the hall, but he could still see fairly well. Vanessa was lying on her side on the bed beneath her sheet. The blankets were folded at the foot of the bed. Containers full of strange animals were everywhere.

Seth took a slow step toward her bed. A low croak disturbed the silence. Seth froze, turning invisible. Vanessa did not stir. Apparently she was accustomed to animal sounds in the night. That should work in his favor.

Her bed was on the far side of the room. He decided that instead of crossing the center of the room, he would work his way along the perimeter. That way if she woke up, there would be less chance of her accidentally bumping into him.

Seth crept along the edge of the room taking small, quiet steps. The sheet did not cover Vanessa's shoulders, so he could see that she had not changed out of her clothes. Staring at her, he had a hard time picturing her as a traitor. She was so pretty, her dark hair spilling over her pillow.

Seth glimpsed a metal pole under her chin. It had to be the artifact key! She was sleeping right on top of it!

A bird chirped and he halted, watching the narcoblix intently. Satisfied that she remained asleep, he worked his way along the wall, passing numerous cages. Vanessa was facing him. All she needed to do was open her eyes while he was moving and all would be lost. Finally he reached the nightstand beside her bed. Her blowgun lay on the nightstand, along with three small darts. What if he picked up a dart and pricked her? Did narcoblixes have immunity to sleeping potions? It wasn't worth the risk. But he picked up a tiny dart anyhow, for backup.

Another step closer and he was standing over Vanessa. If she stretched out her hand she could touch him. If he reached out his hand he could touch her. There was no way he could get to the artifact key. She was partly on top of it. He would have to wait for her to shift positions.

While he waited, he scanned the room for the dungeon keys. There were many surfaces where they could be resting, on top of cages or terrariums as well as on tables or dressers. He did not see them anywhere. They could be in her pocket. Or tucked away in a secret spot. Or Errol might have them.

Vanessa continued to breathe evenly, showing no sign that she would ever change positions. Maybe narcoblixes were really deep sleepers. She might not move all night. There was simply no possible way he could slide the long key out from under her without waking her up. Most of it was under the sheet with her.

Seth noticed a box of tissues on the nightstand. He removed a tissue. It made a slight sound as he pulled it from the box, but Vanessa did not twitch. Seth stared at the tissue, but it vanished along with the rest of him as he held still.

Wiggling his hand, he stared again at the tissue, figuring out the best way to let it hang. This would be risky. He might very well wake Vanessa up. But he had to make her shift positions. She showed no sign of budging on her own.

Leaning forward, Seth moved the dangling tissue toward her face. Slowly but surely it came closer, until a corner of the tissue brushed her nose. Vanessa smacked her lips and scratched her face. Seth jerked his hand away and held still. Vanessa twisted her head back and forth, hummed softly, and then her regular breathing resumed. She did not alter her position. The key remained mostly beneath her.

Seth waited for a long time. Then he leaned forward with the tissue and again let it gently brush her nose. Vanessa snatched the tissue and her eyes opened suddenly. She had been waiting for it this time! Seth froze, his invisible hand less than a foot from her face. She glanced at the tissue, squinted in Seth's direction, then turned to look the other way. When she looked away, Seth jerked his hand back, flickering momentarily into view. Fortunately her eyes were not on him. It reminded him of playing Red Light—Green Light when he was younger. He and Kendra had to sneak up on their dad while his back was to them. If he caught them moving when he turned around, they got sent back to the start. The stakes were higher, but the game was the same.

Vanessa sat up. "Who's there?" she asked, eyes darting around the room. She looked straight through Seth several times. "Errol?" she called loudly, reaching for her blowgun. On the way to her blowgun, the side of her arm brushed against Seth. She yanked her hand back. "Errol!" she yelled, kicking the sheet off of her.

Striking quickly, Seth jabbed the tiny dart he was holding into her arm. Her eyes widened in surprise when he flashed into view, but she had no time to react. She had been rising out of bed, but instead she hesitated, lips compressed, and then collapsed heavily to the floor. Seth grabbed the long key off the bed. It was quite heavy, and several inches taller than him. He was glad to see that it disappeared along with him when he held still.

Seth could hear Errol thumping down the hall. He leapt away from the bed and stood still as Errol raced through the doorway and saw Vanessa on the floor. "Intruder!" Errol shouted.

Seth realized that Errol would probably suspect he had already fled, so he held perfectly still. Errol briefly surveyed the room, then ran out into the hall. Seth heard the front door opening downstairs, followed by heavy footfalls on the stairs. Would the imp smell him? What should he do?

He heard a door downstairs slam shut. The imp on the stairs grunted urgently. Seth heard Errol dashing down the hall. "In the study!" he shouted. "Bring the intruder to me!"

Seth heard Errol racing down the stairs. Kendra had created a diversion, but now she would have everybody right on her heels. Seth didn't like her chances. Leaning the key by the door, he picked up a terrarium full of dark blue salamanders and ran down the hall. He could hear them ramming the door to the study.

From the top of the stairs, Seth heaved the terrarium over the banister into the entry hall. He did not stay to watch it hit the floor, but he heard glass shattering like a bomb and Errol shouting. Seth hastily retreated to Vanessa's room. Picking up the key, he crossed the room, unlocked the window, and threw it open.

Vanessa's room was above the back porch. Seth dove through the window onto the roof of the porch. He could only hope that the commotion had already brought the imps stationed on the porch into the house. Otherwise he was about to be caught. He closed the window, hoping his pursuers might not be sure where he had gone. For all they knew he could have retreated to any of the rooms, or even gone up to the attic.

He heard Kendra screaming for Mendigo from the side of the house. She sounded desperate. Seth hurried to the edge of the porch roof. The porch was raised above the level of the yard, so even the lowest part of the porch roof was a good ten feet above the ground.

Seth tossed the key onto the grass. Then he found a portion of the roof that stuck out over a thick bush. Turning and crouching, he grabbed the lip of the roof and stepped off, hoping to dangle before dropping. The weight of his body was too much, and he lost his grip, falling awkwardly on his side, but landing in the bush.

Hitting the bush sideways turned out to be a lucky way to fall. He mashed the bush down, and it absorbed the brunt of the impact. Shaken, heart racing, Seth rolled out of the bush, picked up the key, and sprinted for the woods, his oversized bathrobe flapping behind him.

✺　✺　✺

After waiting in tense silence, Kendra knew they were in trouble when Vanessa started calling for Errol. She opened the window so she would be ready for a quick exit. Then Errol yelled about an intruder, and she realized Seth had not been caught. She heard the front door open and the imp charge up the stairs.

She had to create a distraction. Kendra ran to the study door, opened it, and banged it shut. She locked it and rushed to the window, wishing she had more to wear than a sheet. She put her legs through first, so she was sitting on the windowsill, then turned around and boosted herself backwards. Her bare feet sank into the rich, soft soil of a flowerbed. She dropped the letter opener in the process.

Through the window, she could hear somebody beating on the study door. Wood splintered as the door was rammed with greater force. Not bothering to look for the letter opener, Kendra started running across the grass toward the woods. She heard a tremendous crash behind her from inside the house, like a huge vase shattering. Glancing back, she still saw nobody in the study window.

On the manicured lawn her bare feet did not impede her speed. In fact, she was pretty sure this was the fastest she had ever run, energized by sheer terror. In the woods it would be another story.

She heard something growl behind her. Looking back, she saw a thin, wiry imp in pursuit, having apparently just come through the window. She was about halfway across the yard to the woods, but the imp was running fast.

"Mendigo," Kendra screamed. "Meet me in the woods and protect me from the imps! Mendigo, hurry!"

Off to her left, Kendra noticed the mellow glow of some fairies, bobbing and weaving in a colorful cluster. "Fairies, please stop the imp!" Kendra called. The fairies stopped moving, as if they were now watching, but did not come to her aid.

At the fringe of the yard, a few paces from the woods, Kendra glanced back again. The wiry imp had gained, but remained twenty paces behind her. Behind the wiry imp, Kendra saw an extremely fat imp scrambling through the window. He barely fit, and fell headfirst into the flowerbed.

Facing forward, Kendra dashed into the outskirts of the woods. "Mendigo!" she cried again. Sharp rocks and sticks jabbed at her bare feet. She crunched through leaves and undergrowth. In some places the ground was squishy.

She heard the imp closing in behind her, snapping twigs and tromping through shrubs. Then she heard a rustling from off to one side. The wiry imp was now only about five paces behind her. Kendra had no hope of outrunning him. She heard footfalls from the same direction she had heard the rustling, only nearer now. Some nearby bushes parted, and Mendigo appeared.

A bundle hit Kendra in the chest, and it took her a moment to realize that it was her and Seth's clothes along with Tanu's pouch. Mendigo took flight, launching himself in a flying tackle that leveled the thin imp just a couple of paces from Kendra. They tussled on the ground.

"Mendigo, stop the imp," Kendra said. "But don't kill him."

Looking back toward the yard, Kendra could see that the lumbering, obese imp had almost reached the trees. Mendigo had wrapped up the wiry imp in what looked like a complex wrestling hold. Clutching the bundle of clothes, Kendra tried to decide her next move. What would happen when the fat imp reached them? He was much bigger than the wiry imp. Maybe she could outrun him; he was certainly slower. Neither was the same imp Kendra had seen in the dungeon. Of the three, the imp in the dungeon was the most muscular and looked the most dangerous.

Something else was crashing toward her through the woods from the opposite direction Mendigo had come from. After a moment, she saw that the something was wearing a bathrobe. "Seth!" she cried.

He was carrying a metal staff that had to be the artifact key. He looked at Mendigo wrestling on the ground and then at the rapidly approaching fat imp. "Mendigo," Seth ordered, "break his arms."

"What?" Kendra exclaimed.

"We have to stop them somehow," Seth said.

Mendigo shifted his grip, placing a wooden knee against the wiry imp's back, and then wrenched one of the imp's arms into an awkward position and jerked it briskly. Kendra looked away, but heard the hideous snap. The imp howled. A second crunch followed.

"Mendigo," Seth said, "break his legs, then do the same to the other imp." Kendra heard more disgusting sounds.

She opened her eyes. The wiry imp was writhing on the ground, limbs askew, and the fat imp had almost reached them, plowing through the undergrowth. Mendigo rushed to meet the fat imp. The oversized puppet dodged a punch and flung himself at the creature. The fat imp caught Mendigo in the air and hurled him aside.

Up close, Kendra realized that this imp was not only much broader and thicker than the other imp, he was at least a head taller. Mendigo, scuttling on all fours, dove at the imp's legs, trying to trip him. The big imp stomped at him, then seized Mendigo and slammed him into a tree. One of the puppet's arms came unhinged and spun to the ground.

Seth, who had been invisible, suddenly appeared and bashed the imp in the side of the head with the key. The huge imp staggered sideways and dropped to his knees, releasing Mendigo. The puppet hastily retrieved his arm. The massive imp turned and rose, wheezing, rubbing the side of his head, and glaring with furious eyes. Seth held still, invisible once again.

"Mendigo," Seth said, "use this key to hurt the big imp." Seth flashed into view as he tossed the metal staff to Mendigo. The imp rushed at Seth, but Mendigo sprang into action, swinging the key with much more force than Seth had been able to muster.

The imp raised an arm to block the blow, but his forearm buckled on impact. Whirling, Mendigo clubbed the imp's bulging belly, and then whacked him across the shoulders when he doubled over.

"Mendigo," Seth said, "break his legs, but don't kill him."

The puppet set about bludgeoning the fallen imp, quickly hobbling him. "That's enough, Mendigo," Kendra said. "Only hurt them more if they keep after us."

"You're going to pay for this," the wiry imp snarled through clenched teeth, glaring fiercely at Kendra.

"You asked for it," Kendra said. "Mendigo, pick us up and get us away from the yard as fast as you can."

"And don't lose the key," Seth added.

Mendigo hoisted Kendra over one shoulder and slung Seth over the other. The puppet ran away from the scene faster than either Kendra or Seth had seen him run before.

"Mendigo," Kendra said softly after they had left the crippled imps behind, "take us to back to the cottage as quickly as you can."

"Did you say the cottage?" Seth asked.

"There's another imp, and he looked like the worst of the three," Kendra said.

"Right, but won't they look in the cottage?" Seth asked.

"Imps can't enter the cottage," Kendra reminded him.

"All right," Seth said. "I knocked Vanessa out with one of her own darts."

"Then they probably won't be after us right away. Mendigo, if somebody chases us and gets close, put us down and beat them with the key."

Mendigo showed no sign that he heard, but Kendra felt sure he had. He continued at a tireless sprint. She did not mind the branches whipping past her and tearing at her sheet. It was much preferable to running barefoot.

CHAPTER EIGHTEEN

Diverging Plans

Kendra and Seth sat at the table with Warren. Seth was finishing a second peanut butter and honey sandwich. Kendra was dumping lemonade powder into a pitcher full of water. She stirred the mixture with a wooden spoon.

The key lay on the table. It was mostly smooth, fashioned out of a dull gray metal. One end had a grip like the hilt of a sword. The other end had little notches and grooves and irregular protuberances. Kendra and Seth could only assume that the complicated end was meant to be inserted into an intricate keyhole.

Outside in the night, Mendigo stood watch, clutching a hoe in one hand and a rusty cowbell in the other. He was under orders to raise the alarm with the bell if any strangers approached, and then to use the hoe to cripple any imps or people who came along.

"We can't stay here," Seth said.

"I know," Kendra replied, pouring lemonade into a glass. "Do you want some?"

"Sure," Seth said. "I have a plan."

Kendra started filling a second glass. "I'm listening."

"I say we go back to the grove, get past the revenant, use the key, and retrieve the artifact."

Kendra took a sip from one of the glasses. "Just barely too strong," she said.

Seth picked up the other glass and took a drink. "A little weak, if you ask me."

"What is your plan again?" Kendra asked, rubbing her eyes. "I'm so tired, I feel like I can barely concentrate."

"We should go after the artifact," Seth restated.

"And how do we get past the revenant? I thought it totally froze you."

Seth held up a finger. "I already figured it out. See, we have that courage potion in Tanu's pouch. You know, the bottled-up emotion. I think if I take a big enough dose, the courage will counteract the fear from the zombie."

Kendra sighed. "Seth, he has to mix in all sorts of stuff to get the emotions to balance each other out right."

"The fear from the revenant will balance it out plenty. You heard Vanessa and Errol. I just have to pull out the nail. I know I can do it!"

"What if you can't?"

Seth shrugged. "If I can't, I end up an albino like the others, and you'll have to make a new plan."

"After everything that has happened, do you think the riskiest plan imaginable is the best way to go?"

"Unless you have a better one."

Kendra shook her head and wiped her hands down her face. She felt so weary that it was tough to focus. But obviously they couldn't just charge off and battle a revenant and then try to survive all the traps guarding the inverted tower. There had to be better alternatives.

"I'm waiting," Seth said.

"I'm thinking," Kendra said. "It's what some people do *before* they talk. Let's consider the other options besides deliberate suicide. We could hide. I'm not wild about that option, because it just prolongs an actual decision, and I'm not going to be able to keep awake much longer."

"You have circles under your eyes," Seth said.

"We could attack. They only have one imp left. Mendigo is a pretty tough fighter. If he had a weapon, he could maybe take out their last imp, and then beat up Errol and Vanessa."

"*If* we can lure them all out of the yard," Seth said. "Which I doubt will happen. After they find the injured imps, they'll be careful. You never know, they might have other tricks up their sleeves. Vanessa could come after us as Dale, for example."

"I hadn't thought of that," Kendra admitted. "Do you think she's doing that right now?"

"I would be," Seth said. "And this is the first place I would look."

"What if Dale shows up and Mendigo hurts him?" Kendra wondered.

"At this point, if Dale shows up, Mendigo better hurt him. His legs will heal."

"We should probably leave Fablehaven," Kendra said. "Escape and find the Sphinx."

"How? You have his phone number? Know where he hides out?"

Kendra rubbed the side of her head.

Seth looked at her adamantly. "And guess who is probably waiting on the driveway just outside those gates? Your friend the kobold. And that big monster made of hay. And about a zillion other members of the Society of the Evening Star, guarding the gates in case somebody tries to do exactly what you're saying. And probably hoping Vanessa figures out how to let them in."

"Do you have a better idea?" Kendra huffed.

"I told you a better idea. They won't be expecting it."

Kendra shook her head. "Seth, even Tanu and Coulter weren't sure how they were going to get past the traps in the tower. Even if you could defeat the revenant, we'd never make it to the artifact."

Seth got up out of his chair. "Outside of Fablehaven, the Society of the Evening Star can send everybody they have after us. We wouldn't last five minutes. In here, they only have Vanessa, Errol, and that imp. Either way is dangerous. But I'd rather take a risk trying to fix everything than take a risk running away."

"Running for help," Kendra stressed.

"You didn't run away when you went to the Fairy Queen," Seth reminded her.

"That was different," she said. "You and Grandma and Grandpa were about to die for sure, and I had nobody to help me. If I had run away, I would have been abandoning you. I knew I could save you if the Fairy Queen was willing to help me."

"And if we get the artifact we can save Grandma and Grandpa," Seth said. "It probably has powers we can use."

"Nobody even knows what it does," Kendra said.

"It does something. They're all supposed to be really powerful, letting us control time or space and stuff like that. You didn't know exactly what the Fairy Queen could do. You just knew she was powerful. Whatever the artifact is, at least it would give us a chance. Would you rather go hide under a log? In the morning, we'd be no better off than we are right now."

"At least we wouldn't be dead."

"I'm not so sure," Seth said. "All it takes is one of us falling asleep, and we'll be in all sorts of trouble."

"I'm not saying we hide under a log. I say we bring Mendigo, and take our chances trying to find the Sphinx. We don't have to use the driveway; we can climb the gate and loop way around, stay out of sight. There's a better probability we'll succeed."

"How is there a better chance? We have no idea what is waiting outside the gates! We have no idea where the Sphinx is! We don't even know if he's still alive!"

Kendra folded her arms. "He's been alive for hundreds of years and all of a sudden he gets killed?"

"Maybe. These artifacts have been hidden for hundreds of years and all of a sudden they're being found."

"You're exhausting," Kendra said.

"That's what you say when I'm right!" Seth said.

"It's what I say when you won't shut up." Kendra stood. "I have to use the bathroom."

"First tell me we'll go after the artifact."

"No way, Seth. We're leaving the preserve."

"I've got it," Seth said. "How about you leave, and I go get the artifact?"

"Sorry, Seth. I thought you were dead once. I'm not going to lose you now."

"It makes sense," he said with more conviction. "I go after the artifact, you go after help. Both might be long shots, but both only require one of us."

Kendra's hands clenched into fists. "Seth, I'm about to lose it. Enough about going after the artifact. It's crazy. Can't you tell when an idea is doomed? Are you programmed to self-destruct? We're sticking together, and we're leaving Fablehaven. There might not even be anybody on guard out there. You're just guessing. We'll be careful, but our best bet is somehow finding the Sphinx. Hopefully he's already looking for us."

"Fine, you're right," he said curtly.

Kendra wasn't sure how to respond. "You think?"

"It doesn't matter what I think," Seth said. "The fairy princess has spoken."

"You're a jerk," she said.

"Then I can't win," Seth said. "I'm a jerk if I agree, I'm crazy if I don't."

"It's *how* you agree," she said. "Can I go to the bathroom now?"

"Apparently you get to do whatever you want," Seth said.

Kendra walked to the bathroom. He was being unreasonable. Going after the artifact was insanity. If they were seasoned adventurers like Tanu, it might be a risk worth taking. But they knew nothing. It was a certain recipe for disaster. Running away from Fablehaven was scary too, but at least those dangers weren't guaranteed. The revenant was there for sure, and so were the traps guarding the artifact.

Kendra massaged her temples, trying to clear her mind. She always got muddled when she was overtired. Part of her didn't want to leave the bathroom. As soon as she rejoined Seth, they would have to run off into the night with Mendigo and flee the preserve. All she wanted to do was curl up and go to sleep.

Kendra washed her hands and splashed water on her face. Reluctantly she returned to the main room. Warren sat alone at the table. "Seth?" she called.

The potion pouch was open. The key was gone. A note sat on the table, with the invisibility glove beside it. Kendra hurried to the note.

Kendra,

I took Mendigo and am going after the artifact. I will send him back once he takes me to the grove.

Don't be mad.

Keep a good lookout and lie low until Mendigo gets back. Then go find the Sphinx. I left you the glove.

Love,

Seth

Kendra reread the note in stunned disbelief. She threw it down and ran outside. How long had she been in the bathroom? Pretty long. She had been thinking, and taking her time. Ten minutes? More?

Dared she yell for Mendigo? The night was quiet. A crescent moon was rising. The stars were clear and bright. She heard nothing. If she ordered Mendigo back, would he hear? Would he come? Surely Seth had commanded the giant puppet not to heed any orders from her to return. And since she had told Mendigo to obey Seth, the puppet probably saw their authority as equal, and would obey Seth's preemptive command.

By now, they were probably out of earshot anyway. Mendigo would be even faster carrying only one passenger.

How could Seth be so selfish? She considered going after him, but had no idea which direction he had gone. If she knew where the farthest corner of Fablehaven was, she would go search for Hugo, but again, she would be wandering blind. Seth was going to get killed, and while Mendigo was gone, somebody would probably show up and capture her as well.

Should she hide inside the house, or outside? If they sent the imp, inside would be foolproof. But they knew the imp would not be able to enter the cottage, so if they sent somebody, it would probably be Dale or someone else controlled by Vanessa. Which meant Kendra should find a good hiding place outside the cottage and lie low until Mendigo returned. The glove would help conceal her.

She ran back into the house to get Tanu's bag and the glove. Warren looked at her, smiling vaguely. He had no idea what was going on. In a way, she envied him.

※　※　※

Seth had discovered that riding Mendigo piggyback was considerably more comfortable than being slung over his shoulder. He had also discovered that Mendigo could run notably faster carrying only one person. In one hand Mendigo held the key, in the other, the courage potion.

Seth had ordered Mendigo to go to the covered bridge, and then to proceed onward to the valley surrounded by four hills. He could only hope the puppet understood where he meant. Mendigo seemed to be running purposefully, so at least the puppet had some destination in mind. Seth had also ordered Mendigo to disregard any instructions from Kendra until he sent him back to her. He had also directed Mendigo to quietly point out any humans or imps that came near them. He hoped the chances were slim of meeting up with any of his enemies in the woods, but it was possible the imp or others were out hunting them.

The crescent moon gave off enough light that Seth could see fairly well, even without special fairy vision. He had found a flashlight in a cupboard at the cottage, so he had insurance that he would be able to see his adversary in the grove. He had also commandeered a pair of pliers that he had noticed in the tool closet when they had grabbed the hoe for Mendigo.

Before too long Mendigo was clomping across the covered bridge. It had been only two nights ago that Hugo had carried Seth and Coulter along this same route to the same destination. This time Seth would be prepared. That revenant had looked pretty flimsy. With the courage potion to counteract the fear, he should have a good chance.

Back under the trees, Seth lost all sense of where they were headed, and had to trust that Mendigo knew the way. "Get us to the valley with the four hills, Mendigo," Seth said softly. "And be careful with the bottle you're holding. Don't let it get damaged."

They rushed along in silence until Mendigo suddenly veered and slowed, heading toward a clearing. Seth was about to reprimand the puppet when he saw that Mendigo was pointing. The puppet came to a stop behind a bush. Looking in the direction indicated by the wooden finger, Seth saw a silhouetted form slowly walking in the clearing.

Who was it? He was big. Was it Kendra's imp? No, it was Tanu!

Seth burst from hiding and ran into the clearing. Tanu

continued shuffling along, oblivious to Seth's approach. Seth ran up to Tanu and stared in amazement. Seeing Warren and Coulter as albinos was one thing. Seeing the large Samoan, whose skin had been so dark, was another. Illuminated by the ghostly moonlight, his pallid skin and white hair were shocking.

"Hey, Tanu," Seth said. "Anybody home?"

The big Samoan trudged languidly forward, offering no hint of acknowledgment. Seth looked back at Mendigo. He hated the thought of leaving Tanu to roam the woods, but Warren had showed up back at the house after he became an albino. At least Tanu appeared to be generally heading in the right direction.

The reality was, time was too short, and his mission too urgent, for Seth to do much for Tanu at the moment. Kendra was back at the cottage nearly defenseless. He needed to get to the grove and send Mendigo back to her.

"Mendigo, come get me. Let's keep going to the valley with the four hills, fast as you can." Mendigo raced to him, and Seth climbed on his back. The puppet started running. "But if we come near any other imps or humans, still point them out without giving us away."

Seth glanced back over his shoulder at Tanu making his way across the clearing. At that rate, even if he walked in the right direction the whole way, he would not reach the house for a day or two. Hopefully everything would be happily resolved by then.

Once again, Seth was crashing through the darkness. He was pretty sure Hugo had gotten them to the valley more rapidly. Just when he was about to despair that they would ever reach the grove, they emerged from a thick stand of trees and Seth recognized that they were in the brush-filled valley surrounded by the familiar hills.

Mendigo slowed to a walk. "Mendigo, take me to the grove at that end of the valley," Seth said, gesturing toward their destination. Mendigo started trotting. "Fast as you can." Mendigo sped up.

As the grove drew nearer, Seth contemplated how much he was betting on the potency of the courage potion. The fear potion had made him very afraid, but it was hardly a shiver when compared to the terror radiating from the revenant. Of course, he had sampled only a drop or two of the fear potion, with some other ingredients mixed in to dilute it. He would down a much bigger dose of pure courage, and bring the bottle with him so he could chug more if needed.

Mendigo stopped near the edge of the grove. Seth estimated it was roughly the same place Hugo had stopped. "Mendigo, go just a few steps closer to the trees," Seth urged.

The puppet took several steps, but did not move forward. He was walking in place. Seth slid off of Mendigo, dropping to the ground. "Mendigo, walk into the grove." The puppet appeared to be trying to comply, but instead took more steps without advancing.

"Forget it, Mendigo. Hand me the key and the potion." The puppet obeyed. "Mendigo, return to Kendra as fast as you can." Mendigo started running off, so Seth shouted after him to finish his instructions, cupping his hands around his mouth. "If she's not at the cottage, or is in any trouble, rescue her. Hurt her enemies if they try to stop you. Obey her!"

Before Mendigo was out of sight, Seth turned to face the grove. Under the moon and the stars, the grove was brighter than it had been on his previous visit. Even so, he switched on the flashlight. It had a dimmer bulb than the light Coulter had used, but it still made a difference.

Standing alone in the dark, shining his dim flashlight at the ominous trees and their convoluted shadows, was not good for morale. Seth remembered Kendra's certainty that he would fail, and, alone under the stars, he suddenly felt she might be right.

Seth took a calming breath. This was what he wanted. This was why he had run away from Kendra. Sure, he was a little nervous now, but a good dose of courage would remedy the situation. And when the chilling fear of the revenant began to take hold, he would give himself another boost. He had to do this, just as Kendra had to go after the Sphinx. Both propositions were risky, but both were necessary.

Setting down the tall key, Seth unstopped the bottle and tipped it into his mouth. Even with the little bottle upended, the potion dripped out in a weak trickle. He shook the fluid into his mouth until he had emptied roughly a quarter of the contents.

The liquid burned. Once, in a Mexican restaurant, Seth had downed some hot sauce straight from the bottle on a dare from Kendra. It was brutal. He had to stuff his mouth with chips and guzzle water to stem the burning. This was worse—less taste, more stinging.

Seth coughed and swiped at his lips, eyes watering. His tongue felt like he had licked an iron, and his throat felt like a pincushion bristling with scalding needles. Tears leaked profusely down his cheeks. There was nothing to mute the burning, no water, no food. He had to wait it out.

As the painful sensation subsided, a warmth began to spread through his chest. He smirked at the dark trees. They seemed less intimidating. Had he actually been scared? Why, because it was dark? He had a flashlight. He knew exactly what was in there—a skinny ruin of a man so frail that he could flatten him with a sneeze. A creature so used to victims folding out of fear that it had probably lost all ability to contend with a real opponent.

Seth glanced at the long key. Between the flashlight and the potion and the pliers, his hands were full. The pliers went into a pocket, and he managed to hold the flashlight and the potion in the same hand, while grasping the key in the other. He marched across the space separating him from the grove, and soon found himself amid the trees. He was trying not to smile, but the grin would not go away. How had he been worried? How had he let Kendra's misgivings make him doubt for even a second? This would be absolute simplicity.

Pausing, he set down his things and began throwing punches to warm himself up. Wow, he hadn't realized how fast his right had gotten! His left was pretty good too. He was a machine! Maybe he would give the creature a free swing or two, just for fun. Toy with the freak before he put it out of its misery. Show the pathetic monstrosity exactly what happened to anything that traded blows with Seth Sorenson.

He retrieved his items and continued deeper into the grove. The air became steadily cooler. Seth shone his flashlight beam around, not wanting to give the revenant a chance to sneak up on him. Last time Seth had been helplessly frozen. This time he would dictate exactly how the encounter would go.

Seth began to notice an unusual numbness in his toes. It reminded him of the time he'd gone skiing in ski boots that were too small. He paused, stomping his feet, trying to restore sensation, but instead the numbness spread up his ankles. He started shivering. How had it gotten cold so quickly?

A flicker of motion caught his eye. Pivoting, Seth shone his flashlight at the approaching revenant. The creature was still a good distance away, barely visible through the trees.

The numbness had spread above his knees, and his fingers began to stiffen and feel rubbery. The deadening of his nerves sparked a trace of panic. Was he just going to go rigid without experiencing the same fear as before? Brave or not, if he became paralyzed, he would be in trouble. His vision blurred a little. His teeth chattered. He dropped the tall key.

Seth raised the bottle to his lips. Deciding he should consume all he could while still able, he downed all the remaining potion before tossing the bottle aside. The fluid did not feel as hot as before. Watching the sluggish advance of the revenant, Seth enjoyed the warmth that blossomed at his center and flowed outward, driving away the numbness. Pulling the pliers from his back pocket, he grinned.

No use waiting for the painfully slow zombie to reach him. Seth jogged toward the creature, the beam of his flashlight bobbing. As he got closer, the emaciated figure came into plain view, wearing the same filthy, tattered clothes. The yellow cast to the skin and weeping lesions made the wretch disgusting, but not scary. Sure, the thing was taller than him, but not by much, and it moved like it was on the verge of collapse.

Seth focused on the wooden nail protruding from the side of the revenant's neck. Pulling it out would almost be too easy. Seth wondered if he should do some karate moves to give the revenant a preview of things to come. He had never taken any lessons, but he had seen enough movies to have the general idea.

He stopped jogging about ten paces from the sickly zombie and performed a few fancy punches and a couple of kicks. The revenant kept slowly approaching, mouth twisted in an awful rictus, making no acknowledgment of the martial arts display. Seth flexed both arms, showing the revenant two good reasons to surrender.

The revenant raised an arm and pointed a bony finger at Seth. The shocking cold hit him as completely as if he had fallen into an icy lake. He gasped weakly and his muscles tightened. At his core there remained a warm, confident center, but it was being rapidly eroded. Irrational, gibbering

terror was assailing him at the fringes of his focus, trying to smother his self-assurance.

Part of him wanted to collapse and quail. Seth gritted his teeth. Potion or no potion, magical fear or no magical fear, he wasn't going to succumb, not this time. He willed himself to take a step toward the revenant. His leg refused to function at first. He was numb to the hip, and it felt like heavy weights were holding his foot down. Leaning forward and grunting, he managed a single ponderous step. Then another.

The revenant was still pointing at him, and still coming toward him. Seth knew he could just wait for the revenant to reach him, but something told him it was important to keep moving. He took another step.

The revenant was now within reach. The vaguely malevolent eyes held no personality. A putrid stench polluted the air. The arm of the revenant remained outstretched, and the pointing finger was nearly touching him.

Seth's confidence dwindled. He knew his body was about to shut down. He eyed the black, ragged fingernail drawing closer to his chest. The warm feeling had shrunk to a fading spark. Horrors began to fill his mind. Gripping the pliers tightly, Seth lifted his arm and, with a choppy motion, brought the pliers down on the bony finger. The revenant displayed no reaction to the blow, but the arm lowered a bit, and the finger had obviously been dislocated.

Teeth clenched, Seth fought against what felt like tremendous gravity to take a step to the side. Mustering all his strength, he kicked the revenant in the back of the knee.

The knee buckled and the revenant fell. Seth stumbled forward and knelt on its chest, feeling prominent ribs against his shins.

The revenant glared up at him. Seth could not move. His arms trembled. The final spark of confidence was dying. Seth could feel the deluge of irrational fear waiting to overwhelm him. In a moment it would. The revenant reached up, both hands moving slowly but purposefully toward Seth's neck.

Seth thought about all the people depending on him. Coulter had sacrificed himself for him. Kendra was alone in the cottage. His grandparents and Dale were trapped in a dungeon. He could do this. Courage was his thing. It didn't have to be fast. He just had to get there.

Seth focused on the nail and began moving the pliers toward it. He could not move quickly. It was as if the air had become a gel. If he tried to go fast, his progress halted. Pushing slowly and steadily, the hand with the pliers gradually advanced.

The hands of the revenant reached his throat. Fingers so cold they burned pressed into his flesh. The rest of his body was numb.

Seth didn't care. The pliers kept moving. Strong, merciless fingers squeezed his neck tighter. Seth gripped the wooden nail with the pliers. He tried to yank it out, but it would not budge.

Seth felt like he was drowning. The spark of confidence was gone, but grim determination remained. The only sensation was the searing pain in his neck. Ever so slowly, his arm feeling distant, hardly connected, Seth began withdrawing the nail, watching it slide out centimeter by centimeter. The nail was longer than he expected—it kept coming and coming, bloodlessly emerging from the hole it had long inhabited. His hand slowed. It felt like the air was congealing from a gel to a solid. The strangling grip of the revenant prevented him from breathing. Sweat beaded on his brow.

With dreamlike slowness, the last of the long wooden nail emerged from the neck. He saw a tiny space between the tip of the nail and the empty hole. For an instant, Seth thought he noticed something flicker across the revenant's face, relief in the eyes, the hideous smile becoming slightly more sincere.

And then the air was no longer solid, and he was falling, and everything went dark.

CHAPTER NINETEEN

The Inverted Tower

Wearing a blanket like a shawl, Kendra straddled a thick limb in a tree with a good view of the cottage. The night was just cool enough to make her glad for the blanket, which was currently invisible along with the rest of her. Before climbing to her current perch she had criss-crossed the area touching the boles of several other trees, in case an imp tried to track her scent.

Although she felt exhausted, her precarious position helped motivate her to keep alert. If she nodded off, she would fall about ten feet and receive a very rude awakening from the uncaring ground. She had spent the majority of her time astride the limb either furious at Seth or fretting about him. It was not fair that he had abandoned her and left her vulnerable, nor that he had taken action without consulting her. But she also realized that he was trying to do what he thought was right, and that he would probably pay a heavy price for his misguided bravery, which gave her a reason to rein in her unkind thoughts.

Tense and anxious, Kendra strained her eyes and ears for any sign of an enemy approaching, or of Mendigo returning. She was unsure how she would proceed once Mendigo reappeared. Even though it was too late to save Seth from his fate, a big part of her wanted to go after him rather than flee Fablehaven. At the same time, she knew that if she could find the Sphinx, it might be her best chance to rescue her grandparents and maybe even discover a way to restore Seth, Tanu, Coulter, and Warren from their albino states.

Waiting impatiently on the limb, Kendra was stunned to see Warren climb out onto the observation platform atop the cottage. She watched him in astounded silence as he stretched and rubbed his arms. The night was too dim for her to observe details, but he appeared to be moving about like a normal person.

"Warren!" she hissed.

He jumped and turned toward her. "Who's there?" he asked.

She was so surprised to hear him speak that it momentarily prevented her from answering. "You can talk! Oh my gosh! What happened?"

"Of course I can talk. I'm sorry—who are you?"

"I'm Kendra." She couldn't believe it. He seemed perfectly fine.

"I'm going to need a little more to go on." He squinted

in her direction. The night probably looked darker to him than it did to her, and of course she was invisible.

"I'm Kendra Sorenson. Stan and Ruth are my grand-parents."

"If you say so. What compelled you to hide in a tree in the middle of the night? Can you tell me how I got here?"

"Meet me at the back door," Kendra said. "I'll be there in a second." Warren had somehow been cured! She was no longer alone! She slid off the limb and climbed down from the tree. Taking off the glove, she walked out from among the trees and through the garden to the back door, where Warren met her.

Standing in the doorway, he studied her. He looked even more handsome now that he had possession of himself. His striking eyes were a silvery hazel. Had they been that color before? "It's you," he said in curious wonder. "I remember you."

"From when you were mute?" she asked.

"Was I mute? That's a first. Come inside."

Kendra entered. "You were a mute albino for a few years."

"Years?" he exclaimed. "What year is it?"

She told him and he looked flummoxed. They walked to the table in the main room.

He ran a white hand through his thick hair, then stared at his palm. "I thought I was looking sort of bleached," he said, flexing his fingers. "The last thing I remember was something coming toward me in the grove. It could have been yesterday. I was overcome by a panic like I had never known, and my mind withdrew to a dark place. I felt nothing there, hemmed in by pure terror, disconnected from my senses, retaining a groggy semblance of self-awareness. Near the end I saw you, wreathed in light. But it felt like hours lapsing, not days, certainly not years."

"You've been catatonic," Kendra said. "There is a revenant in the grove, and everybody who goes there ends up like you did."

"I haven't wasted away too terribly," he said, patting himself. "I feel a tad slimmer, but not withered like I should be after years in a coma."

"You could move around, but always in a daze," Kendra explained. "Your brother Dale made sure you got exercise. He took good care of you."

"Is he here?"

"He's locked in the dungeon with my grandparents," Kendra said. "The entire preserve is in danger. Members of the Society of the Evening Star have taken over the house. One of them is a narcoblix, so I've been awake for a couple of days straight. They are trying to get the artifact."

He raised his eyebrows. "You're saying there isn't going to be a Welcome-Back-from-Your-Coma Party?"

Kendra smiled. "Until we rescue the others, I'm all you get."

"Sooner or later, I want cake and ice cream. You mentioned the artifact. Do they know where it is?"

She nodded. "They weren't sure what to do about the revenant. My brother went to fight it. Since you're suddenly awake . . . I think he must have defeated it."

"Your brother?"

"My little brother," she said, suddenly rather proud of him. "He took off with the key to the tower and a crazy plan to use a courage potion to counteract the fear radiating from the revenant. I thought he was nuts, but it must have worked."

"He has the key to the inverted tower?" Warren asked.

"We stole it from Vanessa. She's the narcoblix."

"Your brother intends to enter the tower?"

"He wants to get the artifact before they do," Kendra said.

"How old is he?"

"Twelve."

Warren looked astonished. "What kind of training does he have?"

"Not much. I'm worried about him."

"You should be. If he goes into that tower alone, he will not emerge alive."

"Can we go after him?" Kendra asked.

"Sounds like we'd better." He dropped his gaze to his hands, shaking his head. "So now I'm albino? Don't stand too close; my luck might rub off. I set out, seems like yesterday, to retrieve the artifact. That was what led me to the grove. I knew a danger lurked there, but the overwhelming fear took me off guard. Now, after losing years of my life in a panic-induced trance, I get to pick up right where I left off."

"Why were you after the artifact?"

"It was a clandestine commission," Warren said. "We

had reason to believe the secret of Fablehaven might have been breached, so I was charged with removing and transferring the artifact."

"Who had you do that?"

Warren gave her a measuring stare. "I'm a member of a covert organization that combats the Society of the Evening Star. I can't say any more."

"The Knights of the Dawn?"

Warren tossed up his hands. "Nice. Who told you that?"

"Dale."

Warren shook his head. "Telling that guy a secret is like writing it across the sky. Anyhow, yes, we had reason to suspect Fablehaven had been discovered by the Society, and I was supposed to locate the artifact."

"Ready to finish what you started?"

"Why not? Looks like things fell apart around here without me. Time to put Humpty back together again. None of my gear is where I left it, but ill-equipped or not, we'd better hurry if we hope to catch your brother before he enters the tower. I take it Hugo isn't around."

"Vanessa sent him to the farthest corner of Fablehaven with orders to stay put," Kendra said.

"The stables are far enough from here that getting a horse will save us no time. I know the way to the valley. You up for a night hike?"

"Yes," she said. "Mendigo should return soon. He's an enchanted puppet the size of a man, and can help us get there faster."

"An enchanted puppet? You're not exactly an average teenager, are you? I bet you've got some stories to tell."

Kendra was pleased by the admiration in his voice, and hoped it wasn't showing on her face. Why was she thinking about the moment she had kissed him? She was suddenly very conscious of the way she was standing, and had no idea what to do with her hands. She had to stop noticing how cute he was. This was the wrong time for silly crushes! "One or two," she managed to say.

"I'm going to scavenge for equipment," Warren said, hurrying over to the cupboards.

"I have a glove that makes me invisible when I hold still," Kendra said. "And several magical potions, though I'm not sure what they do."

"Of course you do," he said, rifling through some drawers. "Where did you get all that?"

"The glove belonged to a man named Coulter."

"Coulter Dixon?" he asked urgently. "Why do you speak of him in the past tense?"

"He became a mute albino like you. Which probably means he's fine now, except that he's locked up in the dungeon with Dale."

"Jackpot!" Warren announced.

"What?"

"Cookies." He stuck one in his mouth. "What about the potions?"

"A guy named Tanu. He's a former mute albino too now, but I don't know where he is."

"I've heard of Tanu the potion master," Warren said. "Never met him."

Just then Kendra heard a faint jingling of hooks. She ran to the front door. Mendigo came to a halt beside the porch. "Our ride is here," Kendra said.

"One minute," Warren called. He returned promptly with a coil of rope looped over one shoulder and an ax in his hand. "Best weapon I could find," he said, hefting the ax.

"Mendigo can carry us," she said. "He's stronger than he looks."

"That may be, but we'll travel faster if I run alongside. Off we go, then."

"Mendigo," Kendra said. "Carry me to the place you just took Seth, fast as you can. And don't lose Warren." She pointed at Warren for emphasis. She scrambled up onto Mendigo's back and they set off at a brisk pace.

Warren did a good job keeping up at first, but he was nearly running at a full sprint, and before long he was gasping and wheezing. Kendra ordered Mendigo to carry him as well, and Warren consented. "I don't have the wind I used to, or the legs," he apologized.

Warren was considerably bigger than Seth or Kendra, and Mendigo did not run quite as speedily while carrying him. Occasionally Warren insisted on running for a minute or two, trying to maximize their pace.

The night wore on. At last they reached the valley. The stars in the east were growing faint as the sky began to pale. Mendigo soon reached the unseen boundary that he could not cross.

"He can't enter the grove, just like Hugo," Warren remarked. "If Hugo had been with me that night, I would not have lost those years."

"Set us down, Mendigo," Kendra said. "Guard the grove from all intruders."

"What have we here?" Warren murmured, stooping and examining the ground.

"What?" Kendra said.

"I think your brother was here. Follow me." Warren jogged toward the trees, clutching the ax.

Kendra rushed to keep up. "Could there be other dangers in the grove?" she asked.

"Doubtful," Warren said. "This has been the revenant's domain since the hiding of the artifact and the founding of Fablehaven. Few would dare tread this cursed ground."

"Wait a second," Kendra said. "Here's Seth's emergency kit. He lost it the first time he came to the grove." Kendra retrieved the cereal box from where it lay.

"First time?" Warren asked.

"Long story," Kendra said.

"Look here," Warren said. "The key. Your brother is not inside the tower. He's probably injured or spent. We'd better hurry."

They trotted through the trees. Warren held the ax in one hand, the key in the other. "What's that up ahead?" Warren said. "A flashlight?"

Kendra saw the glow as well, low to the ground. As they hurried nearer, she saw that it was indeed a fallen flashlight. Gauging by the faintness of the bulb, the batteries were nearly depleted. Beside the flashlight lay a skeleton clad in rags. And atop the skeleton lay her brother, facedown.

Warren knelt beside Seth, felt his wrist for a pulse, and rolled him over. One of Seth's hands remained closed around a pair of pliers that held nothing. The flashlight revealed ugly mottled marks on Seth's throat. Warren leaned in for a closer look. "His neck is bruised and burned, but he's breathing."

"Shouldn't Vanessa be in control of him?" Kendra asked. "You know, the narcoblix?"

"This is no natural sleep," Warren said. "She may have power over him, but she can't animate limbs that refuse to function. He paid a severe price to best the revenant—it was evidently a very close contest. Potion or no potion, your brother must have the heart of a lion!"

"He's very brave," Kendra said, tears pooling in her eyes. Her lips trembled. "Can I borrow the light?" Warren handed her the flashlight and she found a small potion in the cereal box. "He was very proud that Tanu gave him a potion that could boost his energy in an emergency."

"That might do him good," Warren said. He uncapped the bottle, propped up Seth's head, and poured some of the fluid into his mouth. Seth spluttered and coughed. After a moment, Warren gave him more, which he gulped.

Seth's eyes opened, and his brow furrowed. "You!" he said weakly, his voice raspy.

"Get out of him, hag," Warren spat.

Seth smiled eerily. And then his eyes rolled white.

"What happened?" he gasped, voice still raspy. "The revenant?"

"You succeeded," Warren said.

"You're healed," Seth murmured perplexedly, staring at Warren. "Didn't know . . . that would happen. Kendra. You came."

"Ask him something only he would know," Warren said. "This could be a ruse."

Kendra thought for a moment. "What dessert did you hate in your school lunch last year?"

"Cherry cobbler," he said weakly.

"What was your favorite shadow puppet Dad used to make?"

"Chicken," he said.

"It's him," Kendra said confidently.

"Can you sit up?" Warren asked.

Seth's head bobbed slightly forward. His fingers twitched. "I feel like I've been run over by a steamroller. Like everything . . . has been squished out of me. My throat hurts."

"He needs time to recuperate," Warren said. "And I need to get into the tower. The narcoblix knows the way is open. The only reason she would have released Seth is because she is already on her way here. Kendra, you mentioned that a great imp is helping her, along with another man, but she may have more contacts than them on the preserve. I should be able to navigate the traps. Let's have Mendigo take you and your brother to a safe place."

"I want to come," Seth croaked.

"You've done enough today," Warren said. "Time to pass off the torch to others."

"Give me more of that potion," Seth said.

"More of that potion won't change your condition," Warren said. "Though Kendra should probably have a dose, to help her keep awake."

Kendra took a sip. Almost instantly she felt a burst of alertness, as if she had been slapped.

Warren scooped his arms under Seth, lifting him in a cradled position. Kendra started collecting the key and the ax, but Warren told her to leave them. He was walking with quick steps back toward Mendigo.

"Should I go into the tower with you, Warren?" she asked, catching up.

"Too dangerous," he said.

"I may be able to help," she said. "Last year, I visited the Fairy Queen's shrine on the island in the pond and raised a fairy army to save Fablehaven from a demon named Bahumat."

"What?" Warren sputtered.

"She did," Seth confirmed.

"You do have stories!" Warren said.

"The fairies left me with certain gifts," Kendra continued, not wanting to specify that she was fairykind. "I can see in the dark, and speak all the languages the fairies can. I don't need the milk anymore to see magical creatures. And my touch can recharge magical objects that are out of energy. The Sphinx seemed to think that might come in handy for some of the artifacts."

"It very well might," Warren said. "It has been suggested that the artifacts were deliberately drained of energy as an additional safeguard."

"Without me you might not be able to use the artifact even if you find it," Kendra said.

"I believe I can successfully negotiate the traps in the tower," Warren said. "But that is without knowing what they are. I'm not infallible, as the grove has aptly proven. Do you understand the possible dangers of accompanying me?"

"We could both die," Kendra said. "But there is danger everywhere at Fablehaven today. I'll come with you."

"An extra pair of eyes and hands could make a difference," Warren conceded. "And the ability to charge the artifact, whichever one it is, could make all the difference. We'll trust Mendigo to watch over Seth."

"This is no fair," Seth muttered.

"Do you want your glove back?" Kendra asked.

"You'll need it more," he said firmly.

They emerged from the grove and hurried to Mendigo. Warren suggested that Kendra have Mendigo take Seth to the stables. Kendra gave orders for Mendigo to take Seth to the stables and watch over him, keep him safe from harm, and not allow him to wander off for a full day unless otherwise instructed. Mendigo trotted away, cradling Seth.

Warren and Kendra ran back to the dry skeleton of the revenant and retrieved the key and the ax. Kendra followed Warren deeper into the grove. There was little undergrowth, but the deeper they went, the closer the trees grew together, and the heavier they were draped with moss and mistletoe.

They reached a place where the trees grew so snugly that their branches interlocked in such a way as to almost form a wall.

When Warren shouldered through the living barrier, they found a small clearing ringed by trees, illuminated by a warm, predawn glow. A sizable raised platform of reddish stone dominated the area, looking almost like an outdoor stage. Stone stairs on one side of the platform granted easy access.

Up the steps Warren charged, with Kendra at his heels. Despite the ubiquitous wildflowers and weeds in the clearing, the stone platform was untouched by vegetation. The smooth surface was flecked with black and gold. At the center of the spacious platform was a round socket, surrounded by multiple circular grooves that radiated out concentrically to the edge of the platform. About four feet separated each of the dark, narrow grooves. From above, the grooves would look like a target, with the socket at the center of the bull's-eye.

Warren placed the complicated end of the key into the round socket. He had to twist the key back and forth, lining up various protuberances with notches in the socket to gradually work it in deeper. Once the tall key was approximately a foot into the hole, it clicked home.

"You sure you're up for this?" Warren asked. "There will be no turning back once we go inside."

"What do you mean?" Kendra asked.

"These sorts of places are designed so that unless you make it to the end and claim your prize, you do not make it out alive. The designers don't want explorers solving the puzzle piece by piece. The traps guarding the way back will be much less forgiving than the traps protecting the way forward. Until we reach the artifact."

"I'm coming," Kendra said.

Face reddening with exertion, Warren gripped the handle of the key tightly and began turning it. The key rotated 180 degrees and stopped.

The platform shuddered. It became apparent that the circular grooves marked divisions between concentric rings of stone when the outer ring fell away into darkness, followed by the next, and the next, and the next. The massive rings thundered as they struck the ground.

Warren pulled Kendra near him, standing atop the innermost circle with the key. Though the other rings all fell, the innermost never dropped. Peering down, Kendra saw that the outermost ring had fallen the farthest, with each ring thereafter plummeting a shorter distance, so that all together they formed a conical stairway. From the outside of the platform, it was at least a thirty-foot drop to the floor of the chamber. From the center where Kendra and Warren stood, the next ring was only four feet lower, the next four feet lower again, and so forth down to the floor.

"They just don't build entrances like they used to," Warren said. He tugged on the key, and, with a musical ring of steel, the portion of the key in the socket separated from the rest of it. Now instead of ending in a complicated series of protuberances and notches, the key ended in a slender, double-edged spearhead. "Would you look at that?"

"Can't be good," Kendra said.

"Yeah, it probably turns into a weapon for a reason," Warren said, looking down into the chamber. "I don't see any trouble yet."

"I'm putting on the glove," Kendra said. She vanished.

"Not bad," Warren said.

Kendra waved at him, reappearing as she moved. "It only works when I hold still."

"Do you know what any of the potions do?" Warren asked.

"I know a couple that would make us about eight or nine inches tall," she said. "And I know some are bottled-up emotions, although I'm not sure which is which. Seth might know a few others. We should have asked him."

Warren began climbing down from ring to ring. "As a last resort, you can always try a random potion," he said. "Hopefully it won't come to that."

The chamber was not much larger than the widest ring of stone. The floor appeared to be a single slab of bedrock. There was nothing in the chamber except a pair of doors at opposite ends. One wall was covered in writings in various languages, including a few repeated messages in English.

This accursed sanctum lies
outside the domain of Fablehaven.
Do not proceed.
Go in peace.

Kendra assumed the other messages restated the same thing in their respective languages.

"Why did they write it in English so many times?" Kendra asked.

"I only see it in English once," Warren said.

"Oh, fairy languages," she said.

They reached the bottom ring. "Stay near me," Warren instructed. "Step only where I step. Be ready for anything." He tapped the ground with the handle of the key before stepping down. Kendra followed him.

"Which door should we try?" Kendra asked.

"You pick," he said. "It's a toss-up."

Kendra pointed at one of the doors. Warren led the way, prodding the floor with the key like a blind man. The door was of plain, heavy wood bound in iron, and appeared to be in good repair. Warren probed the ground off to one side and had Kendra stand there holding the ax. Standing still, she disappeared. Holding the key like a spear, he pulled the door open.

Nothing waited behind the door except a stairway curling downward. Warren got out the dying flashlight. He tried to tap the top stair with the handle of the key, but the handle went right through it.

"Kendra, look," Warren said. The handle of the key disappeared through the first few steps. "False stairs. Probably masking a drop of hundreds of feet."

They crossed the room and repeated their cautious actions at the other door. Again the door opened to a stairway, and again the stairs were only an illusion. Warren leaned out far, testing with the key, to check if perhaps only the first few stairs were counterfeit, but nothing within reach proved to be tangible.

Warren led the way around the perimeter of the room, tapping the floor and the walls. They reached a place where the key passed through the wall. Warren leaned through the illusion, and Kendra heard him tapping with the key.

"Here is the genuine stairway," he said. Kendra passed through the insubstantial wall and saw a stone stairway winding downward. White stones set in the walls emitted a soft light.

"You never know what might be a mirage in places like this," Warren said. He poked one of the glowing stones with the key. "Ever seen a sunstone?"

"No," Kendra said.

"So long as one stone sits under the sun, all the sister stones share the light," he said. "It's probably atop one of the nearby hills."

As they descended the stairs, they found a few places where illusionary steps disguised gaps in the stairway. Warren helped Kendra leap across the empty places. Finally they reached the bottom of the stairs and another door.

Again Warren had Kendra move over to one side as he opened the door. "Strange," he murmured, testing the ground. Warren stepped through the doorway. "Come on, Kendra."

She peeked through the doorway. The room was large and circular, with a domed ceiling. White stones set in the ceiling illuminated the scene. Deep, golden sand covered the floor. On the far side of the room a door was painted on the wall. On the left side of the room murals of three monsters decorated the wall, with another three on the right side. Kendra saw a blue woman with six arms and the body of a serpent, a Minotaur, a huge Cyclops, a dark man who from waist up looked human and from waist down had the body and legs of a spider, an armored snakelike man wearing an elaborate headdress, and a dwarf in a hooded cloak. All the images, though a tad faded, had been rendered with supreme skill.

Warren raised a hand for Kendra to halt. The key sank into the sand in front of him. "There are places where the sand becomes treacherous," he said. "Watch your step."

In order to avoid sinking in quicksand, they took a circuitous path to the painted door on the far side of the room. The painting depicted a door of solid iron with a keyhole below the handle. Hesitantly, Warren touched the painting. The image of the door rippled for an instant, and suddenly the door became real, a mural no longer.

Warren whirled, key held high, and eyed the other murals in the room. Nothing happened. Finally he turned back to the door and tried the handle. The door was locked. "Notice anything all the creatures on the wall have in common?" Warren asked.

Kendra focused on comparing them. "A key around their necks," she said. The keys were not obvious. They were small, and subtly drawn, but each painted being had one.

"Any theories on how we get through the door?" Warren asked, obviously with an answer in mind.

"You've got to be kidding," Kendra said.

"Don't we both wish," he said. "The old guys who designed this place sure knew how to throw a party." He led Kendra around the perimeter of the room, avoiding quicksand, and scrutinized the depiction of each individual creature.

"The keys appear identical to me," he said after studying the dwarf. "I think the game is selecting which foe we believe we can overcome."

"I hate to be cruel," Kendra said, "but I'm thinking the dwarf."

"I would choose him last of all," Warren said. "He carries no weapon, which leads me to believe he must be strong in magic. And he looks the easiest at first glance, which almost certainly means he is the most deadly."

"Then who?" Kendra asked. The Minotaur carried a heavy mace. The Cyclops wielded a cudgel. The blue woman held a sword in each hand. The hobgoblin, as Warren had named the snakelike man, clutched a pair of axes. And the half-spider man bore a javelin and a whip.

"I suspect the Minotaur may be the lesser of these evils," Warren said at length. "I would no sooner choose the woman than the dwarf, and a Cyclops is nearly as adroit as he is strong. Of the others, the Minotaur carries the most cumbersome weapon. His mace will limit his reach and hamper his ability to avoid the tip of my spear."

"You mean your key," Kendra said.

"We'll use one key to get another."

Kendra regarded the Minotaur. Black fur, wide horns,

bulky musculature. He stood a full head taller than Warren. "You think you can take him?" Kendra asked.

Warren was testing the sand and outlining the sinkholes. "I'll want you to stand still," he said. "The Minotaur may catch your scent—I want to keep him in doubt as to your location. You'll keep the ax, and if I should lose the key, you may be able to toss it to me. If I should fall, the Minotaur will roam the room searching for you. If you keep still, you may have one free swing at him."

"But you think you can take him?" Kendra repeated.

Warren looked at the image of the Minotaur and hefted the key. "Why not? I've made it through some tight scrapes before. I would give a lot for a few of my regular weapons. Maybe you could use the ax to help me mark all the quicksand?"

They spent much longer than Kendra liked delineating the areas of treacherous sand. She knew Vanessa and Errol were on their trail. Once the sand had been marked, Warren positioned Kendra so that the largest region of quicksand was between her and the Minotaur. He approached the mural.

"You ready?" Warren asked.

"I guess," Kendra answered, squeezing the handle of her invisible ax, her heart pounding.

"Maybe I can get in a cheap shot right at the start," he said, touching the image of the Minotaur and raising the key, holding it ready to strike. The mural wavered for a moment and then vanished. The sharp tip of the key clinked against the wall, and the Minotaur appeared behind Warren.

"Behind you!" Kendra screamed.

Warren ducked and lunged to the side, narrowly avoiding a blow that would have brained him. The Minotaur swung the mace briskly. The weapon was big and heavy, but the Minotaur was strong enough that it did not look very cumbersome.

Warren faced the Minotaur, staying a few paces away, key held ready. "Why not just hand over the key?" Warren asked. The Minotaur snorted. From across the room, Kendra could smell the beast, an odor like livestock.

The Minotaur charged, and Warren nimbly danced away. Warren pulled back his arm as if to throw the key, and the Minotaur raised his mace protectively. Feinting like he was hurling the key, Warren leapt closer and used the long reach of the key to scratch the Minotaur on the snout.

The Minotaur roared, chasing Warren around the room. Warren ran from his pursuer, trying his best to lead the Minotaur toward quicksand while keeping the beast away from Kendra. Either the Minotaur understood what the lines in the sand meant, or he instinctively knew where not to step, because he skirted the quicksand just as effectively as Warren.

Sniffing the air, the Minotaur turned toward Kendra. "Over here, you coward!" Warren shouted, moving in closer and brandishing the key. The Minotaur strode boldly toward Warren, holding the mace off to one side, tempting Warren by leaving his chest exposed.

After a few feints, Warren took the bait, driving the tip of the key toward the Minotaur's chest. The Minotaur grabbed the key just below the slender spearhead with his free hand and wrenched it from Warren's grasp, yanking him closer in the process, and swung the mace.

Warren saved himself by diving backwards and managing to keep his feet. The blow had missed by inches. The Minotaur quickly reversed his grip on the key and hurled it like a javelin, burying the head in Warren's abdomen despite his attempt to dodge it.

Roaring triumphantly, the Minotaur rushed at Warren, who pulled out the key and stumbled away, the spearhead red with his own blood. Scrambling, spraying sand, Warren managed to get a small area of quicksand between the Minotaur and himself.

Kendra flung the flashlight and struck the Minotaur in the back. The brute turned, but she was invisible again. The Minotaur picked up the flashlight, sniffed it, and then sniffed the air, moving toward Kendra.

Using the key like a crutch, Warren came around the quicksand, approaching the Minotaur from behind. The Minotaur whirled and gave chase. Warren skipped away, ending up with his back to a broad expanse of quicksand.

"Warren, quicksand!" Kendra cried.

Too late, he stepped beyond the line in the sand, one leg sinking to his thigh, the rest of him collapsing forward onto the sturdier sand. The Minotaur dashed forward, mace held high to issue the killing stroke. Quick as a mousetrap, Warren thrust upward with the key, the razor tip of the spearhead entering the Minotaur just below the sternum, angled up to pierce his heart. The Minotaur stood still, impaled, and snorted. The mace fell from his hairy hands, landing heavily on the sand. Warren twisted the key and shoved it in deeper, toppling the Minotaur backwards. Panting, Warren withdrew his leg from the mushy sand.

Kendra ran to him. "That was an amazing trick!" she shouted.

"A desperate one," he said. "All or nothing." His hand covered the wound on his abdomen. He swatted at the damp sand coating his leg. "Probably wouldn't have worked, except the Minotaur thought I was mortally wounded. Course, he might have been right."

"Is it bad?" she asked.

"It pierced me deep, but clean," he said. "In straight, out straight. Belly wounds are hard to read. Depends what got punctured. Go fetch the key."

Kendra crouched beside the supine Minotaur, enjoying the livestock smell even less up close. The key hung on a fine gold chain. She pulled hard, and the chain snapped. "I have it," Kendra said.

"Get the big one too," Warren said. The big key was still lodged in the Minotaur's chest. Kendra had to brace a foot against the beast to tug it free. Warren had taken off his shirt. The blood stood out sharply against his white skin. Kendra averted her eyes. He wadded up his shirt and pressed it against the wound, which was a couple of inches to one side of his belly button. "Let's hope this stanches the bleeding," he said. "Can you cut me a length of rope?"

Using the sharp spearhead of the bloody key, Kendra did as he said, and Warren used the rope to bind his shirt in place over the wound. He wiped the blood from the spearhead onto his pants. "Can you go on?" Kendra asked.

"Not much choice," he said. "Let's see if the Minotaur's key works."

Groaning, Warren used the tall key to pull himself to his feet. He walked to the iron door, inserted the Minotaur's key, and opened it.

CHAPTER TWENTY

The Vault

Another stairway spiraled down beyond the open door. More sunstones, brighter than before, lit the way. Warren prodded the steps and found that they were solid. "Kendra," he said. "Go erase the lines around a few of the sinkholes near the entrance to the room."

When Kendra returned, Warren was feeling the pulse in his neck. Perspiration dampened his forehead. "How are you?" she asked.

"I'm not doing too bad," he assured her. "Especially for a guy who just underwent involuntary surgery. We have the Minotaur's key. If we shut the door behind us, our friend the narcoblix will probably have to earn a key of her own."

"Okay," Kendra said, stepping into the stairwell with

Warren and closing the door. She turned to face him, and vanished.

"Maybe you should just keep the glove handy for the next threat," Warren said. "It is tough losing track of where you are when we pause."

Kendra took off the glove. As long as they were moving around, exploring the tower, it wasn't much of a protection anyway. Slipping it on would be little more trouble than simply holding still. They descended the stairs for some time, finding no false steps until the final few before the very end.

"I like the placement," Warren said, jumping over them and wincing when he landed. He leaned against the wall, one hand clutching his wound. "Just when you assume all the stairs are solid, you plunge to your doom."

No door awaited them. Instead, an arched entryway granted access to a broad chamber with a complex mosaic on the floor. The mosaic depicted an enormous battle of primates being waged in tall trees. The perspective was from the ground looking up, creating a disorienting effect.

Motioning for Kendra to stay put, Warren entered the room. A second archway on the far side of the chamber appeared to be the only way out. Satisfied that they faced no immediate threat, Warren beckoned for Kendra to follow.

The instant she stepped into the room, the ax vanished from her grasp. Below her, high in a tree, a chimpanzee screamed. Twirling Kendra's ax, the manic primate leaped from his high perch and fell upwards toward the ground. The chimpanzee sailed right out of the mosaic, materializing in front of Kendra, brandishing the ax.

Shrieking, Kendra ran away from the ax-wielding chimp, yanking on her glove. Rushing up from behind the chimpanzee, Warren flung the key just as the screeching ape was beginning to give chase. The key sailed true, striking the frenzied beast between the shoulder blades, and the chimpanzee pitched forward onto the floor, long hand twitching, the ax skidding forward over tiny tiles.

"Don't pick up the ax," Warren warned. "This chamber is meant to strip us of all weaponry."

"Except the key," Kendra said.

Grunting, Warren bent over and retrieved the key, again wiping the spearhead on his pants. "Right," he said. "My guess is that to pass this room with any weapon besides the key, we would have to slay every monkey in the mosaic."

Kendra looked down. There were hundreds of apes, including dozens of powerful gorillas. "Maybe it was a good thing you didn't have all your gear."

Warren smiled ruefully. "You're not kidding. Being butchered by monkeys is pretty low on my list of ways to go. Come on."

They passed through the archway at the other end of the room and began winding down yet another stairwell. All the stairs were real, and at the bottom they found another open archway, narrower than the previous ones.

Warren led the way into a cylindrical room where the floor was hundreds of feet below. Widely spaced sunstones provided sufficient light. A narrow catwalk without railings ringed the top of the room, level with the entrance. The roof bristled with barbed spikes. Kendra saw no way to descend—the walls were smooth and sheer all the way to the bottom, where she could barely make out something in the center of the floor.

"I'm not sure we brought enough rope," Warren joked, stepping onto the catwalk. "I believe this is our destination. How are you with heights?"

"Not so good," Kendra said.

"Wait here," he said. He walked along the catwalk, testing the air with the key, as if searching for an invisible stairway. Kendra noticed an alcove in the far side of the wide room. When Warren reached the alcove, he removed something from it. He levitated a few feet into the air, glanced up at the spikes above him, and floated back down.

"I think I get it," he called. He reached into the alcove again and there was a bright flash that flung him backwards off the catwalk. Kendra watched breathlessly as Warren plummeted toward the distant floor. He began falling slower, then stopped, then started rising. He floated slowly as he drew even with Kendra, and finally stopped, hovering in the center of the room.

In addition to the key, Warren was holding a short white rod. "I can't move side to side," he explained. He floated up close to the spikes, carefully took hold of one, and pushed off, sending himself drifting toward Kendra, moving much the way Kendra pictured astronauts would in zero gravity.

Warren alighted on the catwalk beside her. The short rod was carved out of ivory. One tip was black. He had been holding the rod parallel to the floor, but now that he stood on the catwalk, he tilted it so the black tip was facing up.

"That makes you fly?" Kendra asked.

"More like it reverses gravity," he said. "Black tip up, gravity pulls down. Black tip down, gravity pulls up. Sideways, you get zero gravity. Tilt the black tip up a little bit, gravity pulls down a little bit. Get it?"

"I think so," she said.

"Careful of the roof," he warned.

"Have you done this before?" she asked.

"Never," he said. "You learn to experiment in places like this."

He held out the rod. She took it. "I want to try it out in the stairway, without the spikes."

"Go for it," he said.

Kendra went back to the stairway. Slowly she tipped the rod until it was sideways. Nothing felt any different. She jumped slightly, and it felt perfectly normal.

"I don't think it works out here," she said.

"The enchantment must be specific to this room," he said. "Still, strong spell, I've never heard of anything like it. Remember, with the rod, you're changing which way gravity pulls you. If your momentum is going one way, turning the rod won't instantly change your direction. When I was falling and I flipped it over, I slowed, stopped, and then started going up. So leave yourself room to stop, or you might end up a shish kebab."

"I'm not going to let myself go fast," Kendra said.

"Good idea," Warren said. "And, for the record, don't try to grab a second rod. It felt like I'd been struck by lightning."

Holding the rod, Kendra followed Warren around the

catwalk. She kept the black tip pointed straight up, not wanting to risk drifting up to the spikes. When they reached the alcove, she saw that there were nine other rods, each resting in a hole, black tip up.

"What do you say we make sure we can't be followed," Warren said, grabbing a rod and tossing it off the edge of the catwalk. Instead of falling, the rod floated back to the same hole from which Warren had removed it. He picked up the rod again. When he let go of it, the rod again returned itself to the hole.

"We better hold tight to these, or we'll end up stranded down there," Kendra said.

Warren nodded, removing a rod for himself. He turned it so the black tip was only slightly upwards and stepped off the edge, falling gently, again making Kendra think of astronauts.

Kendra tipped the rod slowly, marveling as she felt the pull of gravity diminishing, even without moving. The sensation was strange; it reminded her of being underwater. Tilting the rod so the black tip was slightly downward, she floated up, her feet leaving the catwalk. Tipping the rod the other way a tad, she drifted back down.

Now that she trusted the rod, Kendra stepped off the edge of the catwalk and began a mild freefall. The sensation was incredible. She had dreamed of going into space in order to experience zero gravity, and here she was, in an underground tower, sampling something much like it. The dizzying drop beneath her feet was no longer very intimidating, now that she could control gravity with a twist of her wrist.

Warren rose to meet her. "Experiment with the rod," he said. "Nothing too drastic, but get a feel for how to rise and fall and stop yourself. There's a knack to it. I have a feeling it will come in handy before we finish here."

Suddenly Warren shot downward. Kendra watched him slow to a stop. "I thought you said nothing too drastic," she called to him.

He rocketed upwards, drawing even with her again. "I meant for you," he said before plunging away below her.

Little by little, Kendra tilted the black tip up higher, incrementally increasing the rate of her descent. She abruptly tipped the rod in the other direction, and her descent slowed with a feeling like she was connected to an elastic band. Making the rod parallel with the ground, she brought herself to a standstill about halfway to the floor.

Kendra glanced up at the distant spikes in the ceiling. She tilted the black tip all the way down, and with a sudden rush of acceleration she was shooting up toward the iron stalactites. The sensation was disorienting, exactly like falling headfirst toward the ground, and the spikes came rapidly nearer. In a panic she whipped the rod the other way. The elastic feeling was much stronger this time, although it took long enough to slow that she got much nearer to the spikes than she liked. Before she knew it she was careening toward the floor of the tall chamber. Her body began rotating, and she lost some sense of which way she needed to turn the rod to slow her fall. She overcorrected several times before gaining control, whipping herself up and down erratically.

When she finally leveled out, Kendra was two-thirds of

the way to the floor, hovering near the wall. She kicked off gently.

"And I thought I was a daredevil," Warren called.

"That was a little more daring than I intended," Kendra admitted, trying not to sound as shaken as she felt. She experimented more with rising and falling, growing accustomed to easing herself to a stop and to keeping her body properly oriented. At last she landed softly on the floor next to Warren and normalized the gravity by holding her rod black-end up.

The room was bare except for a pedestal at the center. The floor was polished, seamless stone. Atop the pedestal sat a life-sized likeness of a black cat, made of colored glass.

"Is that the artifact?" Kendra asked.

"My guess is we're looking at the vault," Warren said.

"Do we smash it?" Kendra asked.

"That might be a start," Warren said.

"How are you feeling?" Kendra asked.

"Stabbed," he said. "But functional. Things could turn ugly fast. If it comes to it, you may want to fly up to the catwalk and hope for mercy from the narcoblix. But don't try to exit the tower. I was very serious about the traps set to prevent anyone from exiting prematurely."

"Right," Kendra said. "I won't ditch you."

Warren tipped the rod somewhat and jumped, soaring over Kendra's head and landing gently behind her, wincing slightly and clutching his side. "See, you can also simply reduce gravity to your advantage. Could come in handy."

Kendra tilted the rod, feeling herself lightening, and took a leap, gliding in a long, lazy parabola. "Gotcha."

"You ready?" Warren said.

"What's going to happen?" Kendra said.

"I'll smash the cat and we'll see."

"What if the roof comes down on us?" she asked.

Warren gazed up at the distant ceiling. "That would be bad. Let's hope the spikes are just meant to impale people who are clumsy with their gravity sticks."

"You think there may be something scary inside the cat?" Kendra asked.

"Seems like a safe bet. We better hurry. Who knows how long before the narcoblix shows up? You ready? Glove on?"

Kendra pulled on the glove and turned invisible. "Okay."

Warren prodded the cat with the sharp end of the key. The tip of the spearhead clinked loudly, but the figurine did not crack. He jabbed it a few times. Clink, clink, clink. "I'm not sure we're meant to break it," he said. Moving close, Warren touched the cat with his finger and then skipped away, key ready.

The glass cat shimmered and became a real cat, mewing softly. It had a tiny key around its neck.

Kendra felt some of the tension leave her. "Is this some kind of joke?" she asked.

"If so, I don't think we've seen the punch line yet."

"Maybe it has rabies," Kendra said.

Tentatively, Warren approached the black cat. It hopped down from the pedestal and slunk toward him. Nothing indicated that the feline was anything other than a scrawny domestic cat. Crouching, Warren let the animal lick his hand. He stroked the cat softly, and then untied the ribbon that held the key. Instantly the cat hissed and swiped a paw at him. Warren stood and backed away, puzzling over the key. The cat arched its back and showed its teeth.

"It turned mean," Kendra said.

"It is mean," Warren corrected. "This is certainly no mere housecat. We have not yet seen the true form of our adversary."

The feral cat spat and hissed.

Warren began investigating the big key. He rolled it, examining it from end to end. "Ah-ha!" he said, inserting the tiny key into a hole just below the spearhead. When he turned the miniscule key, the handle at the opposite end of the big key detached and clattered to the ground. Connected to the handle was a long, slender blade. A sword had been hidden in the shaft of the tall key, with only the handle showing!

Warren picked up the sword, swishing it through the air. The handle had no guard. The sharp blade was long and sleek, and it flashed dangerously in the glow of the sun-stones. "We have ourselves a pair of weapons," Warren said. "Take the spear! Without the sword it has a better balance."

Eyes on the cat, Kendra drew near and took the spear from Warren. "How do I use this?" she asked.

"Stab with it," Warren said. "It's probably too heavy for you to throw it effectively. Pay more attention to soaring away if trouble comes near."

"All right," she said, taking a few practice jabs.

Without warning, the cat charged at Kendra. She swung the spear and it veered away, darting toward Warren. His sword whisked down and lopped off the head of the cat. Warren stepped away from the corpse, watching it intently. Both the head and the body of the feline began to boil as if full of writhing worms. The head melted into a soupy pool. The headless body began to heave inside out, revealing wet glimpses of muscle and bone, until the churning finally stopped and the black cat was whole again.

The cat hissed at Warren, fur rising along its arched back. It was bigger now, larger than any domestic cat Kendra had ever seen. Warren took a step toward the cat and it bolted, body stretching long as it raced fluidly away. The next two times Warren came close, the cat streaked away, in the end returning to the pedestal.

Warren approached the pedestal. Baring teeth and claws, the cat sprang at him. A slash of his sword intercepted the feline, and the cat flopped to the floor. Warren stabbed it to ensure the animal a quick demise, and then backed away.

Once again, the lifeless body began to pulse and roil. "I'm not too keen about this pattern," Warren said darkly. Moving in close, he began stabbing the churning mass of fur and bone and organs. With each wound it seemed to grow, and so he retreated to let the process finish.

The reborn black cat no longer looked like a domestic animal. Not only was it much too big, the paws were proportionately larger, with crueler claws, and the ears were now tufted like those of a lynx. Still entirely black, the lynx let out a fierce yowl, showing intimidating teeth.

"Don't kill it again," Kendra said. "It will keep getting worse."

"Then we will never get the artifact," Warren said. "The cat is the vault, and the sword and the spear remain the keys. To get the artifact, we must defeat all of its incarnations." The black lynx crouched, eyeing Warren cunningly. When Warren feinted forward, the lynx did not flinch.

Staying low, the lynx prowled toward Warren, as if stalking a bird. Warren stood ready, sword poised. A dark blur, the lynx rushed at him, low and silent. The sword flashed, opening a gash, but the lynx got through, clawing and biting furiously at Warren's pant leg. A fierce return stroke ended the flurry of claws. The lynx lay motionless.

"Fast," Warren complained, limping away, blood dripping from his tattered pant leg.

"Did it hurt you bad?" Kendra asked.

"Surface wounds. My pants got the worst of it," Warren said. "But it got to me. I'm not sure I like what that says about my reflexes." The hide of the carcass began to bulge.

"Would the spear be better?" Kendra asked. "You could stab it before it gets close."

"Maybe," Warren said. "Trade me." He crossed to her and they exchanged weapons.

"You're limping," she said.

"It's a little tender," he said. "I'll hold up."

The lynx yowled, a heartier, more powerful sound. As it stood on all fours, its head was higher than the bandage on Warren's stomach. "Big cat," Kendra said.

"Here, kitty, kitty," Warren coaxed, edging toward it with the spear. The beefed-up lynx began pacing, staying out of range, moving with sure grace, hunting for an opening. The lynx darted at Warren and then pulled back. It faked a second charge, and Warren danced backwards.

"Why am I starting to feel more and more like a mouse?" Warren complained. He lunged forward, thrusting with the spear, but the lynx sprang to one side and received only a glancing blow before streaking toward Warren, low and impossibly quick, inside the reach of the spear. Warren jumped high into the air.

The lynx instantly wheeled around and raced toward Kendra. Invisible or not, the animal knew her exact location. She reversed the rod and shot upwards, coming to a stop fifty feet above the floor. After halting her ascent, Kendra did not turn invisible. It was impossible to reach a complete standstill in the air. No matter how she held the rod, there was always a slight drifting that apparently prevented the glove from working. Warren hovered about twenty feet below her, glaring at the lynx. He glanced up at Kendra, and then his eyes fixed on something beyond her. "We've got company," he said.

Kendra looked up and saw Vanessa and Errol gliding down from the catwalk. "What do we do?" Kendra asked.

Swinging the spear to ward off the lynx, Warren dropped to the ground and jumped at an angle that let him float near to Kendra. "Give me the sword," he said.

"I propose a truce," Vanessa called down to them airily, as if it were all a game. Kendra handed Warren the sword.

He gave her the spear. The exchange caused them to slowly drift apart.

"A convenient idea, since we have the weapons," Warren growled.

"How many times have you slain the guardian?" Vanessa asked.

"None of your business," Warren said. "Come no closer."

She stopped, hovering with Errol beside her. Errol's suit was torn. One of his eyes was purple and swollen shut, and there were scratches on his cheeks.

"You do not look well, Warren," Vanessa said.

"Neither does your friend," he replied.

"I think you two could use some assistance," Vanessa said.

"What got him?" Warren asked. "The hobgoblin?"

Vanessa smiled. "He was injured before we entered the tower."

"I picked up a bar of gold on the back porch," Errol said. "Apparently it was stolen from a troll. He took it back very impolitely after we left the yard."

Kendra covered her mouth to hide her laughter. Errol glared at her. "Your real name is Christopher Vogel?" Kendra asked.

"I have many names," he said stiffly. "My parents gave me that one."

"We elected to fight the Cyclops," Vanessa said. "Lots of bare skin for my darts. And we deduced from the ax and the ape not to enter the nearby chamber armed. But this cat may pose a problem. How many times has it died? We've seen once."

"You better turn around and clear out of here," Warren said.

"I hope you aren't counting on other help," Vanessa said. "We found Tanu in the woods and took care of him. He will be asleep until this time tomorrow."

"I'm surprised you came in person," Kendra said bitterly.

"Where finesse is required, I prefer my own body," Vanessa said.

"We have no intention of harming anyone," Errol said. "Kendra, we just want to take the artifact and leave all of you in peace. This can still end well for you and your family."

With a flick of his wrist, Warren soared up to their level. "Sorry if we're out of reach," Vanessa said.

Although hovering at the same height, they were separated by a good distance. "Either you will depart, or I will emphatically insist," Warren said, raising the sword menacingly.

"We could fight," Errol said calmly. "But trust me, brave as she may be, it would not take much for me to wrest that lance from the girl." Errol pushed off of Vanessa so that both of them drifted over to opposite walls. They landed softly against the walls, staying near enough to control their direction by pushing off.

"A contest between us will end in injuries none of us can afford," Vanessa said. "Why not first slay the beast together?"

"Because I don't want to be stabbed in the back," Warren said.

"You don't imagine you can walk out of here without the artifact?" Errol asked. "There are always safeguards against such actions."

"I'm well aware," Warren said. "I can handle the cat."

"How many times have you killed the beast?" Vanessa persisted.

"Three times," Warren said.

"So this is its fourth life," Errol said. "Hang me if it has less than nine."

"At your best, uninjured, this guardian is too much for you or any single person," Vanessa said. "All together we may have a chance."

"I will not arm you," Warren said.

Vanessa nodded at Errol. Both of them dropped rapidly along the wall until they were level with Kendra. Warren fell with them, but without a way to control his lateral movement, he could not intervene. Vanessa and Errol kicked off the wall, floating toward Kendra. She tilted the rod, floating upwards, and Vanessa and Errol adjusted to float upwards with her.

They were approaching her from opposite directions. At best she could poke one of them with the spear. Warren had lowered himself almost to the ground, but the fierce lynx was keeping him from touching down. He swatted at it with the sword. In a panic, with Vanessa and Errol closing in, Kendra tossed the spear toward Warren, yelling, "Catch!"

The spear turned end over end and narrowly missed

piercing Warren before it clanged to the floor beside the lynx. Yowling, the overgrown cat guarded the spear, fangs bared. Vanessa and Errol plunged to the ground in pursuit of the fallen weapon. Errol struck the floor much harder than he must have intended, and he crumpled. Vanessa landed perfectly.

It was claw against sword as Warren lowered himself toward the snapping, hissing lynx. Vanessa dashed toward the lynx across the floor. Kendra saw a little white stick fly by her on its way back to the top of the room, and realized Errol had dropped his rod.

With Vanessa approaching from behind and Warren slicing it from above, the lynx darted away, ignoring Vanessa and racing toward Errol, who was rising shakily. Vanessa dove and grabbed the spear at the same time as Warren. Errol screamed, hobbling hopelessly away from the charging lynx, favoring his right leg.

Warren released the spear and jumped toward where the lynx was about to converge with Errol. Vanessa sprinted across the floor. The lynx sprang, and Errol vanished, reappearing a few feet off to one side. The lynx landed and swerved to stay after Errol. Spreading his hands, backing away, Errol create a puff of smoke and a blazing shower of sparks. As the undaunted lynx sprang through the fiery flash, Errol raised his arms defensively. The heavy lynx knocked Errol down and began mauling his forearm, shaking and dragging him. Vanessa arrived before Warren and buried the spear deep into the animal's side. Warren alighted beside her and decapitated the lynx.

Kendra looked on from above in hypnotized horror. She had no love for Errol, but watching anyone get mauled like that was a terrible thing. It all happened so quickly! Smoke curled up from where sparks had singed the lynx.

"Hurry, get him another gravity stick," Vanesssa cried.

"You can only hold one at a time," Warren said, stepping toward her.

"Then back off!" Vanessa panted, holding up the spear defensively. Warren soared into the air. The dead lynx was churning. The severed head was melting. Vanessa glanced upwards, as if considering racing for a stick after all, then looked at the roiling corpse. "Errol, get up," she commanded.

Dazed, the injured magician rose, standing on one leg, his tattered sleeve a bloody ruin. "On my back," she said, turning.

He climbed up piggyback and Vanessa bounded into the air. She rose about twenty feet before slowing, stopping, and drifting back toward the ground. The black tip of the rod was pointed straight down, but still she descended. The revived cat roared. The head was shaped differently, and the body was much more muscular. The cat was now a panther.

"Errol's bigger than her," Warren whispered to Kendra. "Gravity is pulling him down and her up, but he's heavier." Warren compressed his lips. "Hand him the rod!" he shouted.

Vanessa, struggling, either didn't hear or didn't care. "Let go of me!" she demanded. Errol clung to her desperately.

"Don't look," Warren said.

Kendra closed her eyes.

The panther leaped, claws raking Errol and dragging both him and Vanessa to the floor. Errol lost his hold, and Vanessa took off like a missile, escaping unscathed as the panther finished her partner.

Vanessa shot past Warren and Kendra, then slowed and descended, hovering not far from them. "I have the spear; you have the sword," she said, panting, her voice slightly unsteady. "The guardian probably has several more lives. How about that truce?"

"Why did you betray us?" Kendra accused.

"One day those I serve will rule all," Vanessa said. "I do no more harm than I must. At present, our needs align. We must defeat the guardian to escape this place, and neither of us will succeed alone."

"And once we have the artifact?" Warren asked.

"We'll be fortunate to be alive and to have reached the next crossroads," Vanessa said. "I can give you no further assurances."

"Defeating this guardian will be no small task," Warren admitted. "What do you say, Kendra?"

Two sets of eyes were on Kendra. "I don't trust her."

"A little late for that," Vanessa said.

"You were supposed to be my teacher and my friend," Kendra said. "I really liked you."

Vanessa grinned. "Of course you liked me. In the spirit of teaching, here's a final piece of instruction. I used the same approach when we met as Errol did. I rescued you from a supposed threat in order to build trust. Of course, I helped set up the threat. I visited your town the night before the kobold showed up at your school and bit your homeroom teacher while she slept. Later, the kobold put a tack on her chair to put her to sleep, then I took over and gave you quite a scare."

"That was you?" Kendra said.

"We had to make sure you had ample reason to accept Errol's help. And then, once you realized Errol was a threat, I came to your rescue."

"What happened to Case?" Kendra asked.

"The kobold? He's off on some new mission, I presume. His purpose was merely to alarm you."

"Is Mrs. Price all right?"

"She'll be fine, I'm sure," Vanessa said. "We meant her no harm. She was a means to an end."

"I'm not sure I get the moral of this lesson," Warren said. "Don't trust people who help you?"

"More like, be careful who you trust," Vanessa said. "And don't cross the Society. We're always a step ahead."

"So we shouldn't team up," Kendra said.

"You have no other choice," Vanessa laughed darkly. "Neither do I. None of us can flee. If we fight each other, none of us will leave here alive. You can't afford to pass up my help defeating the guardian. Nor can I afford to pass up yours. And, albino or not, Warren is looking paler by the minute."

Kendra looked down at the panther. She glanced at Warren. "What do you think?"

He sighed. "Honestly, we'd better work with her to kill the cat. Even with a combined effort, it will be a challenge."

"Okay," Kendra said.

"Anything good in the pouch?" Vanessa asked.

"Probably, but we don't know one potion from another," Kendra said.

"I'm not sure I could be much help discerning potions," Vanessa said. She looked at Warren. "Your shirt is soaked."

The shirt bound to his abdomen was indeed drenched in blood. His naked chest was bathed in sweat. "I'm all right. Better than Christopher."

"I'm quite good with a sword," Vanessa said.

"I can hold my own," Warren replied.

"Fair enough, finders keepers," she said. "Patience is our best weapon. If we do this right, we can dispatch it without ever touching the ground."

"You be our eyes, Kendra," Warren said, lowering himself. Vanessa sank toward the floor as well. Kendra hovered, watching the baleful panther prowl below, gazing up at the flying people.

Vanessa and Warren floated apart from one another, dipping low enough to bait and tease the panther, rising out of reach when it leaped up at them. Vanessa finally got into a good position and hurled the spear into the panther's ribs. As the panther moved around, the spear eventually dislodged. Warren lured the panther away, and Vanessa retrieved the weapon.

They continued baiting the panther until Vanessa harpooned it again. Soon the animal collapsed, and Warren finished it with the sword. "Sharp blade," Vanessa remarked. "It cuts deep."

Weapons ready, they hovered above the floor, watching as the panther emerged from its own corpse, now the size of a tiger. Before long the glossy black coat had been punctured multiple times with the spear, and the great beast finally succumbed.

"You're not doing much with that sword," Vanessa commented.

"I'll use it when the time comes," Warren said.

"Here comes the seventh life," Vanessa said.

This time, with a mighty roar that echoed through the tall room, the panther was reincarnated standing as tall as a horse, with dagger claws and saber-toothed fangs. Four writhing serpents, black with red markings, grew out of its powerful shoulders.

"Now, that's a cat," Warren said.

Warren and Vanessa started baiting the huge panther, but it did not come at them. Instead, it crouched near the center of the room, keeping the pedestal between itself and Vanessa. They ventured lower and lower trying to tempt the panther to break cover.

Finally, with terrifying suddenness, the panther dashed at Warren and vaulted alarmingly high. Warren fell upwards at full speed, but not before a lashing serpent struck him on the calf. Vanessa was not in an ideal position, but used the opportunity to let the spear fly. It pierced the panther just above a rear leg. Bawling, the panther sprang at her as well, again achieving a phenomenal height, just missing her.

"I got nipped on the calf," Warren said.

"One of the snakes?" Vanessa asked.

"Yeah." Warren rolled up his pant leg to look at the bite marks.

Below them, the panther crouched near the pedestal, the spear still in its leg. Using small bursts of gravity and kicking her legs, Vanessa made her way awkwardly over to Warren, moving vaguely like a jellyfish.

"You'd better lend me the sword," Vanessa said. "It will not be a gentle venom."

"One of these potions counteracts poison," Kendra said.

"And probably five of them *are* poison," Vanessa replied. "Time is essential, Warren. I'll need you with me as we face the final forms."

Warren gave her the sword. Vanessa dropped tantalizingly close to the ground, lower than Warren had been when the giant panther reached him. The ferocious feline charged and pounced. Instead of soaring up to escape, as the panther anticipated, Vanessa dropped, and with a sweep of the sword opened a tremendous wound across the great cat's underbelly.

Vanessa hit the ground hard and instantly took flight, but there was no need—the panther was lying on its side, serpents thrashing, body twitching. Warren dropped to the ground and retrieved the spear, then rejoined Vanessa in the air.

"We've got another one coming," Vanessa announced as the body began to fold in upon itself. "How are you holding up?" she asked Warren.

"So far so good," he said, but he looked exhausted.

Twin roars resounded through the towering room. The

panther, much larger now than any horse, had sprouted a second head. The doubly fierce creature had no snakes or other oddities. It paced beneath them with feral intensity.

"You want to bait or throw?" Vanessa asked.

"I'd better bait," he said, giving her the spear and taking the sword.

Warren went lower, but not much lower. The panther was no longer cowering behind the pedestal; it paced in the open, as if daring them to come closer. Warren still looked to be well out of reach when the panther sprang and from gaping mouths expelled a spray of black sludge. The two-headed panther had not come up directly below Warren, and so the spray came at him diagonally, spattering his chest and legs.

Instantly Warren was screaming. Tendrils of smoke steamed up from where the volatile substance clung to him. He dropped the sword and brushed frantically at the searing sludge. Thrashing and groaning, Warren rose ever higher until he reached the spikes in the roof and used them to make his way to the catwalk, where he collapsed.

Vanessa and Kendra followed Warren and knelt on the catwalk beside him. His body was charred wherever the sludge had splattered. "Acid, or something," he muttered feverishly, eyes wild.

Vanessa cut open his pant leg. The flesh around the snakebite was swollen and discolored.

"We can't get him out of here?" Kendra asked Vanessa.

"The tower will not let us leave without the artifact," Vanessa said. "A safeguard to protect its secrets."

"Can any traps be worse than that thing?" Kendra asked.

"Yes," Vanessa said. "The traps that prevent a premature exit will be rigged to cause certain death. The guardian can be defeated; the traps probably cannot. Hand over the potion pouch. Warren is dying. Blind luck is better than none." Vanessa began considering various bottles, uncapping a few to sniff them. Below, the panther heads roared.

"No potions," Warren gasped. "Give me the spear."

Vanessa gave him a sidelong glance. "You're in no condition—"

"The spear," he said, sitting up.

"This might buy you time," Vanessa said, holding up a bottle. "I think I recognize the potion. It has a distinctive odor. It will transform your body to a gaseous state. During that time, poison will not spread, acid will not burn, and blood will not flow."

Vanessa held it out to him.

Lips twisting into a grimace, Warren shook his head.

Vanessa held out the spear.

Snatching it, Warren rolled off the edge of the catwalk. He was controlling his fall with the rod, but descending rapidly. Warren yelled—a primal, barbaric challenge. The two-headed panther snarled up at him. Warren cried out again, directly above the feline monstrosity. The monster reared up to meet him, jaws agape.

Holding the spear poised, Warren let himself fall at full speed the final thirty feet, and so it was with tremendous force that he plunged the spear between the two necks an instant before striking the unyielding floor. With more than half the length of the spear buried in its body, the mighty beast took a few drunken steps, wobbled, leaned, and slumped to the floor.

Kendra grabbed the bottle from Vanessa and dove off the catwalk. She kept full gravity, and an incredible rush of wind washed over her as she plummeted downward. She whipped the rod around, and her fall began to slow, and then she brought the rod level, coming to a perfect stop beside Warren.

Warren was a wreck, facedown, unconscious, breathing shallowly. Heaving with both hands, Kendra rolled him over, wincing as something inside of him crunched. His mouth was open. Tilting his head up, she tried to ignore the snapping sound his neck made, and dumped the potion into his mouth. His Adam's apple bobbed, and much of the fluid leaked out the sides of his mouth.

Once again, the body of the monster was bulging and undulating, as if it were about to erupt. Vanessa was yanking on the spear, tugging it out a little at a time, leaning into it with everything she had.

"Get clear, Kendra," Vanessa called. "This is not over."

When Kendra looked back at Warren, he was wispy and translucent. She tried to touch him, and her hand passed through him like he was mist, dissipating him slightly. Kendra raced across the floor and grabbed the sword. Behind her, Vanessa finally jerked the spear free.

As Vanessa launched into the air, Kendra watched the ninth version of the guardian emerge. Long wings unfurled. Twelve serpents sprouted from various spots along its back.

Three heavy tails swayed. And three heads bellowed together, a deafening sound even from where Kendra stood behind the beast. The great wings beat down and the beast took flight, pursuing Vanessa.

Kendra gaped in petrified awe. From wingtip to wingtip, the monstrosity stretched across half the cavernous room. It rose swiftly.

Running out of room to ascend, Vanessa started falling instead of rising, hurling the spear as she neared her pursuer. The weapon merely grazed the monster and tumbled toward the floor. All three heads snapped at Vanessa, and all missed. She rebounded off its well-muscled body, snakes striking eagerly, and tumbled toward the ground. Vanessa managed to slow her descent at the last moment, but she still landed heavily only a moment after the spear struck the floor.

Like Errol before her, she lost her grip of the rod, and it floated away toward the ceiling. Quivering, snake-bitten, dragging a broken leg, she crawled for the spear. Above, the three-headed fiend descended, roaring exultantly. Beyond the monster, Kendra saw a pair of figures falling toward her.

Propping herself up with the spear, Vanessa stood and faced the three-headed monster cat as it landed before her. The cat watched her from well out of reach. Kendra recognized Tanu and Coulter descending swiftly, both albino, and she waved her arms at them.

Even as scalding sludge fountained from three mouths, dousing Vanessa in blistering agony, Tanu alighted beside Kendra, snatched his potion pouch, and upended a bottle into his mouth. He accepted the sword from Kendra. As

Vanessa screamed, Tanu expanded, clothes splitting as he doubled in height, a huge man becoming a giant, the sword looking like a knife in his enormous hand.

Too late the three-headed monster turned, as Tanu raged, stabbing and slashing, hacking off wings and serpents even as he was clawed and bitten. Tanu's heavy arm pistoned mercilessly until the monster crumpled, and Tanu collapsed atop the beast, bleeding from bitter wounds.

Kendra watched in horror as the carcass of the monster began to boil. Tanu scooted away from it. But this time, instead of folding in upon itself, the corpse melted away and simmered into nothingness, as if it had never been.

Coulter and Kendra ran to Tanu, who lay on his side. The white Samoan pointed at the space the monster had occupied. There sat a bright, copper teapot worked into the shape of a cat, with the tail forming the spout. Coulter retrieved it. "Doesn't look like much," he said.

"I may need to touch it," Kendra said, taking the pot from him. Light at first, the pot started getting heavier. The exterior of the pot did not change, but Kendra recognized the difference. "It's filling up."

"Pour it," Tanu gasped.

Tanu had three deep, ragged gouges across his beefy forearm. Kendra poured golden dust from the teapot onto the wounds. Much of the dust seemed to dissolve on contact. The gouges vanished, leaving no scar. An enormous chunk of flesh was missing from Tanu's shoulder, but when Kendra filled the gaping wound with dust from the teapot, it closed and the skin above it looked like new.

As Kendra shook the feline teapot over Tanu, his white flesh returned to a healthy brown, and all his wounds closed and vanished. Tanu shook his head, powdery dust rising from his hair.

Kendra hurried over to Vanessa, who lay moaning, withered, unrecognizable, incapable of movement or speech. "I should heal her," Kendra said.

"I would love to say no," Tanu said. "But it is the right thing to do."

"Technically we're not on the preserve," Coulter reminded them. "What happens in here, stays in here."

"Don't let her near any weapons," Kendra warned them.

Coulter kicked the spear away as Kendra coated Vanessa with the dust from the teapot. The healing dust renewed itself and continued to flow until Kendra stopped pouring, leaving Vanessa perfectly whole and unscarred. She sat up, staring at the teapot in wonder. "Nothing could have cured those burns," she said in amazement. "I was blind and nearly deaf."

"This is over," Tanu told Vanessa. "There are others stronger than us waiting just outside the entrance."

Vanessa said nothing more.

Coulter remained near her, sword in hand. "I suppose it goes without saying, if you slip into a trance, you'll never come out of it."

Kendra went over to Errol and dumped dust on him. Nothing changed. He was dead.

"We may be able to save Warren," Kendra said.

"I noticed he was gaseous," Tanu said, having tied his

torn clothes together into a loincloth. "Which means he is alive. The potion would not have worked if he were dead. He must be nearly gone, or he would be able to move around freely in his gaseous state. Instead he lies in a daze. Considering the power of the dust in that artifact, I'm sure we will be able to restore him. Dale will thank you forever."

"Vanessa said she found you in the woods and put you to sleep," Kendra said.

"Then she was lying," Tanu said.

"Bluffing," Vanessa rephrased.

"When I came to myself, I returned to the house," Tanu continued. "I approached cautiously, and must have arrived not long after Vanessa departed to come here. I picked the locks to the dungeon. It is much easier to sneak into that prison than to sneak out. Your grandparents are fine. They retrieved the register, and we found friends waiting outside the gates of Fablehaven."

Not long after that, Tanu returned to his regular size and adjusted his clothes. They stood next to the ghostly, smoky form of Warren until the gas coalesced and he became solid once more. As soon as he became tangible, Kendra covered him with dust from the teapot, mending broken bones and poisoned tissue and burns and ruptured organs. He sat up, blinking, unbelieving. When he removed the blood-soaked shirt from his abdomen, he found no mark beneath it. Warren was no longer albino. He had dark hair and intense hazel eyes.

Kendra also dusted Coulter, curing his albinism.

"We should hurry," Tanu said. "Dale will be needing some healing himself. The hobgoblin left him lame."

They bound Vanessa's hands with the same rope that had bandaged Warren, and levitated up to the catwalk, Tanu holding Vanessa. They replaced their rods in the alcove. No monkeys stirred as they crossed the mosaic, though they still had to tread carefully on the stairs. They found Dale in the sandy room, where only the blue woman, the half-spider, and the dwarf remained on the walls.

Dale shouted in ecstasy upon seeing his brother revived and well, and they embraced for a long while before Kendra could get near enough to heal his legs. Once his legs were well, Dale stared at the teapot in wonder, wiping away tears of joy, and proclaimed that now he had officially seen everything.

One final surprise awaited Kendra. When at length they reached the uppermost chamber in the tower and climbed the knotted rope to reach the stone platform in the formerly cursed grove, she found the Sphinx and Mr. Lich waiting to welcome them.

CHAPTER TWENTY-ONE

The Quiet Box

Tell me about the cat again," Seth said, sitting on the bed with his legs crossed, trying to juggle three blocks.

"Again?" Kendra said, looking up from her book.

"I can't believe I missed the coolest thing anyone has ever seen," Seth complained, losing control of the blocks after two tosses. "A giant, flying, snake-covered, three-headed, acid-breathing panther. If you didn't have witnesses, I'd be sure you made it up just to torture me."

"Being there wasn't much fun," Kendra said. "I was pretty sure we were all going to die."

"And it hosed down Vanessa with a massive acid blast," he continued enthusiastically. "Was she screaming?"

"She couldn't scream," Kendra said. "She was just sort of moaning. She looked like she'd been dipped in lava."

"All that to guard the lamest thing ever: a shabby old teapot."

"A teapot that cured all your zombie wounds," Kendra said.

"I know, it's useful, but it looks like a bad decision from a really pathetic garage sale. You just like it because your fairy voodoo made it work." He started trying to juggle again and immediately lost the rhythm, one of the blocks falling to the floor.

Grandpa opened the door to the attic bedroom. "The Sphinx says he's ready, if you still want to join us," he reported.

Kendra smiled. It was nice seeing Grandpa walking around again like his old self. To her, healing Grandpa Sorenson had seemed like the most miraculous consequence of retrieving the artifact. The other injuries were so recent that they had somehow not sunk in as being real. It had been as if the teapot were washing away the memory of a bad dream. But Grandpa had been in a wheelchair ever since she had arrived at Fablehaven this year, so watching him cut the cast off and walk around was particularly impressive.

"Heck, yeah," Seth said, bouncing off the bed. "I've missed too much! I'm not missing this."

Kendra got up as well, although her feelings were more conflicted than Seth's. Rather than wanting to witness Vanessa's final sentence as a novelty, or perhaps to gloat, she hoped to reach some sense of closure for the betrayal Vanessa had enacted.

It had been the Sphinx who had recommended the

Quiet Box. The previous day, after Vanessa had been incarcerated in the dungeon, they had all sat around filling in the blanks for each other. Grandma and Grandpa knew almost none of the story. Seth held them enthralled with how he overcame the revenant. Kendra and Warren told of the descent into the tower and the battle with the cat. Tanu, Coulter, and Dale told of the rescue they had mounted, how when they had approached the grove with the Sphinx, the imp who appeared to be guarding it had turned and fled, and how Dale had been injured by the hobgoblin.

The Sphinx explained that he had been on the move because of evidence that the Society of the Evening Star was closing in on his location. Once he was clear, he became worried that nobody at Fablehaven was answering his calls, and doubly concerned when he found the gates locked and nobody responding to his solicitations for entry. He had waited there until Tanu finally answered the phone after freeing Grandpa. Tanu had opened the gates for him.

In the end, the conversation had turned to Vanessa. The problem was, as a narcoblix, she would forever have power over those she had bitten whenever they were asleep. "She must be shut away in a prison that will inhibit her power," the Sphinx had said emphatically. "We cannot expect Mr. Lich to spend the remainder of his life watching her." At the time, Mr. Lich was in the dungeon, stationed outside her cell.

"Can't the sand from the artifact cure those of us she bit?" Kendra asked.

"I have been studying the artifact," the Sphinx said. "Its

healing powers appear to affect only the physical body. I do not believe it can cure maladies of the mind. The dust instantly removed the marks from her bite, but it is powerless against the mental link the bite forges."

"Do you know of a prison that would curtail her power?" Grandpa asked.

The Sphinx paused and then nodded to himself. "I have a simple answer. The Quiet Box in your very own dungeon will suit our needs perfectly."

"What about the current occupant?" Grandma asked.

"I know the history of the current prisoner inside your Quiet Box," the Sphinx said. "He has great political significance, but no talents that require such a mighty cage. I know a place where he will be no more likely to cause harm."

"Who is he?" Seth asked.

"For the safety of all, the identity of the prisoner must remain a mystery," the Sphinx said. "Let your curiosity take comfort in the reality that for most of you, the name would hold little meaning. I was present when he was sealed in the box, trussed up and hooded, disguised and unknown to the others who attended the event. I worked long to ensure his capture, and to keep all knowledge of him hidden. Now I will provide the anonymous captive with new confinement, so the Quiet Box can be used to secure the type of villain for which it was designed. Morally, with her as our prisoner, we cannot execute Vanessa. But neither can we reward her treachery with leniency, or provide her the slightest opportunity to inflict further harm."

All had agreed that it was a sound plan. Seth had asked

to be present for the prisoner exchange. Kendra had seconded the request. The Sphinx said he saw no harm in it, since the current occupant of the Quiet Box was unrecognizable beneath his mask and bindings. Grandpa had granted permission.

As Kendra followed Grandpa and Seth down the stairs, she reflected that this punishment was in many ways worse than an execution. From what she had gathered, imprisonment in the Quiet Box meant centuries of uninterrupted solitude. The Box put the occupant in a suspended state but did not render the prisoner entirely unconscious. She could not imagine complete sensory deprivation for a day, let alone a year, but this was potentially many lifetimes standing upright inside a snug container. She could only guess at the psychological consequences of such extended isolation.

Kendra was hurt that Vanessa had betrayed her, and glad to see her come to justice, but the prolonged confinement of the Quiet Box struck her as a heavy price for even the most heinous crime. Even so, the Sphinx was right—Vanessa could not be permitted to exert further control over those she had bitten.

They met Grandma in the kitchen and descended together into the dungeon, where they found Mr. Lich escorting Vanessa from her cell, with a firm grip on her upper arm. The Sphinx nodded gravely. "Once again we prepare to part ways," he said. "Hopefully our next meeting will be under less duress."

Tanu, Coulter, Dale, and Warren had all opted not to attend, so the small party set off down the hall in silence toward their destination. Mr. Lich led the way with Vanessa, so Kendra could not see her face. Vanessa was dressed in one of Grandma's old housecoats, but she held her head erect.

Before long they reached the tall cabinet that reminded Kendra of magicians making lovely assistants vanish. The Sphinx turned and faced them. "Let me stress one last time what exemplary courage and character all of you showed in thwarting this insidious attempt to steal a potentially ruinous artifact. Kendra and Seth, both of you displayed remarkable valor. Words cannot convey my sincere admiration and gratitude. Once we release the prisoner, Mr. Lich and I will need to make a hasty departure. Rest assured that we have a safe home in mind for both the artifact and the captive from the Quiet Box, and that we will telephone you, Stan, to confirm that all is safe and secure. When the prisoner emerges, make no sound until we are gone. My cautious nature would rather he not hear your voices or receive any other clues about who you are."

The Sphinx turned to face Vanessa. "Have you any final words before you learn why we call it the Quiet Box? Take heed—any utterance that passes your lips had best be words of apology." His voice held a menacing edge.

Vanessa looked at them in turn. "I apologize for the deceit. I never meant any of you physical harm. A false friendship is a terrible thing. Kendra, though you might not believe it, I remain your pen pal."

"Enough," the Sphinx said. "Make no professions of continued fidelity. We pity your fate, and collectively wish you had not brought this evil upon yourself. You have sought forbidden knowledge and committed unforgivable betrayals. You once had my trust, but it is now irretrievable."

The Sphinx opened the cabinet. The inside was lined with purple felt. The box was empty. Seth craned his neck, then gave Kendra a befuddled glance. Where was the current occupant?

Mr. Lich ushered Vanessa into the box. Her eyes were cold, but her jaw trembled. The Sphinx closed the door, and the cabinet rotated 180 degrees. Mr. Lich opened a door identical to the first, providing a view of the same space from the opposite side. But the view was not of Vanessa.

Instead, a figure clad entirely in burlap stood in the box. A coarse sack covered his head, chained snugly around his neck. Thick ropes bound his arms to his sides. Shackles gripped his ankles.

Mr. Lich laid a hand on his shoulder and led the mysterious captive out of the box. The Sphinx closed the door. Kendra, Seth, Grandma, and Grandpa watched as the prisoner shuffled away down the hall between the Sphinx and Mr. Lich. Grandma put an arm around Kendra, giving her a comforting squeeze.

※　※　※

That night, Kendra found she could not sleep. Her mind was whirling with the events of the past few days. They had been through so much, it seemed she had returned to Fablehaven a lifetime ago.

Midsummer Eve was a few days away. Grandpa had emphasized to Seth that they were putting their lives into his hands by permitting him to remain on the preserve during that perilous evening. Her brother had assured everyone that he had learned his lesson, that he would stay far from the windows unless otherwise instructed. Kendra was almost surprised to discover that, like her Grandpa, she absolutely believed him.

One particular thought kept recurring as Kendra lay awake in the dark. Vanessa's last words kept striking her as increasingly peculiar: "I remain your pen pal."

Kendra knew she might be crazy, but she felt certain the statement was more than a platitude. It sounded like Vanessa might be hinting at a secret message.

Deciding she had to know, Kendra kicked off the covers. Opening the nightstand drawer, she removed the umite wax candle that Vanessa had given her. She padded across the attic floor and down the stairs to the hall.

Kendra eased open the door to Grandpa and Grandma's room. Like everyone else in the dark house, they were sleeping soundly. There were the dungeon keys, on a peg near the bed. Grandpa had sworn he was going to make copies and hide them in strategic locations in case of another takeover.

Kendra hesitated. This was a disturbingly Sethlike thing to do. Shouldn't she just tell her grandparents her suspicion and have them accompany her? But she was worried they would not want her reading a farewell message from Vanessa. And she was worried they would be right, that the message would be cruel. And she was also worried that she was wrong, and there would be no message, and she would look foolish.

Quietly removing the keys from the peg, Kendra left the room. She was getting good at sneaking around. Being able to see in the dark certainly helped. Kendra tiptoed down the stairs to the entry hall.

Would there really be a message? In many ways, she would be relieved if the cell wall was blank. What could Vanessa have to say? A sincere apology? An explanation? More likely something spiteful. Kendra steeled herself against the possibility.

Whatever the message, it was hers to read. She did not want others going through her mail, at least not until after she had a look.

Kendra took matches from a kitchen cupboard and descended the stairs to the basement. Getting to Vanessa's cell would be simple—they had held her in the fourth cell on the right, not far from the dungeon entrance.

With Mr. Lich watching her, could Vanessa have written much of a message? Maybe. He was only there to prevent her from going into a trance and taking over people. He might not have had his eyes glued to her every second.

Kendra unlocked the iron door to the dungeon and entered. The goblins could make no complaint against her. They had received six dozen eggs, three live geese, and a goat for aiding Kendra and Seth when they had showed up in miniature. As long as she went straight to Vanessa's cell and then left, visiting the dungeon secretly could not possibly cause any harm. Maybe the idea wasn't quite as Sethlike as it had seemed.

She unlocked Vanessa's cell and entered. As had become

routine for Kendra since the fairies had altered her vision, it was dim but not terribly dark. The cell was like the others she had seen—stone walls and floor, crude bed, hole in the corner for waste. She struck a match and lit the candle, suddenly certain there would be no message.

Beneath the glow of the umite candle, words flared into view, cramped but legible, covering multiple patches of the floor—a much longer message than Kendra had anticipated. The words were oriented so that they must have been written while Vanessa crouched with her back to the door, with most of the writing concentrated in areas that were hard to see from the little window.

In mounting wonder and alarm, Kendra read the following message:

> *Dear Kendra,*
>
> *I have vital information to share with you. Call it a final tutorial, and a parting shot at my treacherous employers. You should have learned the lesson I shared when we first met. What is the textbook Society infiltration? Set up a threat, then come to the rescue in order to build trust. Errol did it to you and Seth. Then I did the same thing to you and your grandparents, pretending to be part of the solution rather than the cause of the problem, legitimately helping most of the time until the moment of betrayal arrived. Others have been using that model for a long time, with infinite subtlety and patience. Namely, the Sphinx.*
>
> *Your reflex will be to doubt me, and I cannot*

prove that I am right. My gifts made me privy to secrets that piqued my curiosity, and when I dug deeper, I unearthed a truth that I should have left undiscovered. He suspects I know his secret, which is why he will confine me to the Quiet Box. He would prefer if he could have me executed. I work for him, but I am not supposed to know the identity of my employer. Few know the enigmatic leader of the Society of the Evening Star. For months, I believe, the Sphinx has suspected that I have guessed his true identity. The kind of fraud he is perpetrating could endure only with supreme discretion and meticulous attention to detail. In his mind, I have become a liability.

The Sphinx could have claimed he had a prison that would hold me and impede my powers. He could have taken me with him. And if he had, he would have earned my undying loyalty. At present, I would still be in doubt as to his intentions, but Lich, not fully understanding the dynamics of the situation, hinted about the Quiet Box, and so I scrawl my revenge on the floor.

Consider the coup this is for the Sphinx. As a known traitor, I am a spoiled asset for the Society, and therefore of much less use. He gets to look like the hero and the sure friend of Fablehaven as he locks me in the most secure prison on the property, further obscuring the duplicitous truth. In case his suspicions are correct and I know his true identity, I am permanently out of the equation.

What else? He frees a prisoner who is undoubt-edly a powerful ally! And he walks away with the arti-fact I was sent here to retrieve for him!

This could be a fabrication. Keep your eyes open, and time will confirm my version of things. The rea-son the Sphinx knows so much, and anticipates danger so well, is because he is playing both sides. He is caus-ing the danger, and then providing relief and advice until those perfect moments of betrayal arrive. Who knows how many artifacts he has collected? He has been at it for centuries! Considering his actions at Fablehaven and in Brazil, he has apparently decided that the time for aggressiveness has arrived. Beware, the Evening Star is rising.

Had he trusted me, his secret would still be safe. But he spurned me, and underestimated me, and so his secret is revealed. My loyalty is no longer his. I know much more that could be useful to you and your grandparents.

If not your friend, your disillusioner,
Vanessa

THE FABLEHAVEN
ADVENTURE CONTINUES
IN BOOK THREE

To contact the author, request a school visit,
or find out more about the Fablehaven series,
visit FABLEHAVEN.COM

ALSO AVAILABLE:

THE CANDY SHOP WAR
A NEW CHILDREN'S FANTASY BY BRANDON MULL

COMING FALL 2007

CANDY WARNING:
Consumption may cause magical side effects. In case of enchanted
reaction, consult your local confectionery magician immediately.

Acknowledgments

Writing a book is a private endeavor, but sharing a book with others becomes a public enterprise. There are many people to thank who have helped the Fablehaven series come this far.

My wife is the person closest to the process. She reads my work chapter by chapter, providing my first feedback and encouragement. Not only is she my best friend, she also helps me find time to write and makes our household function—the thanks I owe to her are incalculable.

Chris Schoebinger at Shadow Mountain spearheads the marketing and keeps everything on track. Emily Watts edits the book—the polish she adds really helps it shine. Brandon Dorman turns words into striking images, and designers Richard Erickson and Sheryl Dickert Smith use those images and their own skills to give the book a visual identity. Jared Kroff and friends make Fablehaven.com look cool. My sister Summer coordinates the tour and travels with me, helping me raise awareness about Fablehaven while encouraging students to strengthen their imaginations through reading.

I can never read my own work without an intimate knowledge of the story and the events to come. This can pose a problem when I struggle to distinguish the information in my mind from the information actually on the page. To help me gauge whether the story is unfolding effectively I solicit feedback from trusted readers. For this book I had help from Jason and Natalie Conforto, Mike Walton, Scott and Leslie Schwendiman, Chris Schoebinger, the Freeman family, Emily Watts, Mike Crippen, Lisa Mangum, Pam, Gary, Summer, Cherie, Nancy, Tamara, Tuck, Liz, Randy, and others.

There is a lot to learn about the business side of being an author. I'm grateful to Orson Scott Card for some sound advice and kind mentoring, Barbara Bova for getting involved as my agent, the people at Simon and Schuster who are publishing the paperback edition of the book, and the wonderful folks at Shadow Mountain who are helping me share the story of Fablehaven with readers everywhere.

Writers live or die by readers telling others about the books they enjoy. I'm grateful to Robert Fanney for helping to get the word out online, Donna Corbin-Sobinski for going the extra mile in Connecticut, and numerous family members, friends, bookstore employees, teachers, and librarians for helping increase awareness of the series.

In the end, I most rely on readers who suspend their disbelief and let the story of Fablehaven come to life in their minds. Thanks for sharing your time with me!

On a final note, my cousin Nicole Aupiu told me that some of her friends don't believe I'm her cousin. I am! In fact, a character in this book is named after her brother Tanu.

Keep an eye out for Book 3 of the Fablehaven series coming in 2008, and my first non-Fablehaven fantasy novel, *The Candy Shop War*, in stores before the end of 2007.

Reading Guide

1. In the first chapter of the book, Kendra's power to recognize magical creatures allows her to see Casey Hancock for what he is, an evil kobold. Do you think she made the right choice not to tell her friends about him? What would you do if you felt like you should warn a friend about something or someone, but you were embarrassed or afraid to do so?

2. Which of the "experts"—Coulter, the magical relics collector, Tanu, the potions master, or Vanessa, the magical creatures expert—would you be most interested in learning from? If you could be an expert in one of these areas, which would you choose? Why?

3. On pages 108–11, Kendra samples one of Tanu's bottled emotions, shame. After it has worn off, she realizes that the emotion made her blow little problems all out of

proportion. How can our emotions make things seem worse than they really are? What can we do when we're caught up in the "spell" of a negative emotion?

4. On page 124, Seth asks Dale what he'll do if he can't find a way to cure his brother, Warren. Dale answers, "I'll never know that day has come, because I'll never stop trying." How do you keep your hope up when you've tried lots of different solutions to a problem, and nothing seems to work? Have you ever kept trying and ended up succeeding at something that you failed at to begin with?

5. Pages 136–39 describe Grandma Sorenson's interaction with the jinn that resulted in her being changed into a chicken. Have you ever felt that you could "handle" a situation that you knew would be dangerous?

6. If you had a magical glove like Coulter's, how would you use it? How could you help people? What magical relic would you most like to invent? What would it do? Why would you like to have that power?

7. Chapter 9 describes Kendra's and Seth's encounters with the Sphinx. Why do you think he treated them differently, especially in the Foosball game? Is it best to always treat everyone the same, or are there times when certain individuals may need special handling? Why?

8. Every good and lasting relationship must have trust. However, Kendra finds herself betrayed by people whom she trusted. How much are you willing to trust someone? If you found out someone lied to you, would you be willing to forgive him or her? If so, what would that person have to do to earn back your trust?

9. Seth and Coulter encounter paralyzing fear from the revenant. Is fear always a bad thing? Can fear ever be good? Why or why not? If you could overcome one fear, what would it be?

10. In book 1, Seth's boldness caused problems. In book 2, his courage helped save the day. What is the difference between bravery and recklessness? Is it always easy to see the difference?

11. When Slaggo and Voorsh, the goblins, are about to cook Kendra and Seth, Kendra persuades them that her grandparents will reward them for letting the children go. The goblins recall, "Stan and Ruth have repaid loyalty in the past," and "[Stan] has a history of fair rewards." How does a person gain a reputation for fairness or other good qualities? How might you be helped by your good reputation, or that of your parents?

12. In Seth's battle with the revenant, when his courage is almost gone, he remembers all the people who have helped him and are depending on him. Has thinking about people you love ever given you more courage than you thought you had? How does remembering your loved ones help you make better choices in your life?

13. What do you think of the end of the book? What reasons are there to believe the final message? What reasons are there to disbelieve it?